The
HIGHWAYMAN
of
TANGLEWOOD

Center Point
Large Print

Also by Marcia Lynn McClure and available
from Center Point Large Print:

Dusty Britches
Weathered Too Young
The Windswept Flame
The Visions of Ransom Lake
The Heavenly Surrender
The Light of the Lovers' Moon
Beneath the Honeysuckle Vine
The Whispered Kiss
The Stone-Cold Heart of Valentine Briscoe

**This Large Print Book carries the
Seal of Approval of N.A.V.H.**

The HIGHWAYMAN *of* TANGLEWOOD

MARCIA LYNN McCLURE

CENTER POINT LARGE PRINT
THORNDIKE, MAINE

The text of this Large Print edition is unabridged.
In other aspects, this book may vary
from the original edition.
Printed in the United States of America
on permanent paper.
Set in 16-point Times New Roman type.

ISBN: 978-1-68324-925-2

Library of Congress Cataloging-in-Publication Data

Names: McClure, Marcia Lynn, author.
Title: The highwayman of Tanglewood / Marcia Lynn McClure.
Description: Center Point Large Print edition. | Thorndike, Maine :
    Center Point Large Print, 2018.
Identifiers: LCCN 2018022927 | ISBN 9781683249252
    (hardcover : alk. paper)
Subjects: LCSH: Large type books. | GSAFD: Love stories.
Classification: LCC PS3613.C36 H54 2018b | DDC 813/.6—dc23
LC record available at https://lccn.loc.gov/2018022927

To Amanda Heath,
My sweet, young friend . . .
You are a beautiful angel, a damsel,
a princess, a romance heroine!
You inspire me!
All My Love,
Marcia Lynn McClure

———*and*———

To my husband, Kevin . . .
The Highwayman of My Dreams!

The
HIGHWAYMAN
of
TANGLEWOOD

Prologue

Lady Maranda Rockrimmon watched with guarded interest as the pretty young woman went about her duties. A maid in the manor house of Lord and Lady Tremeshton, the young woman set the sweets-laden silver serving tray on the table, forced a friendly smile, dipped a respectful curtsy, and went to stand near the doorway.

During her recent visits to see Lady Tremeshton, Lady Rockrimmon had often observed this young maid, noting an uncommon elegance about the girl, a somewhat ethereal beauty in her features. Lady Rockrimmon had also silently noted the girl's nervous state—the flicker of fear ever present in her dark eyes. It seemed the girl was continuously on her guard against something— and Lady Maranda Rockrimmon knew plainly what. The young masters of great households knew well of the ill and shameless behavior that more often than not haunted a pretty young serving girl. When a manor house in which she labored harbored an arrogant young master, a young woman of no means could be made quite miserable—or even ruined. Furthermore, Lady Rockrimmon knew that if there were an arrogant young master to be suspicious of, it was most certainly and none other than Kade Tremeshton.

Kade Tremeshton was not only handsome and wealthy; he was egotistical and corrupt. Perhaps it seemed a harsh description, but it was true. Hardly a single serving girl over the age of fifteen had passed through the halls of Tremeshton Manor without being accosted in one way or another by Kade. Lady Rockrimmon kept a concerned and caring ear to the conversations of those who labored under her husband's employ. She knew Kade Tremeshton was a scoundrel of the lowest sort. Even the roguish Highwayman of Tanglewood, who had been impishly robbing the wealthy for nigh unto a year, was known as a gentleman, never to have sullied any woman in any way—and the Highwayman of Tanglewood was a thief! A well-intentioned thief, perhaps—the likes of Robin Hood of old and with the same motivations—but a thief all the same. Still, even the local Highwayman seemed to respect womanhood, for stories had been told of his gallant and chivalrous deeds where women were concerned. Kade Tremeshton, however, was just as well known for his disrespect of women. Everyone was aware of Kade's lowly character—everyone save his mother and father.

It was not an uncommon thing—parents ignorant of their progeny's preposterous behavior. Whether for pure ignorance or simple denial and a lack of ambition to see their children to admirable adulthood, it seemed the children of the noble and wealthy were often of the worst character to be found. Kade Tremeshton was one of these—spoiled, arrogant, and without a shred of moral fiber to atone. As she watched the Tremeshton Manor maid stand anxious and fearful at the doorway waiting for Lady Tremeshton to return and dismiss her, Lady Rockrimmon knew—the girl was fearful of Kade.

Maranda cleared her throat. She pressed a graceful, lace-gloved hand to her lips and glanced about before saying, "Young woman—would you come to me for just a moment, please?"

The young woman startled at the sound of Maranda's voice, nodded, smoothed her dark hair, and dutifully came to stand before the grand lady—a guest in her mistress's home.

"Yes, milady?" the young woman asked.

Maranda smiled, pleased the girl's voice carried the softness and lilt of a songbird. "What is your name, dearest?" Maranda inquired.

"Faris, milady," the girl answered. "Faris Shayhan."

"Faris," Maranda repeated. "Oh, I love it!"

The girl smiled, obviously pleased for the moment. "Thank you, milady," she said. High cheekbones and long eyelashes gave the girl more the look of a princess or fairy sprite than that of an overburdened serving maid.

"Now, Faris," Maranda continued, lowering her voice and motioning the girl closer, "how do you find your position here at Tremeshton Manor?"

The girl's dark eyes widened, fear and anxiety all too apparent. Maranda realized at once the carelessness in her manner of posing the question. The girl could not answer truthfully, for if her mistress were to hear of an unenthusiastic response, no doubt she would be sent on her way in an instant.

"I mean to ask . . . would you—would you consider coming to Loch Loland Castle? I've need of a careful young woman such as yourself, and I've noticed you for some time. You're careful in your duties—very attentive and polite." Maranda saw the girl's eyes widen and sparkle with hope. This encouraged her, and she continued, "I know you're probably more than happy here, dear," she said, retrieving a small piece of parchment and a quill from the nearby desk. "Still, I would like to have you over to Loch Loland, if you ever find . . . that you desire an alteration of venue."

Maranda wrote several sentences on the parchment, elegantly penned her name, and handed it to Faris. "There now—if you should feel a change is in your own best interest, simply come to Loch Loland. Won't you?" Maranda asked.

"Milady . . . I . . . I . . ." the young woman stammered, tears filling her eyes.

Maranda reached out, taking Faris's trembling hands in her own. "I've a kind and good family, Faris," she whispered. "A gallant husband and a son who understands the importance of . . . of virtue."

"So I have heard, milady," Faris admitted. "Though there are those who wish the young master wasn't so—" The girl gasped and clamped one hand over her mouth, horrified at what she had begun to say.

Maranda smiled and laughed. She understood far too well and said, "There are those young ladies who wish . . . who wish the handsome devil of my son . . . was a bit more *of* a devil, eh?"

The young woman smiled and nodded, obviously relieved at Maranda's understanding.

"Well," Maranda said, still holding Faris's hands. "I'm sure there's a woman out there somewhere who can bring out the imp in him, at least—if not the devil."

Faris smiled.

"But for now, come to Loch Loland Castle, Faris. It is a safe haven. I promise."

"Do you—do you make such offers on a regular basis, milady?" Faris asked.

Maranda laughed and shook her head. "No, I do not," she said. "But somehow I feel I want you at Loch Loland, dear—if you ever find your way."

"Oh, I will find my way, milady," Faris

said, smiling. Hope had returned to her lovely countenance—her eyes flashed with excitement. "I will find my way."

"Faris!" Lady Tremeshton exclaimed, entering the room just at that moment. "Haven't you finished serving yet?"

"Yes, Mistress," Faris said, smiling as Maranda winked at her.

"Then go about your business, girl. Lingering is simply idle," Lady Tremeshton grumbled, waving Faris aside as she curtsied.

Lady Maranda Rockrimmon settled back in her chair. She breathed a heavy sigh of contentment. She may not be able to save every young woman from the dastardly grip of Kade Tremeshton, but perhaps she could save one. She closed her eyes for a moment, silently thanking God for a good son who did not heap shame upon others, and praying Faris Shayhan would find the venue to leave Tremeshton Manor before any harm came to her.

"Now, Maranda, do tell me about the new tapestries in the grand hallway at Loch Loland," Lady Tremeshton began. "Are they bright and full of color?"

"They are, Christina. They are, indeed."

Faris hastened to the kitchens. Finding a corner void of prying eyes, she withdrew Lady Rockrimmon's note from her pocket. She read it over and over, smiling as she did so. She could not believe her good fortune!

" 'This is Faris Shayhan, and she will be joining us at Loch Loland Castle. Please bring her to me at once upon her arrival. With Sincerity, Lady Maranda Rockrimmon,' " Faris read in a whisper.

Clutching the note to her bosom, she let several tears trickle down her cheeks. How she had dreamt of and prayed for something to happen—something, anything to help her escape Tremeshton Manor and its vile young master.

Since the moment she had arrived, Kade Tremeshton's eyes had followed Faris. Every step, every movement in his presence was unsettling. The entire staff of Tremeshton Manor knew the young master was ever aware of Faris. Certainly every serving member of the household felt sorry for her. Yet, with the next breath, the other serving women at Tremeshton were glad his attentions were not on them. It was nightmarish for Faris, living under the same roof as Kade Tremeshton. What had begun as vile insinuations from him were quickly billowing to intention, and Faris knew it. Only the day before, the young master of Tremeshton Manor had detained her in the great hall, attempting to force a kiss upon her. He seemed to enjoy the game of cat and mouse—his startling her with a sudden appearance, her attempting to escape him without losing her position on the staff. In the end, he had let her go without so much as a grip to her wrist. This would not forever be the case, however. Faris knew it, and she feared for her own well-being.

The tales abounding at Tremeshton Manor of the young master's "conquests" were appalling. Many girls had been victims of his lecherous behavior. Several unfortunate victims had been sent away—reputations and innocence altered for life. Furthermore, it seemed very few of the ruined girls had been willingly ruined. In her very soul, Faris knew for certain—she was his next intended prey. Everyone at Tremeshton knew it. Everyone save Lord and Lady Tremeshton.

It was apparent the Lord and Lady Tremeshton worried nothing over the abominable behavior of their son. Indulged and spoiled at every turn, Kade Tremeshton knew nothing of hard work— nothing of character, chivalry, compassion, courtesy. Kade Tremeshton had been raised to think himself above any other person simply because of his name and would-be title and therefore deserving of anything he desired, without payment or consequence. Why should he assume anything other than this? He had been given everything he demanded without exerting any sort of effort, other than voicing the demand itself. He treated others as if they were pestilence, as if every other human being were indentured to him simply because he existed— simply because his father was Lord Tremeshton.

Kade Tremeshton had never been told he could not have—that he could not conquer. Simply, he had never been told *no,* and now his wanting had turned to Faris.

Yet fate or heaven had intervened. Faris felt deliverance close at hand. Carefully, she folded the note and returned it to her apron pocket. There was not time to waste! She would leave that very night. She would not even speak to Lady Tremeshton about the matter—simply write a note of leaving and have the house mistress deliver it. All those who labored under Kade Tremeshton's arrogance would understand. Most of all, Kade Tremeshton would understand. Faris smiled, delighted at the thought of his fury at having been foiled.

Faris turned, intent on leaving the kitchen to write her note and gather her things to ready for her impending escape. She gasped as she found Kade Tremeshton standing before her. In the low lighting of the kitchens, his dark hair and light-blue eyes appeared unearthly in their wicked essence. Faris imagined this was how the devil appeared—handsome, alluring, the favored appearance of deception.

"My pretty—very pretty Faris," he said, his voice lowered, his hands instantly at her waist. "What are you about in the kitchens this afternoon?" He leaned forward, nuzzling his face in the dark brown of her hair.

"Your mother's requirements," she said, struggling out of his grip and moving past him.

"Ah, but I have requirements of you as well," he whispered, catching hold of her wrist. He moistened his lips as he looked at her, and a wicked grin spread across his face.

"But—but I shall be missed in another moment, Master Kade. It would go badly for me," Faris told him as she began to tremble. She knew she could attempt a struggle—perhaps run from him. Yet she further knew any attempt at escape would be in vain. He would overtake her in a moment. It was best to try and ease out of his clutches. This she had learned in the most difficult way, having been caught and brutally struck by the back of his hand for trying to run from him on her first afternoon at Tremeshton Manor.

"Perhaps it would," he mumbled. "But I will be Lord of Tremeshton one day, Faris—so who should you labor most to please? My mother? Or me?" He moved his head toward hers, moistening his lips. His mouth was open as he attempted to kiss her.

"Your mother," Faris said, pulling away from him. "For it is she who bore you, and I know you would see her well served and happy."

Kade straightened. Glaring down at her he said, "Very well. But I am growing impatient with waiting for you to warm to me, Faris. You would be wise to consider surrender. It may go easy, and you will be safe—or it may go quite the opposite. The choice is yours."

"I must see to your mother, Master Kade," she said, twisting her wrist from his grip and hurrying from the room. She listened for any sound he meant to follow her, but there was none. It had been a narrow escape. She knew there would be no escape when next he chose to waylay her. She must flee. She must flee when night fell.

Once inside the chamber where she slept, Faris closed the door behind her, buried her face in her hands, and wept for a moment. Kade Tremeshton was a monster, and she could not wait to be out of his reach. Settling her wits, Faris brushed the tears from her pretty cheeks, careful not to rub her eyes too much. Faris never rubbed her eyes too harshly, for if she did, she found one or two of her unusually long, dark lashes would invariably turn under, painfully scratching her eyes. She remembered the way her mother would scold her for rubbing her eyes when she cried as a child, frustrated with the tantrums Faris would then embark upon because of the pain due to the turned-under lashes. Faris fancied what a strange reminiscence it was to linger on. She was near the brink of escape, and neither tears nor turned-under lashes were of any importance when liberation was waiting a breath away.

Quickly, Faris gathered the few items she possessed, stuffing them rather carelessly into the worn satchel once belonging to her mother. Wages were due Faris. A full week's worth, but she would not wait to collect them. A week's worth of wages wasn't worth a moment more in Kade Tremeshton's company. The sun would be setting soon—the perfect time to embark. Loch Loland Castle was more than five miles from Tremeshton Manor, but Faris cared not. She would walk all night if she had to. She would not spend another sunset under Kade Tremeshton's roof. She would bide her time until twilight and write a note—a note that left not a clue as to where she was about. Indeed, she would not endanger Lady Rockrimmon's reputation by labeling her a thief of servants. In her note, she would simply state she had left in search of another position. Three hours until dusk descended, and Faris would wait. She would avoid Kade Tremeshton and wait.

Bright pink and warm lavender on a canvas of night blue was the painted sky of sunset as Faris Shayhan walked through the Tanglewood Forest. She was glad for the glimpse of a meadow ahead—a break in the trees that would allow her to look heavenward into the beauty of nature's twilight painting above.

The moment she had left Tremeshton Manor, her heart had begun to swell with renewed hope and joy. Her lungs even seemed better able to draw breath. Faris felt lighter, freer, and happier than she had in months. As she stepped out of the forest and into the Tanglewood Meadow, she marveled at the beauty of the evening. Soon the pinks and lavenders of sunset would turn to great curtains of purple, folding over the world as night gathered. Already the hum of the crickets' song soothed her senses; the scent of wildflowers and lilacs in the meadow caressed her tattered nerves with their comforting perfume.

She paused in awe of the colors of the meadow, soft greens of grass, sweet yellow buttercups, lavender of lilacs, creamy sprigs of pussy willow. All of it, the color, the freshness of the air, the melody of the crickets—all of it served to calm Faris, to gladden her heart.

Yet as she set her satchel down, closing her eyes to revel in the beauty of the evening, the soft breezes brought something else to her—a rhythm—a horse carrying a rider. At first it seemed far off, and Faris remained calm, but fear leapt to her bosom at the thought of Kade Tremeshton! Perhaps the house mistress had delivered her note to Lady Tremeshton too early! Perhaps Kade Tremeshton had been provoked to fury and now rode after her!

Faris knew by the sound of the mad gallop there was not time to hide. She stood vulnerable, unprotected in the midst of the evening meadow—as helpless as an injured rabbit. It was senseless to run. Through the trees she could see the shape of a horse and rider approaching in furious haste!

Faris's eyes widened as she saw the rider's black hood, his midnight cape billowing in the wind as he rode toward her. His mount was as black as moonless night and angrily snorted as it reared up before her. Instinctively, Faris raised her arm to cover her eyes, certain she would next be trampled by powerful hooves. Yet she was not, and she ventured a glance at the rider.

The hooded man seemed to be looking at her—his horse pacing back and forth as its companion studied her. The rider was an enormous man, covered from head to toe in black clothing—from his black hood and cloak to his blackest of breeches to black boots cuffed just under his knee. For a moment, Faris wondered if perhaps the grim reaper were upon her, come to claim her before Kade Tremeshton did. For long moments, the only sounds were the horse's heavy breath, the strain of leather as the rider shifted in the saddle, and the whip of his cape as he flung one length of it over his broad shoulder.

"Who are ya, lass?" the rider asked in a low, raspy growl. "And what are ya about here in the night?"

"I-I . . . I'm only Faris, and . . . I'm on my way to Loch Loland Castle," Faris managed.

"At sunset?" the rider asked. "Only ghosts and

highwaymen wander at dusk and sunset, lass," he said.

Faris sensed his raspy whispered growl was intentional, a method of hiding the true intonation of his voice, but his accent was unmistakable—a man from the green isle. It was only then she realized with whom fate had matched her in that moment.

"The Highwayman!" she gasped.

The Highwayman of Tanglewood was legendary through all the land. With the will and purpose of Robin Hood, the Highwayman of Tanglewood set upon only those who were wealthy—further, only those who had come by their wealth in deceitful and hateful ways. The Highwayman of Tanglewood never murdered, and it was said he never robbed any honest person—only dishonest and arrogant persons who used the poor and less fortunate to further fleece their gold-lined pockets.

"Hush, lass!" the Highwayman ordered, dismounting and striding toward Faris.

Faris shook her head and took several steps backward, certain she had escaped Tremeshton Manor only to find her doom.

"Know ya not the trees have ears, they do," he whispered. He stood directly before her now—tall, dark, menacing. Reaching up, he pushed his black hood from his head, revealing a black mask, dark mustache, and goatee. Faris Shayhan found herself looking into the smoldering black eyes of the Highwayman of Tanglewood. The mask he wore covered his head and perfectly concealed any feature of his face around his eyes, nose, and cheeks. The mustache and goatee completed the concealment. It would be impossible to determine the true identity of the Highwayman of Tanglewood.

"Why is it ya travel under the cover of evenin'?" the Highwayman asked.

"I-I . . . It was the most convenient time to leave," she stammered.

The Highwayman growled low in his throat and began walking around her, prowling like a panther stalking his prey. He studied Faris— looking from her head to her feet and then from feet to head again. His study was thorough.

"Leave where, lass? What reason would a bonnie young lass the like of ya have to leave a place?" he asked.

"Are . . . are you going to harm me, sir?" Faris asked. Though she felt he meant her no damage, she was yet driven to ask.

"It is unwise to travel at night, lass," the Highwayman said as he stopped his investigation of her and stood straight before her once again. "Rogues and criminals and wicked men of every sort roam at night, they do—even highwaymen who might steal something from a young lass sooch as yarself," he whispered.

Faris was mesmerized by the flash in his eyes, by the sheer height of his head and breadth of his shoulders.

"Are . . . are you going to steal something from me, sir? I . . . I haven't much, but I will gladly give you all that I do have," Faris said, certain she was about to be robbed.

"I might indeed steal something from ya, lass," the Highwayman said, grinning a rogue's grin. "It might be I'll steal yar satchel there," he said pointing to her satchel. "Or I might instead steal away yar innocence."

Faris gasped, covering her mouth with her hand. Could it be she'd only just escaped the grip of one evil man to fall carelessly into the grip of another? The Highwayman laughed, no doubt amused by her astonished expression. His smile flashed in the night like starlight—white teeth against all the blackness of his wardrobe.

"But methinks tonight," the Highwayman began, reaching out and taking Faris's face between his large, gloved hands. "Methinks tonight I'll steal yar kiss instead."

Faris's eyes widened with surprise, and her heart hammered with fear mingled with some sort of wild exhilaration.

"Only yar kiss tonight, bonnie lass," the Highwayman of Tanglewood whispered. "Only yar kiss."

Faris couldn't breathe! She felt faint—but

not from fear. Somehow her breathlessness, the weak sensation in her knees, was not the product of fear but of some sort of unthinkable, unfathomable delight! She fancied she had lost her senses—gone mad. Delight—in anticipation of a thief stealing her kiss? She should struggle! She should! Yet her limbs would not obey her mind's command, and she stood still, unmoving, frozen with a strange, enchanting sort of fear.

"Ah, pretty little lass," the Highwayman whispered as his gloved thumb caressed her lower lip for a moment. "Close yar eyes, and let the Highwayman of Tanglewood rob ya now."

Faris shook her head, unable to believe what was happening. But as the Highwayman's head descended toward hers, the spell he had woven around her—the magic of the night breeze—all of it enveloped her, and she did, indeed, close her eyes.

"Ya smell of the heather, of the meadow, of lavender and rose petals," the Highwayman whispered as his breath, hot on her neck, caused Faris's body to tingle with unusual bliss. "Yar skin is soft and sweet," he breathed.

Faris trembled as she felt his lips brush the bare flesh of her neck.

"And do ya taste as sweet, lassie?" he asked. Faris was breathless, sent trembling as his lips pressed to hers in a firm but tender kiss. "Do ya taste as sweet as the lavender of yar skin smells?"

Faris gasped as the Highwayman kissed her once more. His lips lingered soft against her own. Of a sudden, his hand gripped her chin, his kiss abruptly more intense, hot, and moist. This was a rogue's kiss! Faris knew it was, for although she had never before experienced the like of it, she had seen it once—seen the milkmaid at Tremeshton kissed in like manner by a visiting coachman. In truth, Faris had always longed for a rogue's kiss, for it seemed somehow more genuine, more passionate than the quick, properly administered kisses she had witnessed otherwise.

But this—this was a stranger! The thought shouted in Faris's mind, and she pulled away from the Highwayman—away from his strong grasp and rogue's kiss.

The Highwayman of Tanglewood smiled—his white teeth bright in the moonlight. "Ah, yar sweet as honey warmed in the summer sun, ya are, lass," he whispered. Faris's entire body was still erupting with goose bumps as he continued to look at her. "Sweet as honey," he repeated. "And thrice as bonnie."

Faris could only stand staring up at him in astonishment. The Highwayman of Tanglewood! He had come upon her in the meadow and—and stolen something from her! Yet Faris knew he hadn't really stolen anything, for something that was given so freely could not be considered stolen.

"Now, off with ya to Loch Loland Castle, lass," he said, striding from her and mounting his black steed. "But not alone," he added, "for I'll see ya safely there myself—though ya may not know it." The magnificent black beast he sat reared up, neighing madly as the Highwayman of Tanglewood pulled his hood back over his head.

Breaking into a gallop, the Highwayman rode past Faris to a nearby lilac tree. Snapping off a sprig of fragrant blossoms, he then rode to her once more. His black beast of a stallion impatiently stomped the ground as its rider paused, tossing the sprig of lilacs to Faris.

"Goodbye, fair Faris of Loch Loland Castle," the Highwayman said. Faris again saw the white of his teeth flash as he smiled at her. "And I thank ya, I do—for the wares which I've stolen from ya this night!"

He was off again in a mad gallop across the meadow. Faris looked up into the purple curtains of night's sky. The Highwayman of Tanglewood! It was as a dream! And such a kiss was the stuff of dreams too! Oh, what a blessed day it had been—deliverance from Tremeshton Manor and its arrogant young master and a chance, romantic rendezvous with the Highwayman of Tanglewood. Faris shook her head, knowing she would never again be the same girl she'd been before that moment—before that blissful, dream-borne moment in the meadow when the Highwayman of Tanglewood had stolen a kiss.

At Loch Loland Castle

Summer faded into autumn, and autumn slept through winter. Spring melted winter's cold embrace, and once again the lilac and meadow flowers were abloom. As the Tanglewood Meadow was alive with early summer, so Loch Loland Castle was alive with merriment and grand anticipation. The young miss of the manor, Lillias Rockrimmon, was betrothed to the dashing Lord Gawain Kendrick. Furthermore, after an absence of near to two years, the young master of Loch Loland, Lochlan Rockrimmon, was expected to return for his sister and Lord Kendrick's blessed event. Lord and Lady Rockrimmon were resplendent—joyous in expectancy at the return of their son as well as the marriage of their daughter. All others who labored and lived within Loch Loland's strong walls were near to giddy for the beauty of summer and anticipation of the events pertaining to the Rockrimmon children.

Faris Shayhan had never known such happiness and contentment as she had come to know at Loch Loland. An honorable and just lord and a compassionate and kind lady were the Lord and

Lady Rockrimmon. Though she did not know the young master—for he had been away since long before Faris's arrival—the young mistress, Lillias, was as kind and as lovely as ever her mother was. The staff at Loch Loland Castle were likewise unusual in their good character. Faris had made fast friends of many of those with whom she labored.

Still, there was one circumstance, one detail of her coming to Loch Loland that she yet held high above all else—the Highwayman of Tanglewood. As Faris arranged lilac sprigs in a delicate crystal vase, the sun shone bright and warm through the window of the chamber in which she labored. Yet it was not the day filled with sunshine that owned her thoughts—but the memory of a purple-curtained sky in a fragrant summer meadow.

Drawing one large set of lilac florets to her face, Faris inhaled deeply the sweet scent of it. Closing her eyes, she could almost hear the rhythmic approach of the Highwayman's mount—almost sense the cool of evening, see the amethyst of evening's drapery being drawn over the Tanglewood Meadow.

It had been a year—an entire year since Faris had quit Tremeshton—an entire year since the Highwayman of Tanglewood had stolen a kiss under the cloak of darkness. Yet the cherished memory had lingered in Faris's mind, heart, and soul every day since. Often she fancied she heard the Highwayman's raspy brogue—fancied her lips still warm and tingling from his kiss. In leaving Tremeshton, in meeting the Highwayman of Tanglewood, it seemed Faris's life had begun anew—her heart awakened.

Yet Faris had not set eyes on the Highwayman since the night she had traveled to Loch Loland Castle. Each night of the year's passing, Faris's head lay on her pillow, her eyes closed as she reminisced upon her chance meeting with the fascinating rogue. Over and over, she dreamt of his broad shoulders, strength of body, and tantalizing kiss. Many were the evenings she had ventured to the Tanglewood Meadow at night—hoping, praying for another chance meeting with the dashing Highwayman. In vain she had hoped and prayed for it: she had never seen him again. Though the Highwayman of Tanglewood continued to battle the corrupt noble and wealthy, though his legend thrived as fast and as strong as the ivy clinging to the outer walls of Loch Loland Castle, it seemed Faris was doomed never to see him again. At least twice a week the Highwayman of Tanglewood was seen riding over the countryside—seen by others, but never again by Faris. Having stopped a rich man's carriage or waylaid a corrupt nobleman, the Highwayman of Tanglewood continued to strip greedy and dishonest men of undeserved gold and riches—gold and riches taken by means of inflated rent charged to struggling tenants or by other equally treacherous means. Such pompous men, dishonest or not, were outraged at the very existence of the Highwayman of Tanglewood—furious at being bested by a common thief. Many deserving victims had hired men of questionable character to track down and detain Tanglewood's famed Highwayman. All failed. The Highwayman of Tanglewood remained free, roaming Tanglewood and the surrounding countryside, championing the bitterly oppressed and unfairly abused.

Adjusting one fragrant sprig of lilac, Faris sighed, pleased with the results of her labors. Miss Lillias would find her chamber sweet-scented and brightened by the arrangement of lavender loveliness. Faris was happy in knowing she had contributed to the young woman's being comfortable. Satisfied she had adequately finished with Miss Lillias's chambers, Faris made her way down the hall to the abandoned, yet ever maintained, chambers of Miss Lillias's brother, Lochlan.

Upon arriving at Loch Loland, Faris had been charged with the maintenance of three sets of chambers, as well as various other duties pertaining to the efficient running of the household. She had been flattered as well as humbled when Lady Rockrimmon had charged her with the bedchambers of both her children, and Faris maintained them well. The third chamber in her charge was the empty rooms across the hall from Miss Lillias. Having finished the empty chamber and then Miss Lillias's, Faris opened the door and stepped into the large rooms of the absent Rockrimmon heir.

It was understood that Lochlan Rockrimmon—sole heir to the Rockrimmon titles and fortune—had been laboring far away managing his father's affairs. It was nigh unto two years since the young heir had quit Loch Loland at his father's bidding, yet Lady Rockrimmon begged his chambers be kept in readiness of his eventual return. At times, Faris thought her efforts to keep the young master's room futile. Yet each time Lady Rockrimmon would thank Faris for her efforts, Faris's heart would swell with contentment at having pleased her lovely benefactress.

"Shall I tidy your chambers today, young master of the manor?" Faris said aloud to herself as she looked about the lifeless chamber. "Has yesterday's dust settled as yet?" Running one index finger across the water basin table nearby, she smiled. "Ah!" she said. "I see dusting is, indeed, in order."

"Faris! Faris!"

Faris startled only slightly at the sound of Lillias calling her name. It was quite a common thing—Miss Lillias scurrying through Loch

Loland Castle in search of Faris. Faris smiled, happy in knowing the young miss often sought her advice and assistance.

"Oh, there you are, darling!" Lillias exclaimed, bursting into the chamber, eyes bright with excitement.

"Yes, Lady Kendrick," Faris greeted, sending Lillias's eyes to even brighter illumination.

"Oh, how I love that you call me that, Faris!" Lillias giggled, green eyes lit pure with delight. "But you must not let father hear it. It does upset him so."

"Because he loves his only daughter and is already missing her," Faris said. She smiled.

Lillias Rockrimmon was the perfect image of youthful beauty. Eyes like soft green opal, hair as nut-brown as any chestnut, rosied cheeks, rubied lips. In short, Lillias Rockrimmon was the loveliest young woman Faris had ever seen. Her heart was good and kind as well. Lord Kendrick could count himself very fortunate indeed. Faris's smile faded slightly—a wish flitting through her mind that she were such a beauty.

"Hush, Faris," Lillias said. "You'll well my eyes with tears, and I shall look a fright." Lillias paused, looking about the room. "I do not know why mother insists you keep Lochlan's rooms at the ready. It is yet two months before the wedding. He will not return until the very last possible moment." Lillias smiled at Faris, reached out, and clasped her hands in her own. "But it is not Lochlan's room that concerns we two at this moment." Lillias looked about the room as if expectant upon finding they were not alone. Lowering her voice, she said, "The Highwayman of Tanglewood has been seen! Only an hour ago—in the broad light of day!"

"What?" Faris exclaimed in a whisper. Her heart increased the pace of its rhythm, for indeed it was an unprecedented event. "Surely not, miss!" Faris added. "He has never been seen in daylight before! Surely it would be too perilous for him to appear so!"

"Indeed! Yet it is true! Graybeau saw the Highwayman himself, as did two of Lord Tremeshton's stablemen," Lillias explained in an excited whisper.

"Lord Tremeshton's men?" Faris asked.

Lillias laughed, her opal-green eyes flashing. "Yes! He's done it again, Faris! Our beloved Highwayman has bested Lord Tremeshton once more. And in the bright light of day."

Faris giggled, covering her mouth with one hand to stifle the delighted sound.

The arrogant Kade Tremeshton had fallen prey to the tricks of the Highwayman of Tanglewood once before. Bested at swords and fists, Kade Tremeshton had known the humiliation of being beaten by the Highwayman some months earlier. Lord Tremeshton had fallen ill and died only months after Faris had left Tremeshton Manor. His arrogant son, Kade, had inherited his title and wealth, as well as his greed. In his ravenous gluttony, Kade had more than doubled the rent he demanded from his tenants and had even begun to tax their livestock. How Faris had delighted in listening to the telling of the Highwayman of Tanglewood's besting Kade Tremeshton. Now it seemed she was to enjoy another tale of Lord Kade Tremeshton's humiliation at the Highwayman's hand.

"Tell me, Miss Lillias!" Faris whispered. "Tell me the tale—in its entirety! Do not leave one word of it to be missing!"

Giggling with excitement, Lillias turned and closed the door to her brother's chambers. Taking Faris's hand, she led her to the massive bed before them, promptly sitting down on the sapphire velvet coverlet and pulling Faris to sit beside her.

"The tale was told to me thus," Lillias began. "Lord Tremeshton—Kade the Heinous, as I prefer to refer to him—"

Faris could not help but giggle at Lillias's favorite title for Lord Kade Tremeshton.

Lillias smiled and continued. "Kade the Heinous was out with two of his stablemen. It seems he has acquired a new mount and wished to try it—poor, miserable animal. Kade the Heinous, being the coward that he is, demanded two stablemen accompany him—in case the new mount was not to his satisfaction, so he said."

Faris breathed a sigh of exasperation, rolling her eyes as well.

"Just what I feel," Lillias continued. "To continue, they were there, the three of them, riding through the Tanglewood Forest. It is true, for Graybeau saw them, having been riding at the same time in exercising Jovan."

Jovan was Lord Rockrimmon's favorite mount. The magnificent bay was aging, however, and Lord Rockrimmon had lessened the frequency of riding the animal. Therefore, it was often Bainbridge Graybeau, Lord Rockrimmon's favored stablemaster, who was asked to provide mild exercise for the beloved horse when Lord Rockrimmon himself did not have the time to do so. Bainbridge Graybeau was a strikingly handsome man, perhaps ten years Faris's senior. A man to be admired—a man of honor. If Bainbridge Graybeau had seen the Highwayman of Tanglewood take Lord Kade Tremeshton to task, then it was the truth.

"There they were—Kade the Heinous, his two stablemen, and Graybeau just a ways beyond them, when from the direction of the meadow he rode, the Highwayman of Tanglewood—his black cape rippling in the breeze, the heated breath of his black steed bearing down upon them all."

Faris smiled, delighted with the light of exhilaration in Lillias's eyes. Lillias loved the tales of the Highwayman almost as much as Faris did. It was one of their secrets together—Lillias and Faris's—their love for the tales of the Highwayman of Tanglewood.

"Oh, do go on, Miss Lillias!" Faris pleaded. "I am desperate to hear the whole of it!"

Lillias Rockrimmon smiled. How she adored Faris Shayhan! How thankful she was her mother had stolen her away from Tremeshton Manor to become her daughter's friend. Lillias giggled, delighted by the luminous light of excitement flashing in Faris's dark eyes. How plain Lillias felt in Faris's presence. Faris's dark hair, dark eyes, and long, dark lashes gave her the look of some magic being—as if she could gaze into the very depths of a soul, read each person's thoughts and feelings. How glad she was Faris had come to Loch Loland Castle.

Faris seemed to love the tales of the Highwayman of Tanglewood even more than Lillias herself did. To Lillias this was nearly inconceivable— that someone could be more intrigued by the local rogue than she was—for the Highwayman was Lillias's greatest intrigue. It was often Lillias dreamt of meeting the Highwayman, of pulling the infamous black mask from his face in revealing his true identity.

"Oh, isn't this delicious, Faris?" Lillias squealed.

"Delicious!" Faris agreed.

"His steed reared up before Kade the Heinous's new mount, frightening the poor beast into throwing his new master," Lillias continued.

"Wonderful!" Faris exclaimed, clasping her hands with delight.

"Kade the Heinous fell flat on his backside, shouting at his stablemen to defend him from the Highwayman," Lillias said. "They dismounted, drew swords—what lord provides his stablemen with swords for a daylight ride, I ask you?" Lillias said.

"Only a coward," Faris said.

"Indeed," Lillias agreed. Both young women shook their heads, disgusted with Kade's cowardice.

"Pray, go on," Faris said.

"The Highwayman did not dismount, however," Lillias explained. "Rather his boot met with the chin of one stableman, who then found himself fairly sprawling as he fell to the ground, rendered entirely unconscious."

"The Highwayman's boot is not to be taken lightly," Faris said, smiling so broadly her face began to ache.

"No indeed," Lillias agreed. "Nor his rapier— for drawing it quickly, he disarmed the second stableman from astride his mount! Disarmed him, then met his chin with the same boot and sent him sprawling next to the first!"

Faris laughed and clapped her hands! What a story! She thought of her own vision of the Highwayman, and she could see it all in her mind's eye—his boot, his cape, the black steed he sat. Her heart fluttered at the secret knowledge that he had once called her by name—had once stolen a kiss from her very lips.

"Naturally, Kade the Heinous was frightened," Lillias continued. "Graybeau says Kade drew his sword, his hand trembling as he wielded it, and called out to the Highwayman, 'Coward! To ambush such as I when no aid is with me.' "

"Ridiculous fool!" Faris breathed.

"Graybeau says the Highwayman laughed, dismounted in one swift movement, and stood before Kade with his rapier at the ready," Lillias continued. " 'To meet you in the broad light of day with two men at your back and none other at mine?' the Highwayman asked. 'That is no coward, Lord Tremeshton. Yet only a coward would tax his tenants so heavily as to starve wives and children. It is a coward I see before me, and your time has come once more. Hand over your purse, Lord Tremeshton—or see your blood spilt before me.' That is what Graybeau heard the Highwayman tell Kade the Heinous."

"Did Lord Tremeshton strike first?" Faris asked. She must know the tale! She must know if Kade Tremeshton was once again bested by the Highwayman of Tanglewood. Certainly she already knew he had been, but she must know how he was bested. She must hear it all.

Lillias laughed. "It is even worse for Tremeshton than that! He surrendered his purse! Without offering any defense of himself at all! He simply glanced at the unconscious stable-men about him and surrendered his purse to the Highwayman!"

"Are you in earnest, miss?" Faris asked, unable to believe what she was indeed hearing.

"I am!" Lillias answered. "Graybeau said there was no confrontation beyond that. Kade the Heinous simply surrendered his purse, mounted one of his stablemen's horses, and rode away."

"His cowardice knows no bounds! Even in villainy!" Faris said.

"Indeed. Kade Tremeshton has ever sickened me, and news of this only sours my stomach more at the thought of him," Lillias said.

"It is no wonder the Highwayman dared a daylight ambush," Faris said. "No doubt he knew Lord Tremeshton's cowardice would make the besting easy."

"No doubt," Lillias agreed. She was quiet for a moment. Faris watched as Lillias glanced away, to the sunshine pouring warm and bright through the window of her brother's empty chambers. "Do you suppose, Faris," she began, "do you suppose it is possible my own Lord

Kendrick is the Highwayman of Tanglewood?"

"What?" Faris exclaimed.

"I have often wondered it, for it is on several occasions my lord betrothed has spoken to me of the Highwayman's escapades with a certain insightfulness I find curious."

Faris was struck silent for a moment. Could it be? No! It certainly could not! Indeed Lord Gawain Kendrick was young and strong, a worthy nobleman who despised those of Kade Tremeshton's character. Dark-haired and boasting a well-groomed mustache and goatee, Lord Kendrick was unusually handsome as well. Yet Lord Kendrick could not be the Highwayman—for if he were, it would only mean Faris's dreams of meeting the Highwayman in the meadow once more, her dreams of his stealing another blissful kiss—her dreams would be dashed, as waves on a rocky shore.

"I-I am certain he would have told you, miss . . . implied it in the least," Faris stammered. The thought of it was causing her heart to ache the like she had never known. The Highwayman of Tanglewood—her Highwayman of Tanglewood—betrothed to Lillias Rockrimmon? It could not be!

"I'm sure you are right, Faris," Lillias said, looking to Faris once more. "Perhaps it is merely my youthful infatuation with the Highwayman that causes me to think it. Still, sometimes . . . sometimes Gawain seems to know things . . . and I wonder."

"When next your lord speaks something to cause you to wonder," Faris began, "perhaps . . . perhaps we could meet in secret as we do now and . . . and I can hear his words and help you to better interpret their meaning." Oh, Lord Kendrick could not be the Highwayman! He must not be!

"That is a brilliant notion, Faris!" Lillias exclaimed. "And so it shall be that next time Gawain piques my curiosity where the Highwayman of Tanglewood is concerned. I will seek you out, and we will ponder it together."

"We will do it," Faris said, forcing a smile.

Lillias giggled. "We will," she said.

Faris felt a frown pucker her brow a moment. "Do you know, miss," she began, "it even comes to me now that perhaps Graybeau is the Highwayman."

"Graybeau?" Lillias asked.

"The Highwayman is said to be tall—quite tall, in fact. Why—Bainbridge Graybeau is near the tallest man I have ever known," Faris said. And it was true. Bainbridge Graybeau was unusually tall, very handsome, and known for his strength. As Lillias's eyebrows arched in astonished realization, Faris nodded.

"He is that," Lillias said. "And handsome as any rogue ever was. As a child, I followed him around with endless infatuation. He looks to be skilled with horses—then why shouldn't he be skilled with the blade as well? And it would explain his witnessing the Highwayman in the broad light of day." Lillias gasped as if sudden realization struck her. "Do you know, Faris, that Graybeau told me neither Kade the Heinous nor either of his men was aware of Graybeau's presence in the Tanglewood when they were set upon by the Highwayman?"

"Perhaps it was not so much he witnessed the ambush—" Faris began.

"—as much as it was he manipulated the ambush himself!" Lillias gasped.

For a moment, Faris's mind settled on it—Bainbridge Graybeau was the Highwayman of Tanglewood! She could see the same thought alight in Lillias's eyes. Still, in the next instant, both young ladies burst into peals of laughter.

"What a pair we are, Faris!" Lillias sighed once her laughter had subsided. "Meeting in secret to discuss such a rogue—to speculate his identity."

"Well, we are not alone, miss," Faris said. "Every soul in the entire countryside is speculating of it."

" 'Tis true," Lillias said. She breathed a heavy sigh and shook her head as if dispelling a dream. "I'll tell you a secret, Faris—though you may think very little of me for admitting it."

"Then do tell me—if it is so delicious as to

45

scandalize you in my mind," Faris giggled.

Lillias bit her lip and paused, obviously uncertain she should share the mentioned secret.

"Go on then, miss," Faris prodded. "Do not keep me waiting. I am far too anxious to manage patience of any sort!"

"You are my friend, Faris," Lillias said, dropping her voice once more. "But I pause to tell you my secret—for I am not sure you truly value me as yours."

"The greatest I have, miss!" Faris assured. "I promise it with all my heart!"

"Then you must call me Lillias, Faris," Lillias said. "For we have been fast friends for a year now, and still you call me 'miss' when we are speaking thus."

Faris smiled, her heart swelling with happiness. Lillias Rockrimmon was the young miss of Loch Loland Castle. It was soon she would be Lady Kendrick—yet it was ever she begged Faris to call her by her given name. Always Faris had resisted for reasons of her station and for fear of letting Lillias Rockrimmon become too beloved a friend. Still, she could see in the young woman's eyes the need for true friendship.

"Very well," Faris whispered. "Please entrust me with your most delicious of secrets, Lillias."

Lillias smiled, and Faris giggled when her friend reached out, embracing her quickly.

"You are my truest friend, Faris! The truest I

46

have ever known!" Lillias said. "And because it is so, I shall tell you my greatest secret!" Lillias cleared her throat, and Faris giggled as a blush rose to her cheeks. "It is almost nightly I dream of the Highwayman."

Faris giggled—for what shocking confession was this? She too dreamt of the Highwayman—dreamt of meeting him in a fragrant meadow at midnight, of being kissed by the rogue with the Irish brogue.

"Why, that is not so scandalous, Lillias," Faris said, "for I dream of him as well."

"But do you dream of his coming to Loch Loland Castle, stealing you from the warmth of your bed, only to carry you to the Tanglewood and hold you in the warmth of his arms? Do you dream of his ravishing you with kisses?" Lillias sighed, delighted by the reminiscence of her own dreams.

"No, indeed, I do not," Faris said. "For I dream of wandering through the Tanglewood Meadow, the air fragrant with dew-laden grass and new flowers. I dream of a purple-draperied sky at midnight and a chance meeting with the Highwayman where he steals a kiss from me—a kiss the like you and I may only dream of."

Lillias smiled. "I dream he is Gawain and that he dare not tell me the truth for fear of discovery."

Faris giggled. "He has no true identity in my dreams," she said. "In my dreams, he is only the

47

Highwayman of Tanglewood—though sometimes I hear his voice in my mind."

"Indeed?" Lillias asked. "And what is the nature of his voice?"

"Deep in intonation, masked with a rough rasping to secure the truth of his identity, and thick with a brogue—like they who travel here from the green isle." Faris hoped she had not revealed too much to Lillias. Still, the words had been over her tongue before she could stop them.

"I like your dream, Faris," Lillias said.

"And I yours," Faris said.

"Then let us be about our day—both with our secrets cached safely away in our hearts," Lillias said.

"Yes," Faris said. She thought again of her chance meeting with the Highwayman of Tanglewood—of the kiss he had stolen from her. "Both with our secrets cached safely."

Lillias embraced Faris once more, and Faris returned her embrace. Her heart was warmed by friendship, the safe and happy life at Loch Loland Castle.

"Oh!" Lillias exclaimed. "It was nearly I forgot to tell you—Mother asked me to beg you to place a vase of lilacs in her dressing chamber the like you arrange in mine each day."

"Of course," Faris said. "I will do it at once, for the day is young, and she may enjoy them still."

"Thank you, Faris," Lillias said as the stood.

"For what?" Faris asked as she smoothed the sapphire velvet of the coverlet upon which they had been sitting.

"For being my friend," Lillias said. "For coming to Loch Loland Castle to be my truest friend."

"Thank you, Lillias," Faris said, holding the tears in her eyes that begged for release. "For being mine."

They stepped from the chamber and into the hall. What met their eyes caused them both to gasp—for there, in the hall near the stairway, stood none other than Lord Gawain Kendrick and Bainbridge Graybeau in hushed conversation.

Faris felt the hair on the back of her neck prickle, and she looked at Lillias to see her mouth agape.

"It is mere coincidence," Lillias whispered.

"Of course," Faris agreed. "Mere coincidence."

Yet Faris could not rid herself of the unsettled feeling that had washed over her at the sight of Lord Kendrick and Graybeau steeped in curious conversation.

Even after Lord Kendrick had greeted Lillias, kissed her sweetly on the cheek, and taken her arm—even as she walked down the long hall of the east wing toward Lady Rockrimmon's dressing chambers—the unsettled sensation lingered.

She fancied she would not mind so much if the

49

Highwayman were Graybeau. Bainbridge Graybeau was handsome, quite perfectly masculine, and quite perfectly unattached. Lord Gawain Kendrick, however, though handsome enough, would soon be married—and to Faris's best friend. Faris decided in that moment the Highwayman of Tanglewood was not Lord Gawain Kendrick—for the truth of it would break her heart. No! The Highwayman was no one of her acquaintance. The Highwayman of Tanglewood was an Irish rogue with no other attachments save to a girl he had once met in a meadow in the moonlight. Faris was certain of it.

The evening was summer-warm. A soft breeze played through the meadow grass, and twilight was just beginning. Faris gazed up into the violet of the evening sky—inhaled the fragrance of meadow flowers and moist grass.

How long should I wait for fate to appear? Faris wondered. How long should she stand in the midst of the meadow waiting for a chance glimpse of the Highwayman of Tanglewood? Yet such a man was worth waiting forever to see again. Was he not?

It was her conversation with Lillias—the conversation they had shared concerning their mutual dreams of the Highwayman that found her in the meadow. In all the times she had visited the meadow in hopes of seeing the Highwayman again, she had never felt so desperate to see him as she did now.

All the day long she had agonized, wondering whether the Highwayman of Tanglewood was truly Lord Gawain Kendrick in disguise. Further, she was certain he was not—certain that if she could chance to meet the Highwayman again, she would be even more certain. Thus, she had waited until all was dark and quiet at Loch Loland Castle—waited until even Old Joseph, Lord Rockrimmon's loyal first man, was retired to his chamber. It was then she had set out for the meadow. It was then she hoped—Faris Shayhan hoped the stars or heaven would bless her with another stroke of good fortune.

Faris reached up, pulling the pins from her hair and running her fingers through her long, dark tresses. Drawing a ribbon from the tiny pocket in her skirt, she tied her hair back at the nape of her neck, feeling somehow free and refreshed. The fragrant breeze caressed her cheeks, cooling the blush caused from her brisk walk.

Purple seemed to rinse the sky, and the sun was nearly set when Faris fancied she heard the rhythm of a horse's gallop in the distance. She narrowed her eyes, straining to see through the darkness of the settling night, glad she brought a lantern with her. Still, she could see nothing but the outline of the Tanglewood Forest against the violet of falling night.

Faris closed her eyes and listened. Yes! She was sure she heard the drumming of horse hooves in the distance. Her heart began to hammer within her bosom; yet she knew the rider could be one of a million upon the earth with a thousand intended directions—a hundred different purposes. After all, chances were the rider Faris heard on approach was simply a messenger sent from one manor house to another. Or the constable on the hunt for any highwayman he might come upon.

But as the resonance of the drumming hooves grew nearer, louder, so did the mad pounding of Faris's heart. And then, of a sudden, a rider astride his mount broke the tree line. Galloping into the meadow came a rider in black—black hood, black cape, black boots—and a stallion as black as obsidian. Faris knew at once fate had granted her wish—for reining to a mount-rearing halt before her was none other than the Highwayman of Tanglewood!

In Meeting the Highwayman

"Careful, lass!" the raspy voice of the Highwayman of Tanglewood warned. "I nearly run ya over, I did!"

"Forgive me," Faris said. Her palms were moist, her heart causing pain within her so violently did it hammer. He was before her! In the heavy purple of evening, he mumbled to his mount to calm the beast, all the while his attention fixed on Faris. She could feel the blood coursing through her veins, feared her heart might beat itself to quitting. As the breeze caught his cape, ruffling it, blowing it back over one shoulder, Faris silently bit her tongue a bit to assure herself she was indeed awake and not rapt in some wonderful dream.

"Aye, but wait," the Highwayman said, dismounting in one swift movement. Throwing back his hood to reveal his black mask, mustache, and goatee, he strode toward her. "Me and thee have met before, we have."

Faris's heart raced as he approached. She feared her knees might give way beneath her. "Y-yes," Faris managed, swallowing hard. The rogue of her dreams stood directly before her, his smile piercing the night with its dazzling brilliance—far more brilliant than the stars dotting the amethyst sky above.

"Ah, yes! I could never farget a rendezvous such as the one we shared, fair Faris of Loch Loland Castle," he chuckled.

Faris gasped, astounded! He remembered her! Remembered even her very name! Did he remember more of her? Had his memory clung to her the way her memory had clung to him? With his next utterance, her questions were answered.

" 'Twas in this very meadow here that I stole a kiss from ye last summer, I did."

"Yes, sire," Faris said, unable to keep a smile of delight from spreading across her face.

" 'Sire' she calls me?" he chuckled again. "But I be no sire, Faris of Loch Loland. I be a far simpler man than that, far sure and far certain."

"You are no simple man," Faris told him, and he laughed, the silver moonlight catching his smile once more.

"No. No, I suppose I be anythin' but simple," he said. He cocked his head to one side, asking, "But what finds ya out in the meadow at night once more, lass? Have ya quit Loch Loland?"

"Oh, no!" Faris assured him. "I am happier there than ever I have been. I-I only came at the chance to . . . to see you again."

The Highwayman glanced about quickly, seeming suddenly unsettled as he mumbled, "Have ya now?"

"Oh! Not to entrap you, sire!" Faris explained, realizing the reason for his sudden suspicion. The Highwayman of Tanglewood would not have survived so long had he not been wary, suspicious of impending entrapment. Still, it sickened Faris to think he might suspect her of luring him into a snare. Quickly she explained, "I simply wished to—to meet you once more."

His eyes narrowed a moment. He seemed uncertain as to whether trusting her were a wise decision.

"I've told no one about meeting you last summer. Not a living soul. I swear it."

"Why not?" he asked plainly. " 'Tis many a folk would be willin' to tell the authorities in the least, they would."

"Not me," Faris said. "I have no desire to see any harm come to you."

"Yar far me cause then?" he asked.

"As . . . as much as someone of my station is able," she answered. Of a sudden she felt ashamed—ashamed of being only a chamber-maid, ashamed of being one of those for whom the Highwayman of Tanglewood rode out.

"Someone in yar station?" he asked. "What is it ya do out there at Loch Loland Castle?" He strode toward her, and his sudden advance unsettled

55

Faris so that she stumbled, losing her footing. She did not fall, however, for the Highwayman's powerful grip on her arm steadied her.

Inhaling deeply and mustering a bit of courage, Faris raised her eyes to him once more and answered, "I am chambermaid for the Rockrimmon children."

The Highwayman nodded and released her arm. He grinned as he said, " 'Tis a fine position—to be entrusted with the care of the intimate chambers of such a family. 'Tis not a thing to hang yar head about."

Faris smiled, warmed by his tenderness.

"And I hear Loch Loland Castle will lose its daughter to Lord Kendrick."

Faris's eyes widened, and she nodded. "Indeed. In two months' time, Lillias will wed his lordship. Are—are you well acquainted with Lord Kendrick? Is this how you know of their betrothal?" Faris tried to study the size and stance of the Highwayman. Could he, indeed, be Lord Gawain Kendrick in disguise? It was impossible to discern. Her heart hammered with anxiety—fear that the Highwayman of Tanglewood was, in fact, Lillias's betrothed, fear that her own dreams would be instantly destroyed at gaining a sure knowledge of the fact.

The Highwayman chuckled. Reaching out, he brushed a strand of hair from Faris's cheek, causing goose bumps to ripple over her body. His touch, even for the glove covering his hand, was entirely invigorating!

"Oh, I come by much information and in many ways, lass," he said. " 'Tis me duty to keep an eye on the good families in this blessed country, as well as the bad. And yar young miss and her betrothed young lord—they are both of fine character. Lord Kendrick is honorable. Though I will not tell ye how well acquainted with him I am or how well I am not. Still, he is one to help the good folk 'round here in a much more legal manner than I be able."

"Then . . . then you are not he?" Faris ventured. "Indeed, you are not Lord Gawain Kendrick hidden in masked form?" Faris's heart was beating with such a brutal force it caused her voice to tremble.

"I?" the Highwayman asked. "I? Lord Gawain Kendrick?" He laughed then. Laughed so wholeheartedly and with such volume that Faris felt the need to hush him, to quiet him for his own safety.

"Sire! You must take care," Faris said, glancing around into the darkness of the meadow. Bainbridge Graybeau had happened upon the Highwayman once already that day. Faris feared others may be wandering near the meadow at night, and she did not want the Highwayman to be found out.

"Oh, lass! Ya do me heart sooch good," he said. "I could no more endeavor to be the mighty Lord

Gawain Kendrick than he could endeavor to be the thief I am."

Even though Faris experienced a slight relief, still she wondered at the truthfulness of his answer. "Would you tell me if you were Lord Kendrick?" she asked. "Or would you endeavor to distract me into thinking you are not he?"

"Ya own a rare wisdom, fair Faris," the Highwayman said, smiling at her. "And ye use it well to suspect me. Still, if it's proof ya need, then I'll offer proof to ye."

"What proof can you give me without revealing your true identity?" Faris asked. For it was true. How could the Highwayman of Tanglewood possibly prove himself to be someone other than Lord Gawain Kendrick without unmasking and risking discovery?

"It is well you know Lord Kendrick," he said.

"As well as a chambermaid to his betrothed may know him," Faris said.

"Then it is well ya know his heart belongs to yar young miss. Is that so?" he asked.

"Yes," Faris said. Lord Kendrick adored Lillias Rockrimmon. All who witnessed his honorable treatment of her, all who saw the resplendent light of his countenance when she was in his company, knew it.

"Then it is well ya likewise know I am a thief and a rogue," he continued, "and Lord Kendrick, bein' so besotted by yar young miss—would

Lord Kendrick steal a kiss from a lassie in a meadow when his heart is so true to the young Miss Rockrimmon?"

Faris smiled, for she was witty herself. "Yet Lord Kendrick and Lillias Rockrimmon were not betrothed summer last. When last you and I met, you would not be honor-bound to her as you are now—if you are Lord Kendrick."

" 'Tis true enough," he admitted. "But I would honor-bound be this night in the meadow were I Lord Kendrick in truth. And by this tell me—would the Highwayman of Tanglewood steal another kiss from the fair Faris this night if he truly be Lord Kendrick, betrothed of Lillias Rockrimmon?"

Faris was certain every summer butterfly in the land was holed up in her stomach! Would he steal another kiss as her dreams had foretold? Surely it was his implication. She felt her arms and hands begin to tremble with delighted anticipation. "I would daresay Lord Kendrick is far too honorable for such behavior now he is betrothed—even if he were the Highwayman of Tanglewood," Faris answered.

"In that ya have yar answer, ya do," he chuckled. "For I will not leave this meadow this night without havin' stolen me second kiss from ye, lass. That I promise. And though I be a rogue, me promise holds true. There is yar proof of it then—I am not Lord Gawain Kendrick

59

masked and riding the Tanglewood at night."

Faris released a heavy breath, relieved. She was certain he was telling the truth—for if he meant to kiss her, if he did kiss her, it was well she knew Lord Kendrick would never be so disloyal to Lillias—even to protect the true identity of the Highwayman of Tanglewood.

"So there it is. I am not Lord Kendrick," he said. "I am only a thief. A thief of gold, of silver—"

"And of kisses?" Faris ventured. She blushed at her own boldness but was pleased when he chuckled.

"Aye," he said, smiling. "Perhaps a thief of hearts, as well."

Faris glanced away—shy at his implication. Oh, it was far too true. The dashing Highwayman of Tanglewood had no way of knowing how completely he had already stolen her heart.

"And yar bein' shy with me now, Faris?" he asked, reaching out and lifting her chin as to make her look at him. "Here now," he said, tugging at the fingers of his glove. Faris watched as he removed his gloves, stuffing them rather awkwardly into a pocket within his cape. "Will ya give me yar hand a moment, fair Faris of Tanglewood Meadow?" he asked.

Faris felt as if a river of delight flowed through her being as she nodded and tentatively let him take her hand between his. His hands were warm, a bit calloused, and powerful, and she trembled at his touch.

"I've the desire to know ya better, I have," he told her as his thumb caressed the back of her hand. "I've had the desire in me far this entire year past—for it has been yar face I see in my dreams every sleepin' moment since last we met here in the meadow."

Faris was breathless! Could he possibly be in earnest? Surely not! He was a rogue, after all, and rogues were never in earnest. Rogues were known for their flowery speech and wily ways.

"You but tease me, sire," she said. "For that cannot be. No man such as you can be captured in any regard—especially by a chambermaid in a meadow."

"Then there in that thinkin' ya show yar true innocence, fair Faris. For though I am as cunnin' as a fox and as intangible as the night, yet me heart is held in yar sweet hand," he said. Raising her hand to his lips, he placed a lingering kiss on the back of it.

"That—that cannot be," Faris said, pulling her hand from his. Her body trembled with the blissful effect of his touch as well as with distrust of his rogue's manner. He could not possibly have held her in his heart and mind the way she had held him in hers.

"Why do ye doubt it?" he asked, reaching out and placing a warm palm against her cool cheek.

"Because—because behind the mask, you are another," she said. "Another who lives the day as someone other than the Tanglewood rogue—another who keeps a home, perhaps a family, a lover, a betrothed, or—"

"I have no betrothed," he said. "No hidden wife I disrespect by stealin' kisses from ye here in the meadow. It would be foolish of me to ride as the Highwayman, to risk me life and limbs when a wee family or a sweet lass of a wife was waitin' for me elsewhere." He smiled as she smiled at him.

Faris could not halt the sigh escaping her lungs at the knowledge he was not wed or even promised to another. For a moment, something pinched at her heart: if the Highwayman could have no betrothed or wife, then he could never belong to her either. Faris pushed the thought from her head, however. He was there—standing before her, touching her, and promising to steal a kiss. She would drink in the moment. She would not let doubt poison the beauty of the night and the joy at being in his company.

"And now that ye know I am not bound to another," he began, "now that ye know I am not kissin' yar Miss Rockrimmon in the light of day and kissin' ye in the purple of night—now will ya believe me when I tell ye 'tis you I've been seein' in me dreams for this past entire of the year?"

"I should not," Faris said, her smile broadening as his thumb rested at the corner of her mouth. "For you are a rogue."

"Aye," he chuckled. "A rogue I am. I am yar rogue, fair Faris of Loch Loland Castle."

A soft breeze whispered through Faris's hair, breathing of trust—trust in the rogue who stood before her, the rogue who fought for the weak and afflicted. "I have seen you in my dreams too," she admitted in a whisper. "For with our meeting, it seems my life changed, and every other thing became more beautiful. For in stealing a kiss, you freed my soul."

He smiled and took her face between his strong, warm hands. "Will ya meet me again?" he asked. "Not by chance but by design, lass?"

Faris was nearly overcome to fainting with the euphoric sensation of his hands cradling her face. She was breathless and overly warmed some-how—even for the cool of the evening breeze. Still, she knew no other dream at that moment than to meet the Highwayman again, and so she nodded. The Highwayman of Tanglewood smiled and drew her face near to his.

"Tomorrow night—near the old ruin where the heather runs forever. Do ya know of where I speak?" he asked.

"I do," Faris assured him. She had been to the old ruins only twice before. They were the ruins of an old castle, and it was true the heather seemed to stretch forever there. "They are near to the old cemetery."

"Aye," he said, smiling. "The old cemetery. There's a legend there—a legend of lovers buried beneath two willow trees entwined. Have ya heard it?"

Faris shook her head, distracted by his placing a lingering kiss on her forehead.

"Perhaps I should relate it to ya one day," he said.

"Yes," Faris managed to breathe. Her chest rose and fell rapidly with her quickened breathing. His touch held some sort of bewitchment, an enchanting spell, and she desired nothing ever in the world but to revel in it forever.

"Tomorrow night, then, lass," he said as his hands slid from her face, coming to rest on her shoulders. "At twilight—when the purple shades of night meet the purple heather. There I'll meet ye—and perhaps steal yar heart away."

Faris gasped, trembled as he leaned forward, kissing her neck. His breath was warm and tickled her ear. She felt his strong hands move to her head, his fingers slipping into the softness of her hair. In the next moment, Faris was swept away to bliss by the sense of his mustache on her neck. He was toying with her—allowing his lips to hover a mere breath from her flesh.

"A rogue I may be," he began, "but me promise is sure, and I will have me kiss this night."

His lips gently pressed to hers. The kiss was soft, measured, yet it filled Faris's bosom with such breathless rapture, she sensed her limbs going numb.

"Still, a rogue I am, fair Faris," he whispered as his lips lingered a breath from her own. "And no gentleman's kiss ever satisfied any rogue."

Faris gasped as the Highwayman of Tanglewood gathered her into his arms and against the strength of his powerful body. Instantly his mouth captured hers, his arms binding her securely to him as he administered a kiss of such driven demand as to nearly render her unconscious. Faris heard herself sigh, felt her body surrender and weaken against his as he kissed her. Never had she known such euphoria! To be held by such a man, kissed by the same—it was magnificent! Yet, in the next moment, he ended their kiss all too abruptly, and she gasped for breath.

The Highwayman released her, drawing away quickly and pulling his hood over his head. Faris watched, entirely bemused, as he mounted his steed. Her body still trembled from his touch— her lips still sensed his kiss.

"I must away," he said. His black steed was anxious. No doubt the animal was unfamiliar with any sort of lingering. " 'Til twilight tomorrow, fair Faris," he called. "Where the heather runs forever. I will meet ye there that our adventure together may continue!"

He was gone then—galloping into the forest astride his mount, cape rippling in the breeze as he rode.

Faris let her fingertips trace her neck where the Highwayman had kissed her—pressed them to her lips where his had lingered. It was astonishing! All of it! Not just a chance second meeting with the Highwayman of Tanglewood but the touch of bare hands, a second kiss, and a planned secret rendezvous in the purple-heathered hills.

Faris experienced a momentary wave of guilt. He was, after all, a villain of sorts. Yet her heart cared not, for his crusade was a righteous one. The Highwayman of Tanglewood was the pure stuff of poetic fiction. The purest ingredient of delicious dreams!

She thought of Lillias—wondered if her friend would be angry in knowing Faris had met the Highwayman. Yet Lillias loved Lord Kendrick, no matter her intrigue with the Highwayman of Tanglewood. No—Lillias would be happy in knowing Faris had touched the legendary rogue. Lillias could never know, naturally. Still, Faris took comfort in her own assurance Lillias would be delighted if she could know.

Carefully, Faris made her way across the darkened meadow and back to Loch Loland Castle. How inviting Loch Loland seemed rising in the distance, warm-lighted windows as beckoning as paradise itself. Faris thanked the heavens for Lady Rockrimmon's benevolence, for the good people who otherwise labored under the castle roof, for the soft lace of the pillowcase on which she laid her head later that night—a soft pillow on which to dream of the Tanglewood Highwayman. How charming he was! How strong! How brave and how thoroughly intoxicating!

As Faris drifted into sleep that night, she thought of nothing but the Highwayman—of nothing save him and his rogue's stolen kiss. Nothing—not her duties, not the impending marriage of Lillias to Lord Kendrick, and not the return of Loch Loland's young master. To Faris, there was only soft lace, purple evening, and the vision of the Highwayman of Tanglewood riding over the midnighted meadow.

"Faris!" Lillias exclaimed as she entered the chamber with the grace of a swan.

Faris turned, smiling as she saw her friend hurrying toward her.

"Look, Faris! Simply look what my darling Lord Kendrick has gifted me this morning!"

"Another gift?" Faris asked.

Lord Kendrick was forever showering his betrothed with gifts. Yet for all her sweetness, Lillias Rockrimmon was as ever intrigued and excited about each new gift as she was the last.

"Yes! Indeed, I do know he spoils me so," Lillias said, pausing, a look of guilt puckering her lovely brow for a moment. Her smile returned nearly instantly, however, as she added, "I do admit I adore it!"

"What treasure has he found this day to intrigue you?" Faris asked, anxious to see what token of affection Lord Kendrick had discovered in order to coax Lillias's smile this day.

"Oh, Faris," Lillias said, looking at the bed Faris has been straightening. "Lochlan will not arrive until the very last moment. I do not understand why Mother insists his room be attended to every day. It is two years now he is gone and yet two months until his return."

"She is a mother who misses her son," Faris said. "She has perpetual hope in his sudden and unexpected return." She smiled at Lillias and took her hand as she spoke with intent. "One day you will have a son, and he will grow into a fine man like his father. I daresay you will be stricken with all manner of weeping and heartache when he rides from your nest."

"I shall have a son," Lillias said smiling. "More than one, of course—and I will never let them leave their home!"

"Then they will be silly, frightened boys who will no more be able to find a beautiful woman the like of their mother to take to wife than they will be to properly wield a blade," Faris teased.

Lillias frowned. "A blade is a blade. Yet the rapier is a gentleman's weapon, antiquated though it may be, and I loathe a man who cannot well wield a rapier." She giggled then as did Faris. "Yet, look, Faris! Look what Gawain has given me!"

Faris gasped as Lillias opened her hand to reveal a lovely brooch. Set in gold, the brooch held a piece of amber-colored glass set to protect a lock of dark hair.

"Is it not the most wonderful ornament?" Lillias exclaimed. "How I adore it! A tender lock of Gawain's own hair—to have with me always! Can you imagine he would ever be so romantic?"

Faris giggled, delighted with Lillias's excitement. Hair jewelry in the form of brooches, lockets, or rings was not entirely too rare. Still, Faris knew what a romantic nature Lillias possessed—as romantic as her own. Faris doubted Lord Kendrick even knew how perfectly his gift had touched Lillias's heart.

"How splendid, Lillias!" Faris exclaimed. "No treasure on earth can compare to this."

"It's exactly as I feel," Lillias said, sighing with delight. "How will I ever force myself to wear another brooch when I have this to cherish?"

"Indeed," Faris agreed. "You have little need of any other now."

Lillias smiled and giggled. Sighing, she glanced about the room a moment.

"Faris! Honestly! Fresh flowers?" she giggled, smiling.

Faris smiled as well. "Yes," she answered. "Your mother asked that I freshen the flowers in your brother's room every three days."

"She is far too—" Lillias began. She paused, however, shaking her head with sudden understanding. "She has missed him so terribly. I wonder that Father has kept him away from her so long."

"In order that he may learn to properly wield a blade and find a wife as beautiful as his mother?" Faris offered.

Lillias laughed, her eyes twinkling with merriment. "Oh, what mirth and delight you gift me, Faris," she said. "Yet Lochlan is well acquainted with any blade, and he will have no difficulty finding a wife when he decides it is time. You have seen his portrait in the west wing, have you not?"

"Yes," Faris said.

"And is he not the handsomest devil you have ever laid eyes upon?" Lillias asked.

Faris quickly reflected on the one opportunity she had had to view the Rockrimmon ancestry by way of the paintings in the portrait hall. Inwardly, she admitted to having been very impressed by the painting of Lochlan Rockrimmon. The painting portrayed him in a most becoming light—eyes as green as emeralds, hair a warm and inviting brown. A square jaw and straight nose befriending no hint of smile in the painting gave him the look of a man already titled—a great nobleman. Yet Faris thought his blue breeches, red coat, and white cravat rather boorish. Undeniably handsome he was, yes—still, rather boorish in some manner. Of course, what young man, titled or not, could contend with the vision of the Highwayman of Tanglewood astride his magnificent steed, galloping over the meadow in the moonlight? None of Faris's acquaintance.

Still, she did not wish to hurt Lillias's sensitive nature, and so she admitted, "Handsome, yes—but I hope there is no true devil in him." She paused, astonished by her own next thought. In all her wondering if the Highwayman of Tanglewood were, indeed, handsome rather than plain or unattractive beneath his mask, it was only then she realized there was a bit of a devil in him. For what man could find himself a Highwayman if not for the influence of, in the least, a grain of impish character?

"Oh, no! There is no devil at all in Lochlan. My brother is a good man, an honorable son, and a loving sibling." Lillias explained. "And in business he is perhaps the best I have ever heard of. Father certainly thinks it, and it is why Father has given so much responsibility to him."

"I'm certain he is the best of men," Faris said.

"No doubt it is why your mother longs for his return."

"Oh!" Lillias exclaimed of a sudden. "In my excitement over Gawain's brooch, indeed I forgot to tell you of the Highwayman."

"What of him?" Faris asked. She felt desperate of a sudden—desperate to know anything of her Highwayman.

"Kade the Heinous has claimed he wounded the Highwayman of Tanglewood!" Lillias whispered.

"What?" Faris gasped. She felt as if her heart had leapt into her throat. Yet she had seen the Highwayman with her own eyes the night before. He had held her in his arms, kissed her. He had not appeared wounded in the least. She released an anxious breath at the realization. "But . . . but he was not injured. Graybeau did not mention his being injured yesterday morning when—"

"Oh, no! But it was not then!" Lillias said. "Gawain was told just this very morning that Kade the Heinous set a trap for the Highwayman this night past! He claims to have matched blades with him once more and further claims he wounded the Highwayman in the left leg."

Faris's heart hammered so brutally within her chest she felt certain Lillias could hear its mad beating.

"But it cannot be!" Faris exclaimed.

"I am in agreement with you, Faris," Lillias

said. "Kade Tremeshton is only trying to repair his muddied name."

"We will hope it is so," Faris said.

"I believe it is so," Lillias said. "For Gawain has also told me that the Highwayman bested Lord Barnes only this morning just before sunrise. Lord Barnes was returning from his sister's estate in the south when he was set upon by the Highwayman of Tanglewood."

"But what are we to believe?" Faris asked. She felt ill, sickened by the possibility of the Highwayman's having been injured. Further, a sort of panic was rising in her. What if Kade Tremeshton's story were true? And the worst of it—in meeting the Highwayman, had Faris put him in danger? What if Kade Tremeshton had managed to ambush the Highwayman of Tanglewood because of his dalliance in the meadow with Faris? She might, indeed, be responsible for his being injured! The thought frightened her to near trembling.

"We are to believe Gawain," Lillias said. "For he is honest and above all reproach—while Lord Tremeshton is the worst of men. And is it not the worst of men who weave lies in attempting to elevate themselves in gossip circles?"

"Yes," Faris said, placing a hand to her bosom in an attempt to calm the mad hammering of her heart. "Yes. I am certain Lord Tremeshton is false in his claims."

"Darling!" Lillias exclaimed, taking hold of Faris's arm. "You've gone pale as the moon! Do not worry so over our beloved Highwayman. He can never be bested. I am sure of it."

"I am certain of it as well," Faris said. "I should not allow myself to be so unsettled."

"I was unsettled, also, at first," Lillias said. "But Gawain assures me the Highwayman is well. And I believe Gawain in all things."

Suspicion traveled across Faris's mind a moment. Why should Lord Kendrick be of such certainty where the Highwayman's well-being was concerned? No. She would not think it a moment longer. The Highwayman had assured her he was not Lord Gawain Kendrick in masked form—and she would believe him.

"Excuse me, miss."

Faris and Lillias simultaneously gasped as Bainbridge Graybeau suddenly appeared in the doorway.

"Graybeau!" Lillias exclaimed. "You frightened us near to fainting!"

"My apologies, Miss Lillias," Graybeau said. "But your mother and father wish to speak with you."

Faris frowned. Odd that Lord and Lady Rockrimmon should send the stablemaster into the house to summon their daughter.

"Is it of a serious nature, Graybeau?" Lillias asked.

"I do not believe so," Bainbridge answered.

"Hmm. Very well," Lillias sighed. "We will speak later, Faris?"

"Of course," Faris said.

Her heart was settling somewhat. Still, as Bainbridge Graybeau's dark eyes met hers for a moment, she held her breath. There was something in his countenance—something unsettling. Was something amiss? Did he know the true reason Lord and Lady Rockrimmon had summoned Lillias? Was it grave news? No, it was something else. Faris trembled as an unfathomable thought entered her mind—did Graybeau know? Did Bainbridge Graybeau know of her rendezvous with the Highwayman of Tanglewood the night before?

Lillias took her leave of her brother's room, yet Graybeau remained in the doorway. His gaze lingered on Faris with a strange intensity.

"Is . . . is there something you wish of me, Mr. Graybeau?" Faris asked. She could no longer endure his staring at her.

"Not at the moment, miss," Graybeau said.

He was a handsome man! And so tall! Faris wondered why such a man as he did not have a wife and children. To be stablemaster at Loch Loland Castle—it was an impressive lot. Surely any woman for one hundred miles would think the dark-haired, brooding, and wildly handsome Bainbridge Graybeau, stable-

75

master of Loch Loland, a healthy catch indeed.

"Good day," Graybeau said. He turned and started walking down the hall. Quickly, Faris went to the doorway. Looking after him, she felt her mouth gape open. He was limping! Bainbridge Graybeau was favoring his left leg with a rather pronounced limp.

"Pray, Mr. Graybeau," she could not help but call to him.

He paused and turned to look at her.

"Yes, miss?" he asked.

"Are you . . . are you indeed well?" she asked. "Have you been injured?"

"I—um—I was thrown from a horse this morning, miss. It is nothing to be concerned about," he answered. "Good day to you, miss."

Faris watched Graybeau walk away—counted the measure of his limp. Twilight would tell the tale. Had Bainbridge Graybeau simply been thrown from a horse at Loch Loland Castle's stables? Or had the Highwayman been injured as Kade Tremeshton claimed?

"He's comin' home, he is!" Mary said as Faris entered the kitchen for the evening servants' meal. "I heard his lordship tell milady just this afternoon!"

"Master Lochlan?" Old Joseph asked. "Well, it's at last a relieving thing. It's not good for a young man to be away from his kith and kin so long."

Mary was mistress cook at Loch Loland Castle. Faris knew little about her life before she had come to Loch Loland. Yet she was a kind, nurturing woman, and Faris adored her round rosy face, wiry gray hair, and smiling eyes.

Old Joseph had been at Loch Loland Castle since Lord Rockrimmon's father was a young man. Weathered in his looks and slowed in his ways, still there was a certain dignity in his carriage and manner. Of all the staff at Loch Loland, Mary and Old Joseph were Faris's favorites. She had begun to look on them as one might look affectionately upon an aged uncle and merry-faced aunt.

"When will he arrive?" Sarah asked. "Have you word of when Master Lochlan will attend us?"

Faris watched as Sarah's eyes lit up like fire on a nocturnal lake. It was quite obvious Sarah was overly excited at the prospect of Lochlan Rockrimmon's return. Faris wondered for a moment if the young master of the castle had stolen the hearts of the young maids at Loch Loland before his departure to do his father's bidding. By the look of excitement on Sarah's face, she guessed he had.

Sarah had been somewhat put off when Faris had joined the staff at Loch Loland Castle. Upon Faris's arrival, Sarah had been moved from her post as chambermaid to Lillias and Lochlan Rockrimmon to that of chambermaid to Lady Rockrimmon. Even though the change in post was an honorable one, Sarah had been quite unfriendly to Faris at first. Still, as Lady Rockrimmon began to rain compliments upon her, Sarah's frustration had vanished, and she was now quite friendly to Faris.

"Within the week," Mary answered. "And there was a whisper I caught too," Mary added, lowering her voice. Everyone at the table leaned forward as Mary's voice dropped. "A name," she said.

"A name? What name?" Sarah prodded.

"Tannis. Tannis Stringham," Mary whispered, raising her eyebrows in an expression of disapproval.

"Tannis Stringham?" Sarah exclaimed, disappointment all too blatant on her pretty face.

"Hush, girl!" Old Joseph scolded.

"Oh, but Joseph—Tannis Stringham?" Sarah repeated in a whisper. "Why ever would her name be mentioned in conversation among the family?"

"Why ever, indeed?" Mary said, sitting back in her chair, an irritated purse upon her wrinkled old lips.

"Surely you do not mean to suggest Master Lochlan has . . . intentions toward Tannis Stringham, Mary?" Old Joseph rather chuckled. "Master Lochlan is far too wise a man to give attention in such a direction as that."

"Then why is there to be a visit from Tannis and Lady Stringham next month?" Mary added.

"No!" Sarah gasped.

Faris smiled, entirely entertained by the tittle-tattle of the servants concerning their young master. How she adored to sit in the kitchen in the evenings and converse with Mary, Old Joseph, and the others. It was quite like being part of a family, and Faris savored it more than the sweetest confection.

"Yes!" Mary said. "I heard it with me own ears. Lady Stringham and her daughter, Tannis, are to visit here for a holiday next month."

"Am I to understand this Tannis Stringham is an unfavorable young woman?" Faris ventured.

Old Joseph, Mary, Sarah, and the others at the table exchanged glances. In the end, each disbelieving expression settled on Faris. It was obvious the staff of Loch Loland did not think Tannis Stringham, whoever she was, worthy of their young master.

"Suffice it to say Lord Stringham has frequently received, shall we say, attention from the Highwayman of Tanglewood," Old Joseph said.

At the mere mention of the Highwayman, Faris could not keep the butterflies from rising within her! The sun was low in the sky, and soon she would see him again! Furthermore, she understood why each person at the table disapproved of the young woman who was to visit Loch Loland Castle for a holiday. If her father was the sort to need the reprimand of the Highwayman of Tanglewood, then it did not serve that his daughter should be deserving of having Lord and Lady Rockrimmon as father- and mother-in-law.

"And Tannis Stringham is as haughty as any spoiled she-cat with sharp-ended claws," Mary added.

"Then why," Faris ventured, "if Master Lochlan is as wonderful as you paint his portrait to be— why would he invite her and her mother for a holiday?"

"Mary! Joseph! In fact, everyone!" Lady Rockrimmon exclaimed as she entered the room. Her cheeks were pure pink with excitement. "I've the most wonderful news!"

"Yes, milady?" Old Joseph asked.

"Lochlan is coming home! This very week!" Lady Rockrimmon said.

"Wonderful news, indeed, milady," Mary said, smiling.

"Yes, is it not?" Lady Rockrimmon sighed. "After two long years away! It will be heaven to have him home again!"

"Indeed, milady," Old Joseph agreed.

"Now, Faris," Lady Rockrimmon said. "First thing tomorrow—do not trouble yourself tonight, of course—however, first thing would you please see to Lochlan's chamber and give it a thorough going-over for dust—especially the draperies?"

"Of course, milady," Faris said, full catching the contagious smile resplendent on Lady Rockrimmon's lovely face!

"Thank you, dear," Lady Rockrimmon said. "I'm—I'm just overwhelmed with delight!" All the servants smiled as their mistress left the room in a whirl of satin and excitement.

"How she's missed him," Mary sighed.

"How we all have," Sarah added.

Faris relaxed in her chair, her stomach satisfied by an abundance of Mary's lamb stew and warm bread. Lochlan Rockrimmon. What would he be? Solemn and boorish, as his portrait? Surely not, else what would be the cause for all the excitement at his return?

Faris thought of the Highwayman besting this Lord Stringham, whose daughter Lochlan Rockrimmon seemed to have interest in. She closed her eyes for a moment, remembering the purple light of the evening meadow, the scent of lilacs and green meadow grass. To see him again—it was her greatest wish—a wish which would be granted in less than an hour's time. In meeting the Highwayman, her joy would be at its pinnacle.

"What are you smilin' at, Joe?" Mary asked, drawing Faris's attention from her own thoughts and back to the conversation at hand.

"I'm thinking of Lord Stringham," Old Joe

answered. "How I would have liked to have seen his face when the Highwayman of Tanglewood was upon him!"

"As would I," Sarah said as the others at the table turned to their own conversation. "Lord Stringham is far too arrogant for anyone's good."

"I would give anything to see the Highwayman best any one of the corrupt nobles," Mary mumbled, slathering a large helping of butter onto her bread.

"Oh, thanks be to heaven for the Highwayman of Tanglewood," Old Joseph sighed. "I don't know what poor folks in this country would do without him for their champion."

Faris found herself nodding in unison with Mary and Sarah.

" 'Til there be another way to keep those that prey on the weak and poor in hand, thanks be to heaven for him that does—whatever his methods," Joseph said.

Faris smiled. What a heroic tale the Highwayman of Tanglewood would be to tell one day. Those who had lived in his time would repeat the tales of his adventures, of his heroics, for years and years to come.

Faris glanced out the window. Lavender light was descending; twilight would settle soon. "I fancy an evening walk in the sunset," Faris said, pushing her chair back from the table and standing. "Thank you for the delicious meal, Mary."

"You're welcome, love," Mary said.

"A twilight walk, is it?" Old Joseph asked. "Pray keep an open eye. We wouldn't want to hear of that rascal rogue the Highwayman of Tanglewood kidnapping our pretty Faris, now would we?"

Faris smiled. "Oh, perhaps it would not be a bad thing—to witness the Highwayman about his business."

"I think every girl for one hundred miles 'round dreams of meeting the Highwayman of Tanglewood," Sarah said.

"And your being one of them?" Mary teased.

"Of course," Sarah answered, smiling.

"Well, if I see him as I walk, I'll be certain to send him best regards from all of us," Faris said.

"You do just that," Old Joseph chuckled.

"Goodnight then," Faris said.

As she stepped from the kitchen and into the lavender light of early dusk, Faris inhaled the sweet smell of evening grass. The sky was beautiful! Lavender and pinks, blues of royal hues—all swept across the sky as an artist's brush stroke.

" 'Tis a beautiful evening, this," Graybeau said as he appeared, leading Jovan by the bit. Again his eyes were intent upon her for several moments. Faris fancied she liked the way his dark hair fell across his forehead—windblown and tousled.

"Yes," Faris said. As he passed, Faris noticed he yet limped just as he had earlier in the day. "Have a good evening, Mr. Graybeau."

"And you, miss," he said as he led the horse toward the stables.

The night birds were calling to one another, and Faris could smell the rich scent of the evening fires burning in the hearths of Loch Loland. Glad she had remembered to bring a shawl, Faris started out—started out toward the old ruins near the cemetery and a secret rendezvous with the Highwayman of Tanglewood. The night birds called, the grass lent its fragrance to the air as Faris's feet trod upon it, and lavender light drifted into a shimmering amethyst sunset.

Where the Heather Runs Forever

The silver crescent moon was rising as Faris made her way along the path toward the ruins and cemetery where the heather ran forever. The purple heather grew thick and far-reaching on either side of the small path she trod. Faris wondered if the parent plants of the same heather had been witness to the destruction of the great edifice now lingering in ruin and rubble before her. What battles had been fought on this path? What lives had been born and taken by death during the time before the ruins and rubble of the old castle? Faris imagined gallant knights laden in heavy chain mail, riding heavy horses toward the old castle, banners and colors billowing in the evening breeze as they rode. Perhaps a noble lady had once stood at the towering turrets watching such an advance, hoping for a beloved knight to return with her silken colors adorning his arm. Indeed, as Faris approached the ruins, her mind's eye could almost envision such a scene—almost imagine the outline of a once-grand castle against the amethyst of evening sky.

As she reached the crest of the last small hill and descended toward the ruins, her heart began to hammer. Would the Highwayman of Tanglewood be waiting there for her? Would he come riding through the heather toward her, his dazzling smile flashing in the purple twilight of sun's set?

Her heart fell a moment when she stopped on the hill's crest and looked below to the forever-running heather, the cemetery, and the old castle ruin. The ancient, crumbling castle walls, the worn tombstones, and entwined willows—they stood alone. There was no Highwayman amid them, waiting as a grand and heroic knight of old. With a disappointed sigh, Faris made her way down the hillside, meandering through the heather toward the old castle. How different this was—far different than Loch Loland Castle with its strength, warmth, and inviting appearance. Loch Loland rose like a beacon, while the old ruin before her now lay as the slumbering dead— as those in the graves surrounding it. Though nearly as old as the ruins before her, Loch Loland had weathered the attacks that had destroyed the old castle nearly two hundred years before— so Faris had been told. She felt sad for the old ruin as if it were an aged man—once a strong and capable soldier, now wounded and infirm, waiting to draw final breath.

Faris gasped as a gloved hand suddenly covered her mouth from behind—a strong arm slipping about her waist to hold her fast. A man's low and raspy voice, breath warm on her neck, whispered in her ear, "Be still. The Highwayman of Tanglewood owns ya now."

Faris smiled beneath the man's hand and tried to push it from her mouth that she might turn and look at him. But the Highwayman tightened his grip, coaxing her to lean back against his strong body as he whispered, "Do not struggle. I'll not harm ya, lass. I simply intend . . . to have ya."

Faris's heart beat madly! His breath on the flesh of her neck was titillating, and she wanted nothing more than to stay thus in his hold. She felt the Highwayman's arm tighten at her waist, and he bent, resting his chin on her shoulder for a moment before nuzzling into her neck playfully.

"Come away with me, sweet Faris," the Highwayman whispered. "What say ye?" he added, letting his hand slide from her mouth, caressing her neck, and finally letting it rest at the hollow there.

"I say, who are you, Highwayman?" Faris breathed, unable to believe the euphoric spell he was weaving over her. All romantic thoughts of knights riding to win the fair lady were driven from her mind. A rogue's manner was vastly more delightful!

"Aye! But that ye should know, sweet Faris," the Highwayman whispered. For a moment, Faris searched her shallow knowledge of him, searching for some shred of evidence. Did she indeed know him? Was the Highwayman of Tanglewood Bainbridge Graybeau? Did the Highwayman approach her from behind in order she would not see his familiar limp?

"I know you not, sir," Faris said in a whisper. "Surely I would remember such a shape of a man." He was playful, toying with her, and she was delighted. She would continue as a player in his act.

"Indeed, would ya, lass?" he asked.

"I would, sir," she answered.

"And the taste of his kiss, me sweet lass?" the Highwayman whispered. "Would ya surely remember such a taste of a kiss?" Faris shivered with delight as the Highwayman placed a moist kiss on her neck. " 'Tis well ya know who I am, fair Faris," he whispered, kissing her neck again. "I am the Highwayman of Tanglewood—come to compromise ya here in the heather."

Gasping with delight at his playful manner, Faris turned to face him. Indeed, he wore his black, including his mask. He smiled at her, his white teeth flashing in the evening light of violet.

"But—but how came you here?" Faris asked. "I heard nothing of your approach."

The Highwayman clicked his tongue twice, and Faris saw his black steed appear from behind the old ruin beyond. "It's me way, it is," he said. "Quiet, unseen." He smiled and took her hand in his, raising it to his lips and kissing the back of it. "Come with me now, lass. 'Tis dangerous out in the open heather," he said.

Faris followed the Highwayman as he led her through the heather and toward the old castle ruin. Her heart was beating so fiercely she was most certain she would faint. Yet she did not—even for his touch—for the glove on his hand kept flesh from meeting flesh.

He led her through the crumbling walls of the old ruins to a corner, dark and secluded. Removing his hooded cloak and spreading it on the ground, he motioned her to sit upon it. He joined her, propping one arm on one leg, his head tipping to one side as he seemed to consider her.

"Now, fair Faris," he began, "tell me yar story."

Faris smiled and shook her head, uncertain as to his meaning. "My . . . my story?" she asked.

"That be it," he said, smiling. "If I'm to be meetin' ya in the purple of evenin', if I'm to be stealin' yar kiss the like I have, it's wantin' to know yar story, I am."

Faris smiled, pausing still. He was magnificent! So grand, so dark! In his attire of midnight black, it seemed he was nearly one with the evening. It was difficult to make out any specific feature of him. In those moments, it seemed he was no more than a ghostly voice drifting with the other spirits lingering in the old ruined castle. Still, Faris could feel the warmth of his body, hear his movements as he shifted.

"I'll help ya with the beginnin' of it, I will," the Highwayman chuckled.

"With the beginning of it?" Faris asked. In her study of the dark Highwayman and his shroud of darkness, her mind had wandered.

"With the beginnin' of your story, fair Faris," the Highwayman chuckled. "It begins thus: I am Faris, and I was born."

Faris nodded. "Ah, yes," she said smiling as she began, "My name is Faris, and I was born in a cottage some hundred miles from here in Heathmoor. Do you know of it?"

The Highwayman nodded. "I do. 'Tis well I know it."

Faris smiled, pleased he was familiar with the place of her birth.

"I was born at Heathmoor and lived there until the death of my parents when I was twelve," she explained. "Soon after they died, I was placed in service at the home of a grand lord and lady there, Lord and Lady Middleton."

The Highwayman nodded, seeming to recognize the names.

"They also were lost," he said.

Faris smiled again, further amazed at his range of acquaintance. "Some years later, yes. It was after Lord and Lady Middleton's passing that I found myself at Tremeshton Manor," she explained.

"Near in the evil clutches of Kade Tremeshton," the Highwayman offered.

"Thanks to the heavens and Milady Rockrimmon—for I never found myself fully in his clutches," Faris explained. "Though I knew . . . I knew . . ."

"*He* planned to find ya there?" he said.

Faris felt humiliation wash over her like a heated rain as she nodded and said, "Yes. Had it not been for Lady Rockrimmon . . . I-I shrink to think what might have become of me."

"Ya would've found the courage to evade him—at any cost," the Highwayman stated.

"Yes," Faris said. "Though I fear the cost would've been destitution had Lady Rockrimmon not taken pity on me."

"And so ya quit yar station at Tremeshton, for the greener grasses of Loch Loland Castle?" he asked.

"Yes," Faris said, smiling at him. "And . . . and that's when I first met you."

"Aye. From the clutches of Kade Tremeshton to the clutches of the Highwayman of Tanglewood," he chuckled. "Was it a wise trade do ya think?"

"The very wisest," Faris said. His voice, though masked low and rasping, was of such a comfort as Faris had never known. She smiled, wondering at the odd paradox—for she felt more safe in the presence of a thieving rogue than ever she had in the presence of any other man.

"I bested that blackguard Tremeshton, ya know," the Highwayman said.

"Yes! Twice, and I was glad to hear of it," Faris admitted.

"Not a fortnight ago, I bested him at sabers and then fists and sent him home beaten and bloodied and without the gold he'd stolen from his tenants," the Highwayman said. Faris noted the somewhat of a growl that had entered the intonation of his voice as he spoke of Kade Tremeshton. "And I thought of ya too, lass, in the doin' of it. I beat him worse because of ye." He rose to his feet and began angrily pacing back and forth. "Of the many men who do wrong by the people in this country, Kade Tremeshton is bound to breed into one of the worst, he is. And to think of his coward's manner day before here—demanding two wee stablemen draw swords against me."

"And he surrendered his purse as a coward too," Faris said.

"Aye," the Highwayman said. "I hope to heaven to rein in me temper when next I cross him—for I've never yet murdered a man, even any deserving of it."

"It was the last you saw him? Yesterday—when

you bested him in the broad sunshine?" Faris asked.

The Highwayman paused. He seemed to study her for a moment, and she noticed the way his left hand rested for a moment on his left thigh.

"Yes," the Highwayman said. "Yes . . . yesterday when I bested him and his poor stable hands. I wish it were the last I ever saw of him."

Faris felt the hair on the back of her neck prickle as the Highwayman took his seat on the ground before her once more. She did not imagine the way he seemed to favor his left leg as he did so—the way his hand lingered on his thigh as if he were rubbing at an uncomfortable wound.

"I can well envision it—your besting him," Faris said. She did not wish for him to know of her suspicions. If he had not met Kade Tremeshton the night before, then why did he favor his left leg? Yet if he had met Kade Tremeshton, why did he keep the truth from her?

She did not want to know. Faris did not care. The Highwayman of Tanglewood had rested his eyes upon her, and she would not drive him from her simply because his rogue's ways meant he must keep some secrets.

"Every day I am thankful for Lady Rock-rimmon's benevolence," she said, attempting to draw any suspicion toward her from him. "Every day I am grateful for my timely escape."

93

"Timely it was," the Highwayman said. She could feel his piercing gaze upon her, though she could not see his eyes for the darkness enveloping them.

"Even now, when he visits Loch Loland Castle, I tremble in his presence," Faris sighed.

It was true. It was unfortunate that on several occasions Lord Rockrimmon, forced to deal in business with the man, had accepted the villain into his home. With each visit, Lord Kade Tremeshton would find a way of seeking out Faris, glaring at her with an expression of threat, intended harm. Faris smiled, thinking of Lillias and her referring to Lord Tremeshton as Kade the Heinous. It was the perfect title for him—far more fitting than the undeserved title of Lord Kade Tremeshton.

"He is welcomed into Loch Loland?" the Highwayman exclaimed of a sudden. The rage was instantly apparent in his voice. "Lord Rockrimmon is tolerant of him?"

"N-no," Faris stammered. His outburst and sudden change of demeanor startled her. "Well, yes—only to the point of necessity in the transference of property and tenants. Lord Rockrimmon has purchased several properties from Kade Tremeshton."

The Highwayman breathed heavy—a sigh of obvious relief. "Then 'tis only a great man's way of turnin' the tide, it is. Without resortin' to thievery, your lord acquires the land and thereby the tenants. It improves their lot—much as yars was improved by the great lady's intervention."

Unexpectedly, the Highwayman reached down, took hold of Faris's hand, and pulled her to stand with him. "Still, ya must be wary of Kade Tremeshton, fair Faris," he growled. "No doubt he yet feels bested by yar leavin' Tremeshton Manor summer past. He's known far the ruination of women—for the pure spite of it alone."

Faris smiled and said, "And yet, you . . . a highwayman, a thief of sorts . . . have taken no improper liberties where I am concerned."

The Highwayman chuckled, and Faris was mesmerized by his smile. "Have I not? When first I found ya in the meadow, I stole a kiss, I did. And ya call that not takin' liberties, lass?"

"I gave you that kiss, gallant Highwayman," Faris said.

"Aye, ya did. It's well I remember it," he said, smiling at her. "As well as the one I took from ye last purple evenin'."

Faris felt her cheeks go crimson with blushing. What a memory—the Highwayman's kisses! There could be no better memory in time. "But what of you?" Faris asked—for she was of a sudden more curious than ever before. "Is . . . is there nothing you can tell me of yourself—nothing you may share that will not endanger your safety in secrecy?"

The Highwayman's smile faded. The corners of his mouth seemed to droop as he shook his head.

"Nay. Not a word," he said. "Yet know that I am honorable—even in what I go about in the dark. Far until the men in government can better convince the nobles away from greed and the causes of poverty and unhappiness, I must keep my silence in regard to anythin' which might . . . might reveal . . ."

"I understand," Faris said. And, in truth, she did. Though her disappointment was great in not knowing more of him, she did understand the danger he would be put in were she to falter and accidentally reveal any knowledge of who he might be. "And I will try not to press you." Yet how could she help but ever wonder? Where was he from? Who was he? Was he handsome or plain beneath his highwayman's mask?

"Thank ya, lass," he whispered, brushing a strand of hair from her cheek. "And yet," he began, "I did promise ya the tale of the legend of the two willows. Perhaps that can be me story for you this night."

Faris smiled. "I will be happy to know it," she said.

"Then come with me, fair Faris," the Highwayman said as he gripped her hand more firmly. "The cemetery will tell the tale to ye as much as I."

Faris allowed the Highwayman to lead her out

of the ruined castle and into the cemetery. To have her hand so firmly clutched in his—it was magnificent. She thrilled at his touch, sighed at the sound of his boots along the path, admired the silhouette of his massive build against the deep purple of the evening skies. She was in the company of the greatest champion in the land— of a legend of the times—and it was wonderful! He was wonderful!

The Highwayman stopped as they reached the two entwined willows looming in the old cemetery. It was a quiet, open place. A sense of restfulness, of relief seemed to linger in the place—as if all who slumbered in the soil slept in comfortable knowledge that warring was at an end. Faris knew an odd sensation of peace as she stood beneath the willows.

"Here," the Highwayman, said pointing to the two weathered tombstones beneath the willows. "Here is where they rest—a young lass and a young knight who once fell into a forbidden love."

"Why forbidden?" Faris asked.

"He was knighted, and she was common," the Highwayman explained.

"I see," Faris said. Of a sudden, she felt saddened—for she was common, and her dashing Highwayman was most certainly uncommon.

"Still, the knight truly loved the lass, and he carried her away, secreting her here, at this place," he began. "The ruins ya see now behind ye was then Castle Alexendria, and the knight hid his lover here with his friend, the young king of the castle. When he could, between battles and tournaments, the knight would away to Castle Alexendria to his fair lassie—whom he loved with great desperation. Yet Alexendria's young king began to take notice of the knight's beloved lass, and the king also fell in love with the fair maiden and grew jealous of the knight." The Highwayman paused, looking down at the tombstones. "Look here," he said. "Though engravin' fades, ya can still make it out, ya can."

Faris knelt on the soft grass before the stones. The crescent moon above offered just enough light for her to read the weathered stones before her. "Rockrimmon," she whispered. "I can't make out the rest in this darkness—still I see Rockrimmon here."

" 'Tis true," the Highwayman continued. "The knight and his lassie wed in secret. Yet it was not long before the king received word of the union. The king was enraged, he was. He challenged the knight, and they fought. Indeed, the knight prevailed, and on his deathbed the king's wits were about him once more. He did not condemn the knight for havin' mortally wounded him. Rather, as the king lay dyin', repentant for his covetous manner toward the knight's lady, he bestowed his castles—for he owned two, Castle Alexendria and Loch Loland Castle—bestowed both castles and all his lands on the head of the knight and his beloved lady. The lassie was Fenella, and the great warrior knight who fought for her was Kenner Rockrimmon . . . ancestor of your own Lord Derrick Rockrimmon."

Faris smiled, delighted with the tale of the source of the Rockrimmon wealth and title. She looked to the tombstones, to the trees, utterly enchanted by the story of it all. "But . . . but if the knight and his lady became lord and lady . . . why are they buried here instead of in the great tombs of Loch Loland?" she asked.

"They were aged when the great battles raged over this country. Castle Alexendria was destroyed, and although the Rockrimmon line survived, there were few with them at the end—or so the legend is told. It is said an old servant man put them to rest," the Highwayman explained. "The old man buried them, and the legend goes the willows sprung up unassisted. Though methinks whoever buried them planted the trees, they did."

Faris sighed and smiled. "It is a terribly romantic story, is it not?"

The Highwayman smiled and said, "I thought ya might enjoy it."

"It's comforting to think the family is still near—at Loch Loland," Faris said.

"And how do ya like the family Rockrimmon, fair Faris?" he asked.

"Very well," she said. "They're kind and good people."

"That they are," the Highwayman agreed. "They give me no cause to interfere. In fact, Lord Rockrimmon and his son work toward the same goal as I, they do. Only in a more legal manner."

"I have become fast friends with Lillias," Faris said.

"Friends, is it? With the missy of the castle?" the Highwayman asked.

"Oh, I could never tell another living soul, of course," Faris said. "Only you—for you are a keeper of secrets."

"That I am," the Highwayman agreed. "As are you, fair Faris of Loch Loland." Faris smiled, and the Highwayman took her hand, leading her away from the tombstones and entwined willows.

The sun was gone in completion, and the moon and stars shined from the heavens, casting silver and diamonds upon the heather. The Highwayman quickly glanced about, and Faris sensed he was growing uneasy. It was dangerous for him to linger in such an open space for so long.

"Night has fallen, fair Faris," he said, raising her hand to his lips and kissing it. "I am a wanderer of the night, I am."

"It is not safe for you to linger," she said.

He smiled, raised his fingers to his mouth, and whistled. Faris smiled when she saw his great black steed exit the castle ruin and canter toward them.

"Aye," the Highwayman confirmed. "But I will linger a wee bit longer—if there's a kiss at the end of it."

Faris blushed, her heart racing with anticipation. And yet . . .

"Why . . . why would you choose to pass your time with *me?* A common chambermaid?" Faris could not help but ask.

The Highwayman reached up, patting his mount on the neck to calm it. "Why did a knight and a king battle here—here where the heather runs forever? Why did two great men battle over one the same as you, lass?" he asked in reply.

Faris watched as he removed his gloves, pressing them into the pockets of his breeches. She closed her eyes, overcome with pleasure as he took her face in his hands.

"Strength, virtue, beauty—all are blended together in yar eyes, they are," he said, letting his lips brush hers lightly.

Faris's arms erupted with goose bumps, her heart raced, and her breath abandoned her at his kiss.

"And a kiss tastin' of the sweetest confection a man can savor," he whispered. "I want yar mouth to mine, fair Faris," he said. His voice was deep, resonating seduction. "I mean to have it, I do."

"Then—then have it, Highwayman," Faris breathed.

Instantly, his mouth indeed captured her own in a fiery, driven kiss so burning with passion Faris thought she must surely be rapt in a dream! His arms were around her at once, pulling her tight against his strong body, and she returned his embrace, marveling at the solid form of the muscles in his arms and back.

His mouth was moist, hot as he tutored her in a kiss, which was no less than an artist's rendering. The rough whiskers of his mustache and goatee scratched the tender flesh around her mouth, but she cared not—she only wanted to stay locked in his arms, the taste of his kiss the only nourishment she needed.

The Highwayman of Tanglewood held Faris in utter euphoric bliss—kissing her, embracing her, weaving a spell of enchantment about her until she thought she might die of rapture borne of his affections. Faris melted against him, allowed herself to return his kiss with as much driven passion as his own dominant affection would allow. Never had she known such sensation— such wonder! A rogue he was, with a rogue's manner and abandon of propriety. Yet who was there to see? Who was there to witness their exchange and thereby deem it banished of propriety? No one—only those whose ghosts may have lingered near the ruined castle or cemetery. Certainly the souls of the long-past Lord and Lady Rockrimmon—the knight and his common lover lass who slept beneath the willow—would not be disapproving. And so Faris reveled in the feel of being wrapped in the Highwayman's powerful arms, savored the warm flavor of his kiss, and cared not for anything else in the whole of the world.

When the Highwayman did, at last, break the seal of their lips, Faris wondered how she would ever muster the ambition left to find her way home. As he continued to hold her—smiling down at her, brushing a strand of hair from her forehead—how she wished she could see the color of his eyes, press her palm to his cheek now covered by his black mask.

"I must go, Faris," he said all too soon. "I . . . I put us both in the path of danger in lingerin', I do." Releasing her, he retrieved his gloves, quickly pulling them onto his hands before mounting his horse. He held out his hand to her. "Come, fair Faris. I will see ya safely closer to yar home at Loch Loland Castle, I will."

Faris's heart soared as she took his hand, put her foot in the stirrup, and mounted behind him.

"Put yar arms 'round me, then—for he runs like the wind, he does."

In the next moment, the horse broke into a mad gallop, and Faris leaned forward against the

Highwayman's back. Wrapping her arms tightly about him, she sighed. He smelled of the heather and grasses, of wind and leather, of legends and heroes.

He said nothing as they rode toward Loch Loland Castle, but Faris was not disappointed. To be with him was too wonderful . . . too wonderful to wish for more. The feel of the wind on her cheeks, the sound of the saddle and girth leather as they rode, the rhythm of the steed's gallop—it was a dream—it must be a dream!

Too soon the warm-lighted windows of Loch Loland Castle glowed in the darkness, and the Highwayman reined his steed to a halt. Taking Faris's arm, he let her down from the horse easily, quickly looking about. He was in danger, too close to people to be safe, but her heart began to ache at the realization he must leave her at last.

The black horse that had carried them to safety stomped one front hoof—impatient with its master for lingering.

"Six days hence," the Highwayman of Tangle-wood began as his mount whinnied with anxiety, "I will meet ye if ya are willin'."

"Where?" Faris asked in a whisper.

"The meadow is too far far ye and the ruin too familiar to others," he said. "But do ya know the abandoned cottage at the far edge of the Tanglewood Forest?"

"Yes. Of course," Faris assured him.

"Very well. At twilight, the sixth night from this," he said. He smiled a smile of pure mischief as he reached out, pulling the ribbon from Faris's hair. Drawing it to his mouth, he kissed it before caching it in his shirt. "A thief I was, and a thief I be, fair Faris—and the ribbon from yar hair is mine now!"

Faris giggled, delighted he had stolen the token and in doing so loosed her hair to blow free in the night breeze.

"Until the sixth night when I can taste of your sweet lips again . . . I bid farewell, fair Faris of Loch Loland Castle." Nodding at her, he turned his mount and rode into the night. Faris watched him go, listened until she could no longer hear the rhythm of his steed's mad gallop nor the sound of his cape beating against the breeze.

All at Loch Loland Castle woke early the next morning. The young master of the house would arrive within the week, and the excitement at Loch Loland was as a fever. From Lord Rockrimmon to the stable boys, all who lived and labored at Loch Loland Castle went about their business with joyous anticipation. Yet even for the excitement permeating the castle, Faris found herself nearly indifferent to the anticipated arrival of the Rockrimmon heir. Stars were still twinkling in the night sky of her mind's eye, and the violet of sun's setting would forever remain her favorite color.

As Faris endeavored to go about her duties with calm, directed attention, her heart and all other innards seemed unable to keep from fluttering! The Highwayman of Tanglewood was a thief—a thief who had stolen Faris Shayhan's heart forever—and Faris Shayhan was glad of it! She could think of nothing save his kiss, the warmth of his strong form holding her close, the scent of leather and meadow grasses that was about him. Oh, what delight it would be to spend every moment of each day in his company! How she wished it could be so! And yet, the sixth night would come! The sixth night would come, and with it her joy in the Highwayman's company would be renewed!

Indeed, Faris wondered how ever she would manage to exist for five full nights before the sixth came. Yet she would—she would exist! Further, she would be happy, resplendent in knowing she would see him then. How she wished she could tell Lillias of her meeting, her secreted trysts with the Highwayman of Tanglewood. Lillias would not be jealous or filled with envy the way other young women would be—for Lillias was good and kind and in love with Lord Kendrick. Still, Faris knew it must remain a secret unshared. No one could ever know the Highwayman of Tanglewood had stolen her heart and drawn nectared kisses from her lips.

Having changed the linens and aired the heavy sapphire coverlets of the young master Rockrimmon's long empty bed, Faris had begun the rather arduous process of dusting the bedchamber of Lochlan Rockrimmon. It needed no dusting, of course, for Faris had kept the chamber wholly immaculate for an entire year. Still, Lady Rockrimmon had begged the favor of her, and Faris would see it was done. The hearth, the wardrobe, and the shelving had all been finished, and her attention had turned to the draperies.

The heavy sapphire velvet draperies were quite the efficient gatherers of dust. Still, Faris had learned to manage. This day, however, in her preoccupied state of daydreaming of the Highwayman, she'd forgotten to have Old Joseph bring her the ladder she had intended to use.

Breathing a heavy sigh, Faris looked up, up, and up to the top of the draperies. All unnecessary furniture had been removed from the chamber. The only object providing any sort of sturdy standing surface in order to reach the draperies was the bookcase standing next to the window. Looking from the bookcase to the draperies, Faris deduced it would serve well enough. After all, did not the shelves in the case resemble the manner of a ladder?

Dustcloth in hand, Faris carefully scaled

the bookcase. At last hoisting herself on top, she looked down, noting it stood as tall as the Highwayman of Tanglewood in the least.

"Perfect!" she said out loud to herself, feeling only a wee bit unsettled. A twin bookcase stood at the opposite side of the window. This would allow Faris access to the other side of the draperies, provided she could stretch all the way to mid-window without toppling off.

Warily, Faris began to dust the sapphire draperies of Lochlan Rockrimmon's bedchamber. She smiled, thinking of her beloved Highwayman—her thoughts lingering on his charm, the warmth of his strong hands, and the tingle of his kiss. The radiant joy in Faris's heart caused her to begin humming. The tune had been a favorite of her father's before he had passed, and it came to her now—lightening her heart and helping her work to seem less tedious.

"Once I a weary, bonnie lass was set upon by thieves," she sang.

"I smiled and asked the band of them, upon my bended knees,

'Take pity, lads, upon a lass with not a cent in tow,

And save yourselves from burning with the devil down below.' "

Taking hold of the heavy drapery pole with one hand, Faris stretched her other arm out toward the center of the window. It was precarious, her manner of dusting the draperies. Still, she had performed the task many times successfully enough, and she saw no reason she could not do it again—even without a ladder.

"The thieves they set to grinning and laughing to themselves," Faris continued to sing, frowning as she held tightly to the drapery pole and stretched even further.

"And I enjoyed their merriment, this band of thieving elves.

'I'm glad you are so merry in entering your tomb,

For the devil doesn't tarry'—"

"May I ask—what exactly it is you are about, miss?"

The deep resonation of the unexpected voice behind her startled Faris. She began to wobble, her hand slipping from the drapery pole, thus causing her to lose her balance. With a shrill scream, she tightly clutched the folds of the velvet draperies as she began to topple off the bookcase. Closing her eyes in anticipating the pain of her body meeting with the floor, she was surprised when she felt herself suddenly cradled in two powerful arms instead.

The Heir, The Rider, and The Rogue

Faris Shayhan gasped as she looked into the extraordinarily handsome face of the man in whose arms she was cradled. Instantly stunned at the pure magnificence of his features and form, she determined the man to be nearly as tall as the bookcase from which she had fallen— his shoulders nearly as broad as the expanse of the window whose draperies she had been endeavoring to dust. His eyes flashed green as emeralds; his hair was such a color of brown spice as to cause Faris to wonder if it undeniably tasted as ambrosial as cloves.

"Are you injured?" the man asked.

Faris could only swallow hard and shake her head in response.

"Very well," he said, maneuvering her body so she hung over his shoulder as a sack of potatoes. "Then we shall seek out my mother."

"Y-your mother?" Faris squeaked. Surely not! Surely this was not Lochlan Rockrimmon! Surely this was not the young master of Loch Loland Castle! Yet every part of Faris's body and soul knew it to be true. Acting in such a careless, silly manner, Faris had been caught by the

110

young master of Loch Loland—literally caught!

She would be sent away! Indeed, she would. What other course was left? Faris had been fairly dangling from the draperies, showing such a lack of respect for the furniture in his chambers, and Lochlan Rockrimmon had no doubt been infuriated. She would be dismissed—at once.

Yet hope coupled with pure desperation gripped! She could not leave Loch Loland—it had become her home! What would become of her? Furthermore, where would she go? How would she meet her beloved Highwayman six nights hence if she were not dwelling close to the Tanglewood Forest?

"Oh, sire! Please forgive me!" Faris pleaded, her voice skipping with the rhythm of his stride. "It was an accident! I'm certain the draperies can be mended. I'll mend them myself! I'm quite skilled with a needle. Please, sire," she begged. "Please do not—"

The handsome man chuckled and asked, "As skilled with a needle as with a dusting cloth?"

"No, sire," Faris stammered, uncertain as to what to anticipate where her fate was concerned. In truth, it was an astonishing situation—flung over the shoulder of the young master of the house, on her way to a very severe reprimand, no doubt. Even for his occasional chuckle offering that he was amused, Faris knew it could not go well for her. Yet she must endeavor.

"Please, sire," Faris began. "I was distracted in mind, I do admit it. Yet I beg you not to—"

"Mother. There you are," Lochlan Rockrimmon interrupted.

Faris turned her head to see Lady Rockrimmon approaching. "Look what I've found dangling from the draperies in my bedchamber. What a thoughtful gift you and father have left for me."

"What?" Faris gasped. Was he in jest? Lady Rockrimmon's delighted giggle signaled that he was. Still, she could not believe he would be so merry about her abominable behavior.

"For pity's sake, Loch! Let the girl down," Lady Rockrimmon said through merry laughter.

"Need I remind you, Mother, of father's own words and yours—your very own teachings to me? You and father have ever taught 'what I find and keep in my bedchamber . . . I find and keep in my bedchamber,' " he said.

"Frogs, Loch. Frogs. You found frogs—which you had no doubt secreted into your chambers yourself—and we told you were you to keep them, they must be kept there, in your chamber. And you were but four years aged, Loch—four," Lady Rockrimmon said, holding up four graceful fingers as indication. "Now put the girl down. You'll have Faris thinking you as lewd as Kade Tremeshton."

"Tremeshton?" Lochlan Rockrimmon growled. Taking Faris's waist between strong hands, he slid her body down and over his, finally setting her feet on the floor. "You wouldn't think me the miscreant he is, would you, miss?" he asked her.

His eyes were mesmerizing—the whole of him was! As Faris stared at him for one long moment, she scolded herself for ever thinking his portrait boorish—for he was far, far from it!

"Well?" he prodded as she yet hesitated in answering.

"N-no, sire," Faris breathed. "Of course not."

"Good," he said.

Faris smoothed her apron and tucked a stray strand of hair up under her cap.

"Now," he continued, "if you would be so kind as to tell me the end of the song."

"The . . . the song, sire?" Faris stammered. She looked up at him, feeling her cheeks burn vermilion under his gaze.

"Yes, the song. The one you were singing while hanging from my draperies," he explained.

"Oh! The song," Faris stammered. "Um . . . the end . . . um . . ."

"For the devil doesn't tarry," he said, repeating the last line she had sung before having been startled into falling from the bookcase.

"Oh," Faris breathed. "F-for the devil doesn't tarry in—in sealing up your doom, sire."

The man arched his one eyebrow and nodded. "There's truth in that," he said.

"Oh, leave Faris be, Loch," Lady Rockrimmon

113

said. She reached out, pressing a palm to Faris's crimson cheek. "I sent you to your chamber to change your traveling clothes—not to frighten poor Faris near to death."

"Milady Rockrimmon," Faris began. "The draperies in . . . in Master Lochlan's chamber . . . I'm afraid I tore—"

"She fairly ripped them to shreds, mother," Lochlan said.

But when Faris glanced at him, he wore an impish grin. He was a rascal, Faris determined. A superior one perhaps—bearing no malice—but a rascal all the same.

"For pity's sake, Loch! Have mercy," Lady Rockrimmon said with a giggle. "Faris is not as familiar with your wicked ways as the rest of us are. You've turned her pale as porcelain!"

"Forgive me—Faris, is it?" Lochlan Rockrimmon said. "The draperies are my fault, and mine alone."

"Sire, I—" Faris began to argue, knowing full well she was the fool who had torn them.

"Oh, let him take the blame, Faris," Lady Rockrimmon said, smiling. "We find if we all blame Loch for mischief and misfortunes, it keeps things much calmer here, more often than not."

"But, milady—" Faris began again.

"She is correct, miss," he said. "You'll find that in matters of mischief, it's best for all blame to be placed in my general direction, miss," Lochlan Rockrimmon said.

The green of his eyes burned through the dark of Faris's. She found she was breathless beneath his emerald gaze.

"Faris," Lady Rockrimmon began, "would you know of Lillias's whereabouts? She will so want to know Loch has returned."

"I-I can seek her out quickly enough, milady," Faris whispered with a short curtsy to her mistress and another to her young master.

"Then please do—if you don't mind," Lady Rockrimmon said.

"Yes," Lochlan said, his emerald eye still heavy upon her. "I cannot imagine how she has changed in my absence—already betrothed. It is unfathomable."

"Yes, sire," Faris said. "I will find her."

Turning to leave, she paused, blushing vermilion once more as she heard him say, "Although I cannot imagine enduring life in my bedchamber with the draperies so dull and dreary as they are now." He chuckled and continued, "Pray, mother, do allow me to return your pretty Faris to her place as my favorite drapery embellishment."

"Lochlan! Behave yourself! Where are your manners?" Lady Rockrimmon scolded half-heartedly. "Faris, do not pay him any heed. Please bring Lillias to me, and I will have his tongue straightened before your return."

"Yes, milady," Faris said, hurrying down the hall and away from the unsettling gaze of Lochlan Rockrimmon.

For pity's sake! Her hands were perspiring as well as her forehead! Faris scolded herself for being so unprepared for the young master's return. She scolded herself for being so dim-witted in choosing to scale the bookcase. Most of all, she scolded herself for being so entirely unsettled by his attractive nature.

"You didn't believe us, did you?" Sarah said as Faris met her rounding one corner of the hallway in search of Lillias.

"About what?" Faris asked, feigning ignorance. Faris smoothed her apron again, afraid the blush Lochlan Rockrimmon had brought to her cheeks still lingered.

"About how handsome and charming Master Lochlan is," Sarah said, smiling.

Faris gritted her teeth for a moment. "Oh, he is as handsome a man as was ever born," Faris admitted. "And he knows it. Such conceit!" She could not let Sarah know the true reasons Lochlan Rockrimmon unsettled her. In truth, there seemed no arrogance or conceit about him. Yet she could not let Sarah know she had been proven correct.

"Do you mean to say you don't find him . . . desirable?" Sarah asked. It was obvious by the arch in her brow and her widened eyes that she was entirely astonished Faris had not admitted

Lochlan Rockrimmon to be nearly incomparable in his appeal.

"What I find desirable in a man goes far beyond a pretty face and an ostentatious nature," Faris said. She thought of the Highwayman—of her Highwayman—of his easy manner and overwhelming allure.

"He has unsettled you," Sarah said, smiling. "Do not feel foolish, Faris. He unsettles us all."

"Have you seen Miss Lillias?" Faris asked, praying to end the line of conversation. "Milady wishes me to inform her of her brother's return."

"She's in the east gardens with Lord Kendrick," Sarah said. She still smiled, knowing all too well how uncomfortable Faris remained.

"Thank you, Sarah," Faris said. She would find Lillias quickly—send her to her mother and brother. Then Faris could, once more, allow her every thought to linger on her beloved Highwayman.

"Where did you find that one?" Lochlan asked his mother as he watched Faris round the corner.

"On the rim of disaster at Tremeshton," Lady Rockrimmon sighed. "And Lochlan . . . I-I did something . . . something completely inappropriate."

"Mother, what could you ever do that would be deemed completely inappropriate?" Lochlan asked. He was amused with his mother's expression of mischief. She appeared as guilty as a weasel in Mary's egg basket.

"I had been watching Faris for some time—during my visits to Lady Tremeshton, I would watch her. It was insanely obvious Kade had . . . had intentions toward her," Lady Rockrimmon said.

"Kade has intentions toward anything in a petticoat," Lochlan grumbled.

Lochlan Rockrimmon despised Kade Tremeshton. It was men the likes of Kade who caused the great misery and unrest throughout the countryside—greedy, wicked men who cared for nothing, save their own gratification and gain. He wondered if the local government would ever rein them in. For all his two years away from Loch Loland Castle, he yet bathed in frustration—having done very little, in his own mind, to better the lot of those preyed upon by such as Kade Tremeshton. Politics were slow and wildly frustrating. Still, he was determined and would press forward in his efforts. He liked to think he had made some progress, helped in some small way. After all, he had managed to debate Lord Essex from his political seat; one less greed-monger would be raising taxes for his tenants with that victory.

"Yes," Lady Rockrimmon agreed. "Still, I'll tell you—his designs on Faris were less honorable than usual. So I . . . so I . . ."

"You stole her?" Loch asked, smiling. "You stole her, didn't you, Mother?"

Lady Rockrimmon tossed her head in a gesture of innocence. "I offered her a position at Loch Loland . . . and she came," she said.

"Mother, I'm proud of you," Lochlan said. "Stealing chambermaids—they'll be accusing you of riding as the Highwayman of Tanglewood next."

"Don't be absurd, Loch," Lady Rockrimmon said. "He's a thief! I simply offered Faris a position with . . . with a superior salary."

"And a superior young master," Lochlan teased. "Still, she tempts me, Mother," he added. "She's a pretty petticoat, indeed." How Lochlan delighted in teasing his mother—and his sister, for that matter. It was far too easy a task to spur them to excitability. How he had missed teasing them.

"Lochlan!" Lady Rockrimmon scolded.

Lochlan chuckled and drew his mother into a tender embrace. "I do derive such enjoyment at your expense, Mother," he said. "You're far too easy a teasing target."

"Lochlan!"

Lochlan turned to see his father approaching, arms outstretched. Lord Rockrimmon gathered his son into a warm embrace.

"Father," Lochlan greeted.

"It is good to see you," Lord Rockrimmon said.

"And what have you been about?" he asked. "Your mother is as red as a radish."

"Your son has been about his mischief already," Lady Rockrimmon said.

"Already? I've not seen you 'til this moment, and already you've ruffled your mother's pin feathers?" the great lord chuckled.

Lochlan looked from his father to his mother and back again. It was good to be home.

"He's ruffled Faris's pin feathers," Lady Rockrimmon said.

"Poor girl," Lord Rockrimmon chuckled.

"And now I'm off to see Mary in the kitchens," Lochlan said. "I'm sure she's missed my visits."

"I'm certain she has," Lady Rockrimmon said. She smiled, shaking her head. The expressions on the faces of his parents were easy enough to read—they were glad to have him back at Loch Loland Castle.

Still, as he kissed his mother affectionately on the forehead, Lochlan Rockrimmon could not vanquish the vision of Loch Loland Castle's newest chambermaid. There was a bewitching quality about the girl. She put him in mind of indigo evenings and star-spattered skies. He hoped he would find her dangling from his draperies again during his visit home.

"Pardon me, Miss Lillias, Lord Kendrick," Faris said as she approached the couple.

"Hello, Faris," Lord Kendrick greeted, his smile as dazzling as sunlight. For a moment, Faris studied him. His smile was nearly as enchanting as the Highwayman of Tanglewood's was in the light of the moon. She shook her head slightly, dispelling the ridiculous suspicion that rose in her every time she approached Lord Kendrick.

"Milady wishes to see Miss Lillias, sire," Faris said. "Her brother has returned and—"

"Lochlan?" Lillias exclaimed. Taking Lord Kendrick's hand, Lillias began tugging on his arm. "Come, Gawain! Lochlan is home at last! We must go to him at once."

"He was in the upper east hallway with your mother," Faris explained.

"Then we'll begin in the kitchens," Lillias giggled. "I've no doubt we will find him tormenting Mary near to apoplexy!" Lillias unexpectedly took hold of Faris's hand. "And I've much to tell you later . . . when you have a free moment to converse with me, Faris. Much to tell you."

Faris smiled. By the manner in which Lillias's eyes widened, Faris knew the "much to tell" concerned the Highwayman.

"Then simply seek me out when you are able," Faris said.

"I will," Lillias said. "Come, darling. Lochlan is home, and everything will be even more wonderful now!"

Faris watched them go—watched Lillias tugging at Lord Kendrick's hand in order to urge him on more quickly. They would be a happily wedded couple, there was no doubt. Faris thought Lord Rockrimmon the best of fathers. To have let his daughter choose whom she would marry on her own terms—it was rare among titled people. She tipped her head to one side as she pondered Lord Rockrimmon. She realized only then he looked quite like his son. Not as handsome, nor as boldly mischievous—still, father and son resembled one another in the green of their eyes and the tint of their hair.

"And so the young master has returned."

Faris gasped, so startled at the sound of Graybeau's voice as to feel her heart had skipped in the rhythm of its beating. Turning to see Graybeau leading Jovan by the bit, Faris placed a hand to her bosom to still her hammering heart.

"You startled me near to death, Mr. Graybeau," she said. She caught her breath a moment as he grinned at her. He was so very tall and so very striking in his appearance, and there was quite an unsettling air about him. Faris quickly glanced away when she noticed several of his shirt buttons were not fastened, allowing his shirt to gape open near to his waist. The sculpted contours of his chest were easily visible, and Faris wondered what Lillias would say were she to see Graybeau so casually attired.

"Forgive me then, miss," Graybeau said, stopping before her. Jovan whinnied, and Graybeau patted his jaw with reassurance. "He is returned," he said. "I saw his mount in the stable just now. Jovan was quite excited himself to see Master Lochlan's mount once more. They were good friends before Master Lochlan left."

"Yes," Faris said. "He . . . Master Lochlan is with Lady Rockrimmon."

Graybeau chuckled, and Faris fancied the sound of it warmed her. "Oh, milady must be a whirlwind of delight. She has missed him painfully."

Faris felt her eyes narrow as she studied Bainbridge Graybeau. Yes, he seemed to be as tall as the Highwayman. He was a good horseman—there could be no doubt of that, else Lord Rockrimmon would not hold Graybeau in such high regard. Again, Faris wondered at Graybeau's being the Highwayman of Tanglewood. Yet, if it were so, would he not give some sign to her? Some signal he was the man she had met on three occasions—the man she had kissed on three occasions?

"Do you ride, Miss Faris?" he asked then.

"R-ride?" Faris stammered. "Me?"

"Yes," Graybeau said. "It would not be difficult for you to learn, and if you are to learn, then I am the rider to teach you."

"But—but I have no mount," she stammered. It

was odd he should offer to teach a chambermaid to ride.

"Aye, but I have," he said.

Faris felt the hair on the back of her neck prickle. It was there—she was certain of it—just the faintest hint of accent.

"I have my own mount and would gladly tutor you in riding. All ladies should know how."

Was he setting bait for her? Was Graybeau indeed the Highwayman of Tanglewood and attempting to draw her to him before their planned rendezvous six nights hence?

"I . . . I believe I would enjoy learning to ride," Faris said.

"Good," Graybeau said. "If you would meet me at the stables this evening after you have supped, then we can begin."

"Very well," Faris said.

Graybeau smiled, and Faris was suddenly breathless. In that moment, she had become conscious of something quite astonishing concerning Bainbridge Graybeau's appearance. "Yet might I inquire something of you, Mr. Graybeau?" she asked.

"Of course," he said, the dark of his eyes fixed upon her own.

"When did you rid yourself of your whiskers?" she asked. It was true! It was only in those moments, when her suspicion was at its ripest, that Faris noticed Bainbridge Graybeau had shaven his mustache and goatee. Yes! Before that very moment, Faris had failed to realize Graybeau had always worn a mustache and goatee—and in the same manner as the Highwayman of Tanglewood.

"Just this morning, Miss Faris," he said, his smile broadening. He ran a large, callused hand over his chin. "Yet I will admit, I feel a might exposed somehow without it."

Faris felt her own eyebrows arch with doubt. How could such a man—a man who brazenly walked the grounds at Loch Loland Castle with his shirt unbuttoned and hanging open—feel exposed in ridding himself of a mustache and goatee? Furthermore, it came to her then—the memory of the Highwayman favoring his left leg the night before. As Graybeau's hand rested on his left thigh, as he seemed to rub the spot as if it were sore, she remembered—the Highwayman had done the same!

"And your injury?" Faris asked. "You said yesterday you were thrown?"

"Aye," Graybeau said, still smiling. "But I am much beyond any discomfort today. Thank you."

Faris smiled. Oh, it could not possibly be so! Bainbridge Graybeau was no more the Highwayman of Tanglewood than Old Joseph was.

"This evening then?" Graybeau asked.

125

"Yes," Faris said. "I will meet you at the stables after the evening meal."

"I look forward to it," Graybeau said. "Good afternoon, Miss Faris."

"Good afternoon, Mr. Graybeau," Faris said. She watched him go—watched him walk away, favoring his left leg as he led Jovan.

It could not be he! Bainbridge Graybeau was not the Highwayman of Tanglewood. And yet the thought intrigued her. Graybeau was a handsome man. Something within her thrilled at the thought it might indeed be Bainbridge Graybeau she had met and kissed in the meadow one year earlier. Something in her thrilled at the thought it may have been Bainbridge Graybeau who told her the story of the Rockrimmon ancestors who slept beneath the entwined willows.

Quickly, Faris turned on her heel and headed toward the house. There was much to do before her rendezvous with Graybeau that evening. She must mend Lochlan Rockrimmon's draperies for the first of it. Still she could not believe he had returned to his chambers for the first time in two years to find her dangling from his draperies! Even at that moment, she felt a hot blush rise to her cheeks. How thankful she was not to have been sent away.

"Once I a weary, bonnie lass was set upon by thieves," Faris began to sing. She smiled, thinking of her first walk through the midnight

meadow—of her first meeting with the Highwayman—of being set upon by the rogue
Highwayman of Tanglewood. She thought of
his kiss on that night—and on the two nights so
recent. Splendor! Pure wonderment! In those
moments, Faris could not believe the good
fortune of her heart! The Highwayman of Tanglewood? What resplendent joy rinsed over her at
the thought of him!

As she hurried to return to her duties within
Loch Loland, she began her song once more—
this time mixing up the words to please her own
thoughts.

*"Once I a weary, bonnie lass was set upon by
he,"* she began,

*"He smiled and asked oh if he dared to steal a
thing from me.*

*I told him that I never would attempt to tell him
no,*

*And he then kissed me blissfully in Tanglewood's
Meadow."*

Faris giggled as she entered Loch Loland
through the servants' entrance. She was pleased
with her clever writing of lyrics. She was no
longer afraid of losing her position—Lady
Rockrimmon had simply scolded her son for
endeavoring to tease his chambermaid. She
was no longer suspicious that Lord Gawain
Kendrick might be the true masquerader—he
was not the Highwayman of Tanglewood, she

was certain. And what disappointment could there possibly be if Bainbridge Graybeau were the Highwayman? Handsome, strong, and with quite the chiseled form, Faris could be quite happy knowing Graybeau rode out at midnight to best the likes of Kade Tremeshton. In addition, the Rockrimmon family was complete! Lochlan Rockrimmon had returned, Lillias would be married, and Lord and Lady Rockrimmon's joy would be complete! Furthermore, the day was fast waning. Faris scolded herself for wishing the days to wane more quickly. Yet what woman would not, if a meeting with the Highwayman of Tanglewood were at the end of five days waned?

Faris giggled to herself, pure in her delight as she hurried up the staircase toward Lochlan Rockrimmon's room. She would mend his draperies! Further, as she had done when she had endeavored to dust them, she would sing to herself for company.

And so she began anew,

"Once I a weary, bonnie lass was set upon by he.

He smiled and asked oh if he dared to steal a thing from me.

I told him that I never would attempt to tell him no,

And he then kissed me blissfully in Tanglewood's Meadow."

● ● ●

The Highwayman of Tanglewood smiled as he stepped from his concealment in the lush east gardens of Loch Loland Castle. He had been witness to Lillias Rockrimmon's tryst with her lover Lord Kendrick, and he had been witness to Faris's arrival in the gardens to summon the Rockrimmon daughter to her mother. Further, with his own ears, he had heard Faris's song. He knew the song well—a favorite from his childhood. Moreover, he had heard Faris's changing of the lyric, and it encouraged him. Perhaps she did care for him. Perhaps it was not just the adventure of his having come upon her in the meadow one year previous.

"Fair Faris of Loch Loland Castle," he mumbled. " 'Tis rapt you have me with yar charmin' ways, ye do." Slipping through a large break in the otherwise impenetrable stone wall of Loch Loland's east gardens, the Highwayman of Tanglewood chuckled to himself as he began to sing,

"Once she a weary, bonnie lass was set upon by me.

I smiled and asked her if I dared to steal a thing from she.

She told me that she never would attempt to tell me no,

And we then kissed most blissfully in Tanglewood's Meadow."

A Question of Saxton

"Graybeau tells me he is to teach you to ride," Old Joseph said.

"Yes," Faris said, retuning the old man's smile. "He seems to think I should learn to ride well— though only providence knows why I should ever need to know how."

"It's a good thing, learning to ride well," Mary added with one strong nod. "And if you're going to learn, Faris, then Bainbridge Graybeau is the one to teach you."

"I think Mr. Graybeau is nearly as handsome as Master Lochlan himself," Sarah sighed.

"Fffp!" Mary breathed. "Always going on about what man is handsome and what man is not. There's more to living than a handsome face, miss."

Sarah ignored Mary, however. She smiled at Faris and asked, "Do you think Graybeau is taken with you, Faris?"

Faris felt blushed warmth rising to her cheeks. Yet shaking her head, she answered, "Oh, indeed, not."

"Then why teach *you* to ride?" Sarah asked. There was no envy or malice in her voice or upon her countenance—simply curiosity. "Why not teach any other chambermaid to ride? Bethany, Willeen, or even me?" Sarah smiled. "No . . . no, I think Mr. Bainbridge Graybeau may be taken with you."

Faris tried to force the red upon her cheeks to cool. Yet in her own heart, she'd wondered the same all day. Why had Graybeau offered to teach her to ride? There could be only one answer: Bainbridge Graybeau was the Highwayman of Tanglewood!

Certainly, Bainbridge Graybeau had always been polite toward Faris. He was polite toward everyone! Yet to suddenly offer to teach her to ride—after a year's long acquaintance with no seeming interest in her before—it was odd. Further, there was the matter of his limp—his favoring his left leg in the same manner as the Highwayman. Further still was the matter of his accent in speech. Although hard to discern, Faris did not doubt he could call up the full brogue the like of the Highwayman if the desire so struck him.

Therefore, after having pondered all the day long on the matter, Faris was quite suspicious that Graybeau's sudden interest in teaching her to ride was because he may well be the Highwayman of Tanglewood. It quite enchanted her to think her Highwayman could not wait for their planned rendezvous—that Graybeau had found a way to meet with her beforehand.

"I'm certain Mr. Graybeau would be happy to teach you to ride as well, Sarah," Faris said, forcing her thoughts to her companions. Oh, it was a half-hearted suggestion—for if Graybeau was the Highwayman of Tanglewood, Faris had no desire that he should teach Sarah anything!

"That may be," Sarah said. "Yet I would have to *ask* to be taught. He would make no offer the same to me, I am sure."

"For pity's sake!" Faris exclaimed. "It is only an offer of learning to ride."

"And it's a good thing, learning to ride well," Mary said once more.

"That it is," Old Joseph said.

"Faris?"

It was Lillias's voice.

Faris glanced behind her to see Lillias standing just inside the kitchen. What a look of mischief was about her! Her face was a lovely pink, bright with excitement.

"Faris, may I have a moment?" Lillias asked.

"Of course, miss," Faris said. Smiling at the others seated at the kitchen table, Faris pushed her chair back as she stood. "Thank you for supper, Mary. It was delicious—as always."

Mary smiled, pleased with the compliment.

Faris giggled when Lillias took her hand and pulled her from the kitchen and into the hallway leading to the grand dining hall.

"What is it?" Faris asked in a whisper. "You are fairly blooming with excitement. Has Lord Kendrick gifted another wonderful treasure?"

"No," Lillias said, eyes illuminated with delight. "I've news of our friend."

"The Highwayman?" Faris whispered.

"Indeed, yes!" Lillias whispered.

When she had been sent to summon Lillias earlier in the day, Faris had been certain Lillias held news of the Highwayman of Tanglewood. Her arms spread over in goose bumps with wondrous anticipation. Five days stretched out endlessly before her—five days more until she would meet the Highwayman at the old cottage near the Tanglewood Forest. That is, unless her suspicions were founded and Bainbridge Graybeau was, in fact, the Highwayman of Tanglewood—in which case, she was mere moments from meeting with him again! Still, Faris was certain any news of the Highwayman provided by Lillias would be wondrous.

"Then you must tell me, Lillias," Faris whispered. "Oh, do tell me, at once!"

"It seems there is some talk," Lillias whispered.

"Talk?" Faris asked.

"Yes. Among the townspeople in Saxton," Lillias said. "It is said the Highwayman of Tanglewood will ride to Saxton to best Lord Brookings."

"Lord Brookings?" Faris asked. "It is whispered that he—"

"Murdered his wife!" Lillias interrupted. "And it is true! I believe he did murder her. The circumstances were so terrible and so very odd and—"

"You know how Mother feels about rumor and hearsay, Lilly."

Faris gasped as Lochlan Rockrimmon stepped from the shadows. The deep green of his eyes flashed in the low lighting, his face and form as perfect as any hero of legend.

"It is not hearsay, Lochlan," Lillias said. She seemed completely unaffected by her brother's sudden appearance. "He murdered his wife, and you well know it."

"Still, it unnerves Mother—the story of Lady Brookings's untimely demise," he said, his eyes lingering on Faris. "So you best not let Mother hear you speaking of it."

"Why then, dearest brother, do you think Faris and I are lingering here—in privacy—rather than right under Mother's nose?" Lillias asked.

Faris was suddenly panic-stricken! Caught gossiping with the young miss of the household? Certainly she would be blamed for attempting to corrupt Lillias with such trivial tittle-tattle.

"And I see you have my drapery bauble in tow," Lochlan said.

Faris felt herself breathless, utterly trembling in his handsome presence—under his mesmerizing gaze.

"Good evening, Faris," he said.

Faris felt her mouth open—attempted to return the greeting. Yet her voice was lost as well as her wits, and all she could utter was, "Yes, sire."

"I see Lilly is corrupting you with her wicked gossiping," he said. He reached out, playfully tweaking his sister's nose.

"I am not corrupting Faris," Lillias said. "We were only speaking of the Highwayman."

Lochlan Rockrimmon's eyebrows arched, a teasing grin spreading across his face. "Ah," he said, his gaze lingering on Faris. "Then am I to understand that you are among the giddy girls swooning over the tales of our local rogue?"

Faris was grateful when Lillias spoke next, saving Faris from having to answer.

"We were speaking of the gossip in Saxton," Lillias said, lowering her voice once more.

"What gossip is that?" Lochlan Rockrimmon asked.

"They are saying the Highwayman of Tanglewood will ride out to best Lord Brookings," Lillias answered.

"To best Brookings?" Lochlan asked.

"Yes!" Lillias exclaimed.

Faris bit her lip, attempting in vain to conceal her amusement. The dashing, handsome heir to Loch Loland Castle appeared quite thoroughly intrigued—as taken by Lillias's news of adventure as Faris had been.

"He's a devil, that one," Lochlan said, lowering his voice.

"I think he did murder his wife," Lillias said, "no matter what the magistrate in Saxton says."

"Indeed he murdered her," Lochlan agreed. "The magistrate in Saxton is as corrupt as Brookings himself. No doubt Brookings paid the traitor to cover it for him."

Faris felt goose bumps erupt over her arms as Lochlan Rockrimmon placed one strong hand on his sister's shoulder and the other on Faris's.

Bending toward them, he said, "And besides . . . if a woman were going to kill herself . . . I very much doubt she would slit her own throat from ear to ear with her husband's dagger."

Faris and Lillias simultaneously gasped in horror at the tale. Lochlan straightened to his full height, nodding his assurance of the truthfulness of his information.

"Oh, surely you are simply trying to astonish us, Lochlan," Lillias said. "You'll give us nightmares with such tales!"

"I assure I am telling the truth," Lochlan said. "Father and I were witness to the body when it was delivered to the undertaker."

"What?" Faris gasped.

"It is true," Lochlan Rockrimmon said. His eyes fixed upon her caused an odd delighted sensation to travel down Faris's spine. "Father and I were in Saxton two years past when Lady

Brookings died. It was rumored Lady Brookings had argued with her husband about his raising their tenants' taxes. Nearly all the servants at the Brookings's manor house heard the argument. The next morning, Lady Brookings was found dead in her chambers, her throat slit ear to ear, her husband's jeweled dagger in her hand."

"But why ever would you and Father be witness at the undertaker's?" Lillias asked.

"A constable suspected Lady Brookings did not slit her own throat," Lochlan explained. "He asked us to witness the body and sign our own statements as to its condition."

Faris looked from Lillias to Lochlan and back, her smile broadening. What a pair the two siblings must have made as infants and children. It was pure plain as sunshine they each had a flair for adventure and dramatics.

"Yet why would our Highwayman concern himself with Lord Brookings?" Lochlan mumbled, pondering aloud to himself. "And why so long after the murder of Lady Brookings? Has Brookings overtaxed his tenants once more?"

"This I already know," Lillias said. "For Gawain told me only this morning that Lord Brookings did not inherit his wife's fortune immediately upon her death!"

"Oh yes!" Lochlan exclaimed in a whisper. "I remember it—Lord Brookings had gambled away the fortune left him by his father. It was Lady

Brookings's family wealth on which he existed."

"Yet he did not inherit the whole of it immediately upon her death," Lillias continued. "Gawain tells me her will stipulated that, in the event of her untimely death, a waiting period of two years should pass before the entirety of her wealth descended to him."

"The Highwayman does not want a man to profit from murder," Faris said. She blushed as Lochlan looked to her and grinned with approval.

"Indeed," Lochlan said. "Yet I have never heard of the Highwayman of Tanglewood besting anyone as great a distance away as Saxton."

"Well, it is the murder of an innocent woman," Lillias said.

"Perhaps the Highwayman champions her as she reportedly did her husband's tenants," Faris offered.

"Perhaps," Lochlan said.

"Bainbridge Graybeau is born of Saxton! Is he not, Loch?" Lillias asked with renewed excitement.

"He is, indeed," Lochlan confirmed. "I believe he lived there the whole of his life until he came to Loch Loland Castle."

Faris felt the hair on the back of her neck prickle with excitement. Graybeau was from Saxton? Of course the Highwayman would consider the affairs of the township to which he was born!

"Let us ask him, then," Lillias said, her eyes brilliant with anticipation. "For would he not know further the details of Lady Brookings's death and why our own Highwayman would take such an interest in it?"

"That he might," Lochlan said. His gaze settled on Faris then—a grin of mischief across his most handsome face. "Why don't you inquire of him, Faris?"

"M-me, sire?" Faris stammered.

"Of course," Lochlan Rockrimmon said. His emerald eyes flashed with rascality. "Is he not providing you with a riding lesson this very evening?"

"Y-yes, sire," Faris breathed. She feared she might faint, so shallow was her breath from her surprise at his knowledge of her planned meeting with Graybeau.

"Oh, Faris!" Lillias exclaimed, taking hold of Faris's shoulders. "What a wonderful idea! You will enjoy learning to ride. Riding lends itself to a certain freedom I cannot begin to explain."

"I-I am certain you are right," Faris said. And she was certain—for she had felt the midnight breeze her in hair, the sense of liberation given from riding; she had felt such winsome freedom the night she had ridden with the Highwayman of Tanglewood. Still, she was quite unsettled Lochlan Rockrimmon should know of her planned meeting with Bainbridge Graybeau.

"Then we will leave it to you, Faris," Lochlan said. "You will inquire of Graybeau as to why our own Highwayman of Tanglewood might take such an interest in Lord Brookings of Saxton."

"If—if you truly wish that I do so, sire," Faris stammered.

"I do," Lochlan said. "And you may deliver the information he gives you to me at first sunlight when you come to my chambers to mend my draperies."

"But, sire," Faris began, "I have mended your draperies already."

"Indeed?" Lochlan asked. "Then you may deliver the information to me at first sunlight when you come to my chambers to ensure I have not overslept."

"You never oversleep, Loch," Lillias said. "You are ever awake and rambling long before the cock crows." Lillias giggled and took one of Faris's hands in her own. "He only endeavors to force you to tell him what Graybeau tells you as soon as he can make you."

"I only endeavor to find your pretty Faris in my chambers once more," Lochlan Rockrimmon said.

Faris swallowed the astonished lump in her throat. What a teasing rascal Loch Loland's young heir was!

"Oh quit, Loch!" Lillias scolded her brother. "Faris is not as familiar with your pestering ways as the rest of us. She will think you entirely in earnest!"

"I am in earnest," Lochlan said.

"You are not! And cease in pestering my darling friend," Lillias said.

"You will inquire of Graybeau for us—will you not, Faris?" Lochlan asked.

Faris was rather breathless. What woman could ever deny Lochlan Rockrimmon anything he asked of her?

"Yes, sire," she managed to answer.

"Good!" he said. "Then Lillias and I will not bar your way to the stables any longer."

"Thank you, sire," Faris said, dropping a slight curtsy to the young master.

"Still, I would beg of you, Faris," he added, "please do not let our mother know what a terrible gossip Lillias has become. It would greatly disturb milady to be made aware of such a thing."

Faris giggled as Lillias then drove one delicate fist into her brother's midsection.

"You are the one speaking of corrupted magistrates and the cutting of throats, Lochlan Rockrimmon!" Lillias exclaimed.

"Off with you now, Faris," Lochlan said, chuckling as his sister continued to pelt him with her dainty fists. "Before I am further humiliated in your presence by my sister's brutal pummeling."

"Yes, sire," Faris said, smiling with amusement. "Good evening Miss Lillias, Master Lochlan," she said.

"You may as well endeavor to flog me with a feather as with such tiny fists, Lilly," she heard Lochlan tease as she left them to seek out the stables and Bainbridge Graybeau.

The evening air was warm, fragrant with trees, grasses, and the night-blooming flowers of the Loch Loland Castle gardens. As Faris made her way to the stables, she smiled. Why would the Highwayman of Tanglewood take such an interest in the goings-on in Saxton? There could be only one answer: the Highwayman of Tanglewood had some connection to the place. Bainbridge Graybeau had been born in Saxton. There he had lived until finding himself at Loch Loland Castle. Bainbridge Graybeau had reason to care for the goings-on in Saxton. Faris smiled. With each passing moment, her suspicion of Bainbridge Graybeau riding out as the Highwayman of Tanglewood grew.

"There you are, Miss Faris," Graybeau greeted as Faris approached. "I was only just saddling Lady Violet, I was."

"Good evening, Mr. Graybeau," Faris said. She could not help but smile at him—could not stop the increasing rhythm of her heart. It was he! Surely it was! She noted how handsome

Bainbridge Graybeau was—made even more handsome for having shaved his mustache and goatee.

"Lady Violet will do very well for your learning to ride, she will," Graybeau said. "She's a bit older than the other mounts in the stables. When I told him I meant to teach you to ride, Master Lochlan suggested Lady Violet himself. She is even-tempered and patient."

"You are very kind in offering to teach me to ride, Mr. Graybeau," Faris began. "Especially when I will never have any need to—"

"You may well have need in knowing how to ride one day—in feeling comfortable on horseback," he interrupted.

Faris smiled. Was he thinking of the night she had ridden with the Highwayman toward Loch Loland Castle?

"Very well," she said. "Then I am ready to learn."

"Good," Graybeau said. "And you must address me as, Bainbridge, Miss Faris," he added.

"If you like," Faris said.

"Sidesaddle is the manner of riding preferred by most women," Bainbridge began, "though I plan to teach you to ride astride as well."

"For what reason?" Faris asked. She had ridden astride the night she had ridden with the Highwayman. Still, why did Bainbridge desire to teach her both methods? Most women did ride sidesaddle—those who did not often found themselves the subject of many a raised eyebrow.

"For reasons of being a thorough teacher," Bainbridge said. "Now then," he began, "step here—on my leg. In this, I am giving you a leg up to mount."

"Step on your leg?" Faris asked. She had seen Bainbridge help Lady Rockrimmon and Lillias to mount this way. Still, she was suddenly uncomfortable.

"Of course," he said. "Here now," he added, taking her hand, "mount up."

Faris did as instructed and was soon awkwardly sitting in the saddle.

"Good," Bainbridge said. "Now, left foot in the stirrup, right knee round the pommel—there."

Faris felt entirely self-conscious mounted upon the back of one of the Rockrimmon horses. She was not a grand lady! Whatever was she thinking in allowing Bainbridge Graybeau to teach her to ride? She was thinking Bainbridge might well be the Highwayman of Tanglewood—that was what she had been thinking when she had agreed to it all.

"I'll lead you around a bit, now," Bainbridge said, taking hold of Lady Violet's bit. "Just until you're comfortable holding the reins yourself."

"Very well," Faris said. "Though I will admit to being quite unsettled."

Bainbridge Graybeau chuckled, and Faris tried

to discern whether or not the sound of it sounded as the Highwayman's did. She was uncertain, however, and sighed with frustration.

Misinterpreting Faris's sigh, Bainbridge said, "Don't worry, lass—I'll give the reins over to you soon enough."

"Oh, I am not so impatient as that, Mr. Graybeau," Faris said. He had called her lass! The fact caused her heart to race with delight at another characteristic of her Highwayman.

"I . . . I hear you were born in Saxton, Mr. Graybeau," she began then.

"Bainbridge, if you please, Faris," Bainbridge said. "And yes, I was born there—lived there 'til I was hired by his lordship to come here."

"And . . . and do you still receive news of Saxton?" Faris ventured.

"Indeed," he said. "My mother and two brothers still live there. I often hear from them."

"There is some talk concerning our own Highwayman of Tanglewood," Faris ventured. "It is said he plans to best a certain Lord Brookings of Saxton."

"Yes," Bainbridge said. "I am in receipt of a letter from my mother only just this very day. She wrote of the rumors in Saxton concerning the Highwayman of Tanglewood."

"But why would our Highwayman take interest in something amiss in a township so far from us?" Faris asked. She noted she was feeling more comfortable in the saddle. She smiled as Bainbridge turned to look at her, still leading Lady Violet.

"Perhaps the very origin of our Highwayman of Tanglewood is Saxton," he said, smiling at her. She fancied his smile revealed more mischief than he perhaps intended. "Perhaps he was born and grew there as I did."

Faris smiled at Bainbridge. "Perhaps you are acquainted with him and—and simply are not aware of the fact."

"Perhaps," Bainbridge said, his smile broadening. "Still, the Highwayman's interest in Saxton might merely be at having heard of Lord Brookings's murderous nature. Perhaps he simply endeavors to best an evil man."

"Do you think this Lord Brookings murdered his lady?" Faris asked.

"I know he did," Bainbridge said.

"How can you be so certain?" Faris asked.

"My mother was housekeeper for Lord and Lady Brookings," Bainbridge said. "It was my mother who found Lady Brookings's body— throat slit ear to ear, Lord Brookings's dagger still clasped in her hand."

"Surely you are only trying to astonish me," Faris breathed.

"No," Bainbridge said. "My mother heard Lord and Lady Brookings arguing the night before milady's death. Lord Brookings had raised his tenants' taxes. Further, he had sent Lady Brookings's lady's maid away. His reasons for the second are not known; his reasons for the first of it were simple greed. Lady Brookings argued with him over both matters, and the whole of the manor house heard it. The next morning, my mother found Lady Brookings dead in her chambers. Lord Brookings questioned my mother for near to an hour before the magistrate was called—demanding she repeat her story of finding the body over and over. My mother was certain he was assuring himself he had left nothing else amiss, nothing my mother might have seen upon finding the body. Eventually, Lord Brookings was satisfied and called the magistrate—a purchased man himself, I am certain. The magistrate ruled the incident a suicide. Lord Brookings dismissed my mother that very hour, however. She is certain he killed Lady Brookings. Therefore, it is her certainty that makes mine whole."

"It is an astonishing tale," Faris said.

"It is indeed," Bainbridge said.

It seemed to Faris the Highwayman of Tanglewood would need to own a sure knowledge of Lord Brookings's villainy in order that he might ride out to Saxton. Bainbridge owned a certain knowledge of his own. Furthermore, his mother had been ill-treated. It would be enough to provoke the Highwayman of Tanglewood into riding to Saxton. It certainly would be enough.

"Perhaps the Highwayman of Tanglewood will not ride to Saxton at all. It may be the townspeople in Saxton only wish it were so, for there is a great loathing of Lord Brookings in Saxton," Bainbridge added.

"It is understandable in the least," Faris said. "And if the Highwayman were Saxton-born as you are, he would feel a great loyalty to it, no doubt."

"No doubt," Bainbridge said.

"If you knew the Highwayman of Tanglewood," Faris began, "if you knew who he were—if he were indeed of Saxton and of your acquaintance—would you reveal his identity to anyone?" Faris's heart was pounding with anticipation. Was Bainbridge Graybeau the Highwayman of Tanglewood? Would he reveal himself to her if it were true?

Again Bainbridge chuckled. He stopped Lady Violet and walked to Faris, offering the reins to her. His dark eyes flashed with amusement.

"The Highwayman has every lady for one hundred miles 'round wondering over his true identity," he said. "Yet, if I knew him," he said as Faris took the reins, "I would want to ride out with him for his cause—not wreak havoc upon him in revealing his true identity."

Faris smiled even though her heart seemed to

drop into the very pit of her stomach with great disappointment. He had not revealed himself to her though the opportunity had been ripe.

"Aye—but I am no rogue the like of the Highwayman," Bainbridge said. "Only the stablemaster of Loch Loland Castle."

"Yet there is a rogue's character about you somehow," Faris said. Her hope was renewed of a sudden. Perhaps he had not revealed himself to her as yet, but that did not mean Bainbridge was not the Highwayman: it only meant he was not ready to reveal. Further, Faris could see wisdom in his silence on the matter. She had met the Highwayman but thrice. What true trust was there between them yet?

Bainbridge laughed then. "A rogue's character I own, do I?" he said. "It is a welcome compliment somehow—for are not rogues considered most attractive?"

"Yes," Faris admitted. She felt a blush rise to her cheeks and hoped the dim light of evening hid it well enough.

"Now," Bainbridge began, returning his attention to Faris's lesson, "tell her where you wish to go, Faris. Guide her around the stableyard once or twice."

"But how?" Faris asked.

"Hold the reins thus—taut as such," he said, placing the reins in her hands as he wished them to be. "If you wish to turn left, then gently tug the reins left—against the right of her neck. She will obey you, and I will walk beside."

"Very well," Faris said. Inhaling a deep breath of courage, she did as Bainbridge instructed. "She will only walk with me, will she not? She will not endeavor to quicken her pace?"

Bainbridge chuckled. "She will only walk for now," he said. "We will ride for half the hour. When next we meet, we will have a longer lesson."

"Thank you, Mr. Graybeau," Faris said. "It is very kind of you to offer to teach me."

"Everyone should know how to ride properly," Bainbridge said. "And you are to call me Bainbridge, Faris."

"Thank you, Mr. Bainbridge," Faris said.

"You are welcome, Faris," he chuckled.

He had not revealed himself. Bainbridge Graybeau had not revealed himself to be the Highwayman of Tanglewood. As Faris lay upon her pillow, hands tucked behind her head, as she stared up at the great oak beams in the ceiling of her chamber, she frowned. She knew little more about Bainbridge Graybeau than she knew before. The voice whispering in her head told her that were Bainbridge in truth the Highwayman of Tanglewood, he would have at least offered some small evidence to her. He had revealed nothing, however, and Faris was no longer certain of his being the Highwayman—of his being *her* Highwayman.

Breathing a heavy sigh, Faris turned on her side, closing her eyes. In her mind, she could quite see him—the Highwayman of Tanglewood, his cape billowing in the breeze, his dazzling smile illuminated by the moonlight. Five nights more, and she would be with him. She wondered then if he would be clean-shaven as Bainbridge Graybeau now was.

As the fire burned low in the hearth, Faris imagined she heard the heavy rhythm of hooves beating the ground. No doubt it was simply Old Joseph prowling about as was his habit. Old Joseph often lingered in wakefulness long after everyone else in the castle had retired. Still, she would dream it was he—the Highwayman of Tanglewood riding toward Loch Loland Castle. Perhaps he would whisk her away to a life of adventure—a life filled with fragrant meadows, amethyst sunsets, and a rogue's passionate kiss.

"Master Lochlan is requesting your presence in his chamber, Faris," Old Joseph said.

"Me?" Faris asked.

"He says you were to have awakened him first this morning—that you were gathering some information at his behest and that he wishes to receive it now." Old Joseph smiled. "He will not scold you, Faris," he said. "He is a mischievous lad. You will come to know him and his ways."

"Then shall I attend him? Or is he in jest?" Faris asked.

"Oh, he is most certainly in earnest," Old Joseph said. "And you may wish to attend him at once—for he and Lord Rockrimmon are riding out in visiting many tenants today."

"I-I suppose I should attend him then," Faris stammered.

"It would be wise," Old Joseph said. "But do not go in fear, Faris. He is not angry with you— simply impatient to be told whatever it is you have to tell."

"I fear disappointing him," Faris said. After all, what grand information did she gain from Bainbridge? Only that he himself was certain of Lord Brookings's murderous treachery, that the Highwayman may or may not have been born in Saxton, and that indeed rumors were abounding in Saxton of the Highwayman of Tanglewood's potential appearance there.

"He is waiting, Faris," Old Joseph said, gently reminding her of Lochlan Rockrimmon's position in the household.

"Yes. Of course," Faris said. Smiling at Old Joseph, she started toward the large staircase leading to the family's chambers.

Her heart beat with anxious anticipation as she climbed the stairs. She feared she might faint as she approached Lochlan Rockrimmon's chambers. His door stood ajar, and it took every thread of courage she could muster to knock upon it.

"Come," came the deep intonation of his voice from beyond the door.

"Sire?" Faris said as she pushed on the door, entering the room as it opened.

"Ah, Faris," Lochlan Rockrimmon said.

Faris gasped, her eyes widening as she saw he was not yet properly attired. Indeed, he wore black boots and brown breeches—yet the white billowing shirt he wore yet hung opened to his waist.

"Forgive me, sire," Faris said, turning away from him.

"For what?" he asked. "Did I not tell you I was only teasing you about the draperies? Besides, they looked to be perfectly mended."

"Yes, sire—but I meant to beg your forgiveness for intruding when—" Faris began.

"Do not concern yourself," he said. "I awoke easily enough of my own will this morning."

Faris sighed. He did not seem to understand she was uncomfortable in his presence when he was not properly attired.

"See here," he said. "What news have you brought me?"

It was obvious he wanted her to look at him as they spoke. Slowly she turned to see he had finished fastening his shirt. He appeared even more attractive for his casual appearance, and Faris scolded herself when she felt a spray of butterflies take flight in her stomach as she looked at him.

"Well?" he prodded.

"B-Bainbridge Graybeau yet has strong family connections in Saxton," Faris stammered. "He is in agreement with you—that Lord Brookings indeed murdered his wife."

"And what of the Highwayman of Tangle-wood?" Lochlan asked. Faris watched as he tucked his shirt into his breeches at the waist. "Does he have an opinion as to why our Highwayman would ride so far west?"

"Only the same as do you, sire," Faris said. "Either for loyalty to Saxton and its people— or because of the great injustice done Lady Brookings."

"Hmm," Lochlan said, frowning and hastily donning a black vest. "Then we have no more information than Gawain has offered already, it seems." Tossing a coat over one arm and stripping a white cravat from its place on the arm of a nearby chair, he ran a hand through his tousled hair and said, "It is a question of Saxton— of waiting to hear news of the Highwayman appearing there. I suppose we will just have to bide our time where tales of the local rogue are concerned then. Yes?"

"It would seem so, sire," Faris said. She could

not help but return the smile he bestowed upon her then. How his green eyes did flash in the morning light!

"Pray endeavor to make me presentable, Faris," he said then, coming to stand before her. "Mother says I do not take care with my hair. Only yesterday she told me I looked as windblown as any old seadog she had ever seen."

Yet Faris smiled. She preferred his rather disorderly appearance. Further, she would never find the courage to instruct him in any matter—in clothing choice, hair combing, or anything else. Therefore, she paused.

"Come, Faris," he said then. "What is amiss with me this morning and bound to disturb milady?"

"Nothing whatsoever, sire," she told him.

He quirked one eyebrow in suspicious disbelief. "Then when she reprimands me for looking the vagabond, I shall tell her it is no fault of my own—only yours."

"I am quite sure you look as well as any gentleman, sire," Faris said. Oh, he looked far better, if the truth be told. But she would never dare to tell him the truth of it.

"Then I'm off," he said. "Good day, Faris."

"Good day, Master Lochlan," Faris said, dipping a quick curtsy.

As he strode past her into the hallway, Faris frowned as her gaze fell to the young master's bed. Spread up in perfection, Faris would have thought she had already been about the room had she not known better herself. She smiled, however, when she noticed that, although his bed was well spread up, his clothing littered the chair and floor. Indeed, it appeared a toddler may have been visiting the grand chamber of Lochlan Rockrimmon.

"Faris, darling, there you are!"

Faris turned to see Lady Rockrimmon approaching. "Yes, milady?" Faris asked.

Lady Rockrimmon looked past Faris in to Lochlan's chamber, shaking her head. "One would think he were yet six years aged to look at his chambers." Faris smiled as Lady Rockrimmon rolled her eyes. "The boy is near to obsessive about his bedding—found a spider in his bed once as a child and has spread it up himself ever since. But this clothing strewn everywhere . . ."

"I will see to it, milady," Faris said.

"Thank you, Faris," Lady Rockrimmon said, smiling. "But first—would you seek out milord and give him this, please?" The great lady held a basket hooked on one arm. "It is for our friends the McGoverns, on the east tenant farm. I had promised Mrs. McGovern several books from my collection of poetry, and Mary has wrapped up a fresh loaf of bread as well. Will you ask Lord Rockrimmon to see to it? Lillias and I are in with the seamstress at present."

"Of course, milady," Faris said, taking the basket when Lady Rockrimmon held it out to her.

"Thank you, darling," Lady Rockrimmon said. "Now I must return. The wedding dress is almost completed! You must come and see it today when you can."

"Yes, milady," Faris said.

Descending the staircase, Faris made her way to the large room Lord Rockrimmon used for his study. She gasped, however, terrified as Kade Tremeshton suddenly appeared, taking hold of her arm in a fierce grip. Instantly, Faris began to tremble. There was a certain malicious sensation that lingered in the air whenever Lord Kade Tremeshton was present. Furthermore, Faris was entirely startled to see him at Loch Loland Castle. She knew Lord Rockrimmon only allowed him to visit to settle purchasing matters, and she thought Lord Rockrimmon had purchased all the property from Kade Tremeshton that he intended.

"Faris," he said, an evil smile of ill-intent upon his face. "There you are."

"Lord Tremeshton," Faris said, her heart hammering with such fear she thought she might expire. "I-I am on my way to see His Lordship," she said, trying to pull her arm from his grasp. Certainly he would unhand her now—knowing well she intended to speak to his lordship.

"Lord Rockrimmon will wait. It has been far too long since I have set eyes upon you, Faris," Kade Tremeshton said. "Where have you been hiding?"

"I have not been hiding, sire," Faris said. She must escape! She felt sickened merely being in his presence. "I have been laboring here—as you know."

"Yes," he said, an expression of disgust owning his countenance then. "Laboring for Lady Rockrimmon at Loch Loland Castle. My mother was quite vexed at your leaving—and in such a cowardly manner, Faris. Surely you know you owe my mother a greater debt and far more respect than to leave as a thief in the night."

"I did not leave without explanation, sire. There was a note—" Faris began.

"Ungrateful wench that you are—yet my thoughts still linger on you often," Kade said.

His grip tightened on her arm, and Faris's fear heightened. Yet she was safe—safe in Loch Loland Castle. Surely no harm could come to her there—could it?

"Pray unhand me, sire," Faris said, her voice trembling. She sensed she was not so safe as she should be. "I have milady's business to be about."

Instead of releasing her, however, Kade Tremeshton reached forth and took hold of Faris's other arm, holding her fast and drawing her closer to him.

"Unhand me, sire . . . else I should scream," Faris stammered.

He did not unhand her, however, and suddenly his hands were tight about her throat! Faris tried to call out, dropping Lady Rockrimmon's basket as her hands went to his, endeavoring to free herself from his clutches.

"Scream?" he growled, his breath hot on her face. "And who would come for you, Faris? Who would champion a lowly chambermaid in the face of the Lord Kade Tremeshton?"

Faris thought of the Highwayman of Tanglewood—thought of his besting Kade Tremeshton twice before. Her heart swelled at the very thought of him—swelled with courage and anger at her attacker.

"There is one who has easily bested you before," Faris choked.

Kade Tremeshton's face glowed red with fury then. "Silence!" he growled. "And do not think you will slip away so easily this time. I intend—"

Faris felt the grip on her throat relax. She gasped for air but was rendered breathless once again when she turned her head a little to follow Kade's astonished gaze. There, protruding over her right shoulder from behind, was the silver glint of a sharp steel blade.

Faris felt hope, relief, and even elation instantly rise within her. As Kade Tremeshton dropped his hands, she realized it must be he—her beloved Highwayman had come to champion her! But in the broad light of day and from within the walls of Loch Loland Castle?

Chivalry, Speculation, and Impatience

"My father has been far too tolerant of you, Tremeshton," Lochlan said from his stance behind Faris.

It was Lochlan Rockrimmon's sword at her shoulder. She could feel the warmth and strength of his body against her back—his breath in her hair at the top of her head. Faris was simultaneously disappointed and relieved—disappointed it was not the Highwayman of Tanglewood championing her and relieved it was not he, for it would have meant his safety might have been compromised.

Faris looked to her left as Lord Kendrick stepped into the room. Taking hold of Faris's arm, he gently pulled her from under the blade of Lochlan Rockrimmon's sword—pulled her from the place where Lord Kade Tremeshton stood to her front, Lochlan Rockrimmon at her back, with peril in between.

"You dare to draw your sword on me?" Kade growled.

"You dare to enter my father's house and accost one of his own?" Lochlan growled in return.

"She was mine before ever she was his," Kade shouted.

"She belongs to no one," Lochlan shouted in return. "Least of all a coward the likes of you!"

Faris gasped as Kade Tremeshton drew his sword from its sheath at his hip.

"Milord?" she cried. She looked to Lord Kendrick, yet he shook his head and held fast to her arm. Did Lord Kendrick intend to stand by and simply watch as Lochlan Rockrimmon and Kade Tremeshton struck swords? It was apparent that he did, for his grasp on Faris's arm tightened.

"He is a miscreant of the worst sort, Faris," Lord Kendrick said. "Allow Lochlan to best him. It will serve many."

Faris felt tears escape her eyes—her heart beat like a hammer against an anvil. The scene playing out before her was a nightmare! What if the young master were injured? It would be her fault if he were to be injured! Oh, why had she ever agreed to work at Tremeshton Manor? Why had Kade Tremeshton come to Loch Loland Castle?

"What goes on here?" Lord Rockrimmon's voice boomed. Suddenly, he appeared from the direction of his study. "Tremeshton? Why is your presence still staining the very air at Loch Loland? I ordered your prompt departure!"

"He has attempted to accost Faris, Father," Lochlan explained. "I found him fairly choking the life from her just here! Let me slit him open from chin to foot, and he will never again—"

"Rein in your temper, Lochlan," Lord Rockrimmon said. "And do not give him the honor of having his throat slit by one such as you. Rather, throw him out as a rabid dog. Throw him out of Loch Loland Castle!"

Faris brushed the tears from her cheeks. She was so overcome with dread, fear, and disbelief that she did not pause to allow Lord Kendrick to gather her into the protective strength of his arms.

Faris watched as Lochlan seemed to consider for a moment. He did not lower his sword at first—instead stood inhaling and exhaling angry breaths.

"Lochlan!" Lord Rockrimmon shouted.

"As you wish, Father," Lochlan said.

Faris gasped as Lochlan easily disarmed Kade with one quick sword tactic. As Kade's sword clattered to the floor, Lochlan lunged forward, taking Kade by the back of the coat.

"Unhand me!" Kade shouted as Lochlan pushed him toward the grand doors of Loch Loland Castle. Sheathing his sword and opening the great front door, Lochlan turned Kade to face him.

"You owe my father your life, Tremeshton!" Lochlan growled.

"You will pay for this, Rockrimmon," Kade

threatened. "You will pay dearly for such—"

Faris gasped as Kade Tremeshton was suddenly silenced by the force of Lochlan's fist meeting with his nose. Instantly, blood ran crimson over Kade's lips and chin.

"You've broken my nose!" Kade shouted.

"Good! Count yourself fortunate," Lochlan growled, pushing Kade Tremeshton out of Loch Loland Castle and sending him tumbling down the great front steps.

Closing the great castle door, Lochlan tugged on one coat-sleeve and ran strong fingers through his hair—gestures in attempting to restore his temper.

"Perhaps the Highwayman will finish him before he reaches Tremeshton," Lochlan growled.

"Let us hope," Lord Kendrick said.

Faris brushed tears from her face and stood trembling in Lord Kendrick's arms. Realizing her weakness, Faris gently pushed herself from Lord Kendrick's embrace, wiping the tears from her cheeks and smoothing her apron.

She gasped, breathless as in the next moment Lord Rockrimmon himself dropped to one knee before her.

"My apologies, Faris," he began, "for allowing such a man into Loch Loland that he might endeavor to harm you."

"Sire," Faris breathed, "it is no fault of yours. Pray do not lower yourself to—"

Lord Rockrimmon reached out, taking one of Faris's hands in his and kissing the back of it. "All in this house are meant to know safety, Faris. I have failed you in not providing it."

"Please, milord," Faris begged. "It is none of it your fault. I . . . I . . ."

"He will no longer torment you, Faris," Lord Rockrimmon said. "He will not set foot in Loch Loland Castle again. This is my promise to you."

"As it is mine, Faris," Lochlan said, unexpectedly dropping to one knee before her as well. "All who dwell at Loch Loland Castle should, and will, know peace and safety. We will not fail you again."

Faris found drawing breath to be difficult. Lord Derrick Rockrimmon knelt before her—looking as a knight of old pledging loyalty to a great lady—as did his handsome son. She was a mere chambermaid and could no more believe the truth of who knelt before her and why than she could have defended herself from Kade Tremeshton.

"What is all this?" Lillias asked as she entered to see her father and brother kneeling before Faris. "What has happened? Gawain?"

"Kade Tremeshton has assaulted Faris—just here—in Loch Loland Castle," Gawain explained.

"Oh, Faris, no!" Lillias exclaimed, gasping and covering her mouth with one hand.

"Lochlan and your father have driven him out,"

Gawain added, "sworn he will never set foot in Loch Loland again."

"Oh, my poor Faris!" Lillias exclaimed, throwing graceful, caring arms around Faris to embrace her. "He is the devil, I swear it! Sometimes I believe Kade Tremeshton is in truth the very devil!"

"I-I am well, Miss Lillias," Faris said. She received and indeed returned Lillias's embrace, however—grateful for obvious affection and friendship.

"You should have beaten him within an inch of his life, Loch!" Lillias said, releasing Faris and studying her face—an expression of deep worry and concern blatant on her own.

"Father would only allow that I break his nose and throw him out," Lochlan said, rising to his full stance in unison with his father.

"Father!" Lillias exclaimed—a deep scolding tone of disappointment in her voice.

"It was enough," Lord Rockrimmon said. "In the least, for now it was enough."

"I beg your pardon, sire," Lord Kendrick began, "but may I inquire as to what the villain was about at Loch Loland in the first of it?"

Lord Rockrimmon nodded. "This is entirely my fault," he said. "I should never have allowed him to step a foot into Loch Loland. Yet he sent me word yesterday of his desire to sell his eastern properties—the properties on which he keeps

166

five families of tenants in utter misery. I could not refuse the offer. Still, he was determined to strike hands and signatures on parchments here at Loch Loland." Lord Rockrimmon's eyes lingered on Faris a moment. "I think now I understand why he refused to sell me the properties unless I allowed the purchase to take place in my own house."

"He is yet angry at Faris's rejection of him," Lord Kendrick said. "It is more the being bested he minds, rather than the loss of conquest, I daresay."

Faris glanced away as Lord Kendrick's gaze held hers for a long moment. She was far too uncomfortable in the presence of so many titled men.

"Men can be such loathsome creatures," Lillias grumbled. "Kade Tremeshton offers your gender no good due."

Not one of the men present begged to argue with Lillias. Rather they stood in silence for long moments.

"And yet," Lillias sighed, taking Lord Kendrick's arm and smiling up at him, "there are three knights of chivalry yet standing in Loch Loland Castle. Of that I am encouraged and happy."

Lord Kendrick smiled at Lillias, and Faris could not help but be warmed within at the sight of their true and obvious affection for one another.

"Pray, what is in the basket?" Lochlan said.

Faris gasped slightly, remembering then her errand.

As Lochlan stooped to pick up the basket, which had fallen to the floor upon Kade's assault, Faris said, "Milady wishes for you, Lord Rockrimmon, to deliver this basket of books and bread to Mrs. McGovern as you are on your tenant visits today."

Lord Rockrimmon smiled at Faris. "You may inform milady that I will do so promptly upon seeing Mrs. McGovern, Faris." He reached out, taking one of her hands between his two strong ones. "I hope you will forgive us for failing you, Faris. I hope you will not think of leaving us because of this incident."

"It was none of it your fault, sire," Faris said. She was far too uncomfortable and wished only to escape, for Lord Rockrimmon and his handsome son to leave for their destinations and save her from further attention.

"Father," Lochlan said of a sudden. "I cannot allow Tremeshton to simply walk away from this without consequence!"

Faris looked to Lochlan. His temper had flared once more. No doubt it had never completely cooled. His green eyes flashed with fury, and Faris was in awe of the change in him—his playful, teasing nature had vanished, and in its place there was the anger and chivalrous nature of the noble lord he would one day be.

"I will ride him down and best him as I should have!" Lochlan growled, turning to leave. His father's hand on his shoulder suspended his exit however.

"You bloodied him enough for one day, Loch," Lord Rockrimmon said. "We have business to be about. Some of which is the matter of seeing to our new tenants, who once belonged to the blackguard and are, no doubt, in need of much. Leave the besting of such vile villains to those who are best at it."

Lochlan's massive chest rose and fell with the labored breathing of barely restrained anger.

"You mean to say let the Highwayman of Tanglewood manage him while I sit still and in seeming cowardice endure one great political debate after another!" Lochlan growled through clenched teeth.

"You have accomplished much in your debating, Lochlan—much the Highwayman could not accomplish in his way," Lord Rock-rimmon said. "The Highwayman is indeed our ally. He battles in one venue, we in another—both of equal importance in our cause."

"Ride out to Tremeshton's east properties, Lochlan," Lord Kendrick said. "Battle Tremeshton by lifting those he has oppressed from despair and hardship."

Faris watched as Lochlan attempted to rein in

his obviously tweaked temper. Though his teeth were yet clinched with frustration, he nodded. "Very well. Let us ride out then, Father—for my temperament is not favorable to idleness."

"Indeed," Lord Rockrimmon said, winking at Faris. "Then we shall ride out."

Faris could not help but smile. What a wonderful father Lord Rockrimmon was to his children! In those moments, as his kind smile and fatherly wink were bestowed upon her, she felt a wave of endearment wash over her in response.

With a nod to Lord Kendrick, and not one other offered word, Lochlan Rockrimmon turned and stormed from the room.

"What a jolly ride this promises to be, eh, Faris?" Lord Rockrimmon said, offering another wink a moment before he followed his son in exiting.

Lillias released a heavy sigh once her brother and father had left the room. Faris looked to see Lord Kendrick smiling with amusement.

"What an ordeal, Faris!" Lillias said. "I feel as if I want nothing more than to sit down the rest of the entire day! I seem terribly weak of a sudden. Such emotional drama ever takes its toll on me."

"But what of your dress, my love?" Lord Kendrick asked. He smiled at his intended bride as she smiled at him. "Do you not wish to see it finished that we may wed upon the chosen date?"

"Indeed, I do!" Lillias said, smiling.

Faris giggled, delighted in Lillias's sudden renewal of spirit.

"It is why I came in search of you in the first of it, Faris!" she said. "Mother and I demand that you come up and see the dress. I simply cannot allow the seamstress to complete it without your approval!"

Faris felt suddenly tired, worn to a thread. The confrontation with Kade Tremeshton and all that followed had fairly drained her of any vitality and emotion. Yet her friend was asking a boon.

"I cannot wait to see it," Faris said.

"Then we shall go up to Mother," Lillias said, ever smiling.

"Yet, I would wait in telling Lady Rockrimmon of this . . . this incident with Tremeshton," Lord Kendrick said. "Better to have his lordship relate the tale when he returns."

"Indeed," Faris agreed. She knew Lady Rockrimmon would be terribly overcome with fear, guilt, and any other number of sad emotions when the tale was told.

"Yes," Lillias said. "Mother will blame herself—as ever she does. We will wait, Faris—we will allow Father to tell her of it. And until he does return, we will play the excited little girls over my wedding dress."

"We will," Faris said, smiling. Lillias's friendship was true. With each passing day, Faris knew it was so—and prayed it would ever be.

"Then I will ride for my own home," Lord Kendrick said. "I will allow you ladies your privacy—for I have many matters of my own business to attend to."

"Oh, darling!" Lillias exclaimed. "Must you away so early in the day?"

Lord Kendrick smiled and gathered Lillias into his arms in a rather roguish manner, and Faris smiled, enchanted by his unguarded gesture.

"Yes, darling, I must," Lord Kendrick said. "Yet I will return tomorrow to draw more nectar kisses from your berry lips."

"Gawain!" Lillias giggled with delight. "Faris will think you an utter rake!"

"Do you think me a rake, Faris?" Lord Kendrick asked, smiling with a mischief that set her own smile to broadening.

"No, indeed, sire," Faris said. "But I will take my leave—that you might endeavor to disprove my opinion of you."

Lord Kendrick chuckled, and Lillias blushed.

"And . . . and I do thank you for your assistance, sire," Faris said, dropping a slow curtsy.

Lord Kendrick shook his head, holding up one hand in gesture she should not thank him. "I did nothing save stand idly by as two noble lords defended a lady's honor," he said.

"But, sire—" Faris began.

"I will have no more thanks from you, Faris," Lord Kendrick said. "In truth, I did nothing."

Faris began to speak, yet as Lord Kendrick shook his head again, Lillias said, "Faris, please be so kind as to attend Mother and tell her I will join you shortly. If we do not appear, she may come in search of us, and then our secret will indeed be revealed before Father has returned to comfort her."

Faris knew Lillias was attempting to distract her from offering further thanks to Lord Kendrick.

She smiled as Lillias added, "And besides, Gawain will never endeavor to kiss me if you do not leave us. Therefore, I would beg you, as my dearest friend—leave us . . . for I'm near to dying for want of him to do so."

"Very well," Faris said. "I will go."

"And I am grateful," Lord Kendrick said.

As Faris climbed the stairs on her way to the sewing rooms, she thought of the events of the morning. So much had transpired! It was difficult to take it all in. She felt worn and wished there were some way to find respite—a lonesome walk in the gardens or even the opportunity to sit quietly under a tree somewhere off from the castle. What she did find served to distract her thoughts at least—even if rest were not the benefit.

Upon arriving in the sewing room, Faris found Lady Rockrimmon rosy-cheeked and full of excitement.

"Faris! There you are, darling," Lady Rockrimmon greeted. "Lillias's dress is simply lovely! You cannot help but adore it. I'm so glad Lillias is a moderate girl in temper—her dress is simple and elegant, as befits her. And," Lady Rockrimmon prattled on, "Joseph has only just handed me a letter from Lady Stringham!"

"Lady Stringham, milady?" Faris asked when Lady Rockrimmon seemed to pause, expectant of Faris's response.

"Yes, darling" Lady Rockrimmon said. "She and her daughter, Tannis, are meant to visit us in two weeks' time—far earlier than originally anticipated—and I simply cannot seem to feel happy about it."

"Milady?" Faris asked.

"Yet regardless of how I feel, they have managed to coax Lochlan into inviting them, and we must put them up," she said with a sigh. It seemed her excitement over Lillias's wedding dress was cooled at the talk of impending company. "I know you keep the chambers across from Lillias at the ready. Still, I wish you to know that Lady Stringham and her daughter . . . their chambers will be your responsibility when they arrive, as well as Lochlan's and Lillias's," she said.

"Of course, milady," Faris said. "I will be only too glad to serve them."

Lady Rockrimmon looked to Faris, and Faris

almost laughed out loud at the expression of veiled sarcasm upon her lovely face.

"That is because you have not yet met them," Lady Rockrimmon said. "I will tell you, Faris—I am certain Tannis Stringham has designs to marry my Lochlan, and I pray he is not insipid enough to be fooled and consider her. Still, she is a beautiful girl, and I cannot quite explain my aversion. Therefore, I must accept them into Loch Loland—for he has invited them."

Of a sudden, Faris remembered—the night the family and household discovered Lochlan Rockrimmon was to return to Loch Loland Castle, there had been some talk of Milady Stringham and her daughter, Tannis. Mary, Joseph, and Sarah had mentioned an impending visit—mentioned their aversion to the daughter and their hopes Lochlan did not have serious intent toward her. Furthermore, was it not mentioned her father, Lord Stringham, was an enemy of the Highwayman of Tanglewood? Yes! She was sure it had been said.

Instantly, the fiber of Faris's feelings of safety and security were weakened. Kade Tremeshton had managed to infiltrate the safety of Loch Loland Castle, and now it seemed the family of another noble miscreant would invade. It saddened and worried Faris to know another enemy of her secret love was to house under the same roof as she.

"I will see that they are very comfortable, milady," Faris said.

Again she nearly laughed as the lovely woman arched one eyebrow and said, "Not too comfortable, darling. I do not wish that they should linger at Loch Loland long."

"Yes, milady," Faris said, smiling.

"Now come and see the dress, Faris," Lady Rockrimmon said. "Lillias is most anxious you should approve it. Where is Lillias? I asked her to bring you, and now she has gone missing." Faris giggled, knowing Lillias and Lord Kendrick were downstairs sharing *nectar kisses*. "She said she would be here momentarily, milady," Faris said.

"She is, no doubt, somewhere lingering in Gawain's arms, I'd wager," Lady Rockrimmon said. "But you are here and can give your opinion without her."

"Yes, milady," Faris said. She felt warmed in Lady Rockrimmon's presence. She was such a kind woman and possessed of such an entertaining character. Faris was grateful to be at Loch Loland Castle. She hoped to never have cause of finding a new position elsewhere. It would fairly break her heart to leave—unless, of course, she left for the cause of forever being with the Highwayman of Tanglewood. For true love, Faris would leave Loch Loland Castle—but only for the sake of true love.

Lord Rockrimmon and Lochlan spent near to three days wending their way over the Rockrimmon properties, visiting tenants and seeing to things of business. Each morning, Faris had entered Lochlan Rockrimmon's room to find his bed nicely spread up and his clothing strewn hither and yon about the room. Each morning, the sight caused her to smile and giggle with thinking the heir to the Rockrimmon fortune and title was no more than a little lad—too busy about his business to take care in his wardrobe.

Riding from before sunup to long after sun's set, they often rode out before any in the household were awake and returned when only Old Joseph was on his midnight wanderings. Faris had hoped to thank Lord Rockrimmon and his son for their gallant championing of her where the matter of Kade Tremeshton's assault was concerned—yet it was ever they were absent from Loch Loland in the days following the incident. She had even risen very early one morning intent on seeking them out—but it was only Lord Rockrimmon she found in his study moments before he intended to ride out with Lochlan. She could sense he was in a hurry even then and did not have the courage to approach him, even in thanks.

When at last the Rockrimmon men did finish their property rounds, they returned with frustration at having found such poverty and despair on the newly acquired properties. The properties Kade Tremeshton had sold to Lord Rockrimmon were in a sad state of affairs it seemed, and they attempted to help and encourage their new tenants, promising their lots would improve with Lord Rockrimmon as their lord.

Faris then was unable and unwilling to endeavor to thank either man again for having come to her aid. Lillias had assured her both her father and her brother would react as Lord Kendrick did—begging she offer them no more words of thanksgiving. Therefore, Faris did not—even for her great desire to do so—for their minds were much occupied with other matters. She was certain they had both forgotten the incident entirely and reconciled herself to never being able to thank them properly.

Then, as if the heavens knew Faris needed comfort and hope, a tale of the Highwayman of Tanglewood's appearance in Saxton had reached the ears of all at Loch Loland Castle. It was Lord Kendrick who first heard of the news, and it was Lord Kendrick who first arrived at Loch Loland with the story in tow.

As Faris sat with Mary, Old Joseph, and Sarah in the kitchen the night of Lord Rockrimmon and Lochlan's return, her heart felt near to bursting with excitement as the tale was told.

"Two nights past, it was," Old Joseph said. "I

heard Lord Kendrick tell Miss Lillias with my own ears just an hour ago."

"Well, tell us, Joseph! Do not endeavor to try our patience!" Mary demanded.

"Then I'll tell you as I heard it," Old Joseph began, "which was as this—our own Highwayman of Tanglewood rode into Saxton at the stroke of midnight. Mounted on his mighty black steed, he rode up to Brookings's manor house and called him out."

"How?" Sarah asked.

"He shouted," Old Joseph said. "Rapier drawn, he rode back and forth 'cross the lawns of Brookings's manor, calling for Brookings to come out and face him. 'I know what ye did!' he called. 'And I'll not let a murdering thief sit rich and well-fed while his wife lies dead in the dirt because of him!' said he."

Faris felt a smile spread across her face. The Highwayman had ridden once more—ridden the long journey to Saxton in order that he might call out a villain. She was proud of his courage— proud of his cause.

"What then?" Sarah asked.

"It seems the local magistrate was nearby," Old Joseph continued. "No doubt he'd heard the gossip of the Highwayman's intended visit and was staying by at Brookings's manor. So it was the traitorous magistrate who first met the High-wayman of Tanglewood under Saxton's moon."

"Oh, get on with it, Joseph!" Mary exclaimed. "Have a pity and tell us the tale quickly!"

Faris giggled. She understood Mary's impatience all too well—for she too wanted to hear the whole of it told.

Old Joseph smiled and laughed. "I will tell it to you as well as I can, Mary," he said. "And this is what comes next—the traitorous magistrate left the safety of Brookings's manor house and met the Highwayman on the dew-drenched grass. There they dueled with all of Brookings's servants and stablemen looking on. The Highwayman's rapier flashed brilliant in the moonlight, and it was not but few strokes he took to render the traitor magistrate helpless."

"Did he merely lop off the man's head?" Sarah asked.

"No—simply bested him quickly, leaving him with a wound to his sword arm he won't soon forget," Old Joseph answered.

Faris's heart was racing! She could see it—in her mind's eye, she could see the Highwayman of Tanglewood fighting the corrupt magistrate under a dark sky lit only by the silver light of the moon and stars. She was breathless with both excitement for his heroic deeds and fear of his well-being.

"What next?" Mary asked. "For pity's sake, Joseph!"

"Lord Brookings then discovered how ill-favored he was in the eyes of his servants then—for they gave him up. His own first man opened the front doors of the manor house and let the Highwayman enter," Joseph continued. "It was there the confrontation was met—there in the entryway of the grand house that had once belonged to Lord Brookings's sweet wife. 'Confess!' the Highwayman shouted. 'You slit your wife's throat, and now you will confess!' But Lord Brookings stood firm and drew his sword on our Highwayman of Tanglewood."

Faris tried to calm her rapid breath, tried to keep her hands from trembling. "The Highwayman," she began, "he did prevail. Did he not?" She was nearly frightened of hearing Old Joseph's answer.

Yet she sighed with great relief when Old Joseph said, "Is there any doubt?"

"Did he kill Brookings?" Sarah asked.

"No," Old Joseph said. "Such a coward as Lord Brookings did not deserve to die by the Highwayman of Tanglewood's rapier point. No—the Highwayman crossed blades with Brookings—but it was quickly he defeated him and held Brookings's throat at the tip of his blade. It was then the two constables—good honest men, they were—arrived in time to hear the coward Lord Brookings confess his sins to the Highwayman of Tanglewood. He had killed his wife—murdered her as she slept. In a fit of rage over her having argued with him in front

181

of the housekeeper of the manor, he had slit her throat with his dagger and paid the magistrate to provide him an alibi."

"The devil was in him," Mary mumbled.

"It is told that the Highwayman was tempted to slit him—open his gullet with his own rapier's blade—for Brookings had done no less to poor Lady Brookings two years past," Old Joseph said.

"But he did not harm him?" Faris asked.

"He did not harm him in what he deserved," Old Joseph said. "But the tale is told that the Highwayman of Tanglewood drug the tip of his rapier across Lord Brookings's throat, cutting the skin just enough to cause him to bleed and saying, 'This be where the rope will chafe you—where the knot will tighten and break your neck, you murdering thief.' That is what Lord Kendrick told Miss Lillias only an hour ago. The Highwayman of Tanglewood indeed rode to Saxton, drew out, and bested Lord Brookings the murderer. They will hang Brookings, it is sure. Perhaps the magistrate too."

Sarah sighed and smiled. "It is easier than they deserve. Poor Lady Brookings—throat slashed with a dagger."

"Bainbridge will be glad to hear it, I daresay," Mary said. "No doubt he knew of the murder— having been born in Saxton—his mother still there yet."

"We will ask him when he returns," Old Joseph said.

"When he returns?" Faris asked.

"Yes," Old Joseph said. "He rode out to Saxton two days past to confirm his mother is well. It seems he had heard she was ill and was anxious about her well-being."

Faris's breathing stopped—as did nearly her heart. "Mr. Graybeau has been gone these two days past?" Faris asked.

"Of course," Old Joseph said. "He rides to Saxton twice a year or more to ensure his mother's well-being."

"So . . . so he would've been there . . . when the Highwayman was in Saxton. Bainbridge would've been there as well?" Faris asked.

"You don't suspect Bainbridge Graybeau of being the Highwayman of Tanglewood do you, Faris?" Sarah asked. She laughed when Faris could only shake her head in unconvincing assurance. "It is sheer coincidence!" Sarah laughed. "Bainbridge is often in Saxton, and the Highwayman of Tanglewood has never ridden there before." Sarah leaned forward and lowering her voice said, "I, for one, suspect Lord Kendrick."

"What?" Mary exclaimed, laughing as she did so. "Why ever would you suspect Lord Kendrick, Sarah? It's a preposterous notion!"

"Who is it always tells Miss Lillias the tales

of the Highwayman of Tanglewood long before anyone else ever hears of them?" Sarah offered. "How comes Lord Kendrick by this information so quickly? I will tell you how—he was present! It was Lord Gawain Kendrick who bested Lord Brookings in Saxton." Sarah smiled as everyone looked at her, scowling with wonder. "Has he not been absent these two days? Has not today been the first time he has called at Loch Loland Castle in two of those days?"

"He was about his business affairs," Mary said. "Or so milady told me when she gave me the dinner menus these past two nights."

"My money's on a commoner," Old Joseph said. "What titled man would risk life and limb in championing those who are of common status?"

"Master Lochlan debates in earnest for—" Mary began.

"*Debates* in earnest, perhaps," Old Joseph said. "But would a titled man risk prison and even death in defense of the farmer? No." Joseph smiled at Faris. "No. If I were a betting man, I'd put my money firm on Bainbridge Graybeau."

There was a light in Old Joseph's eyes, and Faris wondered—did he know something of the Highwayman of Tanglewood's true identity?"

"Lord Kendrick it is," Sarah said. "I'll put my money on Lord Gawain Kendrick—for the Highwayman is a skilled swordsman, an excellent rider—"

"You're both as silly as two summer geese," Mary said. "The Highwayman of Tanglewood is a farmer's son—a local farmer's son—one sick to dying of watching the rich steal from the poor."

"A farmer's son?" Sarah asked. "A farmer's son who just happens to possess the same skill with a rapier that the nobles do?"

Faris's head was pounding. She did not want to speculate! For all she knew, Mary was right, and the Highwayman of Tanglewood was a common man who had grown tired of tyranny. Yet her own heart wondered at the mystery so hard it pained her. Speculation was rarely a pleasant pastime, and she was worn out by it.

"I-I think I'll go for a walk in the evening air," Faris said, pushing her chair back from the table. It was merely two nights more—two nights, and she would see him again! Yet her heart ached for him, her body longed to thrill at his touch. What harm was there in walking—in perhaps meeting him by chance before their planned rendezvous?

"It is a lovely night for walking," Mary said. "But take care you do not linger too long, Faris. You need your rest."

"Thank you, Mary," Faris said. "I will not linger long."

Anxious, Faris hurried toward the abandoned cottage at the edge of the Tanglewood Forest. No doubt her silent prayers begging for a chance meeting with her Highwayman would not be answered—still she hoped. It seemed an eternity since last she had met with him—since he had held her in his strong arms and rained passionate kisses on her tender lips.

Yet as she neared the cottage, as the moonlight shone down upon its abandoned emptiness, her hopes faded as fast as the amethyst of sunset. As darkness enveloped her, Faris knew bitter disappointment. Still, she would wait—wait a day, a night, and a day—then she would see him again. Would she not? Impatience thickened the doubt in her mind—doubt in ever seeing the Highwayman again. What if he could not meet her at the hour they had planned? Worse—what if he *would* not meet her? What if the Highwayman of Tanglewood had experienced a change of heart or mind since last they met?

Still, Faris shook her head. He cared for her, she was certain of it! Whoever he was by day— whether stableman, titled lord, or farmer's son—Faris was certain he sincerely cared for her. He would meet her two nights hence—he would!

Faris gasped as a hand covered her mouth, a powerful arm encircling her waist from behind. Yet her startle was brief, for she recognized the scent of leather, wind, and meadow grasses.

"And why be ye out near the forest so late of night, fair Faris of Loch Loland Castle?"

Such a feeling of relief and joy spread over her, Faris went limp in the Highwayman's arms as he turned her to face him. Burying her face against the powerful contours of his chest, she began to weep.

"I feared I would never see you again!" she sobbed.

"But why?" he asked, gathering her into his arms. "We planned to meet two nights hence. Why do I find ye here now?"

She could not tell him! She could not tell him she had doubted. And yet, surely her emotions betrayed her. But to tell him of her doubts—doubting was weak, and she would endeavor to be stronger in the future. Therefore, she would not confess her weakness. How then would she explain such tears?

"I-I heard the tale of your besting Lord Brookings, of your ride to Saxton," she said at last—and it was true. "I was fearful of your safety and—"

"Here ya find me, lass—unharmed and holdin' ya in me arms, I am," he said. The rasping, masked sound of his voice comforted her, and the severity of her sobbing lessened.

"But to Saxton you rode," she said. "Why?"

"Ya know well of Lord Brookings it seems," he said.

"I-I do," Faris stammered.

"Then ya know why I rode—why I rode to see him put into the hands of honest men," he said.

"Yes," she said. "But why so far? Why so far

away from the Tanglewood? Why so far away from me?"

"It's weary I am of the tale, fair Faris, and I'm weary of not holdin' ye in me arms," the Highwayman said. "I am weary beyond belief this night, and it's why ya find me here—for I rode here in hopin' ye would be wanderin' nearby, that I might find ya and hold ya and taste the very nectar of yar kiss."

Faris stiffened for a moment. She pulled away from him slightly, gazing up into the black mask covering his face—the black mask covering his entire head save his mouth and chin, save his mustache and goatee.

Nectar? Hadn't Gawain referred to Lillias's kiss as *nectar kisses?*

"You have promised that you are not Lord Kendrick," Faris said. "And yet . . ."

"I am not Lord Kendrick, Faris," he said. "This I have confessed before. Do ya not trust me?"

"I do," Faris said, collapsing against him. "It is only I wish I could be with you more often—in truth I wish . . . I wish . . ."

"To be with me every moment as I wish to be with ye, lass?" he interrupted.

"Yes!" she breathed, allowing her arms to go around his waist in returning his embrace.

"Well, it is we are together in this moment, we are," he said. "So we will forget Saxton and Lord

Brookings the murderer. We are together in the moonlight at last."

Faris smiled, nuzzled against him, and breathed a sigh. It was true—he was with her now. She would not worry about the danger he had been in previously. He was with her now.

"You are so quiet in your approach," she told him.

"Far I want not to find me neck in a noose," he chuckled.

Faris gently pushed herself from his embrace, suddenly shy at having been so willing to be in his arms.

"Far these past days I've thought of nothin' but ye, lass," he said. She felt such elation as to send her heart into fluttering.

"That's not true," Faris told him, delighted by his touch, his confessions of thinking of her. "You've been a busy highwayman, and that takes forethought enough."

He smiled, his teeth dazzling in the darkness. "And each time I bested a rich man, I thought of ye. 'She's me prize,' I'd be thinkin', and next wantin' to taste of yar mouth again," he said.

"Do . . . do you think less of me because I've fallen so easily into your grasp?" she asked him. She had found herself pondering the matter quite often over the past few days. For it was true— what effort had the Highwayman of Tanglewood exerted in winning her? None!

He slowly shook his head and whispered, "No. We were meant to be, we were. 'Twas heaven led me to ya that night in the meadow, it was, and now thrice since. 'Twas heaven led me to ya . . . like a moth to a flame."

"And you promise there are no other flames you are drawn to, Highwayman?" Faris asked, as yet uncertain. "Still, it is difficult for me to . . . to believe such a man as you would choose me when surely any woman on earth would gladly be owned by you." And it was true. Faris knew the Highwayman of Tanglewood could choose any woman for himself. Why then had he chosen a simple chambermaid?

"No other flame burns as bright and as lovely as ye, lass," he said. "What cause would there be to fan another?" He smiled at her, caressing her lips with his gloved thumb. Dropping his hands from her face, he said, "Come with me now, fair Faris. 'Tis time ya understood completely that me heart is in yar hands."

The Cottage in Twilight

Cupping his hands to his mouth, the Highwayman of Tanglewood made a sound like that of a dove. Instantly, his black steed appeared from the edge of the forest. Taking Faris's hand, he began leading her toward the cottage, the loyal steed following silently behind them.

The cottage stood just outside the tree line of the Tanglewood Forest, and as they approached, Faris fancied it appeared warm and inviting, even for the darkened windows. Twilight had descended, and the old cottage door creaked as the Highwayman gently pushed it open. As Faris followed the Highwayman into the cottage, she noticed the thick dust on the windows. Very little moonlight penetrated such old accumulation. The darkness of the cottage, the perfect privacy, was ideal for a lovers' tryst. Faris felt certain the Highwayman would not linger within the cottage did he not feel safety was with him.

Yet Faris felt disappointed somehow all the same—for the deepened darkness of safety meant the Highwayman's features were even less visible than before. Furthermore, the Highwayman yet wore whiskers; the dark mustache and goatee about his mouth and chin implied the Highwayman of Tanglewood was not Bainbridge Graybeau. Still, could not a mustache be falsified? A goatee as well?

"Have ya met the returned young master of Loch Loland yet, then, lass?" the Highwayman asked as he closed the cottage door behind them.

"Yes," Faris said. "It was an odd meeting—the first time we met. I was quite afraid I might be dismissed and find myself residing here in this abandoned cottage."

"Why would his bein' odd find ya dismissed?" the Highwayman asked.

"Oh, he is not odd," Faris began to explain. "Our meeting was odd."

"And how was yar meetin' with the young master odd, fair Faris?" the Highwayman asked, taking one of her hands in his.

"I was seeing to his chambers and . . . and he entered his bedchamber to find me fairly dangling from the draperies."

"What?" the Highwayman chuckled. His smile was dazzling even for the dark of the room.

"I . . . I was dusting, you see—and thinking I was too busy to call for a ladder, I suppose. Therefore, I scaled the bookcase in his bedchamber as I often have before and was dusting the draperies. Yet when he entered so unexpectedly, it startled me so that I . . . I lost my footing." She sighed and added, "I thought certain he would set me

192

outside on Loch Loland's grand steps and tell me to be gone."

"Aye, but he did not, I see," the Highwayman said.

"No. He did not," Faris confirmed. "But let's not speak of it. It was, after all, so horridly humiliating."

The Highwayman laughed low in his throat. "What better thing I could not imagine than findin' ye in my bedchamber," he said.

Faris blushed, delighted with his flattery. Even for the scent of dust in the cottage, Faris could sense the aroma of leather and wind of him. She was warm—warmer than she had been since last they had met. She felt safe and happy in his company.

"Did ya find him handsome then?" the Highwayman asked next.

"Master Lochlan?" she said.

"Yes," the Highwayman said, smiling. "I already know ya think Lord Kendrick is handsome, I do—lest ya wouldn't be wishin' so hard he was me."

"I've never wished you were Lord Kendrick!" Faris exclaimed. "I only thought you might be he because . . . because . . ."

"Because he is a handsome devil, and ya're hopin' I am as well," the Highwayman chuckled.

Faris felt her cheeks blush crimson. Of course she wondered if he were handsome! Every woman for a hundred miles wondered at the same of it.

"In truth," she began, "I had a notion you might be Bainbridge Graybeau in disguise." There! She had confessed it, and now she would listen well—try to discern if he was unnerved in the least—if he truly were Bainbridge Graybeau.

His easy laughter—his instant and obvious amusement—discouraged her, however. "Graybeau?" he asked, still chuckling. "So I've gone from being lord of the manor to the best stableman in the country, I have. Methinks I like that idea."

"Are you Graybeau?" she asked. "Graybeau hails from Saxton, you realize."

"I do realize it. I've heard great things concernin' yar Bainbridge Graybeau, I have—and, in truth, I am flattered ye would think of me in his light," the Highwayman said.

"But you are not he?" Faris asked.

"I did not say I was not he," the Highwayman said. "I only said I am flattered you would think I was such a man."

"But you were not so flattered in my thinking you are Lord Kendrick?" Faris asked. Why would a man be flattered at being recognized as a stableman but not a titled one?

"Aye, I was very flattered! Lord Gawain Kendrick is the finest of men," the Highwayman said.

"Lillias wishes you were Lord Kendrick," Faris said. "Or rather that Lord Kendrick were you."

"Lillias Rockrimmon wishes her betrothed was the Highwayman of Tanglewood?" the Highwayman said, his smile broadening.

Faris gasped, covering her mouth with one hand. "I have betrayed Lillias!" she said. "I have said too much!"

"Do not worry yarself so, fair Faris of Loch Loland Castle," the Highwayman said. "Her secret is safe with ya still—for it is safe in me."

"Still, I should not have said it aloud," Faris said, feeling tears springing to her eyes. Her dearest friend was Lillias. How could she have betrayed her secret? "Every woman has her own idea . . . her own dream of who the Highwayman of Tanglewood is in the light of day and—"

"Then do ya have yar own idea?" he asked. "Do ya wish I was Bainbridge Graybeau? Have ya feelin's for the man?"

"No!" Faris exclaimed. "In truth . . . if you are he . . . then I do. But if you are not he . . . I do not. Though he is a good man. He is teaching me to ride."

"Is he now?" the Highwayman chuckled.

Faris felt her own eyes narrow with suspicion. Truly, she wondered if Bainbridge Graybeau stood before her now dressed in the black attire of the Highwayman of Tanglewood. Why else would he find her riding lessons amusing? Should not he be jealous if he were not Graybeau? He had not claimed he was not Graybeau. In truth, he had never answered to the fact or the contrary.

"I think you are Graybeau," she said. "I think you are only trying to trick me."

"Tryin' to trick ya, am I?" the Highwayman laughed.

"Perhaps," Faris said. Her own smile broadened. What a rascal the Highwayman was! What a delightful rascal!

Faris was breathless as the Highwayman of Tanglewood unexpectedly reached out, gathering her into his arms.

"Aye, fair Faris," he mumbled. His lips were only a breath from her own, and Faris shivered as goose bumps broke over her arms. "I may well be yar Bainbridge Graybeau," he said. "Or I may well be the son of a farmer—or the younger son of a titled man with nothin' but a modest livin' to me name. But one thing is true—in all of it—I am a man captured by yar beauty and wit, enchanted by yar goodness and strength of good character. And I will kiss ya now—whether farmer, gentleman, or true rogue—I will kiss ya and have the taste of yar mouth for me own."

"As you wish," Faris said a moment before his mouth captured her own in a deep and driven exchange.

Instantly, all fear, all uncertainty vanished as Faris melded against the Highwayman. Wrapped in the strength of his arms, his hot moist kiss fanned through her as a fever, and she was careless of all else. He broke the seal of their lips a moment, a low chuckle emanating from deep within him. "I challenge Lord Gawain Kendrick, yar own Bainbridge Graybeau, or any other man ye might suspect of bein' me—I challenge any man to kiss ya as well as I do—to cause yar mouth to water and yar very flesh to begin tinglin' the way the Highwayman of Tanglewood does."

"Admittedly, no man could," Faris breathed, her body trembling with wanting his further kiss.

"Aye," the Highwayman said. "Only I will own yar true kiss, lass. And by that ye shall know me. I give ye me permission to try him whom ya think I may be."

Faris frowned, uncertain as to his meaning. "What is your implication?"

The Highwayman smiled. "If ye yet think I be Lord Gawain Kendrick, or if ya truly think I be Bainbridge Graybeau of Saxton, then I give to ya me word that I will not strike either man dead should the one or the other ever try to taste of yar sweet kiss. Each man may kiss ye once, and I will not run him through for it—but only once."

"Then I do not think you are either man," Faris said. She frowned then. "Either you are not them or you do not care enough for me. For I want no other woman to have your kiss. Yet

197

you would allow another man to kiss me thus?"

"I see the doubt on yar pretty face, fair Faris," the Highwayman said, brushing a loose strand of hair from her cheek. "Even for the dark I see it. Would that I could tell ye what horse I ride by day—what name is mine in the sunlight. But I fear danger for ye were I to tell ya these things. I want no other man holdin' ya in his arms. I want no other man tastin' of yar sweet kiss. I fear the consequence of me own anger were I ever to witness either. Yet I understand yar curious nature, yar fear I might belong to another. Therefore, I grant ya easement in this. Until the time comes it is safe for ye to know me true self, I grant that if ya think ye can guess me, I will not run the good man through if ye mistake him."

"But I never want to kiss another man—not in the whole of my life I do not! Only you!" Faris exclaimed in a whisper.

The Highwayman smiled. "Then bring yar mouth to mine, fair Faris of Loch Loland Castle—that I might endeavor to have me fill of the sweet nectar of yar kiss."

Faris smiled, her entire body awash with warmth and joy as the Highwayman's mouth met her own once more. He was ambrosia to her senses! His arms were strong, and he held her firm against him. His mustache and goatee tickled the flesh about her mouth. The scent of leather, wind, and meadow grasses filled her lungs, set butterflies to swirling in her stomach as he kissed her. Faris's mind burst with every beautiful color, every wonderful sensation, and she wished to stand in the cottage locked in the Highwayman's arms forever!

He broke the seal of their lips a moment, holding her to him.

"I have such a feeling of safety in your arms," she whispered. "As if nothing could ever harm me."

"Would that I could hold ya, lass—far every moment of every day. Would that I could keep ya safe," the Highwayman said.

"Even Lord Tremeshton holds no fear over me here," Faris said.

"Lord Tremeshton?" the Highwayman asked. "Why should Lord Tremeshton hold any fear over ye?"

"It . . . it is nothing," Faris lied. "Only a silly worry from the past."

But the Highwayman was more perceptive than an average man—else he would not have kept safe so long. This Faris knew. Further, she would not withhold some of the truth from him if he pressed her about Lord Tremeshton—and he did.

"There is somethin' yar not tellin' me, Faris," the Highwayman said. "And ya will tell me it now."

The Highwayman loosed his embrace, and Faris stepped back from him. Would he be angry?

Most certainly he would, but not with her—of this she was certain.

Therefore, inhaling deep, she said, "Lord Tremeshton was let in to Loch Loland these three mornings past," she began, "to allow Lord Rockrimmon to purchase some tenant lands."

"And?" he urged. His broad chest rose and fell with the heavy breathing of restrained anger.

"He did cause me alarm—but only for a moment," Faris quickly explained. "Master Lochlan intervened, and I was only a little frightened—and only for a little moment." Faris frowned, slightly disturbed in the sudden elation that rose within her at the memory of Lochlan Rockrimmon's championing her.

"He must not be allowed in Loch Loland!" the Highwayman growled. "He yet means ye harm—of this I have no doubt. Why does Lord Rockrimmon continue to—"

"He is cast out," Faris interrupted, placing a dainty palm to the Highwayman's chest in a gesture of calming him. "Master Lochlan disarmed him quickly, and Lord Rockrimmon bade Master Lochlan throw him from the house."

"Disarmed him?" the Highwayman shouted.

"Ssshh," Faris gently soothed. "We must not be found out—and all is well after all. I have Lord Rockrimmon's promise—offered on bended knee—that Lord Tremeshton will never set foot in Loch Loland again."

"I will best him once more," the Highwayman said, rubbing his temples with one gloved hand. "I will best and beat him to such a bruisin' to keep him abed for a month!"

Panic leapt to Faris's bosom. She would not have the Highwayman put in danger's path for her sake—not any more than their secret meetings already did.

"No!" she whispered. "He has been bested—for Master Lochlan broke Lord Tremeshton's nose with his own fist before he sent him tumbling head over heel."

Yet the Highwayman shook his head and said, "He must be better bested! And by me!"

"Please, sire," Faris said. "I beg you. Master Lochlan has bested him—truly. Kade Tremeshton will no longer frighten me."

The Highwayman cocked his head to one side. "Your Master Lochlan—do ya find him to be a handsome man?"

"I-I don't understand why it should matter," Faris said.

"He has championed ye when I have not," the Highwayman said. "Do ya find him handsome? Is he to be me rival where yar heart is concerned?"

He was jealous! Faris smiled with impish delight in the sudden knowledge the Highwayman of Tanglewood was jealous.

Faris giggled and said, "Surely you do not think me insipid or purely dim-witted enough to fancy his lordship's son! Further, if I were so dim-witted and naive—which I am not—you already own my heart. Do you think me foolish as well as fickle?"

"No," the Highwayman grumbled. "Of course not." He paused a moment and then asked, "But do ya find him to be handsome, lass? I will know if ya tell me false."

"He is handsome, and to deny it would prove me a liar," Faris said. "Furthermore, I do think his character is intact—that he is honorable. He does seem to have a bit of the rascal about him. Still, greater men have a rogue's way and are honorable—is that not true?"

"It is," he said, finally smiling again. "Yet he has championed ye—and a lassie's heart is easily won by champions."

"I already have my champion," Faris said.

At that, the Highwayman took her hand and maneuvered her to sit on the floor with him. Resting his back against the cottage wall, he cradled her in his arms as she nestled against him. Warm and safe and entirely in love, Faris let her head rest against his chest.

"I be farever yar champion, fair Faris," the Highwayman whispered into her hair. "And ye will farever be me lassie."

"How came you to be my champion, Highway-man?" Faris asked. The comfort of being nestled against him was intoxicating. She felt nearly drowsy with delight. "How came you to ride as the Highwayman of Tanglewood? Can you tell me this without revealing what you are not ready to reveal? Can you tell me the tale without revealing who you were before you rode as the Highwayman of Tanglewood?"

The Highwayman chuckled. "I think that I can. And I think that I will. Ya deserve far more, I know—but far now I can at least give ya the tale of the Highwayman of Tanglewood's first ride."

" 'Twas but two years past when I was passin' through the village when suddenly I came upon a wealthy and titled man speakin' with unkindness to a young girl sellin' ribbons. The ribbons had been her mother's, and she was sellin' them to earn enough to buy a loaf of bread for her ailing wee brother. The titled man was landlord to the girl and her fatherless family. Of a sudden, he slapped the girl, confiscatin' her ribbons—far her mother had been remiss in payin' her tenant taxes. I stood stunned, unable to believe I had seen what I had seen," the Highwayman said. "I was too stunned to act in that moment, but I did in the next—far sure and far certain, I did in the next."

"And?" Faris asked, encouraging him to finish the tale.

"I gave the lass every cent I had about me and then . . ." He paused.

"And then?" Faris asked.

"And then I waylaid the filthy landlord in an alley, retrieved the young lass's ribbons, and returned them to her," he said. "It was the start of me criminal profession, it was."

Faris smiled, thinking of the ribbon he'd stolen from her own hair on their last meeting.

"So you began as a thief of ribbons," she giggled.

"And I am still," he said, tugging at the new ribbon in her hair until it loosed. Faris felt her hair fall down around her shoulders. The Highwayman removed his gloves and began twisting one long strand of Faris's hair around his finger.

"Like silk, it is," he whispered, burying his hands in her dark tresses.

Faris fancied the rate of his breath had increased, and she tilted her head to look up at him. Oh, how she longed to reach up, strip his mask from his head, and at last look into the face of her beloved. But she would not betray his trust in her. She would not. She would simply hope for the day he would reveal himself willingly.

"Ya have begun to distract me, fair Faris," he whispered, kissing the tip of her nose lightly.

"What do you mean?" she asked, thrilled by his touch.

"A year past I held no fear in me. No fear of injury, even death. I feared nothin' and thought nothin' could hurt me. But now . . ." he said, kissing her forehead. "Now I know fear—far whenever I'm in the midst of a scuffle, I worry I may be hurt—hurt badly enough to keep me from seein' ye again, lass. And that would take a bad hurt, it would. I worry I may be caught and imprisoned—unable to run me fingers through the silken locks of yar hair—unable to taste of yar sweet kiss."

Faris trembled with fear at the thought of either. "Please do not speak of such things," she told him, suddenly very frightened for his safety.

"Still, I am reasonably invincible," he chuckled. "And there are those in government who have already spoken of grantin' me pardon if I were captured. And with the hope of seein' ye again, I am stronger with each battle—always fightin' far the chance to hold ya in me arms once more."

Faris smiled and snuggled tighter into his embrace. "Do you not think it odd we two are so drawn together? Especially having met only thrice before this?"

"It is not so much odd as it is rare," he admitted. "And a man hears tales, he does—tales of findin' his one true love at first meetin'. Tales of two souls matched in heaven and on earth. It's as we are, it is. Ye and I—Faris and the Highwayman of Tanglewood—lovers the like which spawn legend."

Faris smiled, taking his hand in hers and lacing their fingers. His hands were warm, calloused, not cool and soft as she fancied a titled man's would be, and she smiled. His hands told a tiny tale of his identity: he was a hard-working man, not one pampered and spoiled.

Suddenly, Faris moved from his arms, kneeling just before him. "I've grown weary of talk, Highwayman," she said.

"Have ya now, lass?" he chuckled.

"Yes," she answered. "The hour is late, the cottage is warm, and so is my heart—the perfect moment for a kiss." Faris was a bit surprised by her own brazen manner. Still, she wanted to kiss him, sensed he wanted the same, and she felt comfortable enough with her Highwayman to tell him so.

"So kiss me then, fair Faris of Loch Loland Castle," he said, his brilliant smile piercing the darkness.

"Do you think me too faint-hearted to do so?" she asked. In truth, her body had begun to tremble with nervous anticipation. She wondered if she could truly muster the courage to instigate a kiss between them. Yet he had already kissed her— even that very night he had. Surely he would not refuse her now.

"I think ya as stout-hearted as any lion to walk the green earth, I do," he whispered. "And I think ya can do anythin' ya put yar pretty little mind to, lass."

"You do?" Faris breathed, her heart pounding

so madly within her chest she thought it might break free.

"I do," he said, reaching out and caressing her cheek with the back of his hand. "So seduce me now, little chambermaid," he said. "I will not disappoint ye."

Faris smiled, inhaled a deep breath of courage, and reached out, taking the Highwayman's face between her small hands. She let her thumbs trace the mustache and goatee around his mouth a moment before leaning forward and tentatively pressing her lips to his in the sweetest of kisses. He waited one brief moment before taking her face in his own hands, returning her kiss with delicious and very masculine force.

Faris giggled, and he paused, asking, "What?"

"You're impatient," she whispered.

"That I am, lass. I want yar lips about mine, the taste of yar mouth far me own, and I see no good reason to deny it," he said.

"Then do not deny it," Faris whispered, her arms going around his shoulders as she pulled herself into his embrace.

There was nothing tentative in the manner in which his mouth captured hers then. Nothing withheld or hidden, nothing restrained. He kissed her with a hot, moist passion, sending goose bumps erupting over her body, a sensation of butterflies fluttering about her heart, and an idea of complete surrender echoing through her mind.

As his mouth occupied her own, Faris wondered at his skill, his seemingly artful aptitude in kissing. Surely the man had been instructed somehow! Surely he had been told or taught how to completely conquer a woman's emotions through such an exchange. Surely his way of whisking her into rapturous bliss was not simply instinctive. Yet her ability to return such an amorous trade was purely instinctive—therefore, why should she doubt his was not?

He held her first tightly, then loosely, his arms banding around her with astonishing power. He kissed her mouth, her cheeks, her neck, sending visions of pink sunsets and purple heathered hills through her impassioned mind. He held her to him, whispering words of adoration into the softness of her dark hair.

Finally, as his labored breathing began to calm, he whispered, "Were that I could take ya with me now, lass—keep ye always far me own."

"I am yours," she told him, blissful in his arms. "Whether here with you or at Loch Loland all alone—I am yours."

"But it is selfish, I am," he said. "To keep ya from the possibility of a man who could be with ya every day and hold ya safe in his arms—instead of leadin' ya along the edge of danger the way I do."

"If that's true, then I'm selfish as well," Faris said, "for I put you in danger each time we meet, causing you to linger when you should not—causing you to risk discovery."

"Aye, then we are truly lovers, lass," he said. "To risk such consequences to be together means truly that we love, it does. I ye and ye me."

Faris smiled and nestled against him. Although her mind reeled with trying to understand how she could have fallen in love with a man after only meeting with him a few times, she knew she did love him. Furthermore, she believed he loved her—sincerely and singularly.

"But ya must return to Loch Loland now. The hours have passed quickly, and ye must rest," he told her.

Faris did not want to leave him. She wanted to stay in his arms, held warm against his body, safe with him forever. Still she knew it was impossible. For that, she loathed the greedy lords of the land all the more.

"Yes," she admitted. "It is time."

"I will see ya close to the house, I will," the Highwayman said, rising to his feet and assisting Faris to stand as well. "I would not want another such as I to find ye in the night."

"There is no other the like of you, sire," Faris said, smiling at him.

"Sire?" the Highwayman repeated, chuckling.

Faris laughed and shook her head. "Forgive me—it is habit."

The Highwayman took her hand, raised it to his lips, and kissed the back of it tenderly.

"Habit I hope it is—and not some secret desire ya own toward Lord Kendrick or yar young master," he said, his dazzling smile breaking through the darkness.

"No, no, no," Faris assured him. "Just habit. That and the lack of knowing what to name you when I speak to you."

"Handsome rogue or lover—my darling or the like—any endearment will do," he said, leading her from the cottage and into the night. "Anythin' but sire."

"Agreed, Highwayman," Faris said. The Highwayman whistled, and his black beast of a horse appeared from behind a large tree.

"Come now, lass," he said, effortlessly lifting her onto his mount before mounting behind her. "The night air is magic, and we will share it again soon."

"Promise?" Faris asked, loath to leave him.

"I do," the Highwayman said.

As they rode through the night toward Loch Loland, a certain discomfort began to overcome Faris. She did not want to return. She wanted only to linger with the Highwayman of Tanglewood forever. Yet she knew it was impossible to do so. He was driven in his cause, and a rogue wanted for thievery. He would not put her in harm's way.

And so she rode with him—the night breeze

whispering through her hair, kissing her cheeks. She was, all of a sudden, very glad Bainbridge Graybeau was teaching her to ride. She wondered again if Bainbridge and the Highwayman of Tanglewood were one and the same. Still, shaking her head to dispel the thought, she leaned against him and closed her eyes, hoping never to awaken from the loveliest of dreams.

"When will we next meet?" Faris asked once the Highwayman had helped her down from his horse. "Shall we still meet as we before planned? Here? Two nights hence?"

"We will meet here but perhaps not in two nights hence—for I must be wary. I will send word to ya about our next meetin', I will," he said. "And it will be soon. This I promise."

"But how will you send word?" Faris asked. How could he possibly send word to her without risking discovery?

The Highwayman laughed, his smile radiant in the moonlight.

"I will send word. Fear not, fair Faris of Loch Loland!" And with that, he rode into the darkness, his black cape flaring out behind him.

Faris watched him until the horse and rider blended with the dark of night and she could see him no longer. He was gone. Her Highwayman was gone once more, and she knew not when she would see him again.

The windows of Loch Loland were dark, except for those of the kitchen and Old Joseph's chamber. No doubt Old Joseph was prowling about, and Faris did not feel ready to return to life as she knew it. Therefore, she lingered—lingered near the outer wall of the east gardens—savoring the taste of the Highwayman's kiss still fresh upon her lips, the feel of his hands in her hair.

Still, the air had cooled, and she was chilled. It would do her no good thing to find a chill and be sent to bed ill and unable to receive a message from the Highwayman when he did send one. And so, with resignation and regret, Faris returned to Loch Loland and all there who knew nothing of her secret love.

"And what are you about at such a late hour as this, Miss Destroyer of Draperies?"

Faris gasped as Lochlan Rockrimmon stepped from the shadows near the kitchen servants' entry door.

"I-I . . ." she stammered, distracted for a moment by the fork and plate of pie in his hands. The green of his eyes flashed emerald in the moonlight, his unusual height strangely intimidating. Oh, but what woman would not be startled by such a handsome man?

"Oh, keep your secrets," Lochlan said, grinning with mischief. "You've caught me creeping about pilfering pie—therefore, I suppose you're entitled to your secrets as well."

"Th-thank you, sire," Faris said making to move past him and into the house.

"Still," he said, reaching out and taking hold of her arm.

Faris shivered at his touch, and it was not an unpleasant shiver.

"You've rather the look of a maiden recently seduced. Disheveled hair, crimson cheeks, lips a bit swollen perhaps. What have you been about, Miss Faris? Or shall I say—*whom* have you been about?"

Faris was indeed trembling. He knew! How it frightened her! What if he had been out, away from the house, near where she and the Highwayman had parted? What if he'd seen them? Yet he seemed calm. He did not have the look of a man who had only just witnessed his chambermaid consorting with a rogue. He did, however, have the look of a man who could easily seduce his chambermaid himself, and this unexpected thought unsettled Faris greatly.

"Sire . . . I . . . I . . ." Faris began, but the mirth in his eyes diverted her.

"Each of us with whiskers has kissed each of you without, Faris. It is of no consequence," he said. "Pilfering pie, however, can find one in the worst trouble. Therefore, I would appreciate your silence in the matter."

Faris smiled, secretly delighted at his hiding outside behind the servants' entrance eating pilfered pie. "Of course, sire," she said.

"*Lochlan,* Faris, if you please," he said, winking at her.

Faris felt her eyes widened.

"Lochlan. Yes?" he asked.

"Yes, Master Lochlan," Faris said, quickly slipping into the kitchen by way of the servants' entrance.

Once inside, she leaned against the door for a moment, placing her hand over her racing heart. How thoroughly he'd startled her! This was the reason for the mad pace of her heartbeat—this and the memory of the Highwayman's kiss. She closed her eyes, remembering the warmth of the Highwayman's hands on her face, the pleasure of his kiss. How long must she wait to meet him again? Even an instant seemed an eternity.

Faris started toward her room, smiling to herself. How silly it was—the young master of the house feeling it necessary to hide while eating his pie. He was, indeed, a surprise—in more ways than one.

Faris marveled for a moment. How was it so many such fascinating men would chance to enter her life? She thought of Lochlan Rockrimmon's green eyes—thought of the Highwayman's dazzling smile and roguish manner. She thought of Lord Kendrick's tenderly expressed love of

Lillias—of Bainbridge Graybeau's efforts to raise a chambermaid's worth by instructing her to ride as a lady. She wondered how any woman could resist any one of them.

In pondering each gallant man, Faris thanked the heavens she had met the Highwayman—that her heart had been stolen by him before knowing Lord Kendrick, before Bainbridge Graybeau had taken an inexplicable interest in her, and certainly before Lochlan Rockrimmon had returned to Loch Loland Castle. The Highwayman of Tanglewood had championed her in so many ways—not the least of which was having saved her from falling in love with a "lord of the manor," so to speak. Faris thought of the many girls she had known—the many, many girls she had labored beside in her years of servitude. So many young maidens had found their hearts or lives broken by rapscallion sons of titled men or by dominating male servants. And though a young master had never before tempted her own heart, she could much imagine that if one could, it would be the handsome and dashing Lochlan Rockrimmon. Yes—how thankful she was that the Highwayman of Tanglewood had come upon her first. It had been a narrow escape indeed, for none but the Highwayman could have saved her from such eventual heartbreak, she was certain. Lochlan Rockrimmon overly unsettled her as it was. She could well imagine the fatality her heart might have experienced at his unknowing hands had it not already been captured.

That night as she lay on her lacy pillow, Faris pondered her rendezvous with the Highwayman. She sighed, smiling as she thought of his snatching the ribbon from her hair. What a rascal he was! Faris let her mind linger on the scent of him, on the look of him, on the feel of being in his arms, and on the taste of his kiss.

Turning on her side and tucking her hands beneath her head, Faris closed her eyes, at last ready for blessed sleep. However, she was disturbed by the instantaneous vision of the pie-pilfering Lochlan Rockrimmon that fairly burst into her mind. Squeezing her eyes tightly shut, she vanquished the vision. Tenderly drifting to sleep, Faris thought of her own handsome rogue and lover—of their meeting at the cottage in twilight. She sensed the night wind in her hair and the scent of leather and wind in her nostrils—dreamt of riding astride the blackest of black hero's steed with the Highwayman of Tanglewood.

The Stripe of a Rascal

The next morning found Loch Loland Castle a whirlwind of excitement. Lady May Stringham had again moved forward the date of her planned visit. Lady Rockrimmon, though obviously disenchanted with the expected arrival, desired Loch Loland to be in prime condition. Faris thought it a very arrogant plan—inviting oneself to visit much, much earlier than already settled upon.

Still, she labored diligently to prepare the spare chambers for the lady and her daughter. In truth, she did not mind so much, for it gave her ample time to allow her thoughts to linger on the previous night's meeting with the Highwayman. How dashing he was! How romantic and attentive! The Highwayman of Tanglewood was as a dream, and often Faris feared she had only dreamed of him. What heartbreak indeed—to awaken one morning only to find it had all been a dazzling, beautiful dream. Yet it was not a dream, and Faris was anxious to meet him again. She wondered at how he would send word to her. Secretly, she hoped he would write his word—send her a letter in his own hand telling her when and where they were to meet. Still, it would be a dangerous action for him to take—writing a letter to a chambermaid at Loch Loland. But even chambermaids received post, did they not?

Faris shook her head, scattering her thoughts from musings of the Highwayman of Tangle-wood. Carefully, she finished arranging the fresh flowers in the large porcelain vase in the chambers meant now for Lady Stringham and her daughter. As she studied the lovely spray of flowers and greenery, she frowned as her thoughts moved from the Highwayman to the young heir of Loch Loland.

There circulated much talk among the ser-vants—talk suggesting the young master of Loch Loland was considering taking Tannis Stringham to wife. This talk troubled Faris, and yet she knew not why. Certainly there was the fact no one at Loch Loland seemed to have any fondness for Lady Stringham's daughter. No one save Lochlan Rockrimmon himself perhaps—for it had been he who had extended the invitation, had it not? Yet to hear the other servants speak of her, Tannis Stringham was a very proud and haughty young woman. It was said she was much prone to vanity, conceit, and unkindness. Thus, Faris found herself fretful, worried for her young master's happiness. In the days since his return to the castle, Faris had come to view him as a good man endowed with much strength of character and compassion for others no matter their situation. He laughed often, especially with his mother. The two of them always appeared as if they held some secret delight of which no one else knew. Yet, like his father, he could be firm yet kind in his expectations. Furthermore, he ever offered a good word to anyone happening to cross his path.

Still, Faris had found herself becoming more and more unsettled in his presence, and she knew not why. It seemed he grew more handsome with every sunrise, more alluring with every sunset. Yet, Faris wondered why she should remain so unsettled about him. Everyone else who labored at Loch Loland Castle was quite comfortable in Lochlan Rockrimmon's presence. Again the thought entered Faris's mind that had it not been for her trysting with the Highwayman, she might truly have need to be fearful of her heart's capture by Lochlan Rockrimmon. He was indeed a man above men in every regard. Still, the Highwayman of Tanglewood owned Faris's heart; he ever would, and she scolded herself for such musings.

As she closed the door to the chambers she had prepared for Loch Loland's pending guests, she thought how thoroughly she loved lying on her pillow at night, closing her eyes, and imagining the Highwayman astride his black beast—riding through the purple heather under the amethyst sky. She enjoyed imagining him besting the arrogant, cruel nobles he so often came upon. Faris loved to envision him besting Kade Tremeshton most of all. She thought of the first tale she had been told—of the first time the Highwayman of Tanglewood had bested Kade Tremeshton—thoroughly robbing him and leaving him standing in the middle of the road in nothing but his under-breeches. How she reveled in the idea of Kade Tremeshton being so utterly humiliated and at the very hands of her own Highwayman. How many days more before she would be with him again? Faris fairly ached with the anticipation of seeing him—being held in his strong arms, hearing his mirthful chuckle.

With a heavy sigh of both delight and regret, Faris crossed the grand hallway to Lochlan's room. Oh, she well knew what she would find there—a bed so perfectly spread as to have the appearance of never having been slept in. In opposition, breeches, shirts, and vests would be strewn from one end of the grand chamber to the other. Indeed, she giggled aloud when she entered his chamber to find just such a scene before her. She wondered at how a man could be so particular about the condition of his bedding yet so careless of his attire. She remembered the story of Lochlan's finding a spider in his bed—thus becoming obsessive about spreading his own bed to guard against any future eight-legged beasts finding their way there. Yet could not a spider more easily find its way into a pair of discarded breeches tossed to the floor? Faris always found several pair of breeches strewn about in Lochlan's chambers. Lillias had explained that her brother detested clothing on the whole and often found choosing attire a difficult and frustrating task. Therefore, most mornings Lochlan Rockrimmon would search through his wardrobe, discarding several pair of breeches before finally settling on which pair to wear. Faris found the habit entirely endearing, however, and set herself to the task of returning the scattered clothing to the wardrobe so that the process could begin again on the morrow.

So distracted was Faris by her mirthful ponderings of Lochlan Rockrimmon's boyish habits she did not hear the subject of her thoughts enter his bedchamber.

"Ah! Going through my pockets, I see."

Startled by the unexpected sound of Lochlan's voice, Faris gasped and spun around to face him.

He smiled and added, "I've no sweets or secret love letters to be found there, Faris."

"I-I was simply returning your things to their proper place, sire," Faris stammered. Oh, how he unsettled her! How terribly, terribly, terribly he unsettled her!

"And in going over my things, do you then feel

you know me more intimately?" he asked, still smiling and striding toward her.

Faris felt her eyes widened, and her body begin to tremble as he approached. "I-I do not suppose to trespass on your privacy, sire," she told him.

His smile broadened as he said, "If it were privacy I wanted, I would have bolted the door, Faris."

"Yes, sire," Faris said, lowering her gaze. It was far too difficult to gaze into the emerald flash of his eyes—far too difficult not to blush under the gaze of one so handsome as he.

"Wouldn't you like to know me more intimately, Faris?" he asked.

"Pardon me?" Faris squeaked. He was such a terrible tease—always winning a blush from Faris's cheeks. How she wished he did not affect her so.

"What *do* you know of me, then?" he asked, standing directly before her. "Come—tell me. What do you know of me?"

Faris swallowed hard and stammered, "Um . . . uh . . ." She glanced past him to the open door, wishing she could bolt straight through it.

Having seen her look to the door, Lochlan said, "Oh, of course." He turned and strode to the door, closing and bolting it. Faris was aghast! What did he mean to do? What would the other servants think? Her heart was pounding with mad ferocity! Surely Lochlan Rockrimmon did not mean to seduce her. Surely not!

"Now—privacy assured—what do you know of me, Faris?" he asked, reaching out and pushing her chin up to close her astonish-gaped mouth. "Come now, Faris," he said, taking her arm and directing her to sit on the side of his bed. "Tell me what you know of me?"

"I-I . . ." Faris stammered, too stunned by what was happening to react. Should she cry out for help? Surely not! Lochlan Rockrimmon was not of the same evil froth as Kade Tremeshton. Lochlan Rockrimmon simply liked to tease—this she had been told many, many times since his return to Loch Loland Castle. Surely he was only teasing her—making her uncomfortable because he derived amusement from her discomfort.

"Very well—I'll go first," he said, as he began to unbutton his shirt.

Faris gasped again, certain she was about to be compromised, yet still unable to move.

"You are Faris Shayhan," he began as he stripped his shirt from his body, revealing an astounding, sculptured torso.

Faris pinched herself to make certain she was actually awake and not caught up in some wild dream. She began nervously wringing her hands as she tried to tear her gaze from the muscles of his chest and arms. He reached into his wardrobe and withdrew a different shirt—one she had picked up from the nearby chair and returned to the wardrobe only moments before.

"You came to us from Tremeshton Manor—a vile household with a vile lord over it." He threaded one arm through one sleeve of the shirt, then the other, leaving the front gaping open, still revealing the muscles of his chest and stomach. "Yet you were fortunate enough to escape Tremeshton without falling victim to Kade's treachery," he said, nodding with approval. "It is said, by others who labor here, that you hail from Heathmoor, originally," he continued, "a quaint little village. I am exceedingly fond of it. I've been there many, many times." Lochlan Rockrimmon began fastening the buttons of his shirt as he continued. "You are of a proper age to marry, yet you have declared no intended," he said. Faris smiled as she heard a button hit the floor. "Damn it all!" he exclaimed, stripping the new shirt from his body and tossing it to Faris. "I've lost a button. Would you mind mending it for me? Mother taught me to mend my own, and she'll have my head if she catches me giving it to you—but to see me with a needle . . . it's a painful thing to witness."

Faris smiled. For all the impropriety of the situation, she had begun to realize she was in no danger of being compromised. Lochlan Rock-rimmon was of a different mettle than Kade Tremeshton. Furthermore, what interest would such a man ever find in a simple chambermaid?

Gathering the shirt, Faris said, "Of course, sire." She rose from the bed, taking hold of her opportunity to escape—for he yet unnerved her greatly.

"Oh, not now, Faris," he said, pushing her shoulder and causing her to sit on the bed once more. "Afterward—I've plenty enough shirts to last the day. If you would only mend it for me later, we can continue."

"Yes, sire," she said, nervously sighing. She looked up when she heard him laugh.

"Fear not, Faris," he said. "I have no intention of heaping ruination upon you—at least not here and now."

Faris felt her eyes widen, astonished by his obvious flirting.

He laughed again and added, "And I am no Kade Tremeshton. Were I to want you, I *would* win you—make no mistake—but I would not go about it in any manner akin to his."

It was further affirmation of his noble character. Yet Faris was somewhat miffed at his implying he did not want her. She comforted herself by reminding herself she secreted a liaison with the Highwayman of Tanglewood, and even the dashing Lochlan Rockrimmon could not compete for a woman's affections with such as the Highwayman for a rival.

Yet so miffed did Faris find herself that she in fact found her mouth speaking seemingly without

225

her conscious permission. "And in what manner *would* you go about it?" she asked. Quickly she added, "Sire?"

"Oh, a tender nerve has been plucked," he said, smiling as he pulled another shirt from his wardrobe, threading his arms into the sleeves. "But you mistake me, pretty girl," he added. "I did not mean I flatly did not want you—I meant I did not want to . . . to harm you."

He leaned forward then, placing a hand on either side of her where she sat on the bed. He tilted his head to one side as he studied her, his face mere inches from her own. Faris tried not to look at the bareness of his chest and stomach, but his shirt hung freely open, and it was difficult to ignore.

"I mean to say—lovely girl with soft, berry lips—I would like nothing more than to corrupt you . . . but I won't," he whispered. He lingered before her for a moment, his lips a breath from her own. Then smiling, he stood once more and said, "Still, I've wandered from the subject of our conversation. Now you know my knowledge of you. What is yours of me?"

Faris swallowed hard, still undone by what had just passed. Goose bumps fairly consumed her body! She did not approve of her physical reaction to Lochlan Rockrimmon. She would indeed scold herself thoroughly once he had left her to her own tasks once more.

"Come now," he urged as he began buttoning the new shirt. "Surely you know something. If you know nothing, then tell me what you've heard of me. Still, I would value your own thoughts far more."

Faris did not know how to begin. Could he truly have any care for what her thoughts of him were?

"I-I think you are good," she said, softly. "A bit of a tease, the stripe of a rascal running the length of your back, perhaps—but good at the core." He laughed, and Faris could not help but smile.

"Better a rascal's stripe than a coward's, Faris," he said, smiling at her as he finished the task of buttoning his shirt.

"Yes, sire," she said, smiling. She wondered for a moment why he did not have a valet, and she spoke the thought aloud. "Why do you not employ a valet, Master Lochlan?"

He smiled and asked, "Why do you think I do not? Let us see if you know me that well."

Faris smiled, dazzled by his charm, his attractiveness, his pure masculinity. "I think . . . I think it is because you find . . . that you believe . . ." she stammered, afraid to speak her thoughts.

"Go on, Faris," he said. "You'll not offend me."

Faris inhaled a deep breath of courage and said, "Perhaps you find it weak—a man who must have another to assist him with simple and personal tasks, such as dressing for the day."

"Well done, Faris! Bravo!" he said, smiling and clapping his hands three times. "I find it . . . disturbing—any able-bodied man having another dress him, having another perching about like a sick crow." His brow puckered for a moment, and he said, "But will you still mend the shirt for me?"

Faris giggled, completely delighted by his sudden boyish manner. "Yes, of course, sire," she said.

"Thank you," he said. "And with that . . . we'll have to suspend our conversation for now. I'll be late for my appointment." He leaned forward again and whispered, "I'm off to clean Kade Tremeshton's pockets in a game of cards."

Faris smiled. How could she refuse a smile?

"Naturally," Lochlan continued, "He does not know that Lord Montegue has asked me to join the game, and I hope I am able to keep my temper and avoid breaking his nose a second time." He smiled the smile of a rapscallion and added, "Yet if father will not allow me to defend a woman's honor with my fists, then I suppose my wits will have to do."

"I-I do thank you for your help, sire," Faris said, humbly remembering his championing her where Kade Tremeshton was concerned.

"It is I who should thank you, Faris," Lochlan said. "I've wanted to put a fist to Kade Tremeshton's face for as long as ever I can remember. I should thank you for providing the venue."

"Yet in truth, I thank you, sire," Faris said.

"And thank *you,* Faris," he replied. "And now, I'm off to best the blackguard at cards." He strode to the door and unbolted it, yet paused before he took his leave. "Please don't mention the shirt mending to my mother. She gets terribly put off with me for being all too rough on things." Faris smiled as he nodded at her and took his leave of the room.

Faris remained seated on his bed for a few more moments, trying to smooth her ruffled nerves. He was indeed dangerous, and she was disgusted with herself for letting him unsettle her so. What would her Highwayman think of her weakness?

Quickly, Faris hopped up, smoothed her skirt, and went about her remaining tasks. After tidying Lochlan's room, she found the rogue button from his shirt and tucked it into her apron pocket. Tucking Lochlan's shirt under her arm, she left his bedchamber and made her way to Lillias's room. Oh, how she wished the Highwayman were near. Perhaps he was! Faris was yet suspicious of Bainbridge Graybeau being the Highwayman. At breakfast that morning, Old Joseph had mentioned that Bainbridge had returned from Saxton the night before—the same night the Highwayman of Tanglewood had come upon her near the cottage. Could it be

Bainbridge Graybeau had been riding back to Loch Loland, having bested Lord Brookings as the Highwayman of Tanglewood? Could that be why the Highwayman had happened upon her the way he did? Further, Old Joseph had informed Faris of Bainbridge's request she meet him after supper for another riding lesson. Perhaps this was the way the Highwayman would contact her! Perhaps, now that the Highwayman knew she suspected Bainbridge of being he, perhaps he meant to confess the truth to her! Even if he did not confess, she would test him once more—study him more closely. How wonderful it would be to know her beloved Highwayman was so close at hand. Yet surely she would have known him on their last meeting. Would she not?

"Faris, darling!" Lillias exclaimed as Faris entered her chamber. "Wherever have you been? I could not find you last evening to tell you of the Highwayman and his besting of Lord Brookings in Saxton!"

Certainly, Faris already knew the story of the Highwayman of Tanglewood and his ride to Saxton. Yet why not allow her friend the satisfaction of telling the tale? Furthermore, it was Faris's experience that, in storytelling, one presenter often neglected details another might not.

And so she said, "Tell me, Lillias! You must!"

"Gawain said it was a brilliant besting! The

most brilliant the Highwayman has ever performed." Lillias began.

Faris smiled and listened until Lillias had poured out the tale with far more excitement and detail than had Old Joseph told it the night before. Still, the story was the same—more dramatic in the telling perhaps—but the same.

"Isn't it a marvelous tale, Faris?" Lillias asked.

"Indeed it is," Faris agreed.

Lillias sighed, smiling with delighted excitement. "Of course, I hope Gawain did not neglect any important details in the telling of it," Lillias said. "He was ever so fatigued last evening when he told me—having ridden all the way back to Loch Loland Castle from Heathmoor yesterday."

Faris felt the hair on the back of her neck stand on end. "Heathmoor?" she asked. "Why—why was Lord Kendrick in Heathmoor?" Heathmoor, as Faris well knew, was on the road to Saxton.

"What?" Lillias asked, still dreaming of the adventures of the Highwayman of Tanglewood, no doubt.

"Lord Kendrick," Faris said. "Did he have business in Heathmoor?"

"Indeed!" Lillias exclaimed. "Odd, isn't it—that Gawain should be at Heathmoor when the Highwayman of Tanglewood was at Saxton. They are not so very far apart, I understand—though I have never been to either place. Though—you

231

were born in Heathmoor, Faris, were you not? Did you ever have cause to be in Saxton?"

"No," Faris said. "Never."

Faris was suddenly quite anxious. Was it purely coincidence that Lord Kendrick was in Heathmoor—so close to Saxton—at the very same time the Highwayman of Tanglewood was riding out against Lord Brookings?

"Lord Kendrick is not the Highwayman of Tanglewood. He cannot be," Faris mumbled to herself.

"Oh, I know it," Lillias sighed. "Still, I like to pretend that he is. I like to imagine that my Gawain is the Highwayman of Tanglewood and riding for the livelihood of others."

"Oh, I did not mean—" Faris began.

"No, Faris, you are right to keep me from being so foolish," Lillias said. "Still, I did think it intriguing to imagine Gawain attired in black and astride a black steed calling out Lord Brookings—his rapier at Lord Brookings's throat."

"Graybeau has been absent from Loch Loland as well," Faris said.

"When?" Lillias asked.

"These three days past," Faris added. "He has been to Saxton to inquire of his mother."

Lillias's eyes fairly glistened with merriment and mischief. "Graybeau has been to Saxton?" she asked.

"Yes," Faris said. "I am told he returned last night. I am to have a riding lesson today."

"Oh, Faris!" Lillias squealed in an excited whisper. "You think Graybeau is the Highwayman, don't you?"

"I-I admit to wondering at it," Faris whispered.

"Oh, would not it be simply perfect?" Lillias giggled. "And if Graybeau happened to be the Highwayman—well, he has taken an interest in you, has he not? It may well be you are in line to be the sweetheart of the Highwayman of Tanglewood, Faris! Is that not too delicious for words?"

"Far too delicious for words," Faris giggled. How she wished she could confide in Lillias! How she wished she could! Yet she could not. She could not endanger the Highwayman, or his cause, in any manner.

And so, Faris simply sat in delightful speculation and conversation with Lillias for some time. Such happy times Faris could not remember—for other than the Highwayman of Tanglewood, there was no better companion in her heart or her mind.

"And how fares your mother, Mr. Bainbridge?" Faris asked as Bainbridge Graybeau assisted her in dismounting Lady Violet. The low light of dusk lent a certain warmth and peace to the earth as she smoothed the back of her dress and tucked a stray strand of hair behind one ear.

"She is well," Bainbridge said. "She has her garden and entire flock of cats to keep her company, she does." He chuckled, and Faris smiled at the jolly sound.

Bainbridge was yet clean-shaven, and Faris quickly studied the square angle of his jaw— endeavoring in vain to find some resemblance to that of the Highwayman of Tanglewood. In that moment, she was reminded of how truly vague the Highwayman's features were to her. Having only seen the Highwayman in the least of moonlight, it was nearly impossible to discern whether or not his jaw owned the same angle and square manner as Bainbridge's.

For a moment, she thought, *I'll kiss him! I'll certainly know then!* After all, had not the Highwayman granted her permission to kiss the man she had guessed was he? Still, she was uncertain.

"Still, my sister is not so far away," Bainbridge added, drawing Faris's attention from her musings and to their conversation once more. "She is married and lives in Heathmoor. Perhaps you know her husband—he is William Terry, and he was born in Heathmoor the same as you."

Faris's heartbeat increased in its rhythm. Frantically, she tried to recall whether or not she had ever mentioned to Bainbridge Graybeau that she was born in Heathmoor. Had she? Indeed, she had mentioned it to the Highwayman of Tanglewood, and Lillias knew the truth of it. But had she ever told Bainbridge the fact of it? Had the Highwayman of Tanglewood only just revealed the smallest trace to his true identity? Why could she not find the courage to simply ask him? She had asked the Highwayman himself—asked if he were Bainbridge Graybeau. Then why could she not now ask Bainbridge Graybeau if he were the Highwayman of Tangle-wood?

"I will saddle Lady Violet for you again tomorrow if you have the time, lass," Bainbridge said.

Faris smiled at him. Oh, it must be he! It must be!

"I would like that very much, Mr. Bainbridge," Faris said. "Thank you for this evening's lesson."

"It is ever my pleasure, Faris," he said, smiling at her.

Ask him! Ask him! Ask him! her heart pounded. But she could not find the courage.

"Then . . . then I will leave you to your business," Faris said. Yet she lingered. Would he hand her a letter? Would he whisper the secret of their next meeting to her? Was Bainbridge Graybeau her Highwayman lover?

"Good night, then," he said. Then with another smile in her direction, he led Lady Violet back to the stables.

Faris nearly burst into tears, so frustrated was she. She wanted her Highwayman—wanted him near to her every moment! It was painful to be so separated from him—frightening in not knowing when next they would meet.

Feeling the threat of defeat lingering at her heels, Faris returned to the house. There was not to do but wait.

"Keep your voice, Lochlan!" Faris heard Lady Rockrimmon whisper. The hour was late. Faris had determined to mend Lochlan's shirt before retiring, in the small chance he should inquire about it on the morrow. Now, sitting in the sewing room, mending by candlelight, she heard heavy footsteps in the hallway—heard Lady Rockrimmon's worried whisper.

Curiosity led her to leave her chair and linger in the doorway. She gasped when, in the next moment, Lady Rockrimmon and a very battered and bloodied Lochlan stumbled into the sewing room.

"Oh! Faris!" Lady Rockrimmon gasped, obviously startled herself. "We . . . we came in search of—"

"A needle, Faris. And some thread," Lochlan growled.

"Oh, milady!" Faris exclaimed. "Whatever happened?"

"Cards," Lady Rockrimmon said, irritated. "A

silly, boyish game. Loch's final hand beat Kade Tremeshton's, and this is the result."

"He bested you?" Faris whispered, astounded at the thought.

"Of course not!" Lochlan fairly shouted.

"Hush, Loch!" Lady Rockrimmon scolded. "You'll wake the entire house!"

"He's a coward—drew a dagger when I bested him at the game. He very nearly took my eye in the process," Lochlan explained. He removed the hand he had been holding to his forehead to reveal a devilish laceration just above his right brow.

Faris gasped, her hands covering her mouth in astonishment.

"He won't see a physician, Faris. He insists I can mend it far better," Lady Rockrimmon explained.

"You are perfectly capable, Mother. You or Faris," he growled, snatching the needle and thread Faris had been holding from her hand.

Lady Rockrimmon shook her head and said, "Stay with him, Faris. Keep him calm if you can. I'll bring some warm water."

"B-b-but, milady," Faris stammered.

"He's a filthy bast—" Lochlan began. "He's a filthy blackguard!" he corrected himself. Faris almost smiled, amused by his being careful of his verbiage in her presence. "I bested him in the game!"

"But not in the consequence?" Faris asked.

"In the consequence as well!" he assured her. "But not before the coward drew a dagger."

"Then . . . then he looks the worse than you, sire?" Faris ventured. She smiled when Lochlan smiled and nodded.

"Oh, much," he said, still smiling. "Much worse. His repulsive broken nose is now joined by much bruising and swelling and all manner of damage done by fisticuffs."

"Then I am glad to hear it," Faris said, also smiling. "Still, this is a terrible wound." Faris was trembling with exceeding concern for her master's well-being. She did not like to see him bleeding—to see his handsome features so marred. Though she fancied in her next thought that a scar to his forehead borne of fighting Kade Tremeshton only served to make him all the more fatally attractive.

"A scratch on the head bleeds worse than a scratch elsewhere, 'tis all," he told her. All of a sudden, he was quite unexpectedly enraged. "He infuriates me! Kade Tremeshton! He pushes me to such anger with his arrogance, greed, belligerence, and tales of conquests." The wound at Lochlan's head was still bleeding, and Faris snatched a piece of cloth from the mending basket and pressed it to his head. "His mother has had to send another girl away for her confinement, and yet calmly sat Kade this night bragging, as

238

if the ruination of a young innocent were the best conquest in the world to be proud of."

Faris's stomach churned with nausea at the thought of her narrow escape.

"And your name was mentioned as well," he added.

"What do you mean, sire?" Faris asked, sickened with disgust and trepidation.

"You've bested him in your own right, Faris, and he is furious because of it," he explained. "Further is he incensed because you are here—in my father's house. 'Lay a finger on her before I do, Rockrimmon,' he said, 'and I'll cut your heart out!' "

Faris felt fearful tears well in her eyes, felt the hand which covered her mouth begin to tremble. Could it be Kade Tremeshton still held designs toward her? After such time had passed—after Lochlan and Lord Rockrimmon himself had championed her? Surely he had abandoned her by now! Yet she knew his prideful arrogance. No doubt Kade Tremeshton saw her as the fox slipping away during the hunt—which only served to cause determination to rise, waxing strong in the hunter.

"I should have told him I've had you already," Lochlan growled. "At that his fury would be directed toward me and not toward you." As Faris struggled to retain tears of fear, she was simultaneously moved by Lochlan's thoughts of chivalry on behalf of a simple chambermaid—misguided though they might be.

"Surely, sire—surely he will think no more on me—a simple chambermaid," Faris said.

"You are a beautiful young woman—a lovely prize slipped through his fingers," Lochlan said. "And Kade Tremeshton will not forget it. At least, not until someone else has . . ." Faris swallowed hard, began to tremble as Lochlan's eyes narrowed. He studied her for a moment and then quickly reached out, taking hold her chin in one hand. Faris gasped a moment before Lochlan Rockrimmon's mouth took hers—driven with such a ravenous kiss as to render her breathless. Hot and moist, his kiss drenched her with such astonishment—with such molten pleasure—she feared she would indeed swoon!

"Lochlan!" Lady Rockrimmon scolded upon reentering the room to find her son accosting Faris. "Release that poor girl this moment! This moment, Lochlan!"

The man did as his mother commanded, and Faris stumbled backward. Bumping into a chair, Faris sat down, her mind whirling, her body still warmed by the sensation of his masterful kiss. She wiped tears from her cheeks—tears of residual fear—not tears at having been set upon by Lochlan Rockrimmon.

"What is the matter with you, Loch?" Lady Rockrimmon exclaimed. "I am so sorry, Faris,"

Lady Rockrimmon began, placing a warm palm to Faris's blushing cheek. "I am sorry—he's just not himself, I suppose."

Faris nodded, still trembling from Lochlan's touch—from his powerful kiss.

"Forgive me, Mother. And, Faris, I . . . please accept my apology," he said to her as he collapsed into a nearby chair. "I am only angry—frustrated—so tired of Tremeshton soiling everything he touches."

"So you decided to soil Faris first?" Lady Rockrimmon asked, brushing a loose strand of hair from Faris's forehead.

"No. No. I just—I just . . ." he stammered. "If I tell him I have tasted her first, then his anger will transfer from her to me, Mother. He may abandon his vile intentions toward her."

"Or he might tell every man and woman in the country that you have become a like loathsome creature as he!" Lady Rockrimmon exclaimed. "Such behavior, Lochlan! Such ill-mannered treatment of poor Faris. I brought her here to keep her from such things. And now—now you've heaped it upon her in what was to be her safe place!"

"I am sorry. Truly," he said, burying his face in his hands.

Faris worried at the blood trickling from the wound at his forehead—the blood trickling over his hands—between his fingers.

"I am simply so sickened by it all, Mother—all of the greedy arrogance accompanying Kade Tremeshton and those like him."

"Then you do what you have always done—debate—that you may unseat these men. Champion politically so Kade Tremeshton and those like him lose their power whether through force or their own foolishness. Leave the fighting and the accosting of young women to others. Let the Highwayman of Tanglewood bloody Kade up if you like, but you stay true to who you were born to be!"

"Yes, Mother," Lochlan mumbled half-heartedly. Releasing a heavy sigh, he turned to look at Faris. "I am . . . I am very sorry, Faris," he said. "I beg of you, forgive me. It is not my standard behavior."

Faris's heart was yet hammering with mad confusion. She was astonished, yet fearful and confused by one other emotion—pure elation!

"It is nothing to worry over, sire," she said. "I-I am most humbled and very grateful for your heroic ideals on my behalf—misguided though they may have been."

"Thank you, Faris," Lochlan said.

"Faris, dear," Lady Rockrimmon began, "obviously you have been about your duties far too long today, and with this in addition—please retire for the night. I am more than able here."

"But, milady, he is quite wounded," Faris began.

"He is fine, Faris. Just a scratch. Leave the brute to me," she said, slapping the top of her son's head as penance for his behavior.

"Yes, milady," Faris said.

On weakened knees, she rose from her chair and offered a quick curtsy to Lady Rockrimmon. "Milady," she said. She turned then to Lochlan, who sat in his chair with the countenance of a defeated puppy.

Yet as she moved past the young master of Loch Loland Castle, she was both astonished and oddly delighted when he said, "I know the wrong in it, Faris. Still, I am glad I endeavored to have you before Kade Tremeshton was able to—"

His words were cut short as his mother slapped him on the head again.

"Your lips are as sweet as sun-warmed berries."

Again Lady Rockrimmon slapped him on the head, and Faris returned the smile he bestowed upon her.

"Thank you, sire," she said. Quickly, she fled from the room, hastening to her own chamber.

Once inside, she closed her chamber door. Leaning back against the door, she placed a hand over her bosom where her heart pounded, frantic. Tears filled her eyes, and she allowed them to escape into tiny rivulets over her cheeks.

She placed her hand over her tender lips, still

trembling with the blissful sensation of Lochlan Rockrimmon's kiss. In truth, the kiss had been so fierce it had nearly been uncomfortable in its application—far different than the passionate kiss of the Highwayman, yet wholly passionate in its own right.

Faris sobbed as frustration, self-scolding, and all manner of confusion overtook her. What manner of an appalling, disloyal, dishonest woman allowed such a kiss from her master when her heart already held another man close? Yet she had not allowed it; it had been forced. Had it not? What wickedness was overtaking her that she could experience such pleasure in Lochlan Rockrimmon's kiss when her very soul belonged to the Highwayman?

Perhaps it was the knowledge—the fear—of knowing the Highwayman was so wholly unobtainable. Perhaps, Faris mused, that for the sake of knowing deep in her heart that the Highwayman could never freely belong to her, perhaps her heart had been momentarily tempted by another. But another who could no more belong to her than the Highwayman? There was no sense in it.

She should run—run to Bainbridge—beg him to tell her the truth. Was Bainbridge the Highwayman of Tanglewood? Oh, how she longed for him to confide in her. If she could wake, sleep, and breathe knowing her beloved Highwayman was a breath away—knowing he was there—in the stables at Loch Loland—perhaps it would soothe her confusion and fears.

"Faris?"

It was Sarah. Her quiet knock sounded on the door.

"I-I'm not well, Sarah," Faris said. "May we talk in the morning when I am feeling better?"

"I heard you," Sarah said. "I did not know you were still about. I heard you up and wanted to give you this."

"Sarah," Faris said, wiping tears from her cheeks. "Truly, I am ill. Please—"

"A letter was delivered for you this evening at the back kitchen door, after supper, while you were riding with Graybeau," Sarah whispered.

Faris's heart leapt! The Highwayman!

Opening the door just a crack, Faris looked to Sarah.

"Are you well, Faris? Should I fetch Mary?" Sarah asked.

"No," Faris said. "I-I only need rest. It is a pain in my head. It will pass."

Sarah smiled, still frowning with worry. "Well, here is your letter, Faris. I hope it is good news."

"Thank you, Sarah," Faris said. "Good night."

"Good night, Faris."

Bolting her door to ensure she would not be interrupted, Faris inhaled deeply, attempting to calm the mad pounding of her heart.

A letter! She studied the wax seal before opening it—a symbol, perhaps—family crest? She was not certain for the low light. Quickly she lit the candle at her bedside and broke the seal. Unfolding the parchment, she saw, for the first time, the elegant hand of the Highwayman of Tanglewood.

"What words?" she whispered to herself. What words, indeed. What words would the Highwayman of Tanglewood pen in a secret letter? Allowing her fingertips to caress the first few words on the parchment, she read:

Fair Faris of Loch Loland Castle . . . 'tis I . . . the twilight-lover you own . . .

The Fruit of Provocation

The Highwayman's first words found her tears abundant. He had written to her! He had dared to deliver, or have delivered, a letter to her! How her heart soared with the knowledge he had penned the message himself. What hope it gave her—what respite from her confusion of feelings over Lochlan Rockrimmon's kiss! This was the Highwayman of Tanglewood's own written word. He cared for her. He did! She knew he did, and it warmed her—soothed her fevered mind.

She read the first words of the letter once more.

> Fair Faris of Loch Loland Castle . . . 'tis
> I . . . the twilight-lover you own . . .

Sighing with delight and an odd sort of relief, she continued to read.

> And I can no more delay thoughts of you lingering in my mind than I can delay the rising of the sun. I think only of a violet-curtained dwelling where last I met the evening beauty who holds captive my heart. You own my heart, fair Faris of

Loch Loland Castle. As surely as if you clasp it in your very hands, you own my heart. And in owning my heart . . . you own me. Believe all I tell you—you own me, and my greatest desire is to own you.

I must hold you in my arms once more! I must taste the berry-flavor of your kiss! And yet, my determination to fight great injustice may well place you in the path of danger if I am not full cautious. Therefore, we must plan well: we must be secretive and ever wary. It is even I am anxious in writing to you and feel it necessary to plan our next rendezvous through understanding of the past, rather than in terms any eyes might interpret. Therefore, I propose this: four nights hence we shall rendezvous, yet let us meet where once we met before, where the color of sunset runs forever, where the silver of moonlight illuminates legend, where entwine the branches of true and everlasting love. You know well the place I mean, I am certain. We have met where the color of sunset runs forever. We have conversed where the silver of moonlight illuminates legend, and we have tasted sweet kisses beneath branches of true and everlasting love.

Four nights hence, fair Faris. Meet me

when the sun is nearly set. I will find you and administer to you kisses of such fiery passion as to render you breathless in my arms . . . helpless against my any purpose. Four nights hence, fair Faris. I will find you there.

Your Servant, Your Secret, Your Lover.

Faris sighed, brushing tears from her cheeks. All would be well. She would meet the Highwayman in four days' time—in four days she would be in his arms again! The knowledge renewed her happiness; it settled her mind. After all, Lochlan Rockrimmon had meant nothing in kissing her. The young master of Loch Loland only desired to best Kade Tremeshton at another turn—and in truth, he had. Furthermore, Faris inwardly admitted to herself that if there were to be a nobleman to steal a kiss from her, far better it was the likes of the handsome Lochlan Rockrimmon than a devil the likes of Kade Tremeshton.

Pressing the Highwayman's letter to her lips, Faris kissed it softly. She would cherish the letter all the days of her life—hold it as her greatest treasure. Carefully, she tucked it into the small wooden box she kept, her box of cherished things. There she hid the letter from her lover—the letter from the Highwayman of Tanglewood—beneath the worn ribbons that had once belonged to her mother.

Great fatigue overtook Faris suddenly. Wearily she nestled into her warm bed. Four days—a simple time to pass. She would see the Highwayman once more, and in seeing him, her fears would be soothed once more.

Closing her eyes, Faris tried to envision the Highwayman astride his black steed—tried to imagine him riding through the purple heather near the ruins of Castle Alexendria. She tried to imagine him reining in at Loch Loland Castle's stables, stripping himself of his black attire to don the clothing he wore by day— the clothing of Lord Rockrimmon's master stableman, Bainbridge Graybeau. She thought of Lillias's desire that Lord Gawain Kendrick be, in secret, the Highwayman of Tanglewood. She thought of Lochlan Rockrimmon then— wondered if Lady Rockrimmon had managed to efficiently tend to the wound at his forehead. Her next thought was of Lochlan Rockrimmon's rakish kiss. She inwardly scolded herself when the thought of his kiss brought a tingle to her lips and caused goose bumps to ripple over her flesh. She wondered if Lochlan truly planned to wed Tannis Stringham. The thought disturbed her somehow, and she returned her musings to the Highwayman of Tanglewood. His letter was tucked safely away, and the knowledge soothed Faris as she drifted into slumbering.

"He's only being polite," Sarah said. "That's the truth of it."

"He's planning to ask for her hand, I tell you," Mary insisted.

Faris tried to ignore the conversation between Mary and Sarah, tried to concentrate on finishing her own supper. Yet the speculation as to the reason for Lady Stringham and her daughter's impending visit was running fierce and free at Loch Loland Castle. Most of those who labored therein supposed their young master Lochlan was planning to propose marriage to Tannis Stringham, while the others supposed he was only being polite—extending a coerced invitation.

Whatever the reason—and Faris preferred to believe the second—she felt unsettled, anxious for her young master's happiness. Still, Faris had her own concerns. She glanced at the clock on the kitchen wall—sighed at the slow pace of the pendulum. Four days and three nights until dusk would find her out in search of her lover. Yet after four days and three nights, she would know reassurance as to the affections and adoration of the Highwayman.

How did lovers endure being parted? She often wondered at it. Since meeting the Highwayman one year previous—after his stealing a kiss from her in the meadow—since that night Faris had not known serenity. Since that night, although she had owned a joy beyond measure, she had not a moment of feeling free from care.

Furthermore, it seemed to her now that her moments of peace had lessened all the more since Lochlan Rockrimmon had returned to his ancestral home. The talk of his possible marriage to Tannis Stringham caused everyone to feel unsettled.

"Master Lochlan would never marry with the likes of Tannis Stringham. Of that I am certain," Sarah said. "Although, she is very beautiful," she added, a scowl puckering her brow.

"Beautiful like a perfumed poison," Mary mumbled.

"What do you think, Faris?" Sarah asked.

Faris shrugged her shoulders and answered, "I-I am not as well acquainted with Master Lochlan as are you." She felt the heat rising to her cheeks—for although she did not know the fact of it, she suspected Lochlan Rockrimmon had never stolen a kiss from Sarah. The thought caused Faris to realize she was indeed better acquainted with Lochlan Rockrimmon than was Sarah. "And—and I have no acquaintance with this Tannis Stringham."

"Yet I hear you may know Master Lochlan far better than you have led us all to believe," Sarah said, smiling. Her eyes twinkled with friendship and mischief—twinkled with a secret cached.

"What?" Faris exclaimed, feeling flushed and

uncomfortable. Had Sarah witnessed the event of the night before? Had Sarah seen Lochlan Rockrimmon kiss her?

"Willeen tells us she was walking by Master Lochlan's chambers only yesterday morning when she saw him bolt his chamber door—bolt you in with him," Sarah said. She arched one eyebrow, smiling at Faris.

"He—he is a terrible tease. Certainly, you know him well enough to know it is true," Faris said. Still, she felt overly warm and uneasy. She knew well the dislike that befell a favored servant. Further, she did not like the manner in which her stomach fluttered at the memory.

"And you know Willeen well enough to think better than to believe everything she says, Sarah," Mary added.

"Still, I think Master Lochlan favors his chambermaid," Sarah said. She giggled and patted the back of Faris's hand in the manner of friendship. "I'm only teasing you as well, Faris. I am most certain Maser Lochlan had good reason for—"

"Mary!" All three women startled, gasping as Lochlan entered the kitchen fairly shouting Mary's name. "Mary! I need pie," he growled.

Faris winced at the sight of the wound on his forehead. Indeed, Lady Rockrimmon had done a fair job of sewing, but it still stood bruised and painful in appearance.

"Of course, sire," Mary said, rising from her chair and going to the counter to retrieve a pie.

"A plate is not necessary, Mary," Lochlan said, sitting down hard in a chair at the table next to Faris. "Just bring me a pie and some sort of utensil to devour it with."

Faris sat perfectly still, uncertain as to whether or not to flee. Sarah seemed paralyzed with uncertainty as well, for she did not move even a breath.

"Have you had a taxing day then, Master Lochlan?" Mary said, placing a pie and fork on the table before him.

"I have," he grumbled. "Lord Gettings has taken Robert Gorham's crop! Taken his crop as punishment for unpaid tenant taxes—taxes that are criminal, in point!"

"No!" Mary gasped. "Robert is such a kind and good man. A hard worker too."

Lochlan shook his head and plunged the fork into the middle of the pie. "That he is. And not deserving of such treatment or loss. I have offered him a cottage near Loch Loland, and he has accepted. Still, he is too proud to accept any else. I fear we will be bringing many a food basket to the Gorham tenant this winter."

"If you will excuse me then, sire," Sarah said, finding her voice at last.

"Of course," Lochlan mumbled, waving his fork in her direction in a gesture she was free to

254

leave. "Mary, another fork if you would—Faris is wanting to share my pie."

"Oh, no, no, no, sire," Faris began. "I am not in the least hungry."

"Hunger has nothing whatsoever to do with it, girl," he grumbled. "Another fork, if you would, Mary."

"Of course, Master Lochlan," Mary said, winking at Faris. Her amusement was thinly masked. No doubt she had witnessed the young master in such a state of upheaval before. No doubt it was the reason Mary seemed to have a perpetual supply of fresh pies since his return. "And then, if you don't mind, sire, I'll be about planning tomorrow's meals."

"Yes, yes, Mary. Whatever you need to do," Lochlan said, his mouth full of pie.

Faris shook her head as Mary handed her a fork.

"Enjoy the pie, Faris. It's berry—and my best," Mary said, as she left the room, leaving Faris with their irate master and an assaulted berry pie.

"Just here, Faris," Lochlan said, pointing to one side of the pie. "Pie always makes one feel better."

"But, sire . . . I-I feel fine," she stammered.

"Nonsense, girl!" he exclaimed. "Injustice is plaguing the countryside! And I think pie may be the only answer. Have a bite."

Tentatively, Faris did as she was told. The

255

pie was delicious and did indeed give her a momentary lift.

"Were that I were that rogue Highwayman of Tanglewood and could plunge my knife into Lord Gettings's greedy breast," he mumbled, stuffing another large bite of pie into his mouth.

"Oh, but the Highwayman would not murder Lord Gettings." The utterance was out of her mouth almost before Faris realized it.

Instantly, Lochlan Rockrimmon paused in devouring the pastry before him. His brow puckered in a curious frown. "You speak as if you are acquainted with the Highwayman himself—not just the tales of his activities," he said.

"I-I simply hear the same stories you do, sire. And the Highwayman of Tanglewood has never killed anyone. Robbed those deserving of being robbed, humiliated those in need of humbling, perhaps—but never has he killed. Has he?" Quickly, Faris took another bite of pie, meeting his suspicious stare in an attempt to appear innocent.

Still, she was certain Lochlan was disbelieving of her, for he paused in his attack on the pie, sat back in his chair, and studied her for a long moment.

"Who holds your heart captive, Faris?" he asked.

His question was leading, and Faris knew she

must be wary. "What do you mean to ask me, sire?" she stammered.

"Those who work in this house, they discuss matters with me, and it seems there is ever a question as to who interests you." He lowered his voice and continued, "Though it is said Bainbridge Graybeau has captured your attention in some fashion."

Faris was silent—simply raised another fork-full of pie to her mouth as she looked at him.

"Of recent you came upon me of an evening just outside this kitchen's door. I was eating pie, and you had the look of a woman ravished. Secretive you were about it, unsettled, anxious I should not press you further about your activities. I ask you now—are you and Bainbridge enjoying one another's company often in the evening?"

Faris swallowed hard, closed her eyes for a moment. She was in peril! The Highwayman was in peril! If Lochlan Rockrimmon were to guess it was truly the Highwayman of Tanglewood she had been meeting in secret—oh surely, it would mean danger and ruination for her lover. Yet his thoughts, his assumptions seemed to be that Faris was Bainbridge Graybeau's lover. What different danger did this then pose to her beloved? Even if Lochlan was accepting, it could mean ruin—for if Bainbridge Graybeau were the Highwayman of Tanglewood as Faris oft suspected, then still she could lead him to danger.

"I will not send you away or some such nonsense if you have chosen to place your affections in Graybeau's direction, Faris," Lochlan said. "There is no other man more deserving of a fine young woman."

Faris made her decision in an instant. Better to have the powerful Lochlan Rockrimmon believing Bainbridge Graybeau owned her heart than to have him suspect the Highwayman of Tanglewood did—even if it were true they were one in the same.

"Are you in earnest, sire?" Faris asked. She must deter his thoughts from the Highwayman. "Dependant upon my answer—are you in earnest? May I remain at Loch Loland Castle?"

"No wonder my teasing manner has no effect on you!" he laughed then. "Compared with Bainbridge Graybeau, I must seem as dull as a pudding spoon!"

"Please, sire," Faris begged in a whisper, reaching out and placing her hand over one of his resting on the table. "Please . . . he does not know that I favor him."

"But he favors you in the least of it, else he would not be spending the time in teaching you to ride," Lochlan said. His dazzling smile dazed Faris for a moment. "Bainbridge Graybeau labors with more care and effort than any man I have ever known. If he is spending his precious time in spare with you, then he has a deeper purpose at heart. And you have no need to fear, Faris," Lochlan said, placing a strong hand over hers, which yet lay on his own. "I would ever recommend Bainbridge Graybeau to any woman. Would that I were as hardy and as strong as he. I daresay that were our places the reverse, Bainbridge Graybeau would never have taken the beating I did at Kade Tremeshton's hand. And the Highwayman certainly proves himself Tremeshton's superior. You must think me a weakling fool in standing next to one such as Graybeau and our local rogue."

Faris smiled. He seemed to have swallowed her false implication of being attached to Graybeau. "I think you as brave and as valiant as ever Bainbridge Graybeau is. For that matter, as ever the Highwayman of Tanglewood is," she said. It was not entirely true, a bit too flattering, but she did admire him. "You are at least as strong and as capable as Bainbridge. Further, your wealth and position enable you to help the same people the Highwayman does—simply through different venues."

Lochlan smiled and said, "Ah, but a woman loves a man more who can best his enemy with his fists or a sword. A man who bests another with his wit, wisdom, tongue, and money—oh, he is not the one for whom the women swoon."

Faris frowned, somewhat puzzled. Had not

Lochlan Rockrimmon beaten Kade Tremeshton in fisticuffs as well as cards? And had he not easily disarmed him the day he had assaulted Faris in the grand entryway of Loch Loland? Surely he did not think these tasks were futile or simple.

"All women swoon in your presence, sire," Faris told him in an effort to encourage his self-esteem.

"You are a flatterer of the worst sort, Faris," he chuckled, plunging his fork into the pie once more. This time when he lifted it, however, he held it out toward her.

Faris paused. Could he possibly be offering his fork to her? To eat from the same fork as one's master—it simply wasn't done.

"Here," he urged. "The middle is still warm." Slowly Faris opened her mouth, accepting the bite of warm pie. He smiled as he withdrew the fork, and her eyes widened when he promptly turned the fork over, licking it with his tongue. The man was far too skilled in the art of winning a woman's admiration and desire. Faris could well imagine how impossible it would be for a woman to resist him were he to decisively put his mind to truly seducing her.

"Will you tell Graybeau of my admiration for him?" Lochlan asked. "Will you convey my gratitude to him when next you attend a riding lesson?"

"I will tell him," Faris said.

"Thank you," he said, his emerald eyes flashing. "And do not worry—your secret is safe with me."

"Thank you, sire," Faris said. "If you will excuse me, sire—I truly should be about my duties."

Lochlan nodded as he continued to devour the pie before him. "Yes, yes. I understand." He smiled at her and added, "All the more pie for me then, eh?"

Faris giggled. "Yes, sire."

Faris's smile did not retreat from her countenance once she was gone from Lochlan's presence. Rather it lingered, along with the thought of his boyish manner in devouring an entire pie when being so vexed. Even as uneasiness whispered to her heart—uneasiness at having allowed Lochlan Rockrimmon to believe her heart was captured by the dashing Bainbridge Graybeau—even then her smile lingered at the thought of her young master and his passion for pastry.

His kiss was that fashioned of passion administered by perfect, masculine means. His powerful arms held her tightly against the strength of his warm body. In her dreams, Faris could not draw breath, for his kiss was so entirely unassailable as to nearly suffocate her. But what a joyous suffocation it was! Her mouth watered, unable to quench its thirst for him, unable to satisfy the want of his kiss.

The Highwayman of Tanglewood owned her— mind, heart, body, and soul he owned her. The warm moisture of his mouth was ambrosia to her senses, the sheer power of him magnificent!

All of a sudden, however, he began to transform. His mustache and goatee vanished. Still, she kissed him, reveled in the feel of his mouth on her throat, of his hands at her waist. She placed her hands at the back of his neck, let her fingers travel through his hair until she felt the knot of his mask at the back of his head.

"Go on, lass," the Highwayman whispered. "Strip me of the mask that hides me from ye. Look upon me with fresh eyes, fair Faris of Loch Loland Castle," he coaxed, his warm lips hovering a breath from her own.

Apprehension overwhelmed her. She began to tremble even as she grasped the knot of the mask in one hand.

"Who do ya wish to find beneath me mask, fair Faris?" the Highwayman asked. "Who do ya wish was holdin' ya now? Who do ya wish yar lover to be? Stablemaster, farmer, or lord of the manor?" Faris shook her head, began trembling. Inhaling a long, deep breath, she stripped the mask from the Highwayman's head.

Her breathing stopped, and her heart nearly

stopped as well, as she beheld the unmasked face of the Highwayman of Tanglewood to be . . .

"No!" she cried out, sitting up in her bed. Her face was awash with perspiration, her heart hammering, uncomfortably pent up in her chest. "No!" she repeated in a whisper.

She threw her bedding aside and fairly leapt from her bed and to her washbasin. Splashing cold water on her face, she squeezed her eyes tightly shut and tried to recall the moment before her dream had ended. Nearly her dreams had revealed her deepest desire to her—the true identity of the Highwayman of Tanglewood. Yet something had intruded, halted her mind from revealing her heart's deepest desire to her. Something in her feared the knowledge; something in her protected her from the truth. But why?

"What is the matter with me?" she cried in a whisper.

"Faris! Faris!" came Sarah's voice as she knocked the bedchamber door.

Shaking her head to dispel her frustration and disappointment, Faris opened the door and Sarah stepped in.

"Faris! Are you well? You have overslept, and the hour is late of morning. Master Lochlan has requested you attend him at once! Lady Stringham and her daughter are to arrive this very afternoon, and no doubt he has special instructions for you. You must ready yourself quickly, for he wants to see you in the east library at once," the girl babbled.

"This afternoon?" Faris asked. "Were we not to have near a week before—"

"Milady is very upset and put off," Sarah interrupted. "She received word only an hour ago of Lady Stringham's intended arrival. A great lacking of decorum, if you ask me. Yet we none of us have ever favored her. Therefore, we expect nothing less than the least of her."

Faris's heart was still racing from her dream. "I cannot possibly appear before him so quickly!" she told Sarah. "I-I have only just awakened, and I—"

"You most certainly can possibly!" Sarah exclaimed. "Quickly! I will help you."

Faris closed her eyes for a moment, trying to calm herself, trying to order her thoughts.

"Quickly, Faris!" Sarah said. "Master Lochlan is in a terrible temper! Surely none of us know why—yet he is, and that is that."

"Very well," Faris said, grateful for Sarah's help.

She was trembling yet. The anxiety washing over her because of the dream was near to overwhelming. Further, the Highwayman's words, the question he had posed in her dream, kept ringing in her ears.

Who do ya wish to find beneath me mask, fair

Faris? he had asked of her. *Who do ya wish was holdin' ya now? Who do ya wish yar lover to be? Stablemaster, farmer, or lord of the manor?*

Who did she wish him to be? Her heart and mind were fevered with the question. Yet chances were he was no one of acquaintance to her. Chances were he was not Bainbridge Graybeau, Lord Gawain Kendrick, or any other man she owned a knowledge of. Still, something in her soul whispered she did know him—her very blood ran hot with affirmation.

"Quick as a mouse, Faris!" Sarah said. "Master Lochlan is waiting."

"Lady Stringham and her daughter are to arrive this afternoon, Faris," Lochlan Rockrimmon said as Faris entered the library. He did not look up, only continued to furiously write on a piece of parchment on the desk near the window in his father's study. Faris's heart was pounding so brutally she could hear it in her own ears. She wondered—did it hammer so wildly due to fear of being found oversleeping or from the exhilaration of being in Lochlan Rockrimmon's presence?

"As I understand, sire," Faris said, hoping her face was bright and void of signs of only just awakening.

"My mother has told you that you will be assisting them with their needs while they are

265

here, has she not?" he asked, still writing.

"Yes, sire," Faris admitted. She did not wish to assist them for some reason. Yet she would, for Lady Rockrimmon had asked her to do so.

"I am loath to give you up from my chamber, but you are Mother's favorite, and our guests should be the benefactresses of such."

"Thank you, sire," Faris said. Suddenly, she was even more unsettled—abhorrent to think of serving the young woman who may soon fare as Lochlan's choice of a bride.

"There is more," Lochlan said, finally looking up at her. His green eyes seemed to sear her flesh, for she felt overly warm.

Faris's heart began to thump with fear. Had he known of her slothfulness in oversleeping? Had he spoken with Bainbridge and discovered her deception of the night before?

"My father is away this very day—business in a neighboring township," he explained. "This leaves his local business to me and—and I'm afraid I am not eager about what must transpire here today."

"Sire?" Faris said, uncertain as to what Lochlan Rockrimmon's business could possibly have to do with her.

"Father has purchased more land from Tremeshton," he said.

Faris's innards instantly began to churn.

"He and I will be meeting to sign papers of

transference. I have promised my father that I will not kill him nor beat him—if it can be avoided. Father wants to acquire as much land from Tremeshton as possible. The blackguard must be desperate indeed if he is willing to sell more lands to a man who had thrown him out on his ear. Yet he wrote to my father of his desire to sell, and my father cannot refuse. Good men and women tenant on those lands, and Father is anxious to see them out from under Tremeshton's thumb."

"It is a good thing, to be sure, sire," Faris said. Yet she was confused as to why Lochlan Rockrimmon would inform her of such goings-on. If Kade Tremeshton was never to enter the doors at Loch Loland again, why then did it concern her in the least?

"You are wondering why I have chosen to tell you of such business when Father has forbade Tremeshton to enter Loch Loland," Lochlan said.

Faris felt her eyebrows arch, astonished by his understanding. "Y-yes, sire," she stammered.

"I plan to tell him I have had you," Lochlan said. Slowly his eyes narrowed, their angered intensity glowing green and bright.

"I-I beg your pardon, sire?" Faris whispered.

"Father has demanded I not kill him, not best him—unless provoked, of course," he said. "I will be in receipt of the parchments giving my father claim to his lands, and then I will tell him of the pleasure of the sweet confections of your mouth." The broad expanse of his shoulders shrugged in a boyish gesture as he added, "It will then be up to him—whether he slinks home with his tail between his legs or whether he chooses to have his face further bloodied—or his very guts run through, for that matter."

"Sire, no!" Faris gasped. "You must not provoke him simply for the sake of—"

"He is a dog, Faris!" Lochlan growled, slamming a powerful fist to the top of the desk before him. "He is the ruination of innocence, the torturer of good labor, the very tormentor of morality."

"But, sire, surely," Faris began. "Surely you may leave such dangerous deeds to others." Panic had begun to rise in her—fear for Lochlan Rockrimmon's safety. Oh, it was certain Lochlan could ever best Kade Tremeshton, just as it was certain the Highwayman of Tanglewood could do so. Yet Kade was cowardly. Had he not striven to ambush the Highwayman? No doubt he would sink no less to see the great Lochlan Rockrimmon beaten.

"You speak of the Highwayman of Tanglewood," Lochlan growled. "Yet twice he has bested Kade Tremeshton, and what good has it done? Tremeshton yet continues to spread misery and ruination. It is time someone who does not hide behind a mask bested him—entirely. Better to savor the fruit of provocation than to remain standing idle."

"Sire, surely—" Faris began.

"I only tell you of this so that you may be wary, Faris," Lochlan interrupted. "Kade Tremeshton is a snake, and he has not forgotten his desire for you. If I best him, he may leave you be at last; he may discontinue his ill treatment of his remaining tenants. Likewise, he may not."

"Sire, only allow time," Faris said. "The Highwayman of Tanglewood will best Lord Tremeshton once and for all. In time he will. I only beg you to allow—"

"To allow a true man to deal with Tremeshton. Is that what you mean to tell me, Faris?" Lochlan asked. "You think me weak—think my debating and political position are worthless in this battle against tyranny."

"Of—of course not, sire," Faris stammered. "I only mean to keep you from harm's way and—"

"And allow others to withstand abuse instead," he finished.

"No, sire. You misunderstand me. I . . ." Faris began. She was near awash with panic! Perspiration warmed her temples. Fear for Lochlan Rockrimmon's well-being had gripped her entirely.

"Enough," Lochlan said. "I ride to retrieve the parchments for my father. You will attend Lady Stringham and her daughter, and you will be wary, lest Kade Tremeshton has not purged you from his wanton mind. That is all the instruction I have for you."

"Y-yes, sire," Faris stammered.

"And then why don't you find an hour or two for some extra rest? You look as if you've been burning the candle at both ends," he grumbled.

"Y-y-yes, sire," she said, anxious to escape.

"Thank you, Faris," he said, signaling her dismissal.

"Thank you, sire," she mumbled as she turned, fleeing from his presence.

He knew! She had no doubt he knew! He knew she'd overslept, and no doubt the fact caused his suspicions about why. For a moment, she panicked—did he know of her dreams as well? Could he guess at them too? And what of his plans to provoke Lord Tremeshton? Had he run mad? What would possess him to endeavor to such a thing? Oh, certainly he loathed Kade Tremeshton—yet more than any other of his acquaintance did?

Her heart was pounding—frantic with panic. Oh, how she wished she could speak to the Highwayman, warn him of Lochlan's intention, that the Highwayman of Tanglewood may ride to his defense.

Faris put a hand to her temple. Send her beloved Highwayman to fight Kade Tremeshton in Lochlan Rockrimmon's place? Had she now run mad? To put her beloved in danger in order that her master might be protected—it was the thinking of a mad woman. Yet Faris knew well the Highwayman of Tanglewood could easily best Kade Tremeshton. She did not know so well that Lochlan Rockrimmon could. She thought of the deep cut on Lochlan's forehead—the one she had only just seen upon talking with him. The Highwayman had triumphed unscathed each time he had bested Kade Tremeshton. Lochlan Rockrimmon had not been so fortunate, and she was fearful for his safety. How she wished she could advise her beloved Highwayman of Lochlan's intent. She shook her head—hopeless.

And yet—Bainbridge! What if she were to tell Bainbridge Graybeau of Lochlan's plan to provoke Lord Tremeshton? If Bainbridge were, indeed, the Highwayman of Tanglewood, then her fears might be put to rest where Lochlan's well-being was concerned. If Bainbridge was not the Highwayman, however . . . yet was not it better to try?

She would go to him! At once! She would go to the stables and seek Bainbridge Graybeau's help. Highwayman or not, she knew he held a great regard and caring for his young master.

As Faris hurried to the stables, her mind whirled with thoughts and considerations. Was Bainbridge Graybeau the Highwayman of Tanglewood? How desperately she wished the Highwayman were free to reveal his identity to her, to love her completely and thoroughly. Oh, how she wished she could accompany him during his tasks, run away with him, never to return to Loch Loland Castle. She wondered in that moment if he would take her to wife if he were free. Did he love her enough to spend his life with her? She would gladly marry him, live with him anywhere they chose. The thought of having his children made her smile, but her smile faded when in the next instance she thought of Lady Stringham's daughter bearing Lochlan Rockrimmon's children. It angered her, and she knew not why. She had not even met the young woman. Perhaps she would be a proper and good choice for Lochlan. Still, it bothered her—suddenly ate at her mind like an illness.

Certainly she just felt protective of her young master, she mused. The way he did of her—after all, he had warned her of his intent to provoke Kade Tremeshton, championed her once before in the loathsome man's presence. She thought of the kiss Lochlan had forced upon her, of his licking his fork after having fed her a piece of his pie. Would Lady Stringham's daughter appreciate his chivalry, his compassion to a lowly chambermaid? From what she had thus far heard of the girl, she thought not.

Reaching the stables, Faris searched for Bainbridge. Yet none knew where to find him. He was not with Jovan, for Jovan was stabled. None of the stablemen knew where to find him, and panic gripped Faris once more. Lochlan Rockrimmon meant to provoke Kade Tremeshton, and it seemed there would be no Highwayman of Tanglewood, nor able stablemaster, to aid him.

Faris returned to the house, anxiety holding her in its terrible grip. Silently she prayed for aid—divine intervention that Lochlan Rockrimmon would not be harmed—that he would change his mind and choose not to provoke Kade Tremeshton.

"Quickly, Faris! They have arrived already," Old Joseph said, catching hold of Faris's arm as she entered through the kitchen servants' door.

"Lady Stringham? Already?" Faris asked, smoothing her apron and straightening her cap. She hoped her anxiety was not too apparent in her countenance.

"In rather a hurry to catch her daughter a good husband, I suspect," Old Joseph whispered. "Quickly! We must be present in the main hall."

"Have . . . have you seen Mr. Graybeau, Joseph?" Faris asked.

"Bainbridge?" Old Joseph asked. "Busy tending to Lady and Miss Stringham's coach, I suspect. He is not expected to appear as are we, Faris."

"Of—of course," Faris stammered.

Awash with anxiety and fear, frustration, and

trepidation, Faris endeavored to appear composed. Standing shoulder to shoulder with the other servants of Loch Loland Castle, she waited—waited as Lady May Stringham and her daughter were ushered into the main hall—waited as Lochlan Rockrimmon, heir to the title and heir to Loch Loland Castle itself, rode out to provoke Lord Kade Tremeshton.

In the Broad
Light of Day

"Let us be at our best," Lady Rockrimmon said, as she and Lillias entered from an adjoining room. "No matter who has descended upon Loch Loland—let us be at our best."

"Yes, milady," Faris said in unison with the others serving at Loch Loland Castle.

"I do not envy you, Faris," Lillias whispered aside to Faris. "I do not know if I could endure assisting Tannis Stringham at anything at all—even for one moment!"

Faris bit her lip to stifle a smile, studying Lady Stringham and her daughter as they entered. Tannis Stringham was indeed a rare beauty. It was impossible to deny the fact of it. Her hair was as black as ebony, her eyes as blue as the sky. Her form of figure was exquisite and her height perfect for a man of Lochlan's stature—for she was taller than most young women, and it gave her a look of exceptional grace.

"May," Lady Rockrimmon greeted, embracing Lady Stringham. Faris thought her greeting somewhat less than enthusiastic. "How kind of you to come." The ladies exchanged cheek kisses—as did the daughters. "And, Tannis—"

Lady Rockrimmon said, turning her attention to the daughter. "My, how lovely!"

"Yes, milady," Tannis said. "And may I congratulate Lillias on her betrothal to the dashing Lord Kendrick."

"Thank you, Tannis," Lillias said, forcing a smile. "We are quiet impatient to be wed."

"So says any and all tittle-tattle," Tannis mumbled.

Faris frowned. What a tart! To make such an insinuative remark was intolerable. Yet Lillias bore it well, feigning ignorance.

"These are they who keep Loch Loland Castle in such good repair," Lady Rockrimmon said, motioning to the servants standing behind her.

Lady Stringham and Tannis nodded a greeting, and all the male servants bowed, while the female servants curtsied in unison.

"We would be nothing without our Loch Loland friends," Lady Rockrimmon answered.

Faris did not miss the puzzled, disapproving expression on the faces of both Lady Stringham and her daughter. The arrogance of nobility was thick in them, and they did not take to such compliments of servants—this was obvious.

"Oh! And this is Faris," Lady Rockrimmon said, gesturing to Faris.

Faris stepped forward, curtsied to Lady Stringham, and said, "Milady." She then nodded to Tannis and said, "Miss Stringham."

"I am allowing Faris to care for you during your visit to Loch Loland Castle," Lady Rockrimmon explained. "She is Lochlan's own chambermaid, and though he has been very begrudging in agreeing to give her up for a time, he has—for your sakes," Lillias said.

Faris felt the heat rise to her cheeks. Touché! With one simple remark, Lillias had given Tannis a bit of a comeuppance. Faris noticed the instantaneous fading of smiles from both Lady Stringham's and Tannis's faces.

"Dear me, Maranda," Lady Stringham began, "do you really think it wise to have such a pretty little servant so constantly under Lochlan's nose? Do you not worry she may give him cause to—to falter?"

Faris looked away, irritated and embarrassed by the woman's implication.

"Oh, no, not at all," Lady Rockrimmon said. "He may spirit her away to wife—but he would never threaten her virtue."

Faris's own eyes widened in astonishment, and she looked up when she heard Lady Stringham gasp. The woman stood pale, her hand on her bosom. She was as stunned by Lady Rockrimmon's remark as Faris was. More so, even.

"Oh, for pity's sake, May," Lady Rockrimmon laughed. "Have you indeed lost your sense of jest?"

Lady Stringham forced a smile and said, "Oh—oh, of course not, Maranda. You ever manage to astonish me with your witty manner."

Faris did not miss the glower heaped upon her by Tannis Stringham. She had not made any new allies at this meeting. She wondered at Lady Rockrimmon's teasing. She was, however, the parent most like her son, and Faris could well imagine Lochlan making just such an astonishing remark simply to provoke reaction. She wondered then—had he reached his destination? Did he now remark to provoke Kade Tremeshton? She shivered, momentarily overwhelmed with worry.

"You may all go about your—your goings-about," Lady Rockrimmon said to the assembled servants.

Faris forced a smile as Lillias winked at her. If only Lillias knew her brother's intention, she would not be so free from care as she appeared, perhaps.

"My father is away on business, as is Lochlan at the moment," Faris heard Lillias say as she took her leave. "I suppose you will have to suffer through an afternoon of ladies' conversation, Tannis."

"I look forward to it, Lillias dear," Tannis said.

Faris knew she would need to tend to Lady and Tannis Stringham's things immediately—air out their dresses and petticoats, tend to their vanity. Yet she must attempt to seek out Bainbridge once more. She must attempt to send assistance to Lochlan.

Hurrying through the kitchen, she left the house by way of the servants' entrance door. Perhaps Bainbridge had returned to the stables by now. Perhaps she would find him at last! Her heart pounded with anxiety and worry for her young master's welfare as she started toward the stables.

"I see you've met Lochlan's intended."

Faris gasped as none other than Lord Kade Tremeshton himself stepped from behind a large oak growing near the kitchen door.

Panic mingled with relief in Faris—panic at the sudden appearance of the abhorrent man, relief at realizing his presence at Loch Loland meant he was in no way besting Lochlan.

"E-excuse me, Lord Tremeshton," Faris said. She must escape—not only for her own sake but for Lochlan's. She must find Bainbridge. Making to move past him, she said, "I've—I've duties to attend to."

"Duties, is it?" Kade asked, taking hold of her arm. "You had unfinished duties when you quit Tremeshton, did you not?"

"You will release me at once," Faris told him.

She was frightened, for he was indeed a strong man, and there was no Lochlan Rockrimmon wielding a sword nearby this time. Yet, if he attempted to inconvenience her further, she would indeed give a good accounting of herself. She looked at him, studied his bruised and bloodied face, his swollen nose. It would be her mark. Should she need to defend herself from him, she would strike him where Lochlan Rockrimmon had already tenderized his flesh and bone.

"Do not presume to speak to me in such a manner, girl!" he growled. "I am Lord Tremeshton, and you will succumb!"

"Succumb? To you? Unhand me at once or I shall take to screaming!" Faris demanded.

In the next instant, however, Kade Tremeshton twisted her arm, turning her and holding her back against his body. Faris opened her mouth to scream but was silenced when he covered her mouth with his free hand.

"It was foolish—your coming here, leaving Tremeshton Manor," he growled in her ear. "To think you could escape me by running to Maranda Rockrimmon and her pathetic son. Foolish!"

Determined to escape him, Faris reached back over her head with her free arm. Taking hold of his hair in one desperate fist, she pulled as hard as she could, simultaneously stomping on his foot with the heel of her shoe. It was enough to distract him into releasing her, and she ran.

"You will not run from me again, Faris!" he shouted as she pushed against the servants' door and stumbled into the kitchen.

"Mary!" she cried. "Joseph! Help me!" Frantically she glanced about the room. It was empty, and fear gripped her tighter as Kade burst into the room.

"Do not make this so difficult, Faris," he growled. "Do not vex me further. I warn you!"

He would catch her; she knew he would. Still, if she could just make her way back to the great hall, perhaps Lady Rockrimmon and the others would yet be there. Surely Kade would not assault her with Lady Rockrimmon present.

Faris felt the floor come up fast to meet her—felt Kade's strong hand at her ankle. He had tripped her, and she was sent sprawling to the floor. Taking hold of the back of her dress, he pulled her to her feet, trying to grasp her arm. Faris fought him, slapping his hands and face, beating her fists against his solid chest. She managed to hit him square in one eye, and he winced, letting go of her for a moment. A moment was all she needed, and she leapt from his grasp, dashing away once more.

"Milady!" she cried out as she ran. "Milady!" Surely she was close enough to the great hall to be heard. She felt her head jerk back painfully, the villain having caught hold of her hair. "Milady!" she cried as tears escaped her eyes. Instinct told her to remain still—not to struggle for the moment. Thus, she pretended to be completely powerless as Kade took hold of her chin. Surely someone had heard her calling! Surely Lady Rockrimmon had heard her. Old Joseph and the others would find her any moment. Surely they would.

"What a fuss, Faris," Kade said glaring down at her. He released her hair, but held tightly to her chin. His breath reeked of spirits, and Faris thought she might vomit from the smell of it. "All this to avoid a man most woman endeavor to catch? All this to avoid a kiss?" Faris glared at him as he said, "That is correct, Faris—only a kiss. It is all I've ever wanted of you," he lied. As his head descended toward hers, Faris spit at his eyes. He winced, and she managed to pull free of his grasp.

"I would rather die!" she cried out.

"That can well be arranged!" he growled, lunging at her.

Faris was quick and avoided his grasp, running toward the great hall once more. She could see the light streaming in from the large windows of the great hall. A few more steps and perhaps she would be safe. She could not believe she was running—running through the hall of Loch Loland Castle—running from persistent evil in the broad light of day.

"Milady!" she cried, her voice soft, lost with fear and the fatigue of eluding her predator.

She was stopped short of the great hall, however—stopped short of Lady Rockrimmon and rescue—stopped by the powerful arms of Lochlan Rockrimmon himself as he drew her against the security of his strong body. In that brief moment, Faris clung to him, clutching his shirt in her fists and inhaling the protecting scent of him, leather, cedar and mint.

"You bastard!" Lochlan shouted. "Have you no other wish than to die?"

"Stay out of this, Rockrimmon!" Kade growled. "I have unfinished business with this wench!"

Faris heard the gasps of Lady Rockrimmon, Lillias, Lady Stringham, and Tannis as they entered the hallway to find such a scene awaiting them.

"You have unfinished business with *me!*" Lochlan shouted. As gently as was possible in his current state of rage, Lochlan pushed Faris aside, aggressing toward Kade.

"Lochlan!" Lady Rockrimmon cried out the moment her son's powerful fist met with Kade Tremeshton's jaw. "Beat him to a pulp, and throw him out of Loch Loland! Throw him out!" she cried.

Faris stumbled back until she stood against the wall. She could not believe what was transpiring before her! Kade stooped and lunged at Lochlan, catching him around the waist and forcing him backward. Still, Lochlan's fist came down hard several times in the middle of Kade's back, until the villain was forced to release

Lochlan and take several steps back. Lochlan, however, was not satisfied. With brutal force, Lochlan took hold of Kade's hair, bringing the blackguard's head down to meet his raised knee. Kade fell to the floor, writhing in pain, nose bleeding.

"Your life was spared once for trespassing against me and mine!" Lochlan shouted. "And yet I have given my father my word I will not kill you—at least, not this day. Therefore, leave out of my father's house, Tremeshton! And if you ever step foot in it again, I promise your life will not be spared thrice!"

"She is a chambermaid!" Kade panted, pointing to Faris.

"She is *my* chambermaid!" Lochlan growled, violently kicking Kade in the midsection. "And far beyond that," Lochlan said, taking Kade by the collar of his shirt and pulling him to his feet, "she is a woman!"

His final blow to Kade's jaw appeared nearly lethal, and Faris gasped as Lochlan dropped Kade's unconscious body to the floor. Old Joseph and several other male servants arrived. They stood, jaws agape as they looked on.

"Throw him out, Joseph," Lochlan growled. "Literally, throw him out."

"Yes, sire," Old Joseph said. "However, he is unconscious. Shall I leave him on the steps or have someone escort him home?"

"Find his mount and tie him to it. Slap its hind quarters—no doubt the beast will know the path to its filthy home!" Lochlan shouted.

"Faris? Are you all right, darling?" Lady Rockrimmon asked, placing a comforting arm around Faris's shoulders.

"Y-yes, milady," Faris stammered, unable to meet the woman's concerned gaze.

She gasped when Lochlan took hold of her chin, forcing her to look up at him.

"Did he harm you?" he asked. His eyes were narrowed. Their emerald green burned angry, yet flashed with concern as well.

"Not—not permanently, sire," she told him.

Lochlan released a heavy sigh of relief before running his hands through his hair with frustration.

"Father must end any acquaintance with Tremeshton, Mother! Any bartering even for the sake of good intention!" Lochlan growled.

"I-I do not understand his presence here, Loch," Lady Rockrimmon said. "Were you not to meet him in the Tanglewood to receive the papers of entitlement?"

"Indeed," Lochlan said. "And I rode out. Yet he was not there, nor did he arrive in a reasonable amount of time."

"Do you mean to tell us—do you mean to imply it was a farce, Loch? Did he draw you away from Loch Loland for some reason?" Lillias asked.

"Did he draw you away for—for this?" she asked, looking to Faris.

Faris felt her face brim crimson with the hot blush of humiliation as Lochlan looked at her.

"Father is not at Loch Loland this day," Loch said. "Kade well knew where I would be. It would make it easier to—"

"The Highwayman rides this way!" Sarah exclaimed, fairly bursting into the room.

"What?" Lochlan asked.

"The Highwayman of Tanglewood rides this way! To Loch Loland's very steps!" Sarah repeated.

"In the broad light of day?" Lillias asked.

Faris's heart leapt in her bosom! The Highwayman of Tanglewood was at hand! It strengthened her—gave her courage anew!

"It is long I have heard of your Highwayman of Tanglewood," Tannis said. "I will see him for myself before I believe any more of your tales of Tanglewood's thief!"

"As will I," Lady Stringham said.

Faris watched as both women lifted their skirts and made for the great front doors of Loch Loland Castle.

"Oh, where is Gawain?" Lillias said aloud as she followed. "He has ever wished to set eyes on the Highwayman."

Faris stood paralyzed with awed astonishment

as she watched every other soul present hasten toward the grand doors. Yet she—she who already knew of certain he was genuine—she could not move.

"Are you well, Faris?" Lochlan asked. "Indeed—are you well?"

Startling from her confused and shocked state, Faris looked to him and nodded.

"I-I am well, sire," she said. His eyes still burned emerald with anger.

"I gave my father my word, Faris," he said. "Else I would have run him through for treating you so."

"It—it is of no consequence, sire," Faris stammered. "Pray do not concern yourself so, for I am—"

"He is there! Beyond those trees! Look! There!" Sarah called.

Instantly, Faris's need to see her beloved Highwayman overcame her distress at being assaulted by Kade Tremeshton. She rushed toward the open doors of Loch Loland Castle, followed the others down the massive steps and onto the front walkway.

At the mere sight of him in the distance, her heart leapt! Astride his midnight steed, black cloak billowing in the breeze he shouted, "Lochlan Rockrimmon! 'Twas pinned to a tree in the Tanglewood Forest that I found these parchments!"

Faris smiled. She had never heard his voice raised above a raspy low speech. His angry shouting deepened the intonation of it—strong, demanding, and triumphant was its tone.

Drawing a dagger from his boot, the Highwayman of Tanglewood drove the blade through a set of parchments and into a nearby tree. "They be meant for ye, Rockrimmon!"

At that instant, Kade Tremeshton's mount appeared at a trot—the limp body of Kade Tremeshton draped over the saddle. Old Joseph had not delayed in obeying his young master's orders. Of a sudden, something seemed to startle the horse, and it hastened its pace.

Faris watched, breathless with delight and wonderment as the Highwayman drew his rapier, rearing his steed for a long moment.

"And I thank ye for sendin' the blackguard me way," the Highwayman shouted as he rode out after Kade Tremeshton.

Faris watched the Highwayman ride until she could no longer see him for the thickness of the trees. Her heart was lightened as she thought of their pending rendezvous. Only three days' time and she would be with him again! She smiled, knowing it would be so—knowing Lochlan had returned unscathed—knowing Kade Tremeshton would return to Tremeshton Manor quite thoroughly thwarted.

"Well, I can see you're not at a loss for excitement here at Loch Loland Castle, Maranda," Lady Stringham said.

Faris looked to Lady Stringham and her daughter. Both stood glaring at Faris as if the entire incident were her fault.

"Forgive me, Lady Stringham—Tannis," Lochlan began, running one hand through his hair in an effort to straighten its tousled appearance. "Kade Tremeshton and I have been building toward blows for a very long time. I'm sorry the fact gained summit at the very moment of your arrival."

"Not at all, Lochlan," Tannis said. An entirely bewitching smile spread across her lovely face as she took hold of his arm. "I think it quite chivalrous—your championing your little chambermaid."

"As fate would have it, Kade has harbored an odd obsession with Faris for some time now," Lady Rockrimmon explained.

"I cannot fathom why," Lady Stringham said. "She's a plain enough girl."

Faris took no offense at Lady Stringham's belittling. The woman had earlier made it clear she thought Faris capable of distracting Lochlan and therefore only further endeavored to banish the fact.

"She is lovely, of course," Tannis said, as Lochlan opened his mouth to speak. "I can well see why Kade Tremeshton would fancy her."

"May—may I take my leave, milady?" Faris asked. She wanted only to escape—to tidy her hair, press cool water to her tear-stained cheeks, and most of all flee the cruel, accusing glare of Lady Stringham.

"Are you certain you are unharmed, dear?" Lady Rockrimmon inquired. She brushed a strand of hair from Faris's cheek almost lovingly.

"Yes, milady," Faris mumbled.

"Then by all means, Faris. You may go—still, I want you to rest for the remainder of the day," Lady Rockrimmon said. Her voice was soft, soothing—like that of a mother speaking to a child.

Faris ventured to meet her eyes, smiling with appreciation. Faris turned to go, but she paused as Tannis said, "What's this? Not a word of gratitude and thanks to your champion, miss? How utterly ungrateful."

"It is my fault she was in jeopardy in the first of it," Lochlan said. "She owes me no thanks."

"Th-thank you, sire," Faris stammered, warmed by his kind and rather mischievous grin.

"Would you—as you make to retire, Faris," he began, "would you make certain Mary has my pie made ready by nine this evening?"

Faris could not help but smile, thinking on his passion for pie eaten at various odd hours.

"Of course, sire. I will tell her," Faris assured him.

"Thank you, Faris," he said, still smiling at her. "And be certain to let her know I expect the circumstances of it to be the same as last evening."

Faris was puzzled. Was he indeed implying she should meet him in the kitchen, share his pie with him as she had the previous day?

"Y-yes, sire," she said. "I-I will make sure of it." Faris blushed when he nodded at her, affirming her suspicions.

"I wish you to rest, Faris," Lady Rockrimmon said as Faris took her leave.

"Yes, milady," Faris said as she made her way toward the kitchen.

Of a sudden, she was quite overcome with fatigue. She knew she must look a fright as well. Her struggle with Kade Tremeshton could not possibly have left her any state other than dishevelment. Still, she smiled as she thought of the Highwayman—envisioned his rearing steed, his rapier drawn. He was indeed magnificent to behold! She wished she may have been closer to him, seen him more clearly. She wondered how he had come upon the parchments he had pinned to the tree with the dagger. No doubt the parchments were the documents of entitlement Lochlan had ridden out to obtain. Had Kade Tremeshton pinned them to a tree and then ridden to Loch Loland Castle, knowing no titled man or heir would be present to defend Faris? It seemed this was the case, and Faris shuddered at the realization of his lengths to find her alone and unprotected. Yet the Highwayman of Tanglewood would best him, no doubt! She would not be surprised to hear of Kade's being returned to Tremeshton Manor further bloodied and as bare as the day he was born! She smiled at the thought of his humiliation—sighed with relief at the fact Lochlan Rockrimmon had not tasted the fruit of provocation after all. Indeed, Lochlan was safe, and the Highwayman of Tanglewood would ensure Kade Tremeshton would never think of crossing him or Lochlan again.

Lochlan—her thoughts lingered on him then. How could she meet him in the kitchen? How could she share a pie with him again when her heart, her loyalty, belonged to her Highwayman—her only desire was to be with him once more? Yet how could she decline after all he had done for her? Twice he had championed her against Kade Tremeshton. How could she refuse him the simple request of sharing pie? He asked nothing else of her—expected no thanks other than a simple gesture of sharing pastry.

Collapsing onto her bed, Faris sighed. Overwhelming relief rinsed her with fatigue. Lochlan was safe, and the Highwayman of Tanglewood was well. Yet the thought struck her then—where was Bainbridge? Likewise, where was Lord Kendrick? Ever Lord Kendrick was at Loch

Loland Castle. Unless business kept him away, he was there, ever attentive to Lillias. Yet, today—today when so much had happened, he had not been there. Nor had Bainbridge.

Faris frowned as she turned to her back and stared at the ceiling above her. Was the Highwayman indeed Bainbridge? Bainbridge had not been present when the Highwayman had appeared. Indeed, to appear in the broad light of day—the Highwayman had only done so once before, and it had been Bainbridge Graybeau who had claimed to witness the event. Further, Lord Kendrick had been the sole person to whom Graybeau had confided the incident.

Closing her eyes, Faris called forth the recent vision of the Highwayman of Tanglewood. She could see him—in her mind's eye, she could. There he sat astride his magnificent black, cloak billowing in the breeze. There, just beyond Loch Loland Castle's front lawns, his mount reared as the Highwayman of Tanglewood drew his rapier. Could this have been Bainbridge Graybeau? Faris thought that it could.

Faris trembled slightly as the memory of Kade Tremeshton came to her then. This most recent episode—short though it may have been—had been utterly grueling. Faris fancied her legs ached—her arms as well. She knew, in those moments, she would not have been able to rebuff the monster. Kade Tremeshton may well have triumphed had Lochlan not arrived to her defense. Faris thought of her fear and terror at the hands of Kade Tremeshton—thought of her relief and joy at being gathered into Lochlan Rockrimmon's powerful embrace. He had held her to him for a moment before aggressing on Kade, and Faris remembered scent of him. It had comforted her in a similarity to the manner in which the Highwayman's scent comforted her. Instantly, Faris loathed herself for her comparing thoughts—for her disloyal, deceitful thoughts.

Again she wished she could find her Highwayman at that moment. She determined that if she had been in his presence at that moment, she would no less than beg him to take her away with him. She would pledge her heart, her life to him—to whatever road he was driven to take—to whomever he was. She would swear to follow him anywhere. She determined she would be wife to the Highwayman of Tanglewood or to Bainbridge Graybeau—whichever identity bested him. Yet, in the very same moment, she thought of never seeing Lochlan Rockrimmon. This thought caused an odd aching to take root in her heart, and she scolded her heart for feeling it.

Closing her eyes, Faris determined to find sleep. In sleep she would capture the Highwayman in her dreams. She would dream of him, yes—until the time came to meet Lochlan in the kitchen. Once Lochlan had his fill of pie and Faris was able to convey her gratitude for his chivalry in whatever regard presented itself, she would dream of her beloved Highwayman again.

Slowly she drifted to sleep—the sense of the summer breeze on her face—the sound of the Highwayman's horse galloping across the meadow in her mind's hearing.

"Stripped as the day he was born!" Lillias whispered. "The Highwayman of Tanglewood left not a shred of cloth about Kade the Heinous. Furthermore, he tied his hands atop the pommel, lashed his feet in the stirrups, and bound his mouth!"

"And how came you by these delightful details of Lord Tremeshton's return to Tremeshton Manor, Lillias? Do tell me! You must!" Faris giggled.

"Graybeau was in conversation with a stableman from Tremeshton just an hour ago!" Lillias exclaimed.

"Bainbridge?" Faris asked.

"Yes!" Lillias said. "It seems Bainbridge was out—exercising Jovan—shortly after the Highwayman appeared here. He was riding out on the meadow and came upon a stableman from Tremeshton Manor. It was the Tremeshton stableman who was present when Kade the Heinous's mount returned him."

"Bainbridge was exercising Jovan?" Faris asked.

"Yes," Lillias said. "Why?"

Faris shrugged. "I-I was not sure I had heard you correctly is all." Faris felt a flutter in her bosom. Jovan had been in the stables when Bainbridge was out. Faris had seen Jovan in the stables with her very own eyes—when first she'd gone in search of Bainbridge to inform him of Lochlan's plan to meet Kade and provoke him. Bainbridge had lied! Yet, if he knew of Kade Tremeshton's condition upon his return to Tremeshton Manor, Bainbridge Graybeau was the Highwayman of Tanglewood! He had slipped—made a slight error in his story—and only Faris knew the truth of it! Jovan had been safely stabled while Bainbridge was out riding— riding as the Highwayman of Tanglewood! At last! At last she had proof. Faris smiled, bit her lip attempting to conceal her delight in her own secret knowledge.

"And furthermore," Lillias continued, "when Lochlan retrieved the parchments from the tree the Highwayman had nailed them to using his dagger, they were the documents of entitlement to the property Kade the Heinous had signed over to my father."

"It is as we thought then," Faris whispered.

"Exactly! Kade meant to lure Lochlan from Loch Loland Castle. No doubt so that you would be unguarded."

Faris felt sickened, frightened, awash with

anxiety at the affirmation Kade Tremeshton would go to such lengths to ensure her vulnerability.

"And you should have heard Lady Stringham and Miss Tannis at dinner!" Lillias continued. "On and on they went—on and on concerning their astonishment that Lochlan would so brutalize a titled man over the honor of a chambermaid. You do not think Lochlan truly intends to consider Tannis do you, Faris?"

Another wave of pure nausea washed over Faris at the thought of Lochlan Rockrimmon taking Tannis Stringham to wife.

"I like to think he would not consider her," Faris said. "Yet, why then is she here? If not for the sake of expecting a proposal—why then?"

"Expecting a proposal is far different than receiving one, Faris," Lillias said. Lillias frowned all of a sudden. "You look so tired, darling," she said, placing a loving hand to Faris's cheek. "And after all, why should you not? Such a day! You should retire with haste, Faris—for Lady and the Miss Stringham will arise early, no doubt, and be quite expectant of service."

"I am tired, it is true," Faris admitted. "Yet, I have one—one small attendance to meet before I am found drifting to slumber."

"Then go, my darling friend," Lillias said. She smiled then and whispered, "For I must beg one last kiss from Gawain before he takes his leave of Loch Loland."

"Lord Kendrick is here?" Faris asked. She thought he had been absent from Loch Loland the entirety of the day.

"He arrived only just an hour after we witnessed the Highwayman," Lillias explained. "You should have seen the disappointment of his countenance when we told him we had seen the Highwayman of Tanglewood with our very own eyes. My poor love. He looked just as a little boy disappointed at not receiving a new sword for his birthday." Lillias giggled, quickly kissed Faris on the cheek, and turned to go. "Sleep well, darling! Dream enough dreams of the Highwayman of Tanglewood for us both!"

"I will!" Faris whispered after her.

"Faris."

It was Old Joseph.

"Yes?" Faris asked turning to face him.

"Master Lochlan is on his way to the kitchen and requests that you meet him there momentarily," Old Joseph said. He winked at her with understanding, and Faris blushed. She hoped the tittle-tattle at Loch Loland Castle did not involve their young master favoring his chambermaid.

"Thank you, Joseph," Faris said. Quickly, she fell into step behind him—her heart hammering with something akin to anxiety mingled with excitement.

Following Old Joseph into the kitchen, Faris smiled when she saw a pie and two forks had been laid out on the servants' table. Yet Lochlan was not yet present.

"I will leave you to your pie," Old Joseph said. He nodded and took his leave of the kitchen, leaving Faris all alone with nothing but anticipation.

Faris glanced around the room. It was an inviting place when the day was over—when the bustle of busy cooks had been put to sleep for the day.

She startled when she heard a knock on the servants' entrance door. Had it been locked? It remained ever free of bolting as far as Faris knew—for Old Joseph enjoyed roaming the castle and gardens at night. The kitchen servants' entrance was kept unlocked with no bolt drawn that Old Joseph may enjoy his meanderings.

Going to the door, Faris placed a hand on the large latch. Inhaling a deep breath of courage—for her fear whispered that perhaps Kade Tremeshton had returned to assault her once again—she opened the door.

"Hello?" she called, seeing no one standing on the other side. "Is anyone there?"

"None—save he that would have ye far his own, lass."

Faris was breathless with delight at the sound of his voice. Glancing over her shoulder to ensure no one had yet entered the kitchen, she stepped into the cover of darkness and directly into the waiting arms of the Highwayman of Tanglewood.

Act and Implication

His mouth was hot, moist, and ravenous for want of hers! This Faris knew by the passion of his kiss—the powerful embrace into which he gathered her. All her fear, every shred of anxiety, even the great fatigue she had felt a moment before—all ill feelings had vanished the moment the Highwayman of Tanglewood had taken her in his arms!

"You," she breathed as he broke the seal of their lips for a moment.

"Aye," he whispered. He wasted no more breath in speaking—simply pulled her more tightly against the strength of his body as he endeavored to drink passion from her lips.

Full darkness was upon them as they kissed—yet light and color as bright as any morning sunrise burst forth in Faris's mind! To be held by him, to taste the warm flavor of his mouth—it was magic in quality—enchanting! The sense of his roughly shaven face against her own caused goose bumps to scatter over Faris's entire body. The thought briefly crossed her mind that he donned no mustache and goatee—he was fair clean-shaven. Yet the passion burning between

301

them was fiery and fierce, and the thought was lost to Faris almost as quickly as it had come to her.

He could not quench his thirst for her kiss! As the Highwayman of Tanglewood led passion between him and his beloved Loch Loland chambermaid, he knew he would never have his fill of her—for his fill could never be reached. How he adored her! How he feared for her safety! How furious he had been with Kade Tremeshton! To run the villain through—it had been his first thought. Yet, upon seeing him thrown over the back of his mount, humiliation first seemed the order. Yes, he had heaped humiliation on Kade Tremeshton in plenty! Stripping him bare to his skin, he had tied him upright to his mount, gagged him, and sent the horse trotting for home! Yet now—now as he drank the sweet nourishment that was Faris's kiss—he feared he had been mistaken in letting Tremeshton go so easy.

She melded to him, and the Highwayman of Tanglewood nearly lost all sense of reason at the feel of such succumbing. He must not delay—else he endanger them both. Yet the very act of kissing her was like a wild intoxication—nearly impossible to deny—and he feared it would overtake him entirely should he linger as his heart, soul, and body bade him. With one final savoring of her mouth, he broke the seal of their lips, released his lover, and stepped back into total darkness.

"Me letter?" he asked. "Did ya receive me letter, fair Faris?"

"I did," Faris whispered, still breathless from his attention.

"Then we will meet there—in two nights yet—where the heather runs forever," the Highwayman said.

"Must you go?" Faris asked. She was desperate to stay near to him, desperate to know he wanted to stay near to her. Yet he had come to her. In doing so, he put himself in great peril. It was proof of his caring for her—was it not?

"I have lingered too long, I have," he said. "Yet it was sure I must be that ye are well."

"I am well," Faris said. "I am well in your company."

"Lord Tremeshton has suffered great physical harm and even greater humiliation for what transpired at Loch Loland Castle this day," the Highwayman growled. "Though methinks I should have run him through when I had the chance."

"He does not deserve to die on your blade," Faris whispered. "He is without any honor and therefore not deserving of such an honorable death." Faris smiled as she heard the Highwayman chuckle from his hiding place in the darkness beneath the old oak.

"The day will come, fair Faris of Loch Loland Castle," the Highwayman said.

Faris felt her brow wrinkle with puzzlement. "What day will come, Highwayman?" she asked.

"The day when I will spirit ye, lass," he said. "One day I will spirit ye far me own and cease in sharin' yar attentions with any other."

Faris's heart felt near to bursting with joy—her stomach so full of the feeling of butterflies it took her breath from her bosom!

"Then spirit me now, Highwayman!" she pleaded in a whisper. "Do not leave me again—never leave me again."

"I cannot ye have yet, lass," he said. "But the day will come that I can—and I will. 'Til two nights hence, fair Faris."

She heard the rustle of leaves, the tread of boots on the night grass, and he was gone.

The Highwayman of Tanglewood slipped through the break in the garden wall. He would have her! Neither man nor nature could stop him. Yet he feared what he was, feared Faris's scorn were she to discover his true identity. Still, she was his—he owned her heart—this he read in her kiss. Surely she would not spurn him simply for being what he was born to be. Carefully he made his way. Darkness had become his greatest ally, and he was grateful for its concealing cloak now.

• • •

Faris stepped into the kitchen, closing the door quietly behind her. Her heart yet raced with the excitement of having seen her lover—her lips yet tingled from his kiss! However would she settle into eating pie with her young master when the Highwayman of Tanglewood still lingered in her mind and heart?

She sat down at the table—sat before the pie Mary had left for her and Lochlan. What a trivial thing a pie seemed at that moment. She thought of the Highwayman besting Kade Tremeshton and smiled. Yet had it not been Lochlan Rockrimmon who had bested the beast first? Still, it was the Highwayman of Tanglewood who had heaped such great humiliation on the blackguard, and she was glad.

"Ah, Faris," Lochlan said, startling Faris from her thoughts. "There you are. My apologies for being belated."

"I am sure the pie is glad for a few moments of reprieve before being devoured, sire," Faris said.

Lochlan smiled, and Faris silently scolded herself for the delightful tremble running through her at the sight of him.

Lochlan sat in a chair across the table from Faris and asked, "What is your opinion of Miss Tannis then, Faris?" Faris smiled as he plunged a fork into the center of the pie.

Faris was delighted with his comfortable,

rather boyish manner. She must thank him for his chivalry on her behalf, for her guilt because of his efforts was strong. Still, as she sat across from him, watching him eat from the middle of the pie as was his way, a different sort of guilt battled within her—a guilt in feeling somehow disloyal toward her beloved Highwayman. Oh, how she wished he were with her always. How she wished he would simply spirit her away with him. There would be no reason to be at Loch Loland Castle, no reason to be in the company of the alluring Lochlan Rockrimmon if the Highwayman could only spirit her away.

"M-my opinion, sire?" Faris asked. Suddenly she was conscious of his question and likewise astonished he would inquire it of her.

"Yes, Faris," he said. "Or are you, as yet, too distracted for only having just met with the Highwayman of Tanglewood? He is your lover, I believe. Is he not?"

All breathing that had once begun in Faris's body ceased in its entirety. She felt instead the hot breath of fear as it washed over her. He knew! Lochlan Rockrimmon knew of her meeting with the Highwayman!

"Pray draw breath before you expire, Faris," Lochlan said, plunging his fork into the pie anew. "You have nothing to fear in my knowing—nor does your rogue lover."

"Sire—I-I . . ." Faris stammered. Words would

306

not come to her mind, nor her lips. He knew! He knew, and now Faris's greatest fear was realized—because of her, the Highwayman of Tanglewood was in peril of discovery!

Lochlan waved his fork at her—a gesture she should not be overly distressed. "You have nothing to fear from me, Faris. I will do nothing to endanger either of you. You forget, pretty Faris, the Highwayman and I, we fight on the same battle lines. We fight for many the same purposes," Lochlan said. His emerald eyes narrowed then as he added, "And likewise our desires run to many the same objects."

Faris felt her cheeks blush vermilion. Was his implication to what she understood it to be? Was he implying she was an object of his desire, as she was the object of the Highwayman's?

"Yet he seems the better man than me at every turn, does he not?" Lochlan asked, rather forcing a smile. "He has certainly set Lord Kade Tremeshton to humiliation—far more effective than my pounding him with my fists."

"Sire," Faris began. "How—how did you—"

"How did I know you were the Highwayman of Tanglewood's lover?" he finished for her.

She nodded and watched as he ate another bite of pie. "Yes," she breathed.

"The pie, Faris," he said, pointing to the pastry with his fork. "I cannot possibly finish it all on my own."

Faris frowned, nodded slightly, and pressed her fork into the pie.

"I suspected as much the night you arrived at the servants' entrance here with quite the look of a woman seduced—for Graybeau had only just told me he had seen the Highwayman of Tanglewood riding away from Loch Loland Castle mere minutes before," he said. "And I saw the expression on your lovely face this day, when the Highwayman rode to Loch Loland to deliver the parchments Tremeshton had left pinned to a tree. Your face was simply illuminate with resplendent bliss. Further," he continued, "further, how often have you known me to be tardy in arriving for a meeting with anyone?"

"N-never, sire," Faris stammered. And it was true. Lochlan Rockrimmon was known for his promptness in character.

"Exactly," he said, pointing his fork at her. "Therefore, I tell you—I was not tardy for our pie-meeting this evening. I arrived in this very spot just in time to see the man dressed in black pull you from the door and into his arms."

"S-sire, please," Faris began to beg, "I am ever so grateful for your intervention on my behalf where Lord Tremeshton is concerned—for both instances when you—"

"Your secret is safe with me, Faris," he interrupted. "This I promise you. I would in no way endanger my ally the Highwayman of Tanglewood, nor would I endanger you. If you are not sure of that fact by now, then I suppose my besting of Kade Tremeshton in your defense is of no consequence."

"No, sire! It is of every consequence!" Faris exclaimed. "I can never repay you such a debt. Nor can I repay you for the debt of your silence where the Highwayman of Tanglewood is concerned—where his meeting with me is concerned."

"Do you think it is Bainbridge Graybeau who rides as the Highwayman of Tanglewood?" he asked, pressing his fork into the pie before him.

"Sire?" Faris asked.

"Do you think the Highwayman could, in truth, be Graybeau?" he asked again. "I have thought for some time that he could well be. Of course, perhaps you already know the truth. Perhaps this is the reason Graybeau teaches you to ride—that the two of you may meet in daylight instead of only at night."

"I-I confess, sire—I do not know the High-wayman's true identity," Faris said. She was not lying—truly she did not know assuredly. Though Jovan's presence in the stables when Graybeau claimed to be exercising him . . . it was evidence, was it not?

"But you suspect Graybeau, do you not? Joseph tells me you were quite determined to find him today—just after I left to meet Tremeshton.

He says a young stableboy said you were quite frantic in your search for him. Could it be that you suspect Graybeau of being the Highwayman of Tanglewood and meant to send him to aid me?"

His understanding was uncanny!

"Why else would you seek out Graybeau with such intensity? The Highwayman of Tanglewood stands as your lover. Therefore, you would have no great need of Graybeau, no great confidence in his ability to aid me, unless you suspect him of being the Highwayman as well," Lochlan said.

"Sire, I am fearful beyond understanding at your knowledge of my—" Faris began.

"No wonder you are so indifferent to me," he chuckled then. "Where ranks an heir to title and wealth when a rogue lover awaits at nightfall, eh?"

"But, sire," Faris began, "I am not indifferent to you in the least of it."

"Fear not, Faris," he said. "We all have our secrets. I have secrets where lovers are concerned myself. We all of us do." He leaned forward, the emerald of his eyes burning into the dark depths of her own. "And I will keep yours, Faris. Do not worry."

"B-but, sire—" Faris stammered. She was disturbed—disturbed by his reference to having secrets of his own where lovers were concerned.

"Now," Lochlan interrupted. "I am still awaiting your opinion of Miss Stringham. Pray eat your portion of the pie, Faris, and tell me your thoughts as you do so."

Faris's mind still whirled with confusion, fear, and residual astonishment. He knew! Lochlan Rockrimmon knew of Faris's connection to the Highwayman of Tanglewood. Yet he seemed no more disturbed by the knowledge than if he'd only discovered the pie before them encased apples rather than berries.

"Your opinion, Faris," he said. "I am in earnest in wanting to hear it."

"I-I am not entirely certain as to your meaning, sire," she stammered. Her body yet trembled, yet unsettled by the fact someone knew of her twilight lover. Still, she would endeavor to answer him—to distract him to other venues of thought. "D-do you mean my opinion in regard to her appearance, sire? For if that is what you wish to know, then I cannot deny she is one of the most beautiful women I have ever seen."

"Oh, but that is an easy opinion to form," he said, pointing at her with his fork. "A person can look upon *you* and form such an easy opinion as well."

Faris blushed and could not subdue the rising gladness in her at the compliment. Such a delight fairly overtook her lingering fear.

"However, there is much more to be considered

here," he continued, "at least from where I am standing."

Blush and thrill turned to sickness and fear in Faris once more, for there it was—his admission he was considering her as a wife. Faris considered screaming—considered reaching out and taking hold of his handsome, squared jaw and begging, *No! She is no good for you! She does not deserve to be your wife!*

Instead, she simply swallowed hard, shrugged her shoulders, and said, "I cannot say, sire, for I do not know her well. I have only just this day seen her—met her for the first time."

"Yet what *do* you know, Faris?" he asked. "Be truthful—for I will know if you are answering false to your true feelings."

Faris inhaled and exhaled deeply, taking a bite of the pie when he gestured she should do so. "I-I do not care for her mother. I will confess it, sire," she said.

"Why?" he asked. "Having only just met her this very day, what brings you to such a final conclusion?"

Faris looked to Lochlan. There was something in his countenance. She suspected he held the same feelings toward Lady Stringham. But why?

"She—she seems arrogant and unkind, I think—spiteful and easily envious. She envies your mother, it is clear. It is why she questioned her about my assignment to your chambers," she told him.

"Did she? When did she question it?" he asked, a frown puckering his brow.

"When first they arrived—Lady Stringham and Miss Tannis," Faris told him. "We . . . all of the servants . . . were gathered in the great hall. It must've been while you were—were seeing to your business duties with Lord Tremeshton."

"You may refer to him as 'the rodent,' Faris," he instructed, "for he deserves no other title."

Faris smiled, amused by his wit. She thought of Lillias's title for Lord Tremeshton—Kade the Heinous. She was delighted to see another similarity between her dear friend and her young master. Further, it seemed his mind had entirely shifted its venue. She was certain he had all but forgotten about the Highwayman of Tanglewood and his connection to a chambermaid at Loch Loland Castle.

"Go on, Faris," he urged, eating more pie. "Tell me more of this."

"We were gathered in the great hall to greet Lady Stringham and her daughter, and she—she asked your mother if it was wise to . . . to . . ." Faris stammered, unable to speak to him of what had transpired. It would seem somehow vain to repeat it herself.

"Go on," he urged.

"She questioned your mother, asking was it

313

wise for you to have a chambermaid who . . . who . . ."

"A beauty of a chambermaid who might drive me to distraction? To immoral acts the like committed by Kade Tremeshton?" he finished for her.

"Something the like of it, yes, sire," Faris admitted.

"Hmmm. Interesting," he said smiling. "And what was my mother's response to the implication?"

"Your mother reassured her, of course. We all know you are not capable of such behavior." Faris took another bite of pie.

"Do we?" he chuckled.

"Yes, we do," she said, returning his smile.

"I am glad to hear you have such unwavering faith in me, Faris," he said. "Still, I am awaiting your opinion on Miss Tannis."

Faris paused. She did not like Tannis Stringham. Yet her feelings were not sorted even in herself. She could not fathom whether she disliked the girl simply because she was not likeable—or whether she disliked Tannis Stringham because it was assumed Lochlan meant to take her to wife.

"I think her a younger version of her mother— in face, figure, and character," Faris admitted at last.

"You think she wants to marry me for my wealth and title?" he offered.

"In truth, sire—mostly."

"Mostly?"

"I am certain she finds you an attractive choice all around, sire," Faris told him.

"Flattery. I like it," he chuckled. "But would you like to know a secret, Faris?" he asked her, lowering his voice.

"It depends, sire," she answered.

"On what does it depend, Faris?" he asked, amused.

"On the nature of the secret, sire," she told him.

"Meaning—if I am to tell you I intend to take Miss Tannis to wife—"

"Then I do not wish to know it, sire," she blurted out.

"I see," he said, his eyes narrowing as he looked at her. "Still, what if my secret were this: that the only reason Lady Stringham and her daughter are here is because Tannis pestered me near to madness until I offered an invitation."

Faris was startled by the leap of her heart, the light feeling in her veins, and the smile spread across her face. "Truly, sire?" she could not keep from asking.

"Truly, Faris," he said, smiling at her. "I could no more take Tannis Stringham to wife than I could her giddy aunt!"

Faris bit her lip to keep her delighted smile from bursting into delighted giggles.

"You have no understanding of how it eases my mind, sire," she admitted. "We would all be loath to see her as the young mistress, Master Lochlan."

He laughed and enjoyed a bite of pie. His eyes lingered on her, seeming to consider her. "Speaking of mistresses," he said, lowering his voice, "I *am* sorry Tremeshton has had such designs on you—that he stalks you—causes you to be fearful and unhappy."

Faris frowned, unsettled and suddenly miserable at the mention of Kade's name.

"He would be brazen indeed to appear anywhere near Loch Loland again, sire."

"Indeed," Lochlan said. "Still, I would beg you to be wary. Especially if you have occasion to be away from the house—alone."

"You need not worry, sire," she told him. "For if I am away from the house—"

"You are with your Highwayman and not alone," he finished for her.

"Yes, sire," she said, wishing her Highwayman would walk through the door at that moment and spirit her away.

"How I envy him," Lochlan said.

Faris looked at him, startled. Surely he could not mean he envied the Highwayman because of his liaison with her? But his next words both relieved and disappointed.

"Riding across the countryside, besting the boastful, cruel, and greedy. Bringing joy to those so in need of it. How free he must feel."

"I am not certain freedom is his full feeling," Faris said.

"Is it yours?" he asked.

"No and yes," she said. "He is not free to be with me, which fact makes me a prisoner. And he is not free to wander unmasked, which fact makes him a prisoner. Still, your mother bringing me here—it did free me in many ways. So I am both free and not free."

"He has your heart completely, doesn't he?" he asked unexpectedly. "And why not!" he said when she did not respond. "He is a legend—a living hero in the flesh."

Faris smiled, thinking of Lochlan's championing her—lingering thoughts of the possessive kiss he had forced on her the night in the sewing room. Had not such protective deeds, such a rogue's kiss, been rather that of a hero in its own fashion? Had not his besting Kade Tremeshton twice at Loch Loland Castle shown him to be brave, chivalrous, and a champion in his own right?

"He is a hero, sire—as are you," she told him.

"Flattery!" he said, plunging his fork into the pie once more. "I like it."

Faris smiled and ate from the pie. She could trust in him—this she knew with every shred of her being. Lochlan Rockrimmon would not betray her, nor would he betray the Highwayman of Tanglewood.

"Do you know, Faris," he began, "this is the most delicious pie Mary has ever placed before me."

"It is delicious, sire," she agreed.

"Yes," he said. "I imagine your kiss to be the same—your freely given kiss, that is—the like kiss you bless the Highwayman with, not the kiss I stole from you for vengeance and desire's sake in the sewing room some nights past."

"I beg your pardon, sire?" Faris whispered, coughing as she attempted to keep from choking on her pie. Could she have heard him correctly? Surely not.

He smiled and chuckled. "The first bite of this pie—you remember it, do you not? The very moment the sweetened berries touched your tongue, the manner in which moisture flooded your mouth and all you could think of was tasting that sweet flavor again. That is what I imagine the effect of your kiss to be, Faris. For my mouth warms and waters each time I imagine your own blending warm and moist against mine."

Faris sat awed, stunned into silence by his implication—rather his pure assertion.

"Sire," she whispered. "You only endeavor to tease me."

His smile broadened. "But what is it about rogues? Women beg to belong to them. Yet take a simple man—a man such as myself—and they find nothing worthy of belonging to."

318

Faris relaxed then. He was teasing. "You are no simple man, sire. And you *are* teasing me," Faris said. She smiled as he did. He was a terrible tease—a jester in his own right.

"Yes, yes," he said. "For, in truth, I am glad you have your Highwayman of Tanglewood." He stood then, tossing his fork into the half-eaten pie and striding around the table until he stood near to her. He leaned toward her and spoke quietly into her ear then, "Yet there is something you should know, Faris."

"And what is that, sire?" she asked. She tried to ignore the goose bumps rippling over her flesh—tried to ignore the mad hammering of her heart.

"You should understand well my implication—that were it not for trepidation of provoking the Highwayman of Tanglewood," he began, "I would have already taken your mouth to mine—blending the two in such a rich, moist, and heated kiss as to have stripped the memory of any man from your mind forever—even that of your dashing and heroic rogue lover."

Faris swallowed the excess moisture flooding her mouth—silently demanding her body to cease in trembling with residual delight. What was amiss in her? She loved the Highwayman—truly and wholeheartedly she loved him! Why then could Lochlan Rockrimmon evoke such stirring emotions, such blatant desires in her?

"However, I have no desire to be strapped

naked to my horse and sent galloping for home," Lochlan said. "Therefore, I will concede—for now. Good night, Faris. My regards to Bainbridge—if you please."

Faris sat trembling, fork in hand. Every part of her body trembled, every inch of the surface of her flesh tingling with goose bumps. And yet disappointment flooded her as well—disappointment in sure knowledge she had only just gained concerning herself. Had she not already been in love with the Highwayman of Tanglewood, she would have most assuredly been in love with Lochlan Rockrimmon. She was not stronger than any other chambermaid ever to have walked the earth. In fact, she suspected she was weaker than some.

Self-loathing the like she could never have imagined overtook her. With one such as the Highwayman in her soul, how could she allow Lochlan Rockrimmon to so affect her? She was weak, disloyal, with a traitorous heart! To think of Lochlan when she had already pledged her heart to the Highwayman of Tanglewood—how could it be?

It was his championing of her. This is what she determined. Her soul did not threaten to love Lochlan as it did the Highwayman— only it endeavored to feel indebted to him for his chivalry in championing her against Kade Tremeshton. That was it. Of assurance it was!

She felt nothing more than gratitude toward Lochlan Rockrimmon—indebtedness. She loved the Highwayman! Yet, as she looked at the abandoned pie before her—as her mouth began to moisten at the thought of Lochlan's kiss in the sewing room—she began to weep. She felt it then—the tearing of her heart—the confusion of her mind.

Pushing her chair from the table, she dashed to the kitchen door—dashed out through it and into the night. Perhaps Bainbridge was yet awake. Perhaps he would reveal himself as the Highwayman—if she begged him to, appealed to his sense of desire and passion, perhaps he would reveal. And if he did, then Faris knew she could be saved. To have a face to put with her lover—to know he was near to her—it would save her heart, mend it into one piece again. She knew it would!

An Uncertain Heart

The night was warm and fragrant. As Faris approached the stables, she silently prayed for Graybeau's waking presence there. She must know! This very night she must know whether or not Bainbridge Graybeau was, indeed, the Highwayman of Tanglewood. If it were true—if Bainbridge were he whom she loved in the amethyst of sunsets—then all would be well. If Bainbridge were the Highwayman of Tanglewood, she could rest and find easement of mind in knowing he was ever near to her.

However, if Bainbridge were not the Highwayman—what then? This thought frightened Faris, for there was another her consciousness yet suspected. In the deepest corners of her mind, Faris yet wondered if Lord Gawain Kendrick rode out as the Highwayman of Tanglewood. It was uncanny—his absence ever coinciding with the appearances of the Highwayman. Yet the Highwayman had assured her he was not meant for another—that he was not one to toy with Faris one moment and play Lillias's lover the next.

Certainly there was every possibility the Highwayman of Tanglewood was a man entirely unknown to anyone at Loch Loland Castle, including Faris. Perhaps he was the son of an ill-treated tenant farmer or a simple merchant from the village. Yet Faris's heart whispered differently: she knew him in daylight as she did in the amethyst of sunset.

She would seek him in the stables first. Everyone at Loch Loland knew Bainbridge Graybeau often lingered far into the night in caring for the horses at the castle stables. Perhaps she would have no need of endeavoring to raise him from his quarters.

Quietly, Faris entered the stables. Lady Violet whinnied at the sight of her, and Faris patted the animal's velvet nose as she passed. Her heart leapt as she saw him then, just outside Jovan's stall. Graybeau was there—and alone.

"Mr. Bainbridge?" she ventured. She fancied her softened voice sounded louder than she would have preferred in the quiet of the night-cloaked stables.

Bainbridge seemed startled as he quickly looked at her—as if he had been found going about something he did not wish to be found going about. How handsome he was! His dark hair seemed akin to the night, his dark eyes complemented by the light of the stars.

"Miss Faris," he greeted then. "What brings you to the stables at such an hour?"

Swallowing the anxious lump in her throat,

Faris walked toward him. Would he tell her the truth? Indeed, would he? Had he only just returned from meeting her outside the kitchen door? Had he only just finished changing from the black attire of the Highwayman of Tanglewood and into that of Bainbridge the stablemaster?

"I must know the truth, Bainbridge," she said as she approached.

"The truth?" he asked.

Yet she thought his expression was rather that of apprehension.

"Yes," Faris said upon reaching the place where he stood. "I can no longer bear not knowing! I must know whether you are he whom I love or whether you are not."

"He whom you—whom you love, miss?" Bainbridge stammered.

Faris smiled. He was indeed undone. She was certain of the truth of it then—Bainbridge Graybeau was the Highwayman of Tanglewood!

"You are he, are you not?" she asked, taking hold of his arm. To touch him unmasked at last—it was enchanting! "I will not betray your secret, Bainbridge—our secret. Surely you know I am trustworthy in that. Please confess to me now—you are the Highwayman of Tanglewood."

Faris watched him, studied his expression as he straightened, inhaling a deep breath.

"Faris," he began, "You must understand that I—"

"I will know without your words," she interrupted. Her heart raced wild and frantic in her bosom. "For you once gifted me permission to kiss the man I guessed you were by day—and I have guessed at it now, Bainbridge. Have I not?"

"Faris—I-I . . ." he stammered.

Yet Faris saw the struggle in the alluring darkness of his eyes. He feared confession, but why? Did he think she would not still love him once it was proven he was a stablemaster and not some great and wealthy lord?

"I will love you no matter the circumstance, my Highwayman," Faris whispered, smiling at him.

"In truth?" Bainbridge asked, a mischievous rogue's grin spreading across his handsome face. "No matter the circumstance, you will pledge yourself, lass—to the Highwayman of Tanglewood? I have your word on it?"

Faris smiled. Unable to keep herself from him a moment longer, she threw her arms around his broad shoulders, drawing her slight body against his powerful one. "My word, my heart, and everything else that is me," she said, tears streaming over her cheeks. "Oh, and kiss me now, my love! Do not press me to wait for that which is so blissful between us!"

"As you wish," Bainbridge said.

Faris thrilled as she felt him take her face between his strong hands. Gazing up into the dark of his eyes, she sighed.

"Still, I must tell you the truth," he said, his voice low and warm. "I must speak the words to you in that you may know the truth from my own lips."

Faris's heart beat so brutally within her she feared it might quite break free of her bosom. "Then speak the words, Highwayman," she whispered, her mouth watering for want of his lips pressed to hers.

"Faris," he whispered. "I am Bainbridge Graybeau, stablemaster at Loch Loland Castle, defender of any weaker than I—and though I am fearful to speak the words to you for fear of your knowing the truth of me, I will tell you now that I am—"

She could not wait to hear his words! She could not wait to know his confession! Before the words fell from his lips, Faris raised herself on her toes, pressing her soft, warm mouth to his.

His lips were soft and warm, and she was touched by his tenderness. No doubt he was as yet uncertain as to her acceptance of him. In a moment, however, his arms banded around her, pulling her against him as his kiss pressed firm to hers. He would set his passion free in an instant. She could feel the desire surging through him, and in another instant his full, free, and fervent kiss—the kiss of the Highwayman of Tanglewood—would own her.

"Excuse me, Faris—Graybeau."

It was Old Joseph. Bainbridge released her at once, startled by Old Joseph's sudden appearance.

"Milady Stringham is requesting your presence in her chambers, Faris," Old Joseph said.

He seemed not in the least surprised or unsettled at having found Faris bound in Bainbridge's arms. Faris, however, was quite unsettled. She felt the crimson of a heated blush rising to her cheeks.

"Thank you, Joseph," Faris said.

Old Joseph nodded, turned, and walked away, leaving Faris alone in Bainbridge's company once again.

In an instant, Faris reflected. Bainbridge had not yet aloud confessed to being the Highwayman of Tanglewood. Further, his kiss had not affected her in the like manner the Highwayman's kiss did. In truth, she did not desire to kiss him again.

Turning to face him, she asked, "You are not he then?"

"I cannot speak to whether I am or whether I am not, lass," Bainbridge said. "Not without placing the Highwayman of Tanglewood and all his good deeds in peril."

Faris paused. Would her lover and true Highwayman of Tanglewood keep the truth from her even now—even after her begging for truth? Would he keep the truth and his true kiss from her under such circumstances? Surely her true lover would not. Surely her true lover's kiss would have fanned passion in her in the instant. Graybeau's kiss had not.

She felt the fool and inwardly scolded herself for ridiculous folly. Yet he had lied! Graybeau had lied about exercising Jovan.

"But you were not exercising Jovan when the Highwayman rode to Loch Loland in the broad light of day as you claimed," she said.

"No. I was not," Graybeau said.

"Are—are you he, Bainbridge? I must know," Faris pleaded in a whisper.

"I-I cannot answer, Faris," he stammered. His brow puckered in a frown; he was in battlement with himself, it was obvious. He could neither confirm nor deny the truth to her. But for what reason, she could not fathom.

"Lady Stringham is waiting, lass," he said.

"I pray you are not he," Faris said. "For if you are, you have broken your word to me, and I have wasted a kiss."

"No kiss from you would ever be wasted, Faris," Bainbridge said. "At least not to him who is in receipt of it."

Faris frowned. Bainbridge indeed appeared tormented. Faris was tormented as well. She had come to the stables, sought out Bainbridge Graybeau in search of truth and comfort. What she had found only further confused her.

"I . . . I must go," Faris said. Lifting her skirt, she hurried toward the house.

She would tend to Lady Stringham—even at such a ridiculous hour—and then she would retire. Perhaps sleep would help her to sort it all out. Perhaps rest would clear her mind and order her feelings and thoughts. She was in doubt—in doubt of Graybeau's being the Highwayman of Tanglewood. She was near to convinced he was not the same as her twilight lover. Yet she could not think on it. If her Highwayman was not so nearby as the stables at Loch Loland Castle, how then would she keep her mind and heart on the straight path? How could she combat her secreted attraction to Lochlan Rockrimmon without the regularity of assurance from the Highwayman of her true value to him?

"Had ya held her to ya one minute more, I would have run ya through far certain, Bainbridge Graybeau," the Highwayman of Tanglewood said as he stepped from the darkness.

Bainbridge chuckled. "It was well I knew you were there, laddie," Bainbridge said, smiling at his masked friend. "She has the lips and kiss of an angel, she does."

"Of this I am well aware, my friend," the Highwayman said.

"So it would seem," Bainbridge said. His eyes narrowed as he looked at the Highwayman, and the Highwayman knew well his friend's thoughts. "Yet you will break her heart and her spirit if you do not confess to her soon."

The Highwayman of Tanglewood nodded. He was sick of deceit and fearful of Faris's reaction when the truth was told.

"I must tell her soon," the Highwayman said. "No matter the consequence."

"Yes," Bainbridge said.

"And—and I must tell Lillias as well," the Highwayman added. "For she suspects me I am certain. To keep them both in darkness—to be so deceptive to the women I love—I am hard-pressed to endure it longer."

"It does no good for a man to lie to a woman—especially to those he may love," Graybeau said. "Truth is freedom, lad. Tell your Lillias the truth—and tell Faris."

"But in the telling of the truth I may well lose the love of the woman I cannot live without, Bainbridge," the Highwayman said. "I may lose Faris in the telling of the truth."

"In keeping yourself from her, you surely will," Bainbridge began, "and well I suspect you may lose her to the young master of Loch Loland—for Old Joseph has seen them together, and Master Lochlan plucks at her heart strings with great effect."

The Highwayman of Tanglewood drew a deep breath. His hands yet trembled—residual angst throbbing through him at having witnessed Faris's kiss to Bainbridge. Yet he reminded himself the fault of it was none but his. He had not confessed his true identity to her. Further, he had himself suggested she kiss the man she guessed might be he. Therefore, what right had he to be vexed in any regard?

He was close to losing her—he sensed it. Either to frustration and lack of hope or to another man with more to offer. He must tell her—he must confess. Thus, he determined on the morrow, when he met her at the appointed place and time, there he would reveal himself. She may spurn him, it was true. His own deceit and lying might find his Highwayman's heart as broken as if it had been run through with his own rapier. Yet he must risk her knowing the truth—for he loved her with all desperation and purity.

"In endeavoring to win her, I must risk the losing of her," the Highwayman said. "I will tell Faris when next we meet. I will speak to Lillias even before that—for she certainly deserves no less than to know my secret and where my heart truly lies."

"Yes, lad," Bainbridge said. "Though I'd be willing to let your pretty Faris think a bit longer that I am the Highwayman of Tanglewood—if such kisses are the like the Highwayman enjoys."

The Highwayman of Tanglewood whistled, signaling his midnight steed. The horse appeared from behind a nearby tree, and the Highwayman mounted. "Keep yar lips and yar thoughts from me own fair Faris, Bainbridge Graybeau," the Highwayman called. "For now—now I am off to best Lord Gettings. He rides from Saxton this very night, and what think ye he might find in the Tanglewood as he passes?"

"Fear and besting," Bainbridge chuckled. "Fear and besting to be sure, lad."

The Highwayman of Tanglewood rode out then—out into the cloak of darkness. Yet it was not Lord Gettings's ill deeds that plagued his mind. Rather it was his own deception—his fear he may never hold Faris Shayhan as his entirely own.

Brushing tears from her cheeks, she hurried—hurried into Loch Loland and up the grand staircase to Lady Stringham's chamber. Bainbridge Graybeau was not the Highwayman of Tanglewood. Although her mind fought the truth of it, her heart affirmed the same truth. Fear, anxiety, and insecurity welled within Faris as she knocked on the large oak door of Lady Stringham's chamber.

"Come," Lady Stringham said from within.

Faris opened the door and stepped into the chamber. There sat Lady Stringham at one vanity, Tannis in a chair next to her.

"Did someone neglect to inform you of our need to have our hair brushed before retiring, girl?" Lady Stringham asked.

Her nose was so pointed and raised Faris mused it resembled an arrow aimed at the ceiling.

"Forgive me, milady," Faris said. "Indeed, I was not informed."

"Well, in the least of it we know she is not in the habit of tending to Lochlan at such a late hour," Tannis said. Spite glowed hot in the girl's eyes, and Faris tried to ignore it.

"At once, girl," Lady Stringham demanded. She held a brush in her hand and gestured Faris should take it. "Two hundred strokes at least," the woman said. "And I remind you this should be a comfortable experience for me—nothing uncomfortable about it."

"Yes, milady," Faris said. Her mind still occupied with her meeting with Bainbridge, Faris knew her trembling hands would need to be steady in order to avoid reprimand. She hoped steadiness was possible—hoped she could retrench, find hope, and happiness again. Oh, where was he? Where was her beloved Highwayman? How desperately she longed for him now!

It was afternoon—a lovely enough afternoon for anyone who was not anxious in awaiting nightfall. All at Loch Loland Castle were fairly buzzing with delight in the new day or delight in speculation as to whether or not their young master intended to ask for Tannis Stringham's hand in marriage. All save one—Faris.

Sleep had not come easily to her the night before as she had hoped. Even though Lady Stringham and Tannis had kept her awake long into the night with demands and trivial tasks, she did not rest easy when at last she did retire.

How could she have been so foolish? Running to Bainbridge Graybeau! Throwing herself into his arms and begging his confession! Kissing him as some brazen tart might have! It was far beyond humiliating: it was defeating. Bainbridge was not the Highwayman of Tanglewood. She had accepted the fact of it. Yet the thoughts whispering to her soul now disturbed her nearly beyond endurance. She did not know him! She did not know who rode as the Highwayman, who kissed her with such passion, who promised her his heart. In not knowing for certain, she was adrift in emotion and fear. As if in a boat set upon the sea without oars—she was adrift.

There was one other, of course. One other her mind had long ago whispered of being the Highwayman of Tanglewood. Still, Faris would not believe it—for it if it were true, then true heartache would be hers unmeasured. Yet he had promised! The Highwayman had promised he had no other love, no other attachment.

It was while Faris was caught up in her own thoughts, as she sat in miserable contemplation and heartache, that heartache seemed predisposed to find her.

Faris startled as Lillias suddenly came rushing into the kitchen. Tears stained her face, her eyes appearing red and swollen with the effort of sobbing.

"Lillias?" Faris asked. "Is all well?"

Faris felt the hair on the back of her neck prickle as Lillias paused, looking at her, an expression of great fear, hurt, or near panic on her lovely face. She did not speak, and Faris was further disconcerted. "Are you well? Is Lord Kendrick well?"

At the mention of Lord Kendrick's name, Lillias fairly burst into more sobbing.

"H-have you quarreled with one another?" Faris asked. Never had she seen Lillias so over-wrought. "I am certain all will be well, Lillias," Faris soothed.

"I cannot speak of it now, Faris," Lillias sobbed. "I must—I must gather myself. I cannot speak of it now—especially to you!"

With such an outburst of emotion as Faris had never before witnessed in her dear friend, Lillias dashed out the kitchen servants' door and into the gardens.

Faris stood astonished into silence, paralyzed with not understanding. And yet, it was then her own thoughts of a moment before returned to her—mingled with the realization of what could upset Lillias Rockrimmon so thoroughly.

"No," Faris whispered. Yet it came to her

then—Lord Gawain Kendrick. He had not been present the day before, when the Highwayman of Tanglewood had ridden to Loch Loland Castle. He had not been present when the Highwayman of Tanglewood had been besting Lord Brookings in Saxton. And even still, it was ever Lord Kendrick who appeared at Loch Loland with tales of the Highwayman's antics.

Could this be the reason for Lillias's emotional distress? Had Lord Kendrick confessed to being the Highwayman of Tanglewood? And if he had, what then did it mean for Faris? Certainly Lillias would not have appeared so overwrought with panic emotion had Lord Kendrick simply confessed and not mentioned his connection to Faris. Had he then—had Lord Kendrick broken with Lillias in favor of Faris?

"Quickly, Faris," Mary said upon entering the kitchen. "Milady Stringham and her daughter are demanding tea and cakes."

"Wh-where is Willeen then?" Faris asked, pulling herself from her thoughts and to the present moment at hand. "Do you wish that I should bring her to you?"

But Mary shook her head as she began hastily preparing a service. "No, no, no. Willeen is taken ill. You will have to serve milady and Miss Tannis," Mary said.

"Me?" Faris gasped. In the mere space of one day—most of which she had been told to take rest at Lady Rockrimmon's word—in the mere space of a day, Faris was certain she did not wish to be near the Stringham ladies more than was absolutely necessary to keep her position. "I-I cannot possibly serve their refreshment, Mary! I have not the steady wits about me this day. Cannot Sarah tend to them?"

Mary rolled her eyes and breathed an exasperated sigh. "Sarah? Posh and piddle posh! She has taken the day to visit her sister in town. No. I am afraid you must tend them. They are your lot, after all." Holding the silver tray and service, Mary turned and handed it to Faris. "If they have one complaint about my service or cakes, I do not wish to hear it. Oh, I cannot wait until they have taken their leave. How long will Master Lochlan cause us to endure before he asks for Miss Tannis's hand?" Mary grumbled. She straightened one cup and saucer and said, "There now, Faris. On your way now. We don't want them complaining to Lady Rockrimmon about anything they haven't already."

"Very well," Faris said. "If I must."

Yet Faris felt weak, unhinged somehow—as if the emotion of the previous day and night's goings-on had drained her very life's blood from her. She thought of Lillias sobbing in the gardens. Surely the Highwayman had not so thoroughly lied to her as to keep Lillias his lover by day and

Faris his lover by twilight? Surely he loved Faris better than that?

Stepping into Lady Rockrimmon's parlor, she nodded as Lady Stringham and Tannis looked up from their reading and needlework. Glancing about quickly, Faris was quite unsettled to see that Lady Rockrimmon was not present.

"Maranda has left us here with none whatsoever to entertain us," Lady Stringham said.

"There seems to be some squabble between Lillias and her betrothed, and Lady Stringham is in search of Lord Rockrimmon to soothe it," Tannis added. "Or so I would gather from the recent goings-on and Lillias's childish outburst of emotion."

Faris was loath to serve such arrogant and unfeeling gossips as sat before her now. Yet she admired Lady Rockrimmon, loved her as nearly her own mother. Lady and Tannis Stringham were guests at Loch Loland Castle: welcome or not, she would serve them.

"I have brought your refreshment, milady," Faris said. "Do you wish me to serve it?" She prayed they would serve themselves, for she feared her trembling hands might betray her own tender emotions.

Tannis quirked one eyebrow as she studied Faris from head to slipper. Faris straightened her posture. She did not like being appraised by the haughty young woman. How she hoped

Lochlan had spoken the truth to her when he had said he did not intend to take Tannis to wife. Still, considering Lord Kendrick's deceit and the apparent deceit of the Highwayman, Faris was no longer certain any man wore truth as his emblem of honor.

"You dawdled so, girl," Lady Stringham said. "I hope the cakes are still warm. I cannot fathom why Lochlan favors you as his chambermaid. If that is even the case."

"Oh, surely not, mother," Tannis said. "I think Lady Rockrimmon only meant to tease you when she said as much."

Faris fought the frown begging to pucker her brow, fought the tears pleading for release.

"The service, miss. Now would not be soon enough," Lady Stringham said. "You may serve yourself first, Tannis dearest."

"Thank you, Mother," Tannis said rising and walking to Faris.

"Miss," Faris said, holding the tray out to the young woman. She gasped as Tannis swiftly slapped the tray, causing the cakes and tea to spill out down the front of Faris's dress. Dropping the tray, Faris quickly tore open the fabric of her bodice, for the hot tea scalded her tender flesh. She looked up only when she heard Tannis and Lady Stringham giggle.

"Such a clumsy girl," Tannis said. "Perhaps you should keep to the bedchambers—not to serving tea and cakes to important guests."

"This was intentional," Faris accused, blowing into the opening of her bodice in an effort to cool her scalded flesh. Stooping, she retrieved a napkin from the heap of cakes, broken china, silver tea spoons, and linens at her feet and began dabbing at the moisture on her bosom.

She was rendered breathless in the next moment by the hot sting of a strong slap to her right cheek. Mouth agape in awe, she pressed a hand to the painful flesh a moment before Tannis dealt a second slap to her opposing cheek.

"Impudent wench!" Lady Stringham exclaimed. "Lady Rockrimmon will be very displeased when we tell her of the manner in which you have treated us, girl!"

"Y-you accuse me of mistreatment?" Faris stammered. She could not comprehend it—such treatment of others.

She gasped as the back of Lady Stringham's hand delivered a violent slap to her already offended face. Stunned and unable to order rational thought, Faris turned and fled from the room in a mist of tears.

She could not believe what had just transpired! Tannis Stringham had intentionally knocked the tray from her hand. The tea had scalded Faris's flesh terribly, yet the girl had accused Faris of dropping the tray deliberately. Although she knew Lady Rockrimmon to be wise and understanding, still she feared for her position. What if Lady Rockrimmon believed the Stringhams and she were truly sent away this time? She would never see Lochlan again! Her Highwayman would not know where to find her! She paused in her flight to close her eyes, silently reprimanding herself for thinking of Lochlan in the same moment as the Highwayman. Whatever was the matter with her? Had she lost her wits? In being so entangled in her desire to know the Highwayman of Tanglewood's true identity, had she lost balanced thought? In knowing now that Bainbridge Graybeau was not the Highwayman, that Lord Gawain Kendrick may well be he, had she succumbed to the insanity of a breaking heart?

Inhaling a deep breath and brushing the tears from her tender and sore cheeks, she endeavored to regain a remnant of calm about her. Yet her heart cried out for the Highwayman. If ever she needed championing, it was now! Where was he? Where did he rest in daylight? Why was it she was ever assaulted in the broad light of day when the Highwayman of Tanglewood could not champion her? Why was it ever Lochlan Rockrimmon championing her at Loch Loland and not her beloved?

As she opened her eyes, she gasped, unsettled at the sight of Lochlan himself standing before her. It was an uncanny thing—as if her thoughts of Lochlan had caused him to materialize.

"What goes on here?" Lochlan asked, scowling as his eyes lingered on Faris's gaping bodice. Self-consciously, Faris pulled the fabric together with one hand. "And here?" he asked, lifting her chin to study her.

His touch was comforting and exhilarating in the same moment. From the sense of sting on her cheeks, Faris was certain Tannis's and her mother's abuse had left fiery red welts on her face.

"Who has assaulted you thus?" Lochlan growled. His voice was loud, demanding, and angry in its intonation.

Faris gazed into the hot emerald of his eyes. He was livid with barely controlled rage.

"It—it is nothing to speak of, sire," she lied, attempting to move past him. She did not wish to tell him of the abusive manner of his guests. It was humiliating to her all of a sudden. It seemed at every turn she was being assaulted at Loch Loland Castle. Surely Lochlan must have begun to wonder what a cursed being she was.

"Nothing to speak of?" Lochlan nearly roared. "Your clothing wet and torn, the flesh beneath unnaturally red! The print of a hand on this cheek," he said, brushing her cheek with the back of his hand. "And here, too," he said, pointing to the other.

Faris was rendered breathless, her body rippling with goose bumps as Lochlan pressed the bareness of his hand to the scalded flesh just below her throat.

"Warm and tender. You have been scalded," he growled. His expression was that of rage, and Faris watched as his jaw clinched tightly shut. "You will tell me now, Faris. Who has caused this?"

Faris opened her mouth to speak, but shook her head saying, "I . . . I cannot possibly tell you, sire."

"What?" he asked. "Why not?"

"I-I . . ." she stammered.

"Tell me here . . . now. I demand it. Do not refuse me, Faris," he growled.

"It was first Miss Tannis," Faris whispered. "And—and then her mother."

Lochlan straightened his broad shoulders, ground his teeth, and said, "Tell me all of it, Faris. At once."

Faris frowned. Dared she tell him the truth of it? Surely it would mean her dismissal. Whether or not he meant to take Tannis Stringham to wife, she was his guest—she and her mother. Never would a servant's word usurp that of titled lady and her daughter, guests at Loch Loland Castle.

"I am a chambermaid, sire," she began. "I-I don't usually handle tea service, but Willeen is ill, and Sarah is—"

"You are a woman, Faris," he interrupted. "Now, continue."

343

Faris wiped tears from her sore cheeks and said, "I was serving an unscheduled tea to Lady Stringham and her daughter. Willeen is ill, and Sarah is—"

"This much I have gathered, Faris. Out with it, for my patience is taxed near to being all spent," he said.

Faris was trembling before him. Yet for fear or joy at being in his presence, she did not know. "I simply held the tray for Miss Tannis, that she might serve herself. I was holding the tray, and she pushed at it, causing the tea and cakes to spill on me. I was disrespectful, sire—I admit it—for I spoke improperly, somewhat accusing she had done so on purpose. It was then she first struck me." Desperate that he believe her, Faris reached out, taking hold of his sleeve and pleading, "I beg you to believe me, sire! I am not telling a falsehood! She truly did—"

Faris's words were lost to her, and she began to tremble as Lochlan glanced to where her hand held his sleeve.

"Forgive me, Master Lochlan. I only wanted to make you understand—" she gasped as he took hold of her arm. "Sire, please," she begged, for she knew he meant to throw her out of Loch Loland Castle forever. Yet, as he turned her toward his mother's parlor, pushed her before him toward it, she realized his intent. He meant to make her face Lady and Tannis Stringham!

"Oh, please, sire!" she begged. "I swear I am telling the truth!" She had no choice but to do his bidding, for he fairly dragged her into the room where sat Lady Stringham and her daughter. Both women looked up as Lochlan pushed her toward them.

"Lochlan, darling," Lady Stringham began. "I see you've found our truant serving maid."

Faris wiped the tears from her cheeks only a moment before Lochlan took hold of her shoulders and held her forward, as if assuring Lady Stringham knew she was present. Well expecting another slap, Faris closed her eyes and winced. No slap was administered, however, and her eyes widened as dinner platters when she felt Lochlan pull aside the fabric of her bodice.

"Explain this to me, Lady Stringham," he demanded.

Faris could feel his strong hands trembling with rage as he held the fabric of her bodice. He was indeed enraged—but not so for the reasons Faris had at first assumed.

Lady Stringham smiled. She tossed her head as if innocence were her nature and said, "The girl is as clumsy as any hog, Lochlan. She had an unfortunate episode with the service and spilled the tea and cakes."

"And this?" Lochlan asked, taking Faris's chin in hand and displaying first one cheek to Lady Stringham and her daughter, then the other.

"She is wildly impertinent, Lochlan," Tannis said. "If only you had heard her sharp serpent's tongue."

Faris gasped as Lochlan took hold of her shoulders once more, turned her toward him, and held her firmly against his the protective strength of his powerful body.

"Lady Stringham," he growled. "This—the entirety of it is unacceptable in the very least."

"No apology is necessary, Lochlan," Lady Stringham began. "It was the girl's clumsiness, her inexperience—"

"Milady, you and your daughter have but one hour to gather your things and quit Loch Loland," Loch growled.

"What?" Tannis exclaimed.

At the understanding of his words, Faris could not help but to melt against him. His championing her again was unexpected to her—though it should have been entirely predictable.

"Lochlan," Lady Stringham began, "you cannot possibly be in earnest."

"I am well in earnest, woman," he said.

"Lochlan!" Tannis exclaimed in utter astonishment.

"I will send someone to assist you with your exodus," he said. Then, still holding Faris to him, he turned to leave, yet paused. Looking back at the two women, he added, "I do not believe it necessary, yet I will now inform you that you are no longer welcome in my father's house. No matter the circumstance."

Faris stood in astonished disbelief at what had only just transpired. Had she understood correctly? Had Lochlan Rockrimmon ordered Lady and Tannis Stringham to quit Loch Loland?

Lochlan swept her into the cradle of his powerful arms, rendering Faris further astonished and even more breathless. As he carried her from the room, Faris looked back to see Lady Stringham standing unbelieving, mouth agape. Tannis burst into tears and began wailing about her loss of prospective husband.

"It is your fault, Mother!" Tannis sobbed. "You had to offend his little pet!"

"I?" Lady Stringham screeched. "You struck first, Tannis! Would that you had kept your envy in order for one more day!"

Lochlan closed the door to the parlor with a swift kick of his foot before continuing to walk down the hallway, cradling Faris in his arms. Uncertain as to what action she should take, Faris simply stared up at him. His brow was deeply creased with an angry frown, his jaw still tightly clinched.

"Sire?" Faris ventured. At the sound of her voice, Lochlan stopped and looked at her, though he did not release her. "Sire—I am well," she told him. "Certainly well enough to walk."

Lochlan's massive chest rose and fell with the

heavy breath of anger. Still, after a moment, he nodded. He dropped her feet to the floor, further releasing her when her balance was certain.

"Thank you, sire," Faris said, gathering the fabric of her open bodice into one closed hand.

"I am sorry you endured such treatment, Faris," he said. His teeth were still clinched, his anger yet lingering. She was quite certain the emerald fire of his eyes would next set Loch Loland Castle to flames.

"It was no fault of yours, sire," Faris said.

His frown deepened, and he looked at her. His eyes narrowed, and he said, "It was my invitation that brought them here."

"Yet their character is no fault of yours," Faris reminded him.

He reached forth, taking her chin in one hand and studying the welts on her cheeks. "It wounds me to see your tender flesh so injured," he said.

"It is nothing so lasting as to give you concern, sire," Faris said. Her heart was hammering in her bosom. His presence was unraveling her some-how—rendering her weak and adrift in confusion.

"But I do concern myself, Faris," Lochlan said. His voice was low, alluring suddenly, and Faris was instantly breathless. Again, he tenderly stroked her cheek with the back of his hand, and Faris closed her eyes as he bent, placing a soft, lingering kiss to it.

"Sire, you are not responsible for . . . for . . ."

Faris stammered. Her words were lost as Lochlan Rockrimmon's lips pressed her other cheek. Oh, where was her Highwayman? If he would only come to her more often, give her a thread of hope of spiriting her away, of still loving her as time passed—then perhaps she would not find such unsettling distraction in her young master's presence.

"Sire, please . . ." Faris breathed.

He meant to kiss her, she knew it! And imp that she was, she wanted him to! How could she be so unfaithful to her beloved? How could she be so easily seduced? And yet Lillias was in her thoughts then. Lillias who so desperately loved Lord Kendrick—Lord Kendrick, who had deceived them both. Yet she loved him! Whether Lord Kendrick or not, Faris loved the Highwayman of Tanglewood! How could she be so unfaithful? How could she allow Lochlan Rockrimmon to affect her so? Her undeniable attraction to Lochlan, the trembling that was washing over her body, the moisture gathering in her mouth as she anticipated being kissed by her young master—she knew all of it was simply her wish the Highwayman were standing before her.

"I favor you, Faris," Lochlan whispered, his voice deep and resonate. He lightly kissed the corner of her mouth. "Yet I know your heart is owned by another."

Faris swallowed the excess moisture in her mouth. "It is, sire," she whispered.

"Still, you tremble at my touch, a crimson blush upon your soft cheek each time we meet," he said. "And I think you may not deny me a kiss."

"I . . . I should deny it," Faris whispered as Lochlan cupped her face in his hands. How she reveled in the feel of his hands to her face—the rather rough, calloused feel of his palms against her tender flesh.

"But you will not," he whispered, smiling at her. His eyes held her gaze fast with their bewitching emerald brilliance.

"I-I will," Faris stammered. She felt as if the very threads of her being might ascend instantly to the heavens as Lochlan Rockrimmon caressed her lips with his thumb a moment before pressing them tenderly with his own.

"Sire," Faris began, turning her face from him. His kiss had unnerved her, for its quality was as such to send her mind and senses spinning. She thought of her Highwayman, of his passion's kiss. She winced, furious that her mind and body should be so affected by another man's attention—angry that Bainbridge Graybeau's kiss had not affected her so. She wanted to cry out— to call to him—to cry, *My Highwayman! Come! Champion me now when I am in the deepest depths of peril!*

She did not cry out. She only remained silent,

attempting to muster her courage and resolve to resist succumbing to Lochlan Rockrimmon.

"Share one kiss with me, Faris," Lochlan said. "One kiss, and I will leave you."

"Sire, I cannot. You alone know he whom I—" Faris whispered, entranced by the fire in his brilliant green eyes.

"One kiss," he repeated. "Shared. Then I will let you go."

Faris's mind struggled with her heart, with her mouth, watering for want of his. The Highwayman owned her heart. Indeed she knew he would own her were his circumstances ever to allow it. Still, the imp on her shoulder whispered to Faris in that moment, reminding her she may never belong to the Highwayman the way she dreamed—he may never belong to her. How could he when Lillias stood so beautiful and perfect between them? Further, she knew Lochlan Rockrimmon could never belong to a chambermaid. Still, in the deepest corners of her mind, she gave herself admission—she cared for Lochlan! Cared deeply and lovingly for him— secreted strong desires where he was concerned. Her loyalty to her Highwayman kept her from inwardly facing any further feelings for Lochlan, but in those moments, Faris knew Lochlan Rockrimmon was in her heart as well.

Would one kiss tear the Highwayman from her heart, or her from his? The Highwayman who would not claim her? The Highwayman whom another owned claim to?

"Faris?" Lochlan whispered, placing a hand beneath her chin and tipping her face up to meet his.

"Only one," Faris heard herself breath. "Only one," she whispered.

The emerald fire in his eyes caught blaze as he smiled, and she was undone. Closing her eyes as Lochlan Rockrimmon's head descended toward hers, Faris harshly scolded herself—scolded herself until the instant she felt Lochlan's lips press against her own. She gasped as he drew her body against his with great strength and determination.

His kiss lingered upon her lower lip—lingered against her upper lip. She was near to crying out for want of his mouth full pressed to hers.

He whispered then, "A shared kiss is required, Faris—if you wish to be free of me."

Instantly, his mouth captured hers, coaxing her lips to part. Faris melted against him, her resolve to resist in returning his kiss utterly vanquished as passion caught flame and smoldered between them. He was strong—powerful! His kiss was moist, demanding, overpowering in rendering a sense of intoxication to Faris's full body and mind. Faris despised herself—for she reveled in the bliss evoked by Lochlan Rockrimmon's kiss as deeply as she ever reveled in the bliss found in the arms of the Highwayman of Tanglewood!

His rough whiskers assaulted the flesh about her mouth. His strong hands caressed her arms, tightened about her waist, wove fingers through her hair.

"Will you not touch me, Faris? Will you not embrace me?" he asked in a whisper. "Will you not let me feel the warmth of your full self in returning our kiss?"

Faris knew she must break from him, but not before she had held him in return. His words were as a warm rain, and she melded to him, letting her arms go around him—her mouth working with his to generate a passionate exchange the like she had shared with just one other.

A deep moan rose from his throat as he pushed her back against the wall. His body pressed hers as he kissed her, his hands fisted and hard-pressed on the wall at either side of her head. His kiss was ambrosial in nature—perfect in its heated application and coaxing response.

Faris pulled away at once, stepping out of his embrace and away from him. What had she done? She had never imagined herself capable of such unfaithfulness.

"What have I done?" she cried, burying her face in her hands. "What have I done?"

"You have done nothing," Lochlan said, his voice low and filled with both satisfaction and regret. "It was I forced you to—"

"No, no," she cried, shaking her head as she looked at him. "You are the innocent in this. It was I who—"

"No!" he growled, taking her by the shoulders. "You have done nothing, Faris. He loves you, you love him—it is the truth. You are simply uncertain, I suspect. Uncertain he can ever—"

"Hush!" she told him covering her ears. "It is not his fault!"

"But it is! Do you not see it?" he asked, his hands tightening at her shoulders. "He—he should not expect you to wait—wait until his valiant escapades are over! He should not expect you to spend your life waiting."

"He has never asked me to wait," she said. "I wait because—because I love him."

Lochlan was silent for some moments.

"Then I am the villain," he whispered. "To try and coax you away from him with my weak attempts at chivalry, ridiculous pie conversation, and inept attempt at making love to you. I am sorry, Faris," he said.

Drawing a deep breath, he turned and walked from her. He left her trembling—left her wanting to run after him—left her wanting to throw herself in his arms and beg him to kiss her once more. It was then she wondered—if Lochlan Rockrimmon were a common man, a man with no title, no wealth—if he were such a one as that, would she run to him? In knowing she might have him, would she claim him? Was it because Lochlan Rockrimmon stood more unobtainable than even the Highwayman of Tanglewood— was this what kept her from him? Was this what kept her loyal to the Highwayman of Tanglewood instead—loyal to a man she had seen but five times?

Faris wept bitterly upon her pillow. She had been unfaithful of heart to her Highwayman. She had reveled in the passionate kiss of Lochlan Rockrimmon. Further, she may have caused the greatest heartache of all to her dearest friend—to Lillias. She thought of Lord Gawain Kendrick— wondered could she yet love him if he were the Highwayman of Tanglewood if he had lied to Lillias—and to her. Yet she loved the man she had met in the midnight meadow a year before. Oh, how she loved him! She loved him more than even she loved Lillias, and the thought sickened her. At the end of all her self-loathing, self-doubt, and confusion of thought, Faris simply cried herself to sleep. She dreamt not of purple twilight meadows or of delicious kisses borne of passion. Instead she dreamt of nothing but an uncertain heart lost and wondering in a dark, heavy fog, void of amethyst sunsets or the silver beacon of a rising moon.

A Greater Understanding

Sunlight streamed through the window of Faris's small bedchamber, bright and warm and inviting. Yet as Faris busied herself on preparing for the day, she fancied that even the bright light of morning had done nothing to dispel her confusion, self-doubt, and trepidation. She was to meet him—this very night—near the old Castle Alexendria ruins. What would the Highwayman of Tanglewood say to her? What would he do when she confessed to kissing not only Bainbridge Graybeau but Lochlan Rockrimmon as well? Certainly the kiss she had shared with Graybeau was far less in consequence and feeling than the one she had so willing shared with Lochlan. Still, to have kissed two men since last she saw him—it was abominable.

But what of the Highwayman himself? Was he Lord Gawain Kendrick as she suspected? If he were, his dalliances with her and Lillias were far worse than her own with Lochlan, were they not? And still she loved him—for he had renewed her hope, her dreams, when she was certain there was little dreaming left to be had.

She was wrong, she was certain. All through

the night, she had awakened at residual intervals to thinking Lord Kendrick could not be the Highwayman of Tanglewood! He could not! She was certain the Highwayman would not so blatantly lie to her. She was certain Lord Kendrick loved Lillias as no man had ever loved a woman—loved her as deeply and truly as Faris loved the Highwayman. Lord Kendrick would not betray Lillias, of this she was certain. She believed also that neither would the Highwayman betray her to such lengths. The Highwayman of Tanglewood could not be Lord Kendrick. This assurance was burned into her heart.

And yet, Lillias's outburst of the day before remained unexplained. Perhaps it had simply been a lovers' first quarrel. Perhaps Lillias and her beloved Lord Kendrick had quarreled, and the fact of it had distressed Lillias to tears. Still, why had Lillias asserted she could not to speak of it—particularly to Faris?

Faris's head throbbed with the confusion of it all—the pain of her own guilt in having shared such a kiss with her young master. Even now, as she prepared to leave her chamber in beginning her duties—even now the thought of kissing Lochlan Rockrimmon caused excess moisture to flood her mouth. She sighed, feeling quite defeated.

In the least, she was glad the Stringham women

had quit Loch Loland Castle as commanded. She knew well she could not have faced them after their treatment of her the day before.

Feeling as if she had not found respite in one wink of sleep, Faris left her chamber. She would endure—waft through the day until twilight was upon her. Then she would seek him—confess her mistake in thinking Bainbridge Graybeau was her lover—confess her unfaithfulness in allowing herself to kiss Lochlan on the third occasion of his championing her. Indeed, she feared the Highwayman would quit her entirely, for what man wanted a woman so easily deceived, so easily seduced by another?

Faris comforted herself with the knowledge that it could only be Lochlan Rockrimmon who could ever have tempted her to such betrayal. As she entered his chambers to find his bed neatly spread, his clothing strewn hither and yon, she sighed. An odd sort of ache began in the center of her bosom as Lochlan's emerald gaze appeared in her mind. Her tender flesh raced with goose bumps as she thought of him—as her mind lingered on his delicious kiss.

Closing her eyes for a moment, she silently prayed for release—release from being held captive by his charm, by his kiss, by his very existence! She prayed that, should the Highwayman of Tanglewood forgive her of her loathsome disloyalty, such forgiveness would banish her feelings for Lochlan forever.

"I do not know how you tolerate his untidiness, Faris," Lillias said.

Faris turned to see Lillias standing behind her. She appeared resplendent, happy, and bright. The overwrought emotion of the previous day was entirely gone from her countenance. In its place was a light to her eyes as bright as the morning sun.

"Good morning," Faris ventured. "Are—are you well?"

Lillias's smile broadened. "Yes, darling Faris," she said. "And I owe you the greatest of apologies."

Faris nearly burst into tears! If Lillias was well, then nothing was amiss between her and her betrothed. Furthermore, if nothing was amiss between Lillias and Lord Kendrick . . .

"I am sorry for my behavior toward you yesterday, Faris," Lillias said, taking Faris's hands in her own. "I was only so terribly upset about . . . about . . ."

"You do not have to explain, Lillias," Faris said. Tears brimmed in her eyes—tears of joy at her friend's renewed happiness—tears of relief that all was well between them.

"Of course I do, dearest," Lillias said. "Come—sit with me a moment." Faris sat next to Lillias on Lochlan's bed.

"Something . . . something was revealed to me yesterday," Lillias began. "Something I was quite at first angry to learn of."

"Yet—yet all is well between you and Lord Kendrick?" Faris asked. Her heart pounded wild with trepidation. Something in her yet feared Lord Kendrick may be the Highwayman.

"Yes," Lillias said. "All is very well between us. Still, Gawain confessed to me yesterday of his desire to ride in assistance with the Highwayman of Tanglewood!"

"What?" Faris gasped.

"It is true!" Lillias said. "Gawain spoke to me concerning his desire to ride as the Highwayman of Tanglewood rides—in defense of those in need of championing! I was so overcome with fear and anger I knew not how to compose myself! Imagine the danger before Gawain should he ride out! In all this time of my wishing my darling Gawain were the Highwayman—how foolish have I been? His well-being—rather his lack of well-being—were he to ride . . . oh, Faris! I could not bear such anxiety!"

Faris was stunned into utter and complete silence! She yet feared her worst suspicions may see fruition—that Lord Gawain Kendrick, in truth, was the Highwayman of Tanglewood! Certainly he had not confessed it in full measure to Lillias. Yet was his telling her of his *desire* to ride—was this his manner of leading her into pure knowledge he already did? Still, his wish to ride did not prove Lord Kendrick was, in fact, the Highwayman of Tanglewood. Did it? It was simply an example of his gallant nature. Was it not?

"Still, I was quite out of countenance yesterday—unsettled and quite worried for a moment. This I confess, and I am sorry, Faris," Lillias said. "My worry and frustration—well, it seems to have fallen upon whomever crossed my path. I did not mean to speak so unkindly to you yesterday."

Faris forced a friendly smile. She would settle herself—she would. Lillias had not been angry with Faris the day before—simply fearful of Lord Kendrick's well-being.

"We have all known a temper at one time or the other," Faris said at last. "I am only glad to know your temper was no fault of mine."

"We are still friends then?" Lillias asked. "You are still my best and greatest friend?"

"Of course," Faris said. "As you are mine."

Lillias laughed. "There we are then—the greatest of friends."

"Other than your friendship with Lord Kendrick," Faris said. "In truth, he would be your greatest friend." Oh, how Faris hoped she was correct in her assumptions—that her Highwayman had been in earnest when he had promised he was not Lord Gawain Kendrick.

Lillias smiled. "True. As Lochlan would be yours."

"What?" Faris gasped.

Lillias's eyes sparked with merriment and mischief. "This could be your bed one day, you know," Lillias said running her hand over the soft sapphire velvet of Lochlan's bed coverlet.

"What?" Faris asked again, fairly leaping to her feet.

"Oh, surely you are not going to stand on pretense with me, Faris!" Lillias giggled. "I saw him kiss you yesterday—just after he had ordered Lady Stringham and her insipid daughter to leave Loch Loland. I saw him kiss you—and it was no mere dalliance of a kiss."

"He—he only asked a boon, and I only meant to grant him thanks for his championing me yet again," Faris stammered.

"Oh, do not look so distraught, Faris," Lillias said. "Lochlan does not scheme with virtue or emotion. He is not the like of Kade the Heinous. My brother is ever honorable, and he would not kiss you for triviality's sake."

Faris stood trembling, tears brimming in her eyes. Lillias had been witness to her disloyalty to the Highwayman—to her being quite seduced by the young master of Loch Loland Castle! It was a terrible circumstance.

"He favors you, Faris. I have seen it," Lillias

said. "I believe he would have you if you would have him."

"I cannot!" Faris cried in a whisper.

"Why ever not?" Lillias asked. "Is it his position and title that frighten you? He cares not of it."

"What?" Faris breathed. She could not believe Lillias implication. Did Lillias truly believe one such as her brother, one such as the dashing Lochlan Rockrimmon, would settle his affections eternally on a chambermaid?

"It is the truth," Lillias said. "Lochlan will love whom he will love. He cares nothing for title or wealth. There is no arrogance in him."

Faris shook her head. "No, no. You do not understand," she stammered. "He cannot possibly—your brother cannot possibly . . ." Faris felt overly warm, her throat dry and constricted. "There is another," she said at last. "I have pledged to another."

"Wh-what?" Lillias asked.

"I cannot keep this from you, Lillias!" Faris cried. Burying her face in her hands, she wept as she spoke. "I am a ruin, Lillias! A ruin! A can no more make sense of my feelings than I can keep the sun from rising! I have pledged my heart to another and yet—yet your brother owns me in a like manner! I am near to running mad with anxiety, confusion, and self-loathing!"

"Faris!" Lillias breathed. "Who—who could

363

possibly keep you from surrendering to Lochlan? Is not my brother the perfect example of masculinity—of beauty and honor? Is not he kind and even heroic? Who could possibly own your heart over him?"

Faris raised her face and looked at Lillias. She could no longer endure silence. Lillias was trustworthy—of this she was certain. As she was certain Lochlan would never reveal her secret, so too she was certain Lillias was an able confident.

"You will not believe me," Faris said.

"Of course, I will," Lillias assured her. Lillias took Faris's hands and pulled her to sit on the bed once more.

"Not far over a year ago, the night I came to Loch Loland Castle," Faris began, "I was set upon by a stranger in the Tanglewood Meadow."

"Set upon?" Lillias gasped.

"I was walking through the meadow and—and a rider approached," Faris said. She watched as understanding rained over Lillias.

"Faris," Lillias breathed. "Faris—you do not mean to tell me that it is—that it is the Highwayman of Tanglewood who owns your heart?"

"It is," Faris breathed. "We met under a purple curtain of midnight. He stole a kiss from me," she said, smiling at the memory. "And we have met of recent again."

"The Highwayman of Tanglewood is your

lover?" Lillias breathed, still obvious in her astonishment.

"No one must ever know, Lillias!" Faris pleaded. "For it would put him in danger. Already your brother has guessed at it, and I fear—"

"Lochlan? You confided in Lochlan?" Lillias asked.

"I did not tell him—though I confessed the truth when he guessed at it," Faris said.

She watched as an expression of complete understanding burned radiant on Lillias's lovely face. "What a greater understanding I own now," Lillias said. Lillias's eyes narrowed for a moment. It was obvious a far greater understanding, indeed, was washing over her. "Of course," she breathed. "Of course—I see it now—and how could Lochlan ever compare to one such as the rogue Highwayman of Tanglewood?"

Faris brushed tears from her cheeks and glanced away. She was only somewhat relieved at having confided in Lillias—for her revealed confidence had done little to soothe the struggle in her mind and heart. "He well compares," Faris admitted. "And that is why I am such a loathsome creature."

"You? Why?" Lillias asked.

"For if your brother were not heir to Loch Loland—if he were but a common man," Faris began, "then I fear I would . . . I fear—"

"You see Lochlan as unobtainable," Lillias

finished. "You do not believe he could love you, for you see yourself as beneath him. But I promise you—he holds you in higher esteem than he does himself or anyone else! I saw him kiss you last night! I know he holds you as—"

"I do love the Highwayman, Lillias!" Faris exclaimed. "I do love him! I have loved him from the moment he came upon me in the meadow that night a year past and every moment since!"

"Yet he is also unobtainable in your eyes," Lillias said. "And we women—we need to hold a heart in our own, know it belongs to us, have daily assurance that it is ours. But for now—you cannot own the Highwayman of Tanglewood."

"I will meet him soon," Faris said. "And I will confess my betrayal. He may put me off then. I may find myself abandoned and brokenhearted— and all for passion's sake—for my inability to resist your brother."

"And then you will have no *need* to resist my brother," Lillias said.

"I will have great need," Faris argued. "What sort of woman falls in love with one man and then finds herself so desperately drawn to another? I am not worthy of the Highwayman's heart or affections. Still, I pray he will forgive me."

Lillias was silent for a moment. She inhaled a deep breath and then began, "Two years past, I was betrothed to another, Faris."

"What?" Faris gasped.

"I had fallen quite in love with the son of my father's friend, Lord Shelton," Lillias answered. "John Shelton was the best of men—gallant, honorable, and quite handsome. I was happy in my betrothal—delighted to be marrying the man I loved. And then—one day as I was out riding with John's sister, we were met by Gawain. I was astonished at my instantaneous attraction to him. We were quite thrown together shortly thereafter. I began to realize that although I loved John, I was *in* love with Gawain." Lillias shrugged her shoulders and smiled. "Though I still own guilt over John, I know it is Gawain the heavens intended me for."

"I am in love with the Highwayman, Lillias," Faris said. She understood her friend's offering of the story—she was encouraging Faris toward Lochlan. Yet in her innocence, she still did not see two points: Faris was in love with the Highwayman of Tanglewood, and Lochlan Rockrimmon would not love a chambermaid.

"Oh, I know that you are," Lillias began, "For I may see it even more clearly than you see it yourself. Yet something in me wants you to believe that Lochlan esteems you in his own right. He would not have kissed you in the manner he did if he did not."

"You are afraid I will place him in Kade Tremeshton's sphere," Faris said. She understood then. Lillias wanted Faris to understand that

Lochlan Rockrimmon was not an abuser of innocence the way Kade Tremeshton was.

"I only wish to assure you that Lochlan is in earnest where his feelings toward you are concerned," Lillias said. "I know him. Better than he knows himself."

"I thank you for that assurance," Faris said. "And—and I will admit to you now that it does comfort me somewhat. I would not like to think I was so easily swayed into accepting affections from another rogue."

Lillias laughed, as did Faris. They embraced, and Lillias sighed with contentment.

"He will forgive you, Faris," Lillias said. "I am certain he loves you, and in loving you, he will grant you most any reprieve, I think. Certainly he will understand your fear of never owning him—for he must own the same fear. Yes?"

"Let us hope," Faris said, smiling at her friend.

Lillias giggled, a sudden expression of gleeful delight on her face. "And to think, Faris," she began, "all this time we've been sharing stories and dreams of the Highwayman of Tanglewood—you were living such dreams of him!"

"It was difficult for me—not confiding in you," Faris said. "I so often wanted to."

"You were right to keep him a secret," Lillias said. "Indeed, for his own safety and for yours." Lillias's eyes were bright with mischief once more. "Now—you must tell me—is the Highwayman of Tanglewood as dashing a lover as we always dreamt he would be?"

Faris smiled—her heart swelling with love and affection for her dear friend.

"He is far more magnificent in character, person, and every other regard than we ever imagined him to be!" Faris said.

"And will you tell me more of him one day?" Lillias asked.

"If there is more to tell, then I will tell you," Faris said. Her anxiety renewed. Would there be more to tell? Would the Highwayman of Tanglewood meet her in the forever-running heather and forgive her weakness? Or would the amethyst twilight to come be their last reunion—their final rendezvous?

Faris stood at the kitchen servants' door. The sun lingered low on the horizon. Already the violets and pinks of day's end cast brilliant across the heavens.

Conversing, confessing nearly all to Lillias had lightened Faris's heart somewhat—renewed her hope in receiving the Highwayman's forgiveness. Still, she was apprehensive, fearful that this purple-curtained meeting with the Highwayman of Tanglewood would indeed be her last. She would wait—wait until the sun had nearly set in its entirety before starting out. Her heart pounded as brutal as a hammer on an anvil as she waited and watched—watched the sun's amethyst setting.

"You are in wait of him, are you not?"

Faris swallowed the lump in her throat—rubbed at the goose bumps racing over her arms at the sound of his voice. She was fearful to turn and face him—to lay eyes on his handsome countenance and form. Yet she did turn, gasping at the sight of him—the pure magnificence of Lochlan Rockrimmon.

The kitchen fires had been put out for the night, leaving only the light of the setting sun through the open door as illumination. Lochlan appeared rather disheveled—as if he had only just risen from slumber. His shirt hung open and untucked from his breeches, his hair boyishly tousled. Faris swallowed a second lump in her throat—for he was ever more attractive as such than in the perfect finery of a gentleman.

"Answer me!" he demanded. "You mean to meet your lover this night."

"I-I cannot tell—" Faris stammered.

"You are going to him," Lochlan growled, taking her shoulders none too gently between his powerful hands. "Tell me the truth of it."

"Yes," she admitted. She allowed her gaze to linger on his mouth—allowed her mind to linger on the taste and sense of his kiss.

"And will you return to Loch Loland?" he asked.

Faris was surprised by his question. Why would she not return?

"Or does he intend to strip you from me—from us?" he added.

Faris forced herself to calm breathing. She had not thought of never returning. The only circumstance that could keep her from returning to Loch Loland would be the ability of the Highwayman to spirit her away. Being so uncertain as to whether or not the Highwayman of Tanglewood would even keep her after her betrayal, how could she hope to be spirited by him?

"I am fearful he will cast me off," she whispered, "when I have told him of my weakness and my betrayal. He may ride from me as fast as his mount can carry him."

"He will never ride from you," Lochlan said. His voice was low, his emerald eyes narrowed as he looked at her. "He will not give you up simply because I have forced my own intentions upon you."

"As you said, sire," Faris began, "yesterday— after—after you championed me yet again: it was shared, the exchange between us. It was shared, and this I must confess to him."

"Hmmph," he breathed. "It was not shared, and well you know it. I asked you for one kiss—fairly ordered you to kiss me. That is not a shared kiss, Faris. That is only my desperation playing upon your guilted feelings of indebtedness."

"No!" she exclaimed. "It was shared between us. It was!"

All of a sudden, she wanted him to know of her gratitude. Even she wanted him to know she cared for him, desired his company and his kiss. She wanted him to understand that were it not for the Highwayman, he might well have owned her entirely—that in some regard he already did.

"You are kind to encourage me, Faris," he said, a slight smile spreading across his face. "Yet I think I must accept—what man am I compared with him? What reason would you or any other woman have to consider me over such as him?"

"The kiss was shared, sire," Faris said.

"Then I will endeavor to believe it," he said. "Unless—unless you wish to truly share a kiss with me, not simply allow me to kiss you as the payment you deem necessary for my defense of you. At that I might know you were not false in it."

"I have once already betrayed my heart's desire in offer of gratitude to you, sire," she said. "And yet you would ask me to—"

"I would ask you to offer me the chance to win you, Faris," Lochlan said.

"What?" Faris gasped. What did he imply?

"Grant me one last taste of your lips," he whispered. "In that, I will win you, and you will not run away to meet your Highwayman. Or I will

lose you, and in losing you . . . I will leave Loch
Loland instead."

Faris shook her head. "You are in jest, sire. In
jest or have lost your wits in some manner."

"I will leave you, Faris," he said. "If that is
what you wish. Kiss me. Kiss me, and if I do
not evoke such passion and feeling in you as the
Highwayman of Tanglewood does—then I will
leave."

"You cannot leave Loch Loland for my sake,"
Faris said. "Surely you are only playing at
dramatics, sire."

"One last kiss," he whispered, "before you flee
into the night and into the arms of that damnable
rogue!" He gathered her into his arms, and the
feel of his warm breath hovering over her mouth
caused her to weaken.

"I will go to him," Faris breathed. "I will. I
cannot give him up. I cannot allow you to . . . I
cannot allow myself to—"

"You can," he whispered, and Faris's mouth
burst hot and moist for want of his.

"I-I cannot! I cannot!" she breathed, a moment
before his mouth captured her own. Driven
with passion, moist with desire, Lochlan's kiss
demanded response, and Faris's mouth answered.
She could not keep her hands from seeking out
the broad expanse of his shoulders—she could
not deny her fingers the privilege of weaving
through the warm brown of his hair. His arms

held her with such ferocious intent she thought he might indeed crush her. His mouth worked such a passion of bliss and pleasure against her own she thought she might faint for the wonder of his kiss.

"Do not go to him, Faris," he breathed. "Am I not as good a man as he?"

Faris felt the tears on her cheeks, cursed the mad pounding of her heart within her bosom.

"Perhaps a better man," she said, pushing herself from his arms. "And I am unworthy of either!"

Faris broke from him completely, ran through the kitchen door and into the fading sunset. She prayed he would not follow her, and her prayer was answered.

Some way from the house, as the moon rose silver and full, Faris paused. Brushing the tears from her cheeks, she sobbed as fresh tears rinsed her face anew. She yet trembled with desire for Lochlan's kiss—her heart torn in two with her inward admitted love for him.

The Highwayman of Tanglewood would not forgive her! How could he forgive her such betrayal—such deep and emotive betrayal— betrayal reaching far deeper than the simple act of a kiss. She loved Lochlan Rockrimmon—as she loved the Highwayman of Tanglewood. Yet, she had loved the Highwayman first, and in this he owned her heart, deserved her devotion.

There was not to do but wait—wait and confess—confess and have consequence delivered.

The Highwayman of Tanglewood stepped quiet and unseen in the darkness as he followed Faris from Loch Loland to the forever-running heather. Lochlan Rockrimmon had not won the Highwayman's lover away from him! Still, he loathed the heir of Loch Loland Castle for endeavoring to do so. If it were conceivable—if there were any venue to beating and besting him, indeed the Highwayman would have beaten and bested him. Yet, it was an impossibility.

Thus, the Highwayman of Tanglewood determined to free his fair Faris of Loch Loland Castle—free her from torment, from the self-loathing and thoughts of betrayal she must certainly own. Yes, he would reveal himself! Let truth best him however it would, for his soul was of little worth when weighed with hers. He would free her and allow her to choose—choose to keep him or to abandon him. Her frustration, her weeping as she made her way toward the old ruins of Castle Alexendria, her pain was his doing. A greater understanding he owned of it: her misery was of his own making, none but his. In his soul, he knew it had been wrong to keep himself from her—to keep the truth from her. He had driven her to Bainbridge Graybeau, he had driven her into the arms of Lochlan Rockrimmon, and he could place the blame for it nowhere but on his own shoulders.

As certainly as she bore the heavy guilt of betrayal, the Highwayman bore the guilt of deceit. He had deceived her at each rendezvous. By not revealing the truth, by keeping his whole heart and self from her, he had driven her to another. He would free her—this very night. And if she chose to keep him, he would gather her into his arms, drink the sweet nectar of her kiss, and keep her forever to him. If she chose instead to loathe him for his deceit, then he would free her heart and body. If she chose to loathe him, then such would be his painful, eternal penance for having harmed her.

Quietly, the Highwayman of Tanglewood followed his love—followed her through the heather to the old ruin. There he paused, watching as she knelt before the headstones of the Rockrimmon knight and his lady—watching as a summer's breeze rained willow leaves upon her lovely form.

The Highwayman of Tanglewood

Faris let her fingers trace the worn engravings on the tombstone before her. Had the ancient Lady Rockrimmon—who so long lay at rest in the soil and in heaven—had she been weakened by the king's attention? When her knight was away defending the kingdom and the Alexendria's young king had become smitten with her, had she weakened toward him? Rising to her feet, Faris wondered—had this ancient Lady Rockrimmon melted in the king's embrace, kissed him with such a passion as Faris had kissed Lochlan? Had she betrayed her beloved knight as Faris had betrayed the Highwayman? Faris winced as guilt, shame, and pain gripped her heart. She was certain this great lady had not known confusion and betrayal. She was certain the grand Lady Rockrimmon of the past had stood ever faithful and true— her heart unwavering—her love consistent and strong.

"Surrender yar virtue, milady," came the High- wayman's raspy voice.

Faris could not help but breathe relief as his hands encircled her throat from behind. Yet tears filled her eyes as she turned to face him. Her heart leapt at the sight of him—his black attire from head to boot, the mask covering his head and face, the goatee and mustache he wore. Yes—he wore the goatee and mustache—she was near certain they were false. Had not she felt his clean-shaven face against her own last they had met—on the night he had pulled her from the kitchen doorway at Loch Loland and kissed her in the black of night? He brushed a tear from her cheek, and her body warmed at his simple touch, her heart leaping with hope.

"It's glad ya are to see me then, lass?" he asked, brushing a tear from her chin.

"I-I am," she stammered, more tears escaping her eyes. These would be their last moments together, she well knew it.

"But what be the matter, fair Faris?" he asked. "Yar lookin' at me as if yar never to see me again, ya are."

"I-I have something to tell you," she began, "And . . . and when the tale is told, you may never want to see me again."

The Highwayman's dazzling smile faded. "Then tell me the tale, lass, and let me make me own endin'," he said.

"I love you," she whispered. "You know that is true, do you not?"

"Aye," he said. "I believe it when ya say it to me now."

"I love you. I never imagined I could love someone . . . someone . . ."

"Someone ya may never see—may never know?" he finished for her.

Faris nodded. Mustering her courage she continued, "But . . . but there is something evil in me," she told him, tears streaming over her cheeks. "An evil I cannot purge."

"What manner of evil could possibly find host in ye, lass?" the Highwayman whispered, removing his glove and caressing her cheek with the back of his hand.

She must confess! She must risk losing the Highwayman of Tanglewood, for it was she did not deserve him. "Master Lochlan," she whispered. "He—he has been so kind to me . . . championed me on more than one occasion."

"He is an able man. I do not deny it," the Highwayman said.

Faris could hear the trepidation in his voice. Had he already guessed at her transgression?

"He is a good man, and I . . . I hold a . . . a deep fondness for him," Faris explained.

"A deep fondness?" the Highwayman asked. She saw him stiffen—did not miss the near growling tone in his voice. Yet she must continue. She must confess all.

"Yesterday," she began, "Yesterday he again defended me—my reputation, my person—he defended me. He demanded Lady Stringham and her daughter quit Loch Loland Castle on my account . . . and then when . . . when he asked a simply boon of me in return . . . in fact it was not so simple . . . and I . . . I gave him willingly that which he asked."

"And what be the boon he asked of ye, lass?" the Highwayman asked. His voice was cold, solemn, angry already.

"A . . . a kiss," she breathed. "A shared kiss." Faris squeezed her eyes tightly shut, tears heavy over her cheeks.

The Highwayman was silent. She knew he was angry, hurt, disgusted with her. She had lost him in telling the truth, yet she could not have lived her life with such a secret.

"And so yar tellin' me, the great Lochlan Rockrimmon, well-known for his ability to resist beautiful women such as yarself—the lord of the manor, so to speak—comes to yar rescue and begs a kiss as his reward . . . and ya gave it to him . . . willingly?" he asked.

"I-I did," Faris breathed, wiping at the tears on her cheeks. Her heart was breaking! Still, she looked to him when she heard the low chuckle begin in his throat.

He donned his dazzling smile and said, "Were ya thinkin' I would turn ya out, lass? What chambermaid ever was there who did not dream of kissin' her handsome young master? What woman ever was there who should have withheld such a blessing as a thankful kiss from her rescuer?" His smile faded, and he took her in his arms as he gazed down into her face. "And what Highwayman has the right to claim a woman he has met only on five nights in twilight? A woman he has promised no future to? A woman deservin' of all life's joys?"

"You—you will not abandon me?" she whispered, unable to believe he was forgiving her. Far more than forgiving her—he seemed nearly to be condoning her behavior.

"Never," he whispered, placing a kiss on the tip of her nose. "He has done more than ever I have in rescuin' ya from a ruined reputation and indeed twice from the likes of Kade Tremeshton. Yar pretty young master took him to task on both occasions, he did—before ever I heaped humiliation on him after." The Highwayman paused to press a tender kiss to Faris's forehead. He chuckled and said, "Lochlan Rockrimmon has never been so furious over a woman, it is said in the village, as he was the day at Loch Loland Castle when Kade Tremeshton laid hands on pretty Faris Shayhan."

Faris laid her head on the Highwayman's strong chest, feeling blessed in his understanding forgiveness. Yet as she closed her eyes, it was Lochlan's likeness that grew in her mind. She frowned trying to dispel the vision of his handsome face, the brilliance of his emerald eyes, and the moist passion of his kiss.

"And now, 'tis me own turn, lass," the Highwayman whispered. "One kiss from yar sweet lips—and then I have me own secrets to reveal to ye."

Faris's heart leapt. Could it be? Did he mean to reveal his identity to her? She sensed he did, and as his head descended toward hers, she inwardly vowed to surrender to him—to stay with him—to follow him to the ends of the earth. Lochlan Rockrimmon could never be hers, never. But the Highwayman of Tanglewood, with all his strength and forgiving nature—perhaps he could.

He paused in kissing her, however, a smile of pure mischief spreading across his face. "I do find it a bit disturbin', however," he began.

"Which part of it?" she asked. Was he only just realizing the weight of it—the weight of the manner of kiss she had shared with Lochlan? Her heart seemed to miss several beats, and she was breathless with renewed anxiety.

"The part of it concernin' Bainbridge Graybeau," he said.

Faris gasped as fear anew washed over her.

"Bainbridge," she whispered. She had quite forgotten her moments with Graybeau—her begging of him to confess to her—the kiss she initiated with him. Her mind had been so taken with the fever set upon it by Lochlan Rockrimmon, she had quite forgotten she had once thought Bainbridge to be the Highwayman of Tanglewood.

"I did think he was you," she began, frantic to explain. Had she won his forgiveness only to lose it in the next moment? "I thought so sure he was you that I endeavored to coax his confession."

"I well know it," the Highwayman said. "For I was there when ye did."

"What?" Faris breathed.

"It was I witnessed yar endeavors to Bainbridge Graybeau, and indeed, I am flattered ye would think I be sooch a man as he," the Highwayman said.

Faris frowned. Confusion pricked at her mind. "Then you . . . you are not angry in it?" she asked.

His smile faded, yet his embrace tightened. "What right have I to be angry with ye far any of it, fair Faris?" he said. " 'Tis ye who owns that right, and after I've had me taste of yar kiss—after I strip this mask from me shameful face—it may be me who loses his lover this night."

"Never!" Faris whispered as his lips hovered a mere breath above her own.

"Promise it, Faris," he whispered. "Promise to me that whomever ye find behind this wretched mask . . . promise ye will love me still."

"I promise," Faris sighed as his lips pressed to her own.

The first touch of his lips was tender, gentle, and almost timid. He seemed tentative—as if he thought she might refuse him her kiss. Oh, but she never would! Never! As he kissed her upper lip lingeringly, she sighed. As he kissed her lower lip in the same fashion, she was breathless. He had never before kissed her in so careful a manner. Lochlan's image intruded in her thoughts. She fancied this had been his manner of beginning their first shared kiss. Faris knew it was Lochlan's residual presence in her heart that found the similarity, and she tried to banish him from her mind. As the Highwayman's mouth coaxed hers into a deeper, more passionate exchange, she tried to dispel the memory of Lochlan's similar manner in even this. Yet even as desire rose in her, even as her hands caressed the broad expanse of the Highwayman's shoulders, she could not push Lochlan's image from her soul. Would she ever purge his presence from her being? Yet she must! She must abandon all thoughts of him—for here was her heart's desire, here was the Highwayman of Tanglewood, her rogue champion and lover.

"I should have well known of this!"

Faris gasped, breaking from the Highwayman and whirling about to see Kade Tremeshton standing behind her. He brandished his sword, its blade capturing the illumination of the moonlight.

Panic leapt to Faris's bosom! The Highwayman

was in danger! Her greatest fear for him was at realization before her: in loving him with such desperation, she had placed him in peril. It was for her sake he had appeared. It was for her sake he lingered.

"The favored chambermaid of Loch Loland Castle in tryst with our favored villain." He threw his head back a moment, laughing with utter triumph. "Secretive lovers, is it?" he asked. "And to think, Faris, I had begun to believe you had set your eye on Lochlan Rockrimmon—"

"Ye well know better than to scrap with me, Tremeshton," the Highwayman said. Drawing his rapier, he pulled his black cloak from his shoulders, swiftly discarding it. He was readying for a duel, and the fact frightened Faris beyond imagination.

"Ah, but it's I who have taken you by surprise this time, Highwayman!" Kade laughed. "And you so distracted by Faris. She's has weakened you—weakened your heart, your mind, and no doubt your back."

"The lass but strengthens me, she does," the Highwayman said.

Kade shouted, lunging at the Highwayman. The Highwayman of Tanglewood shoved Faris aside as he leapt backward in defense, Kade's blade just missing his midsection.

Kade laughed. "The blade of a rapier is no match for the blade of a dress sword, Highwayman," he said. "It is a wonder you wield such an archaic weapon."

Faris watched as the Highwayman tipped his head in consideration of his rapier. "It is, in fact, a treasure of me family," the Highwayman said. "And though it has served me well in besting you before—" Faris stepped back as the Highwayman of Tanglewood tossed his rapier to the ground at her feet. "Perhaps I should match a heavier blade with ye this night." Faris eyes widened as the Highwayman of Tanglewood then drew the silver blade of a dress sword from a sheath at his hip. "In fact, it should drain yar blood mooch faster and hurt far worse when I run ya through."

At that, the Highwayman of Tanglewood advanced! Kade's eyes widened with surprise and fear as he defended. The ensuing match of blade against blade caused Faris to stand breathless, paralyzed with trepidation and fear for the Highwayman's safety. She trembled, winced, gasped, watched the two men duel. It was obvious the Highwayman was the better swordsman, yet he seemed to toy with Kade, allowing him to advance on occasion, playing with him as a cat did a mouse before chewing off its head. Furthermore, Faris sensed her lover was indeed distracted, for he kept glancing over at her as if anxious of her well-being.

Minutes passed—long minutes, each of which found Faris near to fainting with fear. At last, the

Highwayman disarmed Kade, sending his weapon tumbling into the thick heather. Faris sighed, relieved at his besting Kade. Yet she gasped when next the Highwayman of Tanglewood tossed his own weapon to join Kade's.

"Aye, but this is not task challenge. I've bested ye at swordplay before," the Highwayman of Tanglewood growled. "I like most to best ye with me fists."

Faris looked to Kade's face—studied the bruising of it, his swollen nose—all evidence of Lochlan Rockrimmon's fists having already bested the blackguard.

"You'll not best me in fists this night, Highwayman!" Kade growled. "For there is in me a deep hatred of you, and it will advance my skill and determination. The stakes are far greater than you imagine this night."

Faris shuddered as Kade looked at her. Her instinct was to flee. Yet fleeing may put the Highwayman in further risk somehow. And so she stood helpless, trembling, and terrified.

"In that ye finally prove ya have one wit in yar head, Tremeshton," the Highwayman growled. "For the stakes of crossin' me here this night . . . may well be yar very life!"

Kade's fist led toward the Highwayman's head. Yet the Highwayman easily avoided it, landing his own powerful fist to Kade's already bruised chin. The force of the Highwayman's strength knocked

Kade to the ground. Yet his fury was great in having been provoked, and he quickly leapt to his feet. Kade bent at his midsection, rushing at the Highwayman and hitting him square in the stomach with his shoulder. The Highwayman of Tanglewood stumbled backward, and Faris gasped, covering her mouth with her hands. The Highwayman fell hard to the ground, and Kade managed two brutal fists, one to either side of his jaw. The Highwayman of Tanglewood's great strength rallied, however, and he pushed Kade aside, rising to his feet once more.

"Me patience is far spent with ye," the Highwayman said. Faris gasped as the Highwayman's powerful fist landed at Kade's left cheek. The great force of the blow sent Kade reeling backward and sprawling to the ground.

The Highwayman of Tanglewood advanced, crushing the sole of one black boot to Kade's throat. Faris could hear the villain choking as the Highwayman's foot kept him pinned on his back.

"Yar no more than a filthy, maggoty dead skunk, Kade Tremeshton!" the Highwayman growled, his breathing labored from the altercation. "I should slit yar throat and leave ya to bleed out on the ground, I should."

"Please! Please!" Kade Tremeshton begged. "I fold! I fold!"

"Coward!" the Highwayman growled as he delivered a brutal kick to the side of the villain's head. Kade the Heinous was rendered unconscious.

With shallow breath and legs weakened from fear, Faris rushed to the Highwayman. She threw herself into his powerful embrace, clinging to his shirt with her small fists, sobbing against the strength of his massive chest.

"He might have killed you!" Faris cried as the Highwayman of Tanglewood held her against him. The feel of his hands weaving through her hair sent goose bumps rippling over her neck and arms.

"Never," he breathed. "Such a coward could never—"

Faris gasped as the Highwayman stiffened, growled as if in great pain.

As the Highwayman shouted, "Aye! Aye!" pain constricting his body, Faris looked down to find the cause. Kade Tremeshton knelt beside them, fully conscious and with his hand on a dagger protruding from the Highwayman's right thigh. The blade was already buried deep in the Highwayman's leg, but Faris screamed as the villain pulled down on the knife, causing it to tear brutally through the Highwayman's flesh.

The Highwayman was yet the more powerful man. Even for the great agony of the wound, he reached down, covering Kade's hand with his own. Overpowering Kade's own strength, the Highwayman of Tanglewood pulled the dagger from his leg, twisting the weapon in Kade's hand, and drawing it quickly across the villain's throat. Kade Tremeshton's body fell limp and lifeless to the ground, his blood staining crimson the heather beneath.

Yet there was other blood seeping into the heather—the blood of the hero Highwayman of Tanglewood.

"He's—he's finished me," the Highwayman breathed as he collapsed to his knees, blood streaming from the wound at his leg.

Panic overtook Faris! She could not think with any coherence! She could not think what action to take! He would die—bleed out in the ruins of Castle Alexendria! She would lose him to heartless death's whim!

"You need a physician," Faris said, dropping to her knees beside him. "I must find assistance else you will surely bleed to death!"

"Ya must help me mount, lass," the High-wayman panted. He was breathless and in obvious, excruciating pain. He whistled, and his great black steed appeared from just beyond the ruins. "I-I must get ya safely back to Loch Loland . . . and meself to some assistance."

"I will see you mount," she told him, brushing the tears from her face. "But we will seek a physician at once. We will not make for Loch Loland!"

Never before had the Highwayman seemed so

massive in his size. He was weak, and it gave him great difficulty in mounting.

"Where do I take you? Is there a physician you trust?" she asked him. She was trying to be brave, trying to be calm and strong, but in truth she was afraid she would faint into a despair.

"The harse will know where to take us," the Highwayman whispered. Even for the dark of the night, Faris looked at the blood spilling from the Highwayman's wound. The loss was quick and profuse. She feared his blood would be spent from him long before they reached a physician.

As if having read her thoughts, the Highwayman said, "Ya must tear a strip from yar petticoat . . . tie it about the wound to slow the bleedin'." His voice was weak and strained.

Faris struggled to tear a long strip of cloth from her petticoat. Her hands trembled and she found she had difficulty drawing breath. Yet she was successful and tied the cloth tightly around the Highwayman's leg just above the wound. Leading the Highwayman's steed to a nearby rock, she mounted behind her lover. For a moment, Bainbridge Graybeau's face passed through her mind. She was more confident on horseback because of his lessons in riding, and she whispered her thanks to him on the night air.

Reaching around the Highwayman's massive form, Faris took the reins, digging her heels hard into the horse's flesh. They were away at once—

away toward Loch Loland Castle! She could see it in the distance—a dark silhouette against an amethyst sky. Its warm-lit windows beckoned— yet there was no physician at Loch Loland.

"He makes for Loch Loland," Faris said. "But there is not help there!"

"He knows where to ride," the Highwayman said.

But who at Loch Loland would help them? Faris knew surely that each soul at Loch Loland Castle was in support of the Highwayman of Tanglewood and his deeds of righting wrongs. Yet would any there risk attending him? She thought of Lochlan—of his knowledge Faris was in league with the rogue of the Tanglewood Forest. Yet would he help Faris's lover?

All of a sudden, Faris felt the Highwayman go limp. She managed to rein in his beast of a steed only a moment before he slipped from his saddle, landing weak and nearly unconscious on the ground.

Faris slid from the saddle, assisting the High-wayman as he struggled to turn to his back.

"You must remount," she told him. "We must find a physician or you will surely—"

"I—I will wait far ya here. I will wait here as ya go to Loch Loland far help," he said.

"Loch Loland?" Faris exclaimed. Indeed, as she looked up, Loch Loland loomed close—a near stone's throw. Faris feared for the Highwayman's safety—feared his being revealed to anyone in Loch Loland. Yet he would bleed out if she did not find assistance soon!

"Leave me here, Faris," he breathed.

Faris wiped the tears from her cheeks, trying to calm her terrified trembling. "I cannot possibly leave you," Faris sobbed.

"Off with ya, lass," he breathed. "Run to Loch Loland Castle now and bring me yar man Old Joe. He'll—he'll know what to do."

"Old Joseph?" Faris asked rising to her feet. "Are you acquainted with him? Is he to be trusted?"

"Aye," the Highwayman said. "He is much trusted."

Old Joseph! Of course! The wisest of men was Old Joseph! If there was anyone nearby to help, it was indeed Old Joseph! Yet she could not leave her love in such agony to bear. Already his breeches at his right leg were completely saturated with blood—the crimson life-liquid fairly streaming down his boot.

"Yet—Faris, wait," he said. She paused, dropping to her knees next to him, and forcing an encouraging smile of hope that all would be well. "I will be havin' yar promise first . . ." he breathed.

"Anything," she sobbed. "Anything!"

"Ye must promise me . . . no matter what comes to ya . . . what knowledge . . . no matter what happens to me . . . I must have yar promise . . . ya must promise ya will love me yet—no matter what ya may witness from here forward."

Faris melted into sobs. She threw herself against his powerful chest, trembling as she felt his weakened embrace. "Nothing could keep me from loving you. Nothing!" she sobbed.

"Swear it to me, then," he breathed, taking her face in his hands and searching her face for sincerity. "Swear to me ya will love me still—that ya will stay with me ever after—no matter what this night may hail upon us."

"I swear it!" she sobbed.

"Then go, now . . . go for Old Joe of Loch Loland Castle. I am nearly done in," he whispered.

Faris knew she could not afford to linger any longer. If her beloved Highwayman was to be saved, she must leave him. She could not bear losing him—he who had so willingly forgiven her, pledged his heart to her. If he died, she was certain her heart would break and kill her in his wake.

Frantically Faris ran to the servants' entrance of Loch Loland's kitchen. Old Joseph spent many a late night in the kitchen. She prayed he would be there on this dreadful one.

Yet what if it were Lochlan she found there? What if he were lingering there over a warm pie? Even he would help—she was certain. No matter his feelings toward her—whether desire or loathing—he was ever chivalrous, a champion. Still, it was Old Joseph the Highwayman wanted, and she prayed he would be there. Attempting to inhale a deep breath of calm, Faris slowly opened the servants' entrance to the kitchen.

The room was dim, kitchen duties long finished. Faris held her breath and prayed for a miracle. As she looked to the kitchen table to see Old Joseph sitting and reading a book, her tears renewed, and she thanked heaven for its benevolence.

"Joseph!" she called in a whisper. "Joseph!"

The elderly man looked around, smiling when he saw her. "Why, Faris!" he greeted. "What has you out and about at such a late hour as this?"

"Joseph, please come to me. At once!" she cried in a whisper. Instantly the old man's brow puckered with concern. "Quickly, Joseph! There is no time to hesitate!"

Joseph was on his feet and at the door in an instant.

Faris burst into tears as she spoke. "You must know of him, Joseph . . . else he would not have sent me to bring you!" she cried, covering her mouth for a moment. Her distress had caused her to speak too loudly.

"Who, dove? Whatever is the matter, Faris?" Joseph whispered in return. He reached out and took her shoulders in hand. "Who?"

"The Highwayman . . ." Faris stammered. "The

Highwayman of Tanglewood. Do—do you know him, Joseph?"

Joseph's eyes narrowed, and Faris knew he was uncertain as to whether or not he should trust her.

"He's been wounded, Joseph! Terribly wounded . . . in dueling Kade Tremeshton. These weeks . . . the Highwayman and I . . . we . . . we have been meeting and—"

"Take me to him," Joseph demanded. "At once!"

Making their way through the dark without the aid of a lantern, Faris felt her heart swell with hope when she heard the Highwayman call out as they approached.

"Joseph!" he called in a whisper. "Quick, man! Ya must spirit me away! If anyone comes upon Tremeshton dead at Castle Alexendria, and I am found to be ailin' . . . it will throw suspicion me way," he said.

"Master Lochlan. What have you stumbled into now?" Old Joseph said, dropping to his knees beside the Highwayman.

Faris stopped breathing. Her hands and arms went cold—numb as understanding rushed over her like a torrential rain. Her mind ached, pounded as if a drum were pent up inside her head. The pieces of the puzzle in which she was entwined began shifting together.

"Faris," the Highwayman breathed. "I—I have your promise. You—you promised me." Gone was the raspy Irish brogue of the Highwayman of Tanglewood—replaced by the all too familiar and beloved intonation of the commanding voice of Lochlan Rockrimmon.

Of Secrets and Wishes

Faris felt her knees give way beneath her. Kneeling before the wounded Highwayman of Tanglewood—kneeling before her wounded champion and lover—she wrapped her arms around her stomach as her body began to heave uncontrollably. She was in love with one man, not two! She was in love with Lochlan Rockrimmon!

As she sobbed, her body convulsing with emotion, Faris shook her head. "No! No! It cannot be!" she cried. Yet she knew it was true. Perhaps she had always known, always dreamt of it, wished for it—always convincing herself otherwise.

As a rush of realization and memory washed over, Faris struggled to hold to consciousness! She saw it now—all of it! Lochlan Rockrimmon—away from Loch Loland Castle in tending to his father's business these past two years. Had it not been two years since village folk had begun to share fantastic stories of the Highwayman of Tanglewood? Since his return—since Loch Loland's heir had returned—had not Lochlan Rockrimmon been absent each time the Highwayman was seen? Even when Lord

Brookings of Saxton had been bested? For a moment, Faris's mind lingered on the Highwayman's appearance at Loch Loland in the broad light of day. Lochlan had been there—Lochlan himself had been watching as the Highwayman of Tanglewood pinned Kade Tremeshton's parchments to a tree. Yet Old Joseph knew Lochlan was the Highwayman of Tanglewood. Was it not possible that others knew as well? She thought at once of Bainbridge Graybeau—of his lie. Lord Rockrimmon's favorite and aged mount Jovan had been stabled when the Highwayman had appeared at Loch Loland. Yet Graybeau had claimed he was not. Graybeau had lied as to his whereabouts at that moment. Could it be Graybeau had ridden as the Highwayman of Tanglewood—and all for the sake of drawing suspicion from Lochlan?

It was why his bed was ever made, Faris realized. Not because Lochlan was so caring about his bedding but because he was often never abed when it was supposed that he was!

"You promised, Faris!" Lochlan shouted, drawing her to full consciousness once more.

Faris reached up, stripping the mask from the face of the Highwayman of Tanglewood. Emerald eyes no longer shaded by a black mask flashed brilliant in the full light of the moon. Lochlan then tore the false mustache and goatee from the flesh surrounding his mouth. "You promised . . . no matter what was revealed!" he growled.

"Calm yourself, Master Loch," Old Joseph said, "lest you want this to be a mortal wound, which now inflicts you."

"Bring her to me, Joe!" Lochlan shouted. "Make her come to me!"

Yet Faris was stiff with fear, heartbreak, and disbelieving, and she could not move.

"Joseph! Now! Bring her to me!" Lochlan continued to shout.

"You must calm yourself, Master," Joe began, "else you'll harm yourself further or draw attention this way."

"Make her come to me, Joe! Now!" Lochlan shouted, as tears appeared at the outer corners of his eyes—traveled over his temples.

Old Joseph turned to Faris. "Faris," he said, his voice kind and soothing. "He'll—he'll bleed out where he sits if I do not tend to this wound at once. Please . . . I understand you're astonished. But, for his life, I ask you . . ."

Trembling, Faris pressed hands to the cool ground on which her knees already lingered. Mustering what little strength was left to her, she began to crawl to her wounded rogue. As she drew near, he reached for her, one blood-soaked hand taking her arm and pulling her full against him.

"You are mine," he growled. "I have won

you! As Highwayman, as gentleman, and as your champion . . . I claim you." His body was wracked with coughing; still he wrapped his bloodied hand in Faris's hair, pressing her cheek to his chest.

"It goes bad for you, sire," Old Joseph whispered. "You need a physician."

"Collect my mother, Joe. Collect the coach . . . but no coachmen. Only you and Mother. We will stop for Physician Standard in the village. You must away with me, Joseph. You, Mother, Faris, and the doctor— or if Lochlan Rockrimmon is to be found so wounded after Kade Tremeshton's death at the hand of the Highwayman of Tanglewood . . . I surely am done for." Lochlan coughed again before adding, "Tell the tale as such—Lady Rockrimmon's Aunt Agatha . . . has . . . has taken ill, and I have accompanied my mother for the visit. We—we took Faris as companion to mother . . . and . . . and did not want to bother the others at such an hour." Lochlan pushed at Joseph's shoulder and breathed, "Go, now, Joseph . . . before my blood is indeed spent. And Joseph . . . tell Father the Rockrimmon rapier is beneath Alexendria's willow. He must retrieve it."

"I go, sire," Joseph said. "Do not let him move, Faris. Not one inch."

Faris watched Joseph disappear into the darkness—her body still trembling, her mind yet unable to completely accept.

"You love me still, Faris," Lochlan breathed.

It was a command, and she knew he doubted the truth of it. "I—I love the Highwayman," Faris whispered, tears streaming down her cheeks as she raised her head to look at him.

"I *am* the Highwayman, Faris," he reminded her.

Her anger, her rage, and her heartbreak at being so deceived caused her to feel as if the very hairs on her head were aflame then. "*You* are Lochlan Rockrimmon! Heir to title and Loch Loland Castle!" she cried. "I—I love the Highwayman of Tanglewood!"

"And you love Lochlan Rockrimmon!" he shouted. "Do not deny it, for I have tasted of your kiss, held you in my arms, felt your heart beating madly—as I was and am both!"

"You are a wicked pretender!" she sobbed. "You—you but deceived me . . . made me believe . . . I—I thought you . . . I thought you truly loved me."

"I do love you!" he said, and she saw the tears anew at his temples. "I love you, Faris. I . . . I . . ."

"You lied to me . . . tried to . . . tried to trick me into betraying the man I loved . . ." she stammered.

"And you did!" he reminded her. "Willingly

and wholeheartedly because you knew he was one in the same! You must have known it to be true!"

"I did not!" she cried.

"You must have known," he whispered, coughing. "At the least, please tell me you wanted it to be true. For I only wished you to love *me*—I only wished to own your heart as Lochlan Rockrimmon. A dashing rogue the like of the Highwayman is he of whom every woman dreams. I knew you could love the rogue—but I hoped you loved me—thought you might love me . . . best."

Her hurt became so painful in its depths to have vanquished her tears. "I did not know," she said. Still, she wondered at her own words, for she fancied in that moment she had known.

"And you would love the thief . . . but not the gentleman?" he asked. He was growing weak.

Faris's fear returned, intensified and beat down her anger and humiliation. "The thief belonged to me," she whispered, "whereas the gentleman never could."

"You won them both," he coughed. "The thief, the gentleman, the rogue, and the heir. You promised—no matter what was spent this night—you promised to . . . to love me . . . thief or . . . or . . ."

Unconsciousness claimed him. Faris marveled at how much pain and crimson loss the powerful man had endured before giving in to the need for reprieve from such exertion and great injury. His fist in her hair relaxed, his arms slackened, dropping from her body, and she pulled herself into a sitting position beside him. She placed her hand to his chest. It yet rose and fell with the breath of life, and her own breath was returned to her.

Slowly her gaze traveled the length of him—over his soft brown hair to the set of his jaw to the blood-soaked boots he wore. The rise and fall of his chest again reassured her he yet lived, but there was no other reassurance to be given her. Her beloved Highwayman, the rogue Highwayman of Tanglewood, was lost to her forever—and yet, there was Lochlan Rockrimmon, her champion and hero. The battle that had raged inside her, the confusion of her heart, was vanquished at the knowledge she had not been untrue to her lover. In fact, what better dream made real could there be? The two valiant men she so desperately loved—the two magnificent men her heart and mind had struggled to understand, struggled to choose between—these two were one. It should have been her comfort—her joy. It should well have been the most wonderful knowledge of her life long. Yet there could be no owning Lochlan Rockrimmon. The Highwayman of Tanglewood may have been anyone—peasant, smithy, or stablemaster. The Highwayman of Tanglewood may have married with a young chambermaid, but Lochlan Rockrimmon was born of greatness, to greatness, and to great expectation. If not Tannis Stringham, he would marry the like of her—beautiful, graceful, wealthy, and with a vast dowry and lineage.

Faris brushed the tears from her cheeks. Still, it was a vain attempt, for more tears followed in their wake. Reaching forth, she dared run her fingers through the soft brown hair of Lochlan Rockrimmon. The sensation was a dream made truth, for she had never seen her Highwayman without the mask covering his head and face. Trailing her fingers over his cheek, his jawline, his lips—she took his limp, lifeless hand in hers, lacing their fingers and placing a tender kiss to its back.

Faris leaned forward, pressing her lips to his— surprised when his feverish voice mumbled, "Faris . . . my fair Faris . . . you promised."

"I promised to love you," she whispered, "not to endure being unable to own you."

She grimaced, tears stinging her eyes as she released his hand. Retrieving the discarded mask he had worn only a short time before, she stood—yet gazing down at him in the moonlight. Faris Shayhan knew not where she would go or how she would arrive there. Still, she knew she would go, for her lover was lost to her. In being assured of the Highwayman's true identity, she had lost the hope of his promised love. When she had seen him safe, knew he was well and cared for—she would flee.

"Faris!" Lady Rockrimmon cried.

Faris gasped when she saw Lady Rockrimmon rushing toward her. The great lady wore only her nightdress. Her hair hung freely about her shoulders.

"Darling!" Lady Rockrimmon exclaimed, reaching out and taking Faris's hands in her own. "Tell me he will live, Faris! Promise me he will live!" Lady Rockrimmon released only one of Faris's hands as she dropped to her knees beside her son.

"Oh, my darling!" she cried. "My darling Loch!"

"She means to leave me, Mother," Loch growled. His eyes opened for only a moment as he commanded in a weak voice, "Do not lose sight of Faris, Mother. Have Joseph bind her if he must—but . . . but do not lose sight of her."

Pulling her hand from Lady Rockrimmon's grasp, Faris was certain she was about to swoon. Her breathing was labored, too rapid. The world seemed about a mad spin.

"Hold her fast, Joseph!" Lady Rockrimmon cried. Instantly, Faris found herself held fast in the surprisingly strong arms of Old Joseph. "Hold her!"

"Let me go, Joseph. Please. I will not leave

until his fate is known," Faris sobbed. She felt weak—knew she had no strength left in her.

"He will surely die if you leave him, Faris," Joseph said. His voice was calm, yet determined.

Faris's fevered mind could resist no longer, and as she slipped into the darkness of unconsciousness, she thought, *Oh, let him live. Please let him live.*

"His lordship Lord Rockrimmon will ride, milady. Graybeau is already too suspect." It was Old Joseph's voice breaking the silence of Faris's unconscious state. "Milord will ride . . . make certain he is seen as the Highwayman."

"Will he be careful, Joseph?" Lady Rockrimmon asked.

"He will, milady. He sends assurance his riding as the Highwayman of Tanglewood will divert suspicion from Master Lochlan."

Faris opened her eyes to see a man she did not recognize enter the small cottage room where she lay.

"I have cleaned the injury, milady," the man began, "Though I do feel searing it is necessary."

"After all he has already endured, Mr. Standard? Can he . . . can he endure your smoldering the wound?" Lady Rockrimmon said. Her fearful voice was nearly a whisper.

"I must cauterize it now, milady, lest infection sets in directly," the man said. The man looked then to Faris, speaking yet to Lady Rockrimmon. "He is feverish and fitful, milady . . . worrisome over the girl, in want of her company. I see she is awake. Might she be persuaded to—"

"Of course! Faris—you must go with Mr. Standard. Lochlan must have you. He has been in such a state ever since he regained consciousness! Such a state, Faris!" Lady Rockrimmon brushed a strand of hair from Faris's forehead, caressing the place lovingly with the back of her hand. "He loves you, Faris. It is long I have known Lochlan Rockrimmon loves you—not so long I have known his Highwayman loves you too."

"He—he cannot love me, milady," Faris said, tears filling her eyes. "For I—I am but a chambermaid."

"As was I, Faris—a chambermaid in the very house you are chambermaid in now. But that was before the young master of Loch Loland Castle fell in love with me—before he made me his bride," Lady Rockrimmon whispered.

Faris squeezed her eyes tightly shut, afraid to believe the woman's assurance. Young masters did not marry chambermaids. They did not. Ill-treated them, as Kade Tremeshton had, teased them perhaps—but never did they take them to wife.

"Quickly, miss. He is in a bad way yet," the physician said.

"Go to him, Faris," Lady Rockrimmon said. "The rest can be sorted out once he is well enough." Faris nodded. Mr. Standard and Old Joseph assisted her in rising from the bed. Her arms and legs were heavy, as was her spirit—her heart.

Lochlan was pallid—as pale as death where he lay in a bed in an adjoining room. Yet his emerald eyes flashed when first he caught sight of her. Faris wondered how she had not recognized the flash of his green eyes when she met him as the Highwayman. Still, their meetings had ever been under the cover of twilight and darkness. Coupled with the mask he ever wore, the two small slits made for his sight—all of it had endeavored to hide the brilliant emerald of his eyes.

"Faris!" his breath called to her. "Come to me at once!" he demanded. "At once!"

Faris went to him. He took hold of her wrist, pulling her against his body. "Oh, Faris—Faris!" he breathed into her hair. "I—I thought you had quit me already . . . not waiting even to see if I lived. And I shall surely die if you leave me."

"Hush," she whispered, laying her head against the strength of his chest. "You must endure . . . and rest."

"Put the branch in his mouth, Joseph," Mr. Standard said. "You must remain as still as possible, sire. Do you understand?"

"Do not take Faris from me, Standard. Do *you* understand?" Lochlan growled.

"I do," the physician said. "Hold his leg . . . there at the ankle, Joseph," he added.

Tears fell from Faris's eyes as she watched the physician retrieve a red-hot knife from the coals of the hearth fire.

"You may lose perception, sire," the doctor said. "But do not give up. Your body must continue to fight."

Lochlan nodded as Joseph placed the small branch of a tree between his teeth.

"Now . . . hold, Joseph!" the physician shouted, driving the hot blade into the wound.

Lochlan shouted. Faris sobbed as she watched the perspiration and pain overtake his handsome face, the sickening smell of seared flesh filling her nostrils. Lochlan's entire body began to tremble. Yet he did not lose consciousness, and Joseph removed the branch from Lochlan's mouth.

"How weak you must think me, Faris," Lochlan breathed, his expression still that of enduring unendurable pain.

"How—how could I ever think you weak?" she sobbed, burying her face against his shirt.

"You must rest, Master Loch," Old Joseph said.

"Yes, sire. A great deal of rest is needed if you are to regain your strength," Mr. Standard confirmed. "Miss Faris needs her rest as well. You may see her after you have—"

"She will rest with me!" Lochlan growled.

"But, sire . . . that is not proper," Old Joseph began.

"I care not for propriety, Joseph!" Lochlan shouted. "She will leave me otherwise."

"I—I will not leave you," Faris told him. She caressed his whiskered cheek with the palm of her hand, reveling in the blessed sensation of his flesh beneath her touch.

"Not now . . . perhaps," Lochlan said. "Still, I see the fear in your eyes. You will try to leave me if I do not keep you here."

"Lochlan, darling!" Lady Rockrimmon cried, entering the room. "Oh, my darling!"

"I am well, Mother," he told her as she threw herself across him. "I am well."

"Will he . . . will he . . ." the grand lady began.

"He will survive and heal," Mr. Standard said. "If he will rest . . . and he refuses to rest unless the girl is with him. But I cannot possibly allow—"

"You will allow it!" Lady Rockrimmon demanded. "You will allow anything he asks!"

"Move me to one side of this bed," Lochlan said. "She will sleep just here."

"This is most inappropriate, milady," Joseph muttered.

"What is he in any condition to do, Joseph?" Lady Rockrimmon scolded, wiping tears from her cheeks.

Joseph shrugged. Mr. Standard and Joseph then moved Lochlan to one side of the bed.

"Shall I—shall I lash her to your arm, sire?" Joseph asked, retrieving a piece of twine from a nearby tabletop.

"Yes," Lochlan began, "Yes, Joseph . . . you must . . ."

"No, Joseph," Faris whispered to Joseph. "I . . . I will not leave him now."

In the latest hours of the night, Faris lay still awake—still staring at the handsome face of her beloved Lochlan—the handsome and unmasked face of her adored Highwayman of Tanglewood. She placed her hand to his cheek. It was cooled yet warm—a fine indication he would be well.

"Who did you love best?"

"What?" she gasped—startled at the sound of Lochlan's voice. "Shhhhh. You must rest, sire," she whispered, caressing his brow with her fingertips.

"Tell me, Faris," he said, opening his eyes to look at her. "I must know. Did you love the Highwayman best—or did you best love me?"

Faris smiled. She could see the torment in his eyes, the guilt in him at having lied to her. Further, she saw love—in the emerald flash of his eyes. He loved her. It was evident and certain he did. Whether he would break and defy propriety to marry her or whether she would have to give him up to the demands of his station, still, she knew he loved her.

"I have been lying here just thinking on it," she whispered.

"And have you come to determination?" he asked. His eyes were tired—yet warm and alive. Their gaze gave cause to goose bumps rising on her arms.

"I loved the Highwayman first," she told him, "for I met him first, kissed him first, loved him first. But—but from the moment I first saw you . . . I began to wish he were you. I wished for it so deeply that I kept my wish to myself—a secret to my own soul. Yet, I—I think I knew it from the moment we met . . . or at least hoped it was so from the moment we met. Therefore, my answer can only be that I love you—the Highwayman of Tanglewood—that I love him, and you are him. I love Lochlan Rockrimmon, and whatever may happen, wherever I may find myself, I will ever love him . . . I will ever love you. It is why I felt such the betrayer," she said. "For I loved him first, and in that I clung to my heart's first loyalty . . . while in truth . . . I loved you best." She had spoken the truth—the truth that had nearly destroyed her in the battle for it.

Lochlan smiled, his emerald eyes flashing with triumph. "Then will you share a kiss with me, fair Faris?" he asked.

Faris smiled, touched by his sentiment. Still,

she worried for his well-being and strength. "You are very wounded, sire . . . and very fatigued," she told him, taking his arm and cuddling closer to him.

"Aye, that I be," he said in the Irish brogue of the Highwayman of Tanglewood. "But I be never too wounded or tired for the taste of yar mouth, lass." He smiled, and Faris raised herself on her elbow. Studying the handsome contours of his face, she hovered over him, tracing his lips with her fingers.

"I . . . I am frightened somehow," she confessed. "You—you are Lochlan Rockrimmon, after all."

"I am he who loves you, Faris. He who would gladly die for you . . . and I am he who will be your husband when next the sun rises," he whispered.

Faris felt tears brimming in her eyes. She shook her head, unable to believe what he was saying. "You mean to tease me, sire," she whispered.

"I mean to marry you, Faris. I mean to *have* you . . . all of you . . . always . . . I promise it," he said. He raised a trembling hand to her face, taking her chin and drawing her mouth to his. His kiss spoke of hope, of life, and of love. Faris realized his kiss had ever been—had ever felt the same. It was her own uncertainty that had deemed Lochlan's kiss dissimilar from the High-wayman's. Yet now she knew him, recognized the flavor of his mouth, the manner in which his hands were lost in her hair.

"Oh, how I love you, fair Faris," he whispered against her cheek.

"Oh, how I love you . . . Lochlan," she whispered.

He took her face between his hands, searching her countenance. "And there it is," he said.

"What?" she asked.

"My own image, reflected in your eyes."

Lochlan drew Faris to him. Taking her mouth with his own, he proved the depth of strength in body and spirit of the Highwayman of Tanglewood—the depth of his own promise to have her—the immeasurable depth of Lochlan Rockrimmon's true love.

Epilogue

Faris Rockrimmon stood over her baby's cradle, gazing lovingly into the peaceful face of her son. Each time she looked at him, whether awake or asleep, as he was now, she was ever amazed at how perfectly he carried his father's likeness. Awake, his eyes were green, flashing like emeralds when he smiled. His hair was ever the same shade of soft brown, and his toothless grin promised to be rivaled only by that of the man who fathered him.

"Good night, sweet Kenner," Faris whispered, kissing the babe's tender brow. At the touch of her kiss to his forehead, Kenner Rockrimmon's lips pursed, his small mouth suckling in his sleep.

Faris breathed a deep sigh of contentment. Never could she have imagined such fulfillment—such blissful happiness. Whether she held her precious Kenner in her arms or her beloved Lochlan held her in his, contentment and happiness were hers.

Faris pondered then all those at Loch Loland—all she knew and loved there. She smiled, thinking on her darling Lillias. Oh, how beautiful Gawain and Lillias's daughter Claire was! With the lovely countenance of her mother and the quiet strength of her father, little Claire Kendrick was as perfect as any sweet princess in a fairy tale. Faris thought then of Bainbridge Graybeau—of his and Lord Gawain Kendrick's selfless loyalty to the secrets and tasks of the Highwayman of Tanglewood—to Lochlan himself. She was happy to think of Bainbridge—admired him for his loyalty and secrecy in order to protect Lochlan as the Highwayman. It was glad she was that Bainbridge had taken Sarah to wife. Sarah's heart and dreams were fulfilled in such a man as was Bainbridge Graybeau.

Suddenly, many memories traveled through her mind. First she thought of the day Lillias had appeared so utterly emotional and out of countenance, causing Faris to suspect Lord Kendrick himself was the Highwayman. Gawain had indeed informed Lillias of his alliance with the Highwayman of Tanglewood. This had unsettled Lillias, causing her great concern over Gawain's safety. Furthermore, Lochlan had confided in Lillias that same morning of his love for Faris. Thus, when Faris had confessed to Lillias of being the Highwayman of Tanglewood's lover, Lillias—having witnessed the passionate exchange between Faris and Lochlan following Lady and Tannis Stringham's comeuppance— at once realized her brother was in fact the Highwayman! Though the sudden awareness had frightened Lillias—caused her anxiety over her brother's well-being—Lillias realized Faris did not yet know the Highwayman's true identity and that it was Lochlan's accountability and place to confess. Therefore, Lillias had remained silent of her sudden knowledge, choosing an attempt to sway Faris toward Lochlan instead. In those moments, Lillias had known Faris was in love with only one man, not two. Yet, she did not, she could not reveal.

Faris smiled. What confusion, wonder, and frustration Lillias must have known in understanding such secrets and being unable to speak of them. How glad she was of such a true friend.

Faris thought tenderly of Old Joseph—of his yet familiar and endearing habit of wandering Loch Loland at night. She thought gently of Mary—of her maternal nature and of the delicious mutton stew she had served for dinner that very evening. Faris's affectionate thoughts lingered then on Lord and Lady Rockrimmon. Subsequent to Lochlan's being so terribly wounded by Kade Tremeshton's dagger, Lord Rockrimmon had thrice ridden as the Highwayman of Tanglewood. Faris giggled as she thought of Lady Rockrimmon's expression the last time he had ridden as the Highwayman—so admiring, so resplendent with love and admiration for her husband and his noble and daring heroics. She sighed as her thoughts lingered on Lady

Rockrimmon then—the woman she now knew as mother, the mother who had once endeavored to save a chambermaid in the house of Tremeshton. These were they Faris loved—these were they she whispered gratitude for each night in her prayers.

Leaving the baby's room, she stood the door ajar as she joined Lochlan in their own bed-chamber.

Faris smiled as she felt two gloved hands encircle her throat from behind.

"Aye, lass . . . ya are in danger of bein' compromised this night, ya are," came the Highwayman's raspy, whispered brogue.

"Is it you then?" Faris asked, a delighted smile spreading across her face. "For legend has it the Highwayman of Tanglewood has not been seen in more than a year. Some say he was killed . . . and some say his cause was for naught when the last of the greedy lords lost their lands and titles by law debated to change by the dashing Lochlan Rockrimmon."

"Aye, 'tis he I be . . . the Highwayman of Tanglewood . . . come back to claim what belongs to me," he said.

Faris giggled as Lochlan's strong hands slid from her neck, over her shoulders, finally settling at her waist. Nuzzling her neck from behind, Lochlan nudged the shoulder of her nightdress with his chin until it slipped, allowing him to place a lingering kiss on her tender flesh. Faris turned in his arms, running her hands up over his shoulders to his neck, letting her fingers caress the soft silk of his black Highwayman's mask.

"Kenner—he looks so like you," she whispered as Lochlan smiled down at her. "Like me?" Lochlan asked. "When that rascal Lochlan Rockrimmon is his father?"

Faris laughed. Reaching up, she stripped the mask from his head, running her fingers through the soft brown of his tousled hair.

"He looks like *you*," Faris repeated.

"Ah, the poor lad," Lochlan sighed, still smiling.

"The poor chambermaids!" Faris said.

Lochlan chuckled for a moment, brushing Faris's hair from her cheek as he gazed at her with infinite adoration.

"What a virtuous good-witch my mother is, eh?" he whispered. "She swears she knew you would win me the moment she saw you at Tremeshton."

"I . . . I still cannot believe that I did," Faris whispered, tears of joy filling her eyes.

"I am every day thankful you forgave my deception, fair Faris of Loch Loland," he whispered. He closed his eyes, wincing, and added, "Every day thankful."

"There was nothing to forgive," Faris told

him, caressing his cheek with the back of her hand. Lochlan smiled, drawing her fingers to his lips and kissing them. Quickly, he retrieved the Highwayman's mask, slipping it over his head once more.

"I be the Highwayman of Tanglewood, lass," Lochlan said. Tenderly he pushed Faris backward, sitting her soundly on their bed. "And I beg no fargiveness for what I am about this night."

"And what might that be?" Faris giggled.

"Aye, ye well know it lass . . . far I be about stealin' far more than a kiss!"

Lochlan gently laid Faris down on the bed, stretching himself out the length of her. He bent, kissing her cheek and pulling a strand of her hair between his lips.

"Oh, how mad I am for you, Faris! How desperately I love you," he whispered.

Faris took his handsome face between her hands, studying its perfection for long moments.

"I think you were in every fanciful, romantic dream I ever in my life had, Lochlan. How came I to be here, in your arms, loving you with every part of my being?"

"Ya've none but the Highwayman of Tanglewood to thank far it, lass," he whispered.

Faris smiled as his lips lingered a breath from her own.

"So, thank him."

As their lips met, their mouths working a spell of perfectly shared affection, Faris Rockrimmon sighed. The stuff of legends was in her arms—she alone owned the Highwayman of Tanglewood.

Author's Note

Several years ago I wrote a story entitled *An Old-Fashioned Romance*. Released as an e-book just in time for Christmas in 2004 (has it really been that long?), I was overwhelmed by the positive feedback I received! Loosely based on me and four of my greatest and most treasured friends, *An Old-Fashioned Romance* somehow managed to strike a nerve with readers. To this day, many friends still tell me *An Old-Fashioned Romance* is one of their favorites of my stories.

Although I'm sure the light-hearted nature of the story, the friendship between the heroine and her "gal-pals," and of course the romance between Breck McCall and her handsome hero were the basis for the popularity of the book, there is one scene in *An Old-Fashioned Romance* that seems to stand as most favored—the scene wherein the "Highwayman of Tanglewood" arrives at Marcelli's Italian restaurant for Breck's birthday.

How do you know this is a favorite scene for readers? you ask. Well, there is a simple enough answer to that question: the receipt of hundreds of e-mails inquiring as to where and when the book mentioned in *An Old-Fashioned Romance*—that being *The Highwayman of Tanglewood*—might be available!

Where can I get it? Is it out-of-print? Did you write it? Is it real?

All of these questions began arriving via e-mail shortly after *An Old-Fashioned Romance* was released in printed form. I was overwhelmed with inquiries! In truth, I had always planned to write a "highwayman" story, but the excitement over the would-be *The Highwayman of Tanglewood* pressed me to pen as soon as possible!

The original version of *The Highwayman of Tanglewood* was, I realize now, a simple, loose, rather skeletal version of the story playing out in my head. Approximately 35,000 words in length, *The Highwayman of Tanglewood* e-book was met with great excitement and delight from readers. Everyone seemed to love it! One dear reader even composed a melody to accompany the lyrics of the song Faris is singing when Lochlan surprises her in his chambers. The 35,000-word e-book version of *The Highwayman of Tanglewood* seemed to bring closure to all who wondered what the book was like after having seen it quoted in *An Old-Fashioned Romance*.

Still, to me it was unfinished. I was not anywhere close to being satisfied with the result and wanted to rework the story to more closely resemble what played out in my mind.

Behold—the 88,773 word novel-version of *The Highwayman of Tanglewood* sitting in your hands at this very moment!

Perhaps the true and complete tale of the Highwayman of Tanglewood will illuminate the reasons for its standing as Breck McCall's favorite book in *An Old-Fashioned Romance*. Furthermore, as an expression of my gratitude to all who encouraged me to write *The Highwayman of Tanglewood*, I give you this author's note—the story behind the story behind the story—the true inspiration for the Highwayman of Tanglewood.

I have always been intrigued with certain heroic characters—the swashbuckling type who do not possess any superpowers or other strange anomalies. Any hero in chain mail wielding a sword and fighting for a good cause (especially a woman's virtue and love) holds my attention and heart captive (Robin Hood—how romantic!). Furthermore, ever since I was a youngster, I've adored the idea of highwaymen! A good highwayman, of course—rogues who battle tyranny and such. Black attire and a mask intrigue me as well. Thus, Zorro—how I have always loved the idea of Zorro! And it was actually my husband (and Zorro too) who inspired the favored scene in *An Old-Fashioned Romance*, giving birth to the Highwayman of Tanglewood.

At the risk of causing my husband to roll his eyes and sigh with exasperation, I give you the tale of my thirty-third birthday, celebrated with a few intimate friends in my favorite Mexican restaurant, Chihuahua's:

Something was amiss—of this I was certain from the beginning. Rhonda, Tara, Kathy, and I were meeting at Chihuahua's Mexican Restaurant to celebrate my turning thirty-three. I noticed the girls seemed a little unsettled—especially Tara. She kept checking her watch and glancing up at the door. In addition, Kathy must've left the table three or four times to "call and check on the kids," and Rhonda's big brown eyes held their familiar "twinkle of mischief" we all know so well. Oh, certainly I knew what was coming—the sombrero! How many times have we each had to endure "the wearing of the sombrero" as the waiters and waitresses in a restaurant sing "Happy Birthday" to us? By thirty-three—a few times, right?

So, there I sat, awaiting my fate—the wearing of the sombrero. Still, as the minutes ticked, Tara seemed to become quite agitated. Finally, she fairly leapt from her seat and rushed from the room with the excuse that she too must "call to check on the kids." Meanwhile, Kathy, Rhonda, and I enjoyed conversation and a generous helping of tortilla chips and pico de gallo. Kathy sat grinning—her rosy cheeks fairly blushing with delight—and Rhonda remained atwinkle with mischief. A few minutes lapsed, and then it happened—the waiters and waitresses arrived with the sombrero, and there I sat—mortified with self-consciousness as everyone sang "Happy Birthday."

Tara returned shortly after "the wearing of the sombrero," and I assumed it had been she who had set the waiters, waitresses, and sombrero upon me. It was over! Whew! I had endured the wearing of the sombrero and seemed none-the-worse for wear.

Suddenly, I sensed someone approach me from behind. An entity, attired all in black—black breeches, black cloak, black shirt, black hat, and a rogue's black mask—whispered something delicious in my ear and pressed a bouquet of fragrant crimson roses 'gainst my cheek. I turned, gasping with delighted awe as Zorro then gathered me into the powerful strength of his embrace! Holding me firm against the solid contours of his body, the handsome and mysterious rogue then captured my mouth in a moist, driven, passion-fanned kiss. Such the stuff of dreams I had never before known in conscious wakefulness!

As each patron of the restaurant applauded—cheered in chanting, "Zorro! Zorro! Zorro!"—my three friends drew the rogue near to them! To be in the company of the dashing rogue Zorro—it was the making of their evening!

With one last kiss to my tender lips, he

vanished—hastening from the restaurant with gallant legerdemain and leaving a cheering wave of awe in his heroic wake! Ah! Such a night it was—the night I first met and kissed him that was, in truth, the Highwayman of Tanglewood!

Now—it is very necessary that all who read of my romantic and epic encounter with "Zorro" understand that my husband (Kevin) is not one to seek after attention or notice. Tall, dark, and handsome, Kevin possesses a unique wit and sense of humor, as well as a sheer naiveté to his magnetism. To dress up as Zorro, race through a crowded restaurant, and deliver such a scene—mortifying! This was the reason for Tara's unsettled appearance—Kevin was an hour late in appearing as Zorro, having had to draw upon every ounce of courage known to mankind!

Dressed in the less-than-perfect rental costume (the only one Tara could find in the tiny town of Bellingham, Washington), Kevin stood for long moments before the mirror in our master bathroom contemplating his rogue's ride! In fact, he made two phone calls to other men—acquaintances who might offer support. Both friends encouraged him, and he was finally able to make it out to the car and drive to the restaurant. It was there that Tara found him—sitting in the car—having been there for over thirty minutes, attempting to find the nerve to run through the crowded restaurant dressed as Zorro.

At long last, Tara was able to convince Kevin to go.

"Is there anyone in there from work?" he asked (as if Tara would be in any way familiar with Kevin's business associates).

Tara assured Kevin there was not (as if Tara would be in any way familiar with Kevin's business associates).

"Just run in, say your line, hand her the flowers, and run out!" Tara ordered.

With a heavy sigh and having to muster more courage than it might have taken for him to face the guillotine, Kevin rushed into the restaurant behind Tara.

Upon entering, however, Tara turned, holding up her hands in a gesture to keep Kevin from approaching our table and exclaiming, "Wa—wa—wait! They're singing to her now!"

There he stood—Kevin the Brave—standing 'midst a sea of restaurant patrons, waiting for the waiters and waitresses to finish singing "Happy Birthday" to me. All around him, people chanted, "Zorro!" Women sighed with delight, men rolled their eyes wishing they could be so bold, and Kevin stood behind Tara dressed as Zorro.

In truth, I know Kevin could best any other man we know at fists, swords, or basketball! Yet, to me, this memory stands out as one of the most heroic deeds of his entire life! What did it take for a man who avoids the limelight, prefers to observe, seeks nothing as far as attention and recognition goes—what bravery indeed—to dress up as Zorro and race through a restaurant filled with people that may or may not be his work associates? That, my friends, is the mark of a true hero!

Oh, he is rapscallion enough—owning the stripe of a rascal, the skill and dexterity of any medieval knight, and a rogue's own power of flirtation, persuasion, and allure. Yet this one brave deed stands out to me—in my mind and heart forever—because I know how challenging it was to perform!

And now, at last, you have the story behind the story—the true inspiration for the Highwayman of Tanglewood's appearance in *An Old-Fashioned Romance*—the true inspiration for the Highwayman of Tanglewood himself!

My thanks to Kathy, Rhonda, and Tara for orchestrating one of the greatest moments of my life!

And, of course, my eternal love and humble thanks to Kevin . . . for loving me enough to follow through with it!

About the Author

Marcia Lynn McClure's intoxicating succession of novels, novellas, and e-books—including *The Visions of Ransom Lake*, *A Crimson Frost*, *The Rogue Knight*, and most recently *The Pirate Ruse*—has established her as one of the most favored and engaging authors of true romance. Her unprecedented forte in weaving captivating stories of western, medieval, regency, and contemporary amour void of brusque intimacy has earned her the title "The Queen of Kissing."

Marcia, who was born in Albuquerque, New Mexico, has spent her life intrigued with people, history, love, and romance. A wife, mother, grandmother, family historian, poet, and author, Marcia Lynn McClure spins her tales of splendor for the sake of offering respite through the beauty, mirth, and delight of a worthwhile and wonderful story.

Center Point Large Print
600 Brooks Road / PO Box 1
Thorndike, ME 04986-0001 USA

(207) 568-3717

US & Canada:
1 800 929-9108
www.centerpointlargeprint.com

r 3/20